2004

ABBEVILLE FAREWELL

by Estelle Ford-Williamson

Estelle Ford-Williamson

ABBEVILLE FAREWELL
©2001 Estelle Ford-Williamson
All rights reserved. Printed in the United States of America
1st printing, May, 2001
2nd printing, November, 2001

Published by Other Voices Press
P.O. Box 2075
Decatur, GA 30031-2075
Telephone 404/299-2271

Cover design by Patricia McDonald with art by Kathy Sea

ISBN 0-9708320-1-X

ACKNOWLEDGEMENTS

Without the help of numerous people and cultural institutions, this book would never have emerged from my antiquated Mac. I would like to thank my husband, Richard, and my family—including my dear daughter, Noel—and all the friends and relatives on whose knowledge and support I drew. My mother and my father, Fannie and Bill Ford, were my original models for storytelling and seeking the history that shaped the world I grew up in. I would especially like to thank the staffs of the many archives and historical collections I consulted; the Hambidge Center, which granted me resident fellowships; and the DeKalb County Library System, whose Decatur Library Author's Room provided dedicated space during part of the writing.

PART ONE

ABBEVILLE FAREWELL

Your people may very safely build houses near us. We shall hurt nothing that belongs to them.

Cherokee leader Attakullakulla, on being honored in London by King George II

Thomas Brown had sentenced Captain Ashby and twelve of the wounded men to death by hanging. He had them immediately strung up in the stairwell at Seymour's....He had his bed moved to a point where he could witness the death struggles of his enemies. Brown...turned about 20 other wounded Whigs over to the Cherokees to be tortured to death as revenge for their braves killed in and around Augusta.

Shocked by reports of Brown's cruelty and knowing that the infuriated Loyalist would wreak a terrible vengeance upon the families of his militiamen, Colonel Clarke had sent his men home to get their families...started leading them to the safety of the Whig settlements beyond the Blue Ridge.

Robert D. Bass
Ninety Six: The Struggle for the South Carolina Back Country

Chapter 1

ABBEVILLE FAREWELL

1826

Joseph John Morgan pulled on the rope that bound his family's household belongings in the open farm wagon. Its sideboards bulged and strained and the wagonload doubled in height as he piled in more goods: chairs, featherbeds, summer paddings for featherbeds, bedsteads.

The wagon was as heavy as the April air, laden with moisture and the smothering pollen of hundreds of blooming trees and grasses. Heavy, too, were the fears Joseph John felt from his father and his mother. Neither parent was in view, but the fear lingered like a wisp of smoky fog in the mountains.

Near the top of the wagonload, the boy had placed a wooden box full of household utensils, many molded and shaped over the red-hot coals of his father's forge. When he heard the clang of an object shifting inside the box, he opened the heavy lid of the box to investigate and pulled out the culprit—a silver bowl that had landed on crockery in the bottom of the box.

Joseph John lifted the bowl to the light. He moved his hand across the concave curves of the eight sections that formed its sides, looking at his image in one of the sections. He stuck his tongue out at the bumpkin he saw in the sliver of shiny metal. People in their new home in Georgia would see a thirteen-year-old with a too-large nose and eyebrows so heavy a bird could nest in them.

He pulled from the box a wad of homespun used for diapering the youngest of his six siblings. He rubbed the bowl with a corner of the fabric and looked at his image again. He sighed, then pushed aside the crockery, the whittled hickory stir spoons, and iron fireplace pot hangers and nested the bowl in the box.

He felt his skin grow clammy with sweat as he closed the heavy wooden box. Resting momentarily from moving furniture, he sat on the box and tried to decipher his father's mood. He turned over in his mind any speck that would provide a clue. Maybe Pa was worried about carrying on his trade in Georgia. The silver bowl was a remnant of his pa's youthful apprenticeship to a silversmith in Charleston. But William Morgan had given up the silverwork and the attractions of the exotic, bustling port city to return to the South Carolina upcountry long before Joseph John was born. The boy wondered if his father had regretted giving up the silver work.

After the War of 1812 and a brief stint pouring cannon, William returned to his father's land and married Rebecca; he then took over running the farm, the gunsmith and blacksmith's works, and the grain mill on the Upper Long Cane Creek in Abbeville District in the upcountry

"Guns," he recalled his father saying. "Ever' man's got to have 'is gun. The more I make 'em for the honest'ns, the more trouble breaks out. Maybe we'll find us a place they won't need 'em so much."

Joseph John looked at his father now, bent over a large group of farm, smithy, and millhouse tools he'd laid out methodically on the ground. The boy felt a queasiness in his own stomach as he looked at his pa. He saw the scowl that came across his father's face as he picked up a set of tongs or pincers and then laid them down, deciding against taking them. It was early spring, too soon for the uncomfortable heat of an upcountry summer, yet Joseph John saw sweat trickling down to his father's collar. William pulled a piece of cloth from his back pocket and wiped his forehead and neck.

Joseph John rubbed his stomach, trying to make the discomfort go away. Maybe when they got to Georgia, he'd get his pa to show him all his silverwork. Maybe they could do that instead of making guns and tools. Right now his father's anger scared him. What kind of place were they moving to?

Joseph John's long arms fell to his sides as he looked around at the packing scene for what to do next. His oversized fingers flexed and straightened rapidly as he anticipated where they'd go to work now that he'd rescued the bowl. He was suddenly not busy, unusual for him. His high cheekbones were flushed, and his intense blue eyes, topped by the heavy eyebrows that were darker than his thick brown head of hair, narrowed as they searched for the next target.

"*Fee*bee, *Fee*bee!" Joseph John heard a chickadee calling nearby. He looked around and spied the tiny bird on the branch of a bush. He saw the sharp black cap on its head moving nervously as it flitted off and then landed on the bud-lined branch of a shadbush. The bird twisted and turned all the way around on the branch in its search for insects.

"Hey, chick," Joseph John called back. "What's got you in a stew?"

Seeing the shadbush reminded Joseph John of the many afternoons he'd escaped chores and sneaked down to the creek to check his fishing line in the water below the dam. The choppy current below the powerful curtain of water, mist, and foam was his favorite place to fish. The shad rose in the creeks with the coming of spring—the blooming bush was always a sign the fish would soon be bending his pole and adding variety to the dinner table.

Joseph John lifted his large feet and stole down the path leading to the dam. His long legs flung behind him and the hair at the front of his head lopped over his eyes as he made for the waterway. Crystal water rushed over the long row of boulders and rocks hauled in to trap the water, roaring in his ears. Mist rose up and coated his hair and face. All of a sudden, a deep sob rose up in his chest, but the sound of the water drowned out his cry. He raised his hand and wiped wetness from his eyes and pushed water off his cheek.

Where would he fish in Georgia? Who would his companions be? What would he do without his cousins and uncles and aunts in the neighborhood? He was angry and sad at the same time. Why did his father want to leave?

His father had told the family gathered around the eating table that they'd be moving in two weeks. William made it sound like Georgia was the land of milk and honey; they would have streams to fish, vast lands to wander and hunt, and untold wealth. But later, Joseph had pumped bits and snatches of information out of his father and he'd begun to suspect there was more to the story.

Rushing streams? Their present home had these. More land? They had enough for his father and the family's two sons and their eventual families here. It was true that in the new home he could buy several times the amount of land he had now. However, he couldn't imagine why his father was predicting untold wealth since he said they'd be doing the same work in Georgia they did here, except they wouldn't run a mill.

Things got more mysterious a few days later, when his father angrily forbade him to ask any more questions about Georgia. Joseph John and the others were left to wonder why they were undertaking a move in less than two weeks rather than the usual months it took to hand over a large operation like theirs. Joseph John knew better than to disobey his father's order to not bedevil him with questions.

By their leave-taking day, William wouldn't discuss Georgia at all—just pursed his lips and squinted his eyes every time the subject of the move came up. Now, as he packed up goods to move, William seemed even more quiet and strained.

"Son!" he heard his father calling from up near the smithy. "Joseph John! Come help me with these tools!"

Quickly, Joseph John took off his neckerchief and wiped his face and nose, folded the cloth over on itself, and replaced it. He ran up the hill to be next to his father. The muscular William stood breathing heavily. His nape hair, black and shiny with sweat, stuck to his skin. Following the motion of his father's hand, the boy went to the rifling bench, which William had partially dismantled by removing the legs. Joseph John gazed at the piece of polished hickory that created the famed rifling down the barrel of a longarm. The rifling guide looked like a huge twist of tobacco leaf but was smoother and shone with the gleam of exceeding age.

Joseph felt tears in his eyes and wiped again, hoping his father didn't see. He had to be strong and not show his shameful tears. He and his father prepared to raise the guide and the boring machine—precious machinery the likes of which couldn't be found for a hundred miles around—to top their load.

"Blamed if I know how I'm gonna get it all on," William sighed. There was more to the sigh than a heavy breath. His father's throat sounded constricted, hardly letting air out. "Gimme a hand with this swage block first," William said.

The quick change of mind was not like William. Was he sick? Joseph John wondered. The boy grabbed the huge black gunsmith's anvil around one of its squared sides. Waiting for his father's greater strength to move the heaviest of all their tools, Joseph John thought the thing looked like a piece of burned toast for some great leviathan, for it weighed a couple hundred pounds and was coal-black all over. Dents for molding rifle barrels lined up where the top crust should be, and small craters of indentations for shaping the curved bowls of spoons and tools lay where the cinder-encrusted heart of the bread would have been.

William heaved the iron piece off the ground. Joseph John barely held onto his own end.

"Quick," his father's voice strained. "Get it over t' the wagon." They fairly ran to the wagon. Joseph John feared dropping his end and crushing his or his father's foot. That would put an end to the move, at least for a while!

They struggled to lift the block on the wagon. After two tries, they let it rest on the ground. Joseph John saw the futility of trying to lift the monstrous weight over their heads. He persuaded his father to let him put two ropes around it so they could stand at the top of the pile of goods and pull the anvil to the top of the wagon.

"How'd you ever get this thing here?" Joseph John asked after they'd finally wrestled the swage block aboard.

"'S always been here—it was Pa's," William gasped. He took a few moments to get his breath back. Joseph John was glad because his heart was thumping loudly beneath his shirt, and he felt blood rushing in his head due to the strain. He remembered how scared he'd been earlier and felt glad the feelings had gone. Hard work cured all woes.

Then his father motioned to the rifling bench and boring machine. "'S get these aboard before we give outa oats."

No doubt these, too, were part of his granpa's tools, Joseph John thought as he moved them. The last two devices were lighter, and he was glad. He'd not known much about his father's father, who died shortly after William took over the farm and shops. He did know that he was named for him, but he and his pa didn't talk much about family—seemed like they were always too busy to work their jaws much.

Joseph John heard the creak of wheels and sniffed the humid, dirt-born smell of a team of horses being driven near him. He heard one of the animals snort and felt the heavy breath on his arm. A stocky black workhorse paired with a gray pulled another wagon loaded with cargo. This wagon was wearing an iron-braced cotton canvas cover that resembled a huge woman's bonnet.

His Uncle Samuel, taller than his father and several years older, called to the team.

"Whoa, Jack," he ordered the lead. Both stopped at the same time. Joseph John reached over to stroke Jack's head.

"Y'ever seen such a fine boy?" Sam yelled to his younger brother. Samuel had sons Joseph's age, so the uncle was special to the boy.

"If y'say so," William mumbled absently.

"Well, y'ought to pay him more mind," said Sam, smiling and winking at Joseph John as he got down to adjust the bridles and harness of the team of horses. Sam was going to drive one of three large wagons filled with the Morgan family goods and then return to South Carolina. However, Sam would take one wagon, his father another, and Gideon would drive the third. Gideon, fifteen, was Joseph John's brother, and the second oldest of the Morgan children. His pa had assured Joseph John that, with just a little more age, he could handle the heavy tasks.

Joseph John smarted some at not being included in the driver group. However, he satisfied himself in the thought that Pa would soon see his value. At least he wasn't unfortunate enough to be a girl. Five daughters, one of whom was older than the two boys, surrounded the two sons in the Morgan family. Alice, the oldest, had tagged along after them when they were younger, even on fishing trips to the creek. She'd tried to copy everything Joseph John did, but that didn't do any good.

"She's still a girl," Joseph John said to the lead mare of his father's wagon as he made a final adjustment to her harness. "Nothing against girls, Mary," he quickly said to the horse. "It's just that females can't do what men like me can." He rubbed the mare's mane playfully.

He looked up to see his mother, Rebecca, on the porch of their two-story homestead nursing his youngest sister Susannah. Rebecca's blue eyes were tight and surrounded by wrinkles. Her voice was sharp as she called down to him.

"Joseph John, make sure everything's out of the cookhouse,"she said.

"Yes, Mama," he replied. He kicked at the rocks in the wall by the family mill as he wended his way up the steep climb to the small house behind the cabin. He felt a need to keep moving himself, to get away from the homestead as soon as possible. If he kept busy, he wouldn't think.

"Father!" Joseph John heard Rebecca call to William. "Please make sure we've got guns where we can reach them, just in case."

"Guns, the mighty guns," William replied. "Wish those characters that use 'em to stir folks up around here would just drop off the face of this green earth."

"More than just neighbors to worry about—there's Indians, too," his wife said, wiping her brow with a plain handkerchief and shifting Susannah closer to her.

Joseph John had never seen an Indian, although he knew people who had. The stories of a huge Indian massacre in which young children had been stolen from settlers there in Abbeville District had been passed on through generations, and the children in the area tried to guess if people they knew were among those who had been kidnapped in that incident.

When they were at play together—at gatherings when a preacher happened into the area or neighbors had a cabin or barn raising—a boy or girl could scare the others by talking about someone who'd been captured and released. Those who'd been captured never spoke of their experience, so it was very tantalizing for an older child to tell the younger ones they *knew* someone. They speculated on various neighbors who seemed odd or secretive.

"Maybe it was Old Man MacLemore," one would say.

"Or Sally Newsome," another would guess, speaking of an old maid with a hunched back and a mean look.

Lots of times the children wondered what had happened to those who never came back. But because it had happened so long ago, the Indian tales were just that—tales.

His father had referred to neighbors stirring things up, but Joseph John didn't know what that meant. Most everybody was pretty nice to him. They spoke to him about his pa and ma, always asking about their welfare. He was going to miss the fishing, the neighbors, the whole place. The creek teeming with shad and brim. The neighbors, mostly farmers, who came by regularly for milling and for blacksmithing and for gun repairs. And even the planters who had smithies, who came by for special work because of William's reputation for quality tools and clever rigs for hard-to-do jobs.

From his hillside location at the cookhouse, Joseph John spied a long saw that had been left behind the house and ran down towards it to make sure it was packed or that Pa knew he was leaving it behind.

After what seemed like hours to Joseph John, the wagons were loaded. They started up the steep hill beyond the mill. No one spoke. Joseph John had rarely experienced a time when everyone in the family was quiet. Here they were, seventy years after the family had settled in the Long Canes, packing up two generations of Morgans and rolling their way to Georgia. They were leaving behind the mill, the creek dam, the house, the forge, the farm—and a lot of hard labor and pain.

Sam was in the lead wagon, followed by a bonneted one driven by Gideon. Joseph John was satisfied that the wagon his brother drove was a lot smaller than the other. Joseph John sat in the rear of the largest wagon, driven by his father. He found a dent in the load of household goods and lowered himself into the opening. He dangled his legs over the side at the rear, careful to make sure his large brogan-clad feet didn't get near the brake reaching the large set of aft wheels.

After draining the sadness he'd felt down by the dam, he was getting excited. Even his pa's face looked less pinched. His ma seemed more at ease as well as she shifted about on her seat, holding Susannah and looking carefully at the wagons carrying her household.

Birds sang from the dense woods. They passed hardwoods of white and red oak, walnut, hickory, and poplar. Cedars, ash, sweet gum, and tall pines, along with wild plums, grew in the forest. Now the plum trees were blooming gloriously white in the midst of the countryside's mostly gray and brown clothing of early spring.

Near the stream they'd left behind, birch trees and acre after acre of cane grew thick and tall, some of it thirty feet high. Joseph John knew from his pa's talk that the thick cane had attracted many settlers to this area. Livestock grazed the cane and nut-strewn undergrowth of the heavy forests, and drank from the waters of the streams so numerous it seemed a boy was never out of earshot of rushing or gurgling water. Animals here in the backcountry required little care for a good return of milk and meat.

Joseph John had learned early that tremendous stands of sky-reaching cane stalks gave names to Long Cane Creek and its large northwest branch, Upper Long Cane Creek. The two streams and their tributaries formed the water-dappled Long Canes area, which stretched southwest towards the Savannah River through a huge portion of South Carolina upcountry. Stories abounded about the thousand buffalo that once stood on one square mile of upcountry land and about great black bears that still beat the trees for bounties of honey.

Joseph John recalled one story the old timers told as though it happened yesterday. A settler was sitting in his doorway with his feet propped on the door brace when a huge black bear jumped across his legs, ran into the cabin, and grabbed a leg of venison that was cooking over the fire in his rock and chink fireplace. Clutching the meat in one paw and running on three others, the bear fled past the amazed settler back into the forest. Those were fearful times, Joseph John told himself. Bears, bobcats, panthers, and Indians would for sure keep a family on edge.

The three wagons neared the junction with the road that would take them north toward Calhoun's Mill, then west towards the Savannah River. Coming toward them on the narrow sunken roadbed was an open farm wagon pulled by a copper-colored horse. The driver of the wagon glowered at them under a wide-brimmed farm hat and kept coming. Finally, after a lengthy delay, the oncoming wagon lumbered up to the high, rounded shoulder of the narrow road. The driver, a neighbor named Thomas Cunningham, hailed William.

"Morgan!" he called. "Gonna run now, huh?"

Joseph John shuddered as he looked at the man's partially hidden face. He could not see Mr. Cunningham's eyes. A deeply tanned, bony jaw projected forward from beneath the shadow of the hat. The shape of the jaw reminded Joseph of the letter "J," so sharp were the lines of the man's jowl. A wedge of thick, black hair poked out from under the dark hat. A prominent Adam's apple moved up and down in a skinny, leathery neck.

The wagons passed in silence. From his post in the back of the wagon, Joseph John heard his mother draw in a deep breath. His father made no sound. Joseph John felt his knuckles digging into his pants waist, just below his shirt. He alone sat looking back after the third wagon lumbered past Cunningham.

After they'd passed, Cunningham remained stopped, slouching over something in his lap. As Joseph John made a final look toward the road to Morgan's Mill, he saw that Cunningham had shifted and turned back toward their wagon train. He had a long barreled rifle in one hand that he raised, in one swift motion, to his shoulder. Joseph John watched, helpless, as Cunningham prepared to shoot right at his head. The boy could not move his hand, his arm, his mouth. Seconds passed, but no shot rang out. Rigidly, Cunningham hunched behind the barrel as though still taking careful aim. As long as Joseph John looked back, he saw the barrel was leveled at his head.

His heart beating fast, Joseph quickly clambered forward in the wagon, climbing over belongings tied down with canvas and secured with various lengths of hemp rope. He passed his mother and Susannah in a wide seat that had been constructed for the trip so they could sit behind his father. He looked back down the hill and saw that Cunningham had lowered the rifle and turned back to the horse drawing his wagon.

"Now, don't go scaring a man to death," said an irritated William as Joseph John straddled the buckboard and sat next to his father. "Give me some warnin' before you spring up from behind!"

Joseph John was frightened, but he decided to bide his time. Why was Cunningham menacing them? Would his pa's sour mood ever go away? Maybe later he could find out what made his pa so testy and why Cunningham threatened him.

Joseph John sat next to William, bobbing and yawing with each thrust of the wagon across the bumpy roadbed.The youngster knew not to distract his father when he was concentrating on keeping the horses moving and avoiding the biggest potholes in the road. Actually, he was well-trained not to bother his father at all unless a cow or a child was about to be killed or hurt. It was the way they lived—close to the land, dependent on the seasons, and beholden to the many demands of a farmer-tradesman's life.

Pa would go out and milk cows before dawn and grab the hens' eggs and clean up after the pigs wallowing in the mud and check the bees' water and let the cows out to pasture and feed the horses and let them out with the cows and pull the hay down for the horses for when they returned to the barn, then go out and, depending on the season, hitch the mules or work horses and plow or plant or plow under crops for restoring the soil. Then he'd go to the smithy and begin the fire that would burn for the rest of the day and the next morning, too—working the iron into spoons and utensils and pots and repairing the same and then maybe working with a gun barrel if the boys could be rounded up and if it was time to be making a rifle for someone.

Pa's day would go past sunset working the fields, often passing by the mill where he and Gideon were in charge. He'd make sure they collected their ten percent tolls and ground the corn satisfactorily. Then he'd go back to tending the smithy and all. He might not come in for the big noonday dinner if the fields required work—in that case he'd carry a meal in a flour sack and tote a jug of water for sustenance.

Rarely was his pa seen again before supper. So, except for the times they might work in the mill or the smithy together, he'd not be with his father and, even when he was, the task before them would always be the first concern.

In the spring, there'd be the planting of seeds and later moving the small plants so they'd grow well. In early summer there'd be honey to extract and in the fall there'd be labors like drying apple slices on the roof for Rebecca. Gathering the honey could take days and competed with felling trees for lumber to repair the sheds or gathering and chopping firewood—a perennial for sustenance spring, summer, winter, or fall.

In winter, they'd repair equipment all over the place. And Pa would go over the arithmetic and science lessons they learned from itinerant teachers who came through the area. There wasn't much time for jawing and passing time. The man who had that kind of time was sorry and no-account. That's what his pa told him and Gideon.

Joseph John, sitting next to his pa in the wagon, watched as the train approached the turn-off to Calhoun's Mill, knowing that soon all three wagons would lumber onto a road traveling west to the Savannah. The road would be easier, as there would be a steady slope down to the river.

As soon as they'd negotiated the turn, Joseph John noticed his father looked relieved. The eyes, which had seemed to be locked in a squint or wince as though his head were in a vice, now showed their color, a dead match for a clear Carolina sky. The boy noticed that the line that had stood guard around his pa's mouth now had melted back into his forge-singed fair skin.

Knowing his pa liked a man of courage, Joseph John decided to ask him questions and stand his ground if Pa was grumpy. He could always climb back to the rear of the wagon.

"Pa," Joseph John said, trying to sound as grown up as possible, "tell me more about this settlement we're headed for."

"Well, Son," William said, turning his head toward the boy for a moment, "you remember the Thurmans that lived over in Chesterfield County; there was David Thurman, his wife, Lavinia, an' ole man Benjamin Thurman."

"Oh, yeah!" Joseph exclaimed. "He was a patriot, just like my grandfather." His eyes lit up, thinking of his ancestor.

"David Thurman won a hundred-sixty acres of Georgia land in the Indian lottery over there, and they moved west earlier this spring. It's a wilderness, but Brother Thurman has sent word that there are a few families there, and it's a fair forest with lots of hardwoods and streams and a great deal of room to grow."

"But why leave everything here?" Joseph John asked. "The mill, the smithy…"

William seemed irritated at the question, and Joseph John decided not to be too curious, as his father might take it as disrespect. But his father went on.

"Son," he said, sighing, "for one thing, we'll be settlin' with people we know're our friends. You won't have the rough characters you've got around here still livin' in the past and not wantin' to live in peace."

Joseph John almost said, "Like Thomas Cunningham?" but he held his tongue.

"Also, I sold this land for a real good sum, and the land I'll buy from Mr. Thurman will be real cheap. We'll have money so we can set up a smithy and depend on newcomers movin' in. People'll need tools to build homes an' keep livestock and farm."

"What's the town's name?" Joseph John asked. He knew the part about cashing in on the land.

"Doesn't have a name. Ain't a town," said William. "There's some people there, 'bout seven or eight families, an' one day there'll be more. It's in DeKalb County, named for Baron DeKalb, killed here in the massacre at Camden."

"What does it look like?" Joseph John asked. "Will there be a stream like the Long Canes?"

"There are lots of streams, and not too far off there's a big river that runs to the end of the state and empties into the Gulf. But Son, remember, railroads will cross this state an' join Georgia and the West eventually. It's the new frontier, just like Abbeville District once was. The way Brother Thurman describes the county, it's prob'ly like this district was when it was all Indian country."

"Indian country? Are there Indians there now?" Joseph John was alarmed. He'd never thought to ask about Indians. They were long gone from Abbeville District, and he assumed they weren't anywhere near.

"Area's been Creek Indian territory till the last few years," said William. "They've sold their land to our government, and it's being given to new settlers moving west."

"Where will they go?" Joseph John asked, incredulous that such fearsome people would voluntarily give up land.

"They're moving far west where it's unlikely any of us will want to go—out in the old French territory on the other side of the Mississippi," said his father.

William pushed back the wide-brimmed hat that shielded the sun from his eyes and looked intently at his second son. Joseph John felt his gaze, even though the youngster was staring straight ahead with the light of excitement in his eyes.

"Y'know, Joseph John, we got opportunities for great blessings in this here Georgia," William said. "Abbeville District's been good to us, gave our family th' chance to work th' land and settle the area. But it's time to move on, create new settlements and push back the frontier. No tellin' what riches lie out in this great land of America. All I know 's that since it's been discovered, every nation in the world has wanted a piece of it.

"Our folks were persecuted for their religion and their property was taken from 'em in the Old Country. Comin' here made it possible to hold onto something and not be forced to pay and pay when the family finally got some land and some good farms. We're here, and we're moving west because there's more to settle, and there's no British king 'r anybody else stoppin' us. We got to claim it and cultivate it. That's what all those before us fought for and died for. I can't tell you how important that is.

"God said in th' Bible to increase and multiply, and He also promised His people that He would provide enough to build His kingdom," William went on. "I've got eight children, five of 'em girls. I have to provide for all of you, and give you the tools and th' land and a way of making a life for y'selves after I'm gone. Mine is not to question how, but God in His providence has provided the way. We have t' respond."

Joseph John figured he'd just heard the most his father had ever said to him about his family, his duty, and his ambition for his sons. Usually his father didn't talk much, for he was a shy man. Joseph John sat quietly, taking in the import of what he'd heard. At the same time, he figured that his pa's outburst of loquaciousness hid the real reasons for the move. A man bound for such bounty didn't button up his lips and forbid his family to discuss the move. And they didn't flee in a fortnight.

He decided he would tell his pa about Thomas Cunningham.

"Pa, back there, when we saw Ol' Man Cunningham," Joseph John blurted quickly. "I don't think you saw, but he aimed his musket at me after we passed."

William turned his body toward Joseph John and looked at him hard. Joseph John could see his forehead crinkle between his eyebrows, the way it did when he bent over the hot coals of the forge, full of concentration.

"I'm afraid he's one of the reasons we're movin', too, Son."

"Why is that, Pa?" Joseph John hoped his pa didn't hear the quaver in his voice.

His question hung in the air unanswered for a time. His pa exhaled deeply, urged the horses on over the rough roadbed, and looked straight ahead at the back of the wagon driven by Gideon.

"Long before you was born there was a lot of unrest back here in the Carolina upcountry, attacks on homesteads, men and women killed, women 'n children left with nothing as their homes burned," he said. "Some of them were in our own neighborhood, Son. Mr. Cunningham an' his farewell were left over from that time.

His eyes showed fire, his hand gripped the reins harder, and he hailed the lead a second time. Joseph John felt his heart beat hard in his chest. He waited to find out all he could about Cunningham. What had his family done to rile him?

"Hyaaah!" William shouted, applying a whip to the mare. Both horses picked up their feet, lurching the wagon forward over the pine needle-covered terrain.

"He didn't even have a reason to be mad. All this happened before he was born, too," his father said while giving a quick look to Joseph John. "Most of it was going on before even I was born."

William began talking about Joseph John's grandfather, who had died before Joseph John was born, and the long-time strife from decades before. Joseph John listened intently, not wanting the miss a detail. His feet, which tended to shuffle and twist around when he rode for long periods, were quiet. Even his questions about Cunningham, which broke out in his head in a fury when the man aimed his rifle at him, took a rest.

"Your granpa was a fine man," said William as the wagon pitched and yawed over a difficult section of road, "—brave, fiery, willing to work to make a home and have a family. *His* father survived a trip overseas from Ulster, in Northern Ireland, to Philadelphia. Then Joseph risked like his father before him, sailing south to the Carolinas from Virginia when he was a young man of twenty."

"But why did his father move?" Joseph John wanted to know. "Why did he come here in the first place?"

"Ah, Joseph John," said his father. "You have a lot to learn. "Don't be so impatient, let me tell m' story."

The boy heard his mother behind him in the wagon as she moved Susannah from one breast to the other to nurse. There was a short cry of objection from the infant, followed by the muffled sound of satisfaction.

"Land was the reason," William continued. "And religion. Famine in Scotland sent your grandfather's family across to the English plantation at Ulster. After some pretty bloody battles, King James took all of Northern Ireland away from th' Irish chieftains. Then he planted Scotsmen and Englishmen there in an effort to civilize the Irish clans."

William related how Joseph's ancestors settled in Ulster. However, the Scots soon found they were treated as badly as the Irish peasants. They were Presbyterians, but they had to tithe to the English church. Penal codes kept them from holding office or making a decent living. They couldn't buy land, and their landlords raised the rent whenever the population grew, just when they needed cheap, good land to feed their families. Crop failures and rackrenting—the practice of jumping rents just when families were growing and needing land—kept them desperate to feed their families.

"What'd they do, Pa?" Joseph John was anxious to know how the story would end.

William told Joseph John that the Scots were quite used to moving on. They'd moved to Ireland from Scotland, and they'd pulled up stakes lots of times in Ireland to find cheaper land, so emigrating to the colonies seemed a natural course.

"There was active trade between Irish ports an' Philadelphia, so the Scotch-Irish started pourin' in there."

"But, Pa, how did the Morgans get to Abbeville District?" Joseph John asked.

"The Morgans followed others of their kind and settled in southern Pennsylvania. My pa said German and Swiss neighbors gave his pap the idea about building cabins from log rather than the stone or mud like they did in the old country. After clearin' the land and workin' the soil and building homes, they sold as soon as they could t' the next immigrant. Then they moved down the Pennsylvania Wagon Road to Virginia. It was from there that Joseph sailed to Charleston."

Joseph John felt a mantle of shame fall over his shoulders. Here he was feeling fearful about the move to Georgia, when his grandfather had had to make a longer, more dangerous trip. Enough of being a baby, he told himself.

"How did they get the land?" Joseph John asked. "If they were poor in Ireland, they must have had nothing here."

William sighed and looked at his son, then back at the horses picking their way on the rutted road west. "That's the hard part. Most got here in the first place by workin' as indentured servants for a landowner or merchant for four to seven years—just to earn their passage. Remember the cost of passage was high, so t' get t' the new country they had to indenture to someone who had th' money."

The boy remembered hearing that Joseph had served out a lease of his labor for several years to pay for his passage from Virginia. Then he followed other immigrants to the South Carolina upcountry. William filled him in on the details: Carolina offered a hundred acres to a man who'd settle the land—even providing tools and seed to start a farm. It pleased the low country planters to have the hardy Scots-Irish and other Europeans as a buffer between the coastal city and the Indians and as a lightening effect in a heavily black colony.

"Why didn't he stay in Virginia, with his pa's family?"

"At that time, it was the law in most of the colonies that the eldest son inherited all the land of the father—an' bein' as he was the second son, Joseph stood t' inherit nothing from his pa."

Joseph John reflected on how the favoring of the first son still went on, even if they didn't inherit all the land. It was his older brother who'd have the chance to learn the gunsmithing and it was his brother who had what attention his father had paid up to now to his children. But maybe that was changing now that he was traveling with his father, Joseph John thought.

"So Joseph got his land in the Long Canes in the 1760s, married, an' started a family," William said.

As the wagon drew closer to the ferry, Joseph John heard his mother sniffling behind him. He turned to look and saw tears streaming down her face. Her eyes were opened with fear, and she looked left and right and straight ahead, then repeated the pattern.

"Mama, what's wrong—"

"I told you ain't nothin' to fear!" William interrupted, flinging his words back at his wife.

"I'm not afraid, dear husband, just mourning for those who went before."

"What do you mean, Ma?" Joseph John asked, aware that his father probably didn't approve of his prying.

At first his mother didn't speak. After a few moments, the tears subsided, and when she spoke, the tears still filled her throat. "Years ago, Son," she began in a strange sounding voice, "there was more than a score of people killed in an Indian attack not far from here, mostly women, some of them kin." She touched her eye with a homespun handkerchief. "I think about them when we're gettin' close to the water. They'd just crossed Long Cane Creek, fleeing to Augusta during an outbreak of Indian raids when the people were attacked. Men didn't have their rifles in a place they could grab 'em. Before the people could escape, many were tomahawked and scalped and killed or kidnapped."

"When did this happen?" Joseph John asked excitedly. The massacre she was describing was the one the children often talked about back in the old neighborhood.

"French and Indian War—'60, way before the War of Independence," Joseph John's father broke in. "French pitted the Indians against the British colonists, and they went on the warpath all over the colonies, especially in the Carolinas.

"Up until then, the English and the Cherokees had attacked each other in bloody raids. There was fear, but there was also trading between th' two groups. The British even took the Cherokee chief to London to present to King George, and the chief and his headmen promised not to hurt the settlers—"

"The Cherokees promised to allow th' whites to build near them," Joseph John's mother interrupted, "but they didn't allow them to take something that wasn't theirs." Her voice had a sharpness Joseph John had never heard. Joseph John was afraid again. He had never heard his parents argue before, and now his mother was almost red in the face with anger.

"Those people in Long Canes, and your grandfather, too," she flung her words at William, "built on the wrong side of Long Cane Creek, going against treaties and longstanding agreements that whites wouldn't settle on the other side of the creek!"

"Rebecca, don't fill the boy's head with foolish notions about something you don't know nothin' about. Joseph Morgan had every right to settle on that side of th' creek!"

"'The dividing waters of Long Cane Creek' is the way the treaty read, way I heard it," Rebecca retorted. "You can't change that. They weren't supposed to settle above the dividing waters."

"Well, what was the dividing waters? You had th' Northwest Fork of Long Cane Creek, and you had Long Cane Creek."

"Well, if the whites decided to call something Long Cane Creek that wasn't Long Cane Creek, can you blame the Cherokees for getting upset?" Rebecca's face was flushed.

"Anyway, Joseph John," his father continued, "there were hundreds of settlers in the Long Canes, as the area came to be called, the area between the regular Long Cane Creek and the 'Northwest Fork of Long Cane Creek.' A hundred and fifty white settlers were fleeing to Augusta when the Indians attacked. After the massacre, nine children were found who'd escaped by hiding in the trees. Many other children were kidnapped and most were never heard from again. In all, twenty-three people, mostly adults, died."

Later, as the wagons prepared to stop for the night, Joseph John grew more apprehensive. He had known that they were to sleep on the ground the first night, but after the talk about Indians and scalping, he was afraid. His father had said there weren't any Indians around. Georgia had signed treaties over a number of years that had gradually pushed the redskins back past where the Morgans were going.

"I've seen a map," William told Joseph John confidently. "The state looks like a slab of streak o'lean, the way the land was ceded—one stripe of fatty meat for each treaty stretching from north to south, parallel to the Savannah."

Joseph John was still thinking about the settlers who were slaughtered in their panic-stricken dash for Augusta as the drivers slowly brought the family's wagons to a stop. After eating a meal prepared over an open fire, the ten Morgans each prepared to sleep on pallets of blankets placed within the triangle of wagons. There was no sleeping for Joseph John. He heard his mother toss in her sleep and sigh. Were there Indians around that might attack them? Despite his father's assurances, Joseph John knew there could still be danger. He decided not to ask any more questions for a while. He was concerned his parents would argue again, and that bothered him.

Joseph John moved quietly from bush to bush, desperate to hide. A fog heavier than the smoke from a fire doused by rain blocked his view. Indians attacked their wagon, overturned in a stream. They pulled his mother from behind the wagon, and through the haze he saw a brave whose skin glistened under the red blotches of bloodroot grab his mother by the hair and hit her in the head with a long, heavy club. The boy screamed, but no sound came out. Why couldn't anyone hear him? Other Indians were clubbing and stabbing his father, his brother. From the second wagon up on the bank, his sisters screamed, but their voices rose and fell as though they yelled through water. The halo of fog shutting him off from the others enraged him. His Uncle Sam shot his rifle at an oncoming Indian, and the brave fell wounded in the chest. Gray, pungent black powder smoke mixed with the pure white fog formed a curtain, thrusting him further back from those he wanted to help. Joseph John watched terrorized as an Indian scalped his mother. Through shreds of mist, he saw the white patch on her head fill with blood. The boy's feet were rooted to the boulders he stood on. He could not move. His ma's dark brown hair loosened from its pins during her struggle with the brave, and fell gracefully, slowly, slowly, down around her shoulders. An ooze and then a crown of a wet crimson cascaded from the white patch across her face and hair.

Suddenly, Joseph John found he could move his feet. He ran through the heavy fog to the wagon and grabbed his father's spare rifle from its nest of bed covering under the buckboard. He pulled back the gun's hammer and flipped open the flash pan cover exposing the powder. He pulled the trigger, firing a shot and hitting a brave in the neck. He ran to William's body and wrested a powder horn from his still figure, then quickly filled the rifle barrel with powder. He inserted a patched ball, pushed it forward in the barrel, poured a finer powder from a second horn into the flash pan, pulled the trigger, and shot a second brave. He could barely see, as the powder backfire covered his eye with grit. Smoke, fog, and black powder odor filled the air around him. Joseph John pulled a large knife from his dead father's waist, waiting for the next attacker. He didn't look at his mother or brother lying in the creek in front of him.

The Indians were gone, except for the wounded and dead. Out of the smoke, Thomas Cunningham appeared, his long jaw rigid, the greasy black hair falling across his face, and the Adam's apple as big as a cannon ball. He raised his rifle, and fired toward Sam. Joseph John yelled and he heard the sound come out. His uncle fell to the ground just in time. Joseph John's scream unbalanced Cunningham. His enemy looked wildly in his direction, then slipped on the moss-covered rocks, tumbling into the water.

Joseph John woke up, his skin wet from sweat. He listened for any noises betraying the still night, and saw his mother, father, and brother sleeping undisturbed in their covers.

"Must've dreamed it," he mumbled to himself, then got up to make sure his uncle was all right in his spot on the other side of his father. He found his uncle's rifle right beside him, and saw his father's was close by his hand as well. He then went to the wagons to see if the spares were in their blanket slings behind the buckboard.

They were safe, he concluded. He checked the older Morgans again, to see if their knives were under their pallets near their heads and saw that the butts of their edged weapons were just visible.

Still shaking from the dream, Joseph John thought about the day's revelations. He somehow felt he was much older than he was earlier in the day. Since he'd been on this journey, he'd learned a great deal about his grandfather and his people. He could still feel the cold fear from the dream-massacre of his family. Even though it was a dream, Joseph John felt reassured that he'd killed his enemies in his imagination. He was a good marksman. And although it might not be needed in DeKalb County, he knew he could take care of himself physically.

The wagon, its wheels exclaiming in pained creaks, rolled onto the crude wooden barge at Barksdale's Ferry on the Savannah River. Its heavy weight caused the plank board platform ferry to list deeply on the riverbank side. The two older men and Gideon held the blindfolded horses by their harnesses and talked quietly to them as they gently led them to the middle of the ferryboat. This allowed the vessel to balance once again.

Joseph John found it hard to concentrate, thinking about his dream. He was afraid of being left without the menfolk. He was relieved when his brother returned to join him on the riverbank; the ferry and its load, along with the two older Morgans, departed. That left the two younger men in charge.

"Mama, is Papa leaving us?" cried four-year-old Becka, perched on the buckboard of the second wagon, where Joseph John attended. Joseph John was suddenly alerted to his wagon master's task. Sensing trouble, he strengthened his grip on the reins restraining the horses that pulled the wagon Becka rode in, then took the ropes of the wagon his mother and Baby Susannah rode in. Looking around, he tried to scheme a possible escape route if the party were attacked.

"No, Papa's not leaving us," Rebecca told her namesake. "You'll be going on the ferry, too, just you wait and see." Holding the baby in her arms, Rebecca looked anxiously at the wagon next to her. By design, Rebecca was riding in the third wagon, and the rest of her girls were in the second wagon, which would be the next to go.

"But I don't want to go on the ol' ferry, Mama." Becka's face crinkled up and she began to cry.

"There, there, Becka, it'll be all right,"Alice, her oldest sister, put her arms around the child and comforted her. At sixteen, Alice took responsibility for Becka and Anne, who was six, as well as two-year-old Laura. "Here's your doll. Talk to her so she won't be scared getting on the ferry."

Becka took a small white handkerchief doll with stitched eyes, nose, and mouth, and rocked it in her arms. Her face returned to its earlier calm, and she consoled her charge. "Now, don't you worry, Virginia," she told the doll. "Just don't you worry at all. We'll be in Georgia soon!"

Becka taken care of, Alice turned her attention to the other two in the back of the wagon. Joseph John watched his oldest sister making sure that the others had a distraction so they could stand the long wait. The ferry would have to take the first wagon to the other side of the broad Savannah River and return to take each of the other wagons in turn.

"Alice, do you have Laura's sugar teat?" Rebecca asked. Laura's accompanying her sister was a delicate matter. At any time, the clingy two-year-old could decide she wanted her mother, and a child's screams could upset the animals. The older, more experienced horse handlers were now crossing the Savannah with the first wagon.

"Yes, Mama. The girls are fine." Alice pulled a teat, a handkerchief with a tied off head that resembled a small doll, from her dress pocket. She'd fixed the concoction of bread soaked in milk and sugar from the hurried breakfast table that'd set before dawn that morning, Joseph John figured. Alice was very responsible.

Standing between the two sets of horses, the boy looked up at his mother sitting in the driver's seat of the third wagon. He thought of a another sister who would have been older than Becka.

"Alice has certainly turned into a little mother," he said.

"Well, I've needed her to," said Rebecca.

"I know," Joseph John said. He pictured in his mind the sad death of his sister Nancy during one winter when he was small. She was two, and she had a very high fever that never went away. Even though he was only four at the time, he recalled seeing his mother bent over the bed where Nancy lay. With blond curls and blue eyes, Nancy was prettier than any of his sisters. He'd helped with her fever by taking rags to the stream outside and dipping them in water too swift to freeze to cool her forehead. Nothing brought the fever down. She died with a horrible rattling in her chest while both parents sat at her side. Joseph John remembered listening at the door in the next room with Gideon pressed close to him.

Many Sundays he had watched his mother walk up the hill to Nancy's small grave behind the cookhouse and not come back for what seemed like a long time. In spring, she usually carried a small crockery vase with some fresh picked buttercups or hyacinths from beside the front porch steps. She would be sad when she returned, but then he or his brother would need food or have a hurt hand or knee to attend. Or a stew would need preparing, or apples would need peeling. So he never saw her stay subdued for very long.

Several years passed before the fall he noticed his mother's belly had grown huge. She started wearing the looser gowns instead of dresses with a waist. Then her belly grew bigger than any pumpkin he'd seen on anyone's farm in Abbeville. After what seemed like a very long time, there was a new Morgan baby, Anne, and Alice became a doting big sister and assistant to Rebecca.

A number of times, he'd seen his mother's eyes become fearful and drawn just about the same time the baggy gowns came on and the closer-fitting clothes disappeared. She never told him there was anything wrong, it was just something Joseph John sensed—like his brother knowing there were deer around when the two of them went hunting. He wondered if each child born brought his mother the memory of that loss all over again.

"Do you remember your little sister?" Joseph John fairly jumped at the sound of his mother's voice. Had she been reading his thoughts? "Her name was Nancy?"

"Yes, ma'am, I remember her. She was real pretty."

"Yes, she was that. I loved brushing her pale yellow hair. It was so unusual in this brown-haired family. But then yours was light when you were little, too."

"Why was she called Nancy?"

"She was named for my mother, Nancy Anderson."

"Nancy Anderson died a long time ago."

"Right. When I was a young girl."

"Tell me about her." Joseph John felt like he was about to be on speaking terms with family—first with his father's and now with his mother's people. He remembered hearing about both sets of family, now long dead, but now he was listening for details he hadn't heard.

"She came from Ireland when she was 14. Her parents came and settled in the upcountry like a lot of people, looking for the land they couldn't have in Ireland. My father, James Anderson, was English. Nancy's first husband died young. Nancy and James married and had brother Stephen and me. She died of the fever when I was about ten. My father remarried, and died a few years later."

"So who raised you?"

"My stepmother, Mother Agnes."

"I guess I'm pretty lucky to have my ma live so long," Joseph John said. "Did you miss your mother?"

"All girls miss their mothers. There's no way to make up for that loss. But, yes, we're fortunate to have so many children and only suffer one loss and be here for the rest of 'em. Each time there's been a child coming, I've had fears that the same thing would happen with them that happened with Nancy. But I've been very blessed. God has been good to us."

Joseph John had plenty of time to think about his grandfather Joseph, Nancy and James Anderson, and his little sister Nancy as they awaited the return of the ferry from the Georgia side. The ferry captain had no cargo on his return trip. Joseph John knew that lines of wagon trains filled with settlers like them pressed from the east going west, not the reverse. More people wanted to push west to get their own land, to provide a way for their growing families to survive. He was glad his father was one of them. Despite the hardships of the move, missing his familiar haunts, and his questions about why the hurry to Georgia, he was beginning to get excited at the prospect of settling in a new area.

Waiting with the two remaining wagons, Joseph John watched as the two ferrymen and the captain used long poles to guide the ferryboat across the wide expanse. He was fascinated with their movements as they briskly pushed off from the other shore with the poles, propelling the platform away from the muddy bottom for as long as they could touch. Then they used paddles and a guide rope stretched across the river to make their way to the South Carolina side before being pushed downstream. One slip, and he knew that the ferry might end up in the big shoals above Augusta, or, worse, snarled in some of the large oaks that shoved their branches into the river.

It was nearly midday before the wagons had all been ferried to the Georgia side of the Savannah, and William Morgan was impatient with the delay.

"Let's push ahead, work the horses a little more, we got a ways to go before Washington," he said.

The party resumed its trek west with Joseph John again riding with his father and his mother and Baby Susannah.

"What'll Washington be like?" he asked his father.

"I've heard it's a very prosperous settlement," William said. Many people from South Carolina had moved over there during the first part of the war and especially after, he said.

"There's shops and tradesmen and it's rivallin' Augusta to be the biggest town in the headright and bounty areas. 'Course, they've had plenty of time to build a town here while waiting for Indian lottery lands to open up in th' rest of th' state."

Joseph John felt the hair on the back of his neck bristle. Bile rose up in his stomach again as he pictured the grisly scene from his dream.

"Where're the Indians now?"

"Joseph John, they're mostly gone, but even if there are a few, the Cherokee are very civilized, and they don't bother the whites. In fact, they've intermarried with the whites and have their own plantations and homes. Even so, many of them continue to move west out to Arkansas to make room for the white settlers."

"Why is that?"

"Well, you know, Son, we're not even sure the Cherokee and Creeks are entitled to be here. There're a lot of people who think they're not of the human race. I don't happen to be one of 'em, but there are a lot who want the Indians totally out of this area, and I think you'll see them disappear from here. Most of the politicians here want them out, want the land totally for the whites. And I'm one of 'em. I don't want to fear for my family. The massacres of the past are just too recent a memory. Besides, they fought against us with the British during the independence struggle."

Joseph John looked back at his mother to see if she'd been listening. Her eyes were wide and she opened her mouth as if she were going to say something, but when she saw her son looking at her, she closed her mouth.

He looked back at his father. "Are they like the slaves, Pa? They can't read or write or do any of the figurin' I can do."

His father winced, then looked at him.

"Boy, you got more questions than a sow has piglets."

The way William responded, Joseph John figured the subject wasn't his favorite. He didn't appear angry, but perhaps sad. Ever since the wagon train turned west, the boy noticed, his going ahead and fearlessly asking questions was working out. His pa hadn't balked yet.

"Yes, they're like the slaves," William said with a sigh. "And yet they were here before the white man came, and they lived freely, so they're not quite the same."

Joseph John watched the roadsides as the wagon made its way along the rugged terrain. Closer to the settlement around Washington, the dense forests on either side of them gave way to vast cotton and grain fields. The lands, which stretched as far as the eye could see, were being plowed for the spring planting. They traveled through gently rolling valleys, admiring shoots of wildflowers by the side of the road and exclaiming over the sizes of plantations lining the way on either side.

Back off the road they would occasionally see a large plantation house or a homestead with numerous outbuildings—tobacco barns, livestock shelters, fowl houses, a smokehouse, and, closer to the dwelling house, a kitchen detached but often connected by a walkway to the main house. In between were numerous sections set off from each other: a kitchen garden, a horse yard, a cow pen. And, sometimes, in back of the main house, usually some ways to the rear tucked into deep woods, they could glimpse one of the Negro houses. They knew that meant it was a large plantation.

The other way they knew it was a plantation was from the attention given to the outside of the house. Some of the houses had white clapboard exteriors, instead of the rough, hewn logs used for homesteads. One house they passed had once been two log cabins connected by a dog trot in between, and its owners were in the process of adding clapboard to the front and all around, then placing a new porch with columns across the front. It was all being painted a gleaming white, and a picket fence was being laid out by a Negro workman in the front yard.

"My, that's a fancy way to turn a humble home into a palace," said Rebecca.

As the wagons pulled into the middle of town, they saw signs of heavy commerce. Wagons loaded with hay and carts filled with livestock crowded by them on the narrow roads. Gentlemen in suits paused to talk on wooden sidewalks across the fronts of stores whose windows held a wide variety of farm supplies, dry goods, and other necessities. A few ladies in fresh cotton dresses with parasols paraded in the afternoon light. There had been a recent rain, and Holland bulbs were bursting in front yards everywhere, their scent mixing with the sweetness of cherry and apple blossoms. The main streets of Washington showed a fine settlement of mostly white clapboard homes with white wood paling fencing in the front yards.

"Ma, it's like Abbeville in the spring, only newer!" Joseph John exclaimed. He looked back and saw his mother looking excitedly at all the buildings.

"Maybe the place we're going to will be like this if enough people move there," she said. She looked from side to side at the splendid homes. "Such a genteel town!"

As they sought out an inn that could accommodate them, Rebecca began reminding Joseph John of all the manners he'd been taught but hadn't thought about since the last preacher's visit in Abbeville District.

"Remember to let your younger sisters go first, when we line up for dinner.

"Be sure and wash your hands before you touch anything in the house.

"First thing when you get down from this wagon, make sure you use the whisk broom all over yourself and your brother, then help your father and uncle get dusted off, too. They'll not appreciate a lot of dirt in these nice, clean homes."

"But, Ma, you know Papa will want to water the horses first. He won't be worried 'bout nothin' else till he gets all six of 'em watered."

"I know, but you make sure he doesn't set foot inside till you've swept him off, d'hear?"

"Yes'm."

"And it's yes, ma'am, and no, ma'am, and yes, sir and no, sir—"

"Yes, ma'am."

Joseph John stood with his mother in the large dining room of the inn. His pa, uncle, and brother were feeding the animals at the livestock pen down the street, and Joseph John had helped bring in a basket of family belongings for his mother. The girls were upstairs already tucked into a number of large beds.

He looked up at the ceiling, and at the walls, which held large oil portraits of what he supposed were important people: a young girl with pink-rose cheeks and lovely long blond hair, an older, wealthy-looking man in black coat and cravat, a matronly woman with dark hair pulled back severely who wore a deep green dress. The ceiling in the room was higher than any Joseph John had ever seen, and the walls and the ceiling were made of dressed planks that had been painted white.

"I heard you questioning your pa," Rebecca said. It was not a reproach, but an observation. "About why we were leaving, and what we're going to." She smiled, and it registered with Joseph John he hadn't seen a smile on his mother's face since before they left. When was the last time?

"Yes'm," the boy replied, then corrected himself. "I mean, yes, ma'am."

"I reckon it's true," she said. "Land is cheaper. We've got the Thurmans writing us about the land and selling it to your pa at a reasonable price." She moved her hand over her long sleeves. Joseph John noticed for the first time: she was wearing her best dress, one he didn't see very often. She had attached undersleeves that were edged with a fine white lace. He'd never seen those.

"But probably the main reason," she said, "is to find a peaceable neighborhood, one where we can stay."

"The neighbors we had were good enough, Ma," Joseph John said. Then, thinking of the last neighbor they saw, he added: "Most of 'em anyway. You heard me telling about Old Man Cunningham. I still don't see why he would aim a rifle at my head."

Rebecca bowed her head and closed her eyes. She hugged herself with her arms, as though protecting herself.

"I know," she whispered. She looked at Joseph John and there were tears in her eyes. "I'll let your pa explain. There's just been so much going on over there. Now we've left it, I don't want to think about it."

She blinked back tears and wiped one eye with her lacy undersleeve.

"It's just so important to have a place that's your home," she said. "A place where you're surrounded with like-minded folks. A place like Washington," she said, extending her arm to show the entire room. Rebecca put her hands on his shoulders. "One day, when you're grown and you have your own family, you'll know what I mean."

She abruptly dropped her hands and walked over to a double chest of drawers that stood against the opposite wall. A large glass window with six panes on top and six panes on bottom was next to the chest.

"Isn't this a beautiful piece," she asked. She ran her hands over the smooth surface of the chest. The walnut wood had been sanded and burnished to a beautiful shine that caught the reflection of the candles burning in silver holders on the dining room table. Rebecca shyly touched the brass pulls on the chest, then traced the elaborate molding at the point where a second set of drawers was set upon the base of the lower three drawers.

"You can take it apart and move it from one room to the next without breaking a back," she said admiringly.

"One day," she said, turning back to Joseph John, "I'll have a nice piece like this in our new home. Your father can make furniture like this, if he has the time."

Joseph John tried to picture his pa, sooty from his work in the smithy, working on a walnut chest of drawers. He couldn't quite see it.

"We'll have a good home in Georgia," his mother went on, almost ignoring Joseph John. "We'll have neighbors of like mind, and we'll find honest and good friends for you and Gideon and the girls."

She was smiling broadly now. This was a new person, Joseph John decided. He'd never seen his mother so excited.

"Joseph John," she said, turning to him. "You're going to need some social graces one of these days. Let me show you how to waltz."

She grabbed his hands, put one lightly around her waist, then raised his other hand to hers. "Now, put your feet just so—"

She showed him where to position his feet.

"It's on a count of one-two-three, one-two-three." She guided Joseph John in a dance. Joseph stumbled.

"Ma, I don't know how," he said, confused. He stood back.

Rebecca broke away and continued waltzing around the room, deftly turning around and around, twisting aside just in time to avoid colliding with the chairs and long table.

"Don't worry," she said brightly. "You'll learn one of these days. After all, Gideon will need to be thinking of courting before too long, and then it'll be your turn. I hope this new settlement will grow, so there'll be lots of fine young ladies from which you can select a wife."

Joseph John watched his mother in amazement. She was just full of surprising thoughts and talents. Does Pa waltz? he wondered.

Suddenly, she stopped, breathless. She smiled again.

"I've got to stop," she said, drawing her hand to her chest. "I forget that I'm an old married lady with seven children."

Joseph John laughed. His mother's lightheartedness was catching. He couldn't remember the last time he'd laughed.

As daylight of the third day dimmed and sunset began warming the western skies, Joseph John and his family's wagons pulled off the road and onto a smaller track heading north into the woods. There, in a clearing not far from the course was a stand, a tavern where they were to spend the night.

For a few moments, Joseph John had to adjust to the scene before him. In contrast to the large, white, two-story Federal style house where they'd stayed the night in Washington, the tavern in front of him was definitely more humble.

The weatherboard stand was neatly built, rose two stories, and was two rooms deep. There was a single window at the top and a couple of windows on the first floor that were hidden by the overhang of the sloped roof over the porch. This porch ran the entire length of the first floor. Joseph John smiled when he saw the openings that served for windows, as yesterday in Washington he saw more glass-paned windows than he'd seen in all his days. This tavern was much more like the frontier homes he knew, with wooden doors to close over the windows in case of rain or cold.

On the left of the tavern was an attached room with a single door that Joseph John guessed was the tavernkeeper's room. The whole structure was perched on a foundation of stacked flat rocks. Further to the left was a lean-to with a pen for livestock.

The wagons stopped in front of the tavern, and the travelling party descended from the large farm wagons. They struggled up the tavern's heavy timber stairs.

Inside a huge fireplace full of pine logs gave off bright, welcome light to the dark room. Three of the four occupants of the room were gathered on heavy log benches pushed up to a single large table. Scraps of food lay on tin plates spread around the table.

"Welcome, strangers," said a large man wearing an apron across a body that Joseph John figured to weigh at least two hundred pounds. "Name's James Darden. Come on in, put your belongin's down, have some food."

"We'd also like lodging for the night and food for the horses if that's possible, neighbor," said William Morgan.

"There's plenty of room, and the feed's in the stables. I got one large room with six beds and two smaller rooms, each can sleep two—or three if you're cozy, heh, heh, heh!" he laughed. His belly fairly jumped as he surpressed a big laugh. "Go on around back and I'll let you in."

Darden reached for a tin lantern holding a candle and moved slowly over to the fire where he used a twig to light the wick, then threw the twig into the fire.

With the proprietor wheezing slightly as he moved past them, Joseph John and his brother, Gideon, followed outside to the back of the cabin where a stairway led up to the second floor. The stairs rose at a sharp incline and were fairly narrow, so the boys let the owner climb up first, giving him lots of room. He paused outside the door to the sleeping rooms on a small porch and handed the lantern to Gideon. He was huffing and puffing as he held the padlock in one hand and inserted a large iron key with the other.

Inside the boys saw two rooms on their right, each holding a square bed big enough for two large or three small people. On the other side was a long room with what appeared to be a half dozen bedsteads. In each of the rooms there was a washstand with a plain white bowl and pitcher and a dingy towel hanging on the overhead bar of the washstand.

"Well, what d'ye think, m'boys? Mr. Darden asked. "As fine a palace as you'll find in these parts, eh?"

"Yes, sir," said Gideon, smirking to Joseph John. Joseph John thought longingly of home in Abbeville District where he'd stored his prized set of dominoes under his bed. But then he thought of his bedroll of the first night and his dream about Indians and Thomas Cunningham.

"Yes, sir, real fine," Joseph John said, smiling at the big man.

Gideon and Joseph John went to William Morgan's wagon to retrieve two large baskets that Rebecca had packed with their travelling clothes. William and Sam Morgan had left the tavern while the boys followed Darden upstairs. In that time, they'd unhitched the three teams, led them to the shed on the left side of the tavern, and found water and oats and corn cobs for the horses. The boys heard the sounds of heavy munching coming from the far side of the tavern.

"There y'go, Mary, eat well, you've earned it," William said to his lead mare. Joseph John could picture his father stroking her. After she'd had food and water, he'd carefully check her shoes to make sure her feet were free of stones and smooth her back to check for burrs. Then the whole process would be repeated with the other horses.

Gideon and Joseph John hauled the baskets upstairs and placed both in the large room. Joseph John pulled several pieces of folded white cloth out of one of the baskets and took them downstairs to his mother, who would diaper Susannah on a makeshift pallet in the corner of the tavern's main room.

"Thank you, Son," Rebecca told him, then turned to shield her daughter from view with her body while exchanging diapers. She would be busy for awhile after dinner, Joseph John knew, rinsing the day's collection and hanging them to dry outside in the dark, if she could find a proper place.

Within a few moments, Darden had put on the table large platters full of what looked like blackened carcasses of poultry. Joseph John couldn't be sure about the identity. It was only after he had cut into one portion and pulled apart a bony piece that he could definitely identify it as the wing of a chicken. A blackened substance fell out of the cavity of the large bird. After a couple of bites and giggles back and forth, Joseph John and his brother decided it was onions and potatoes, extremely well cooked with bits of soot from the fireplace for good measure. Uncooked dough that passed for bread lay uneaten at their plates.

Joseph John tried not to think about what he was eating. He was so hungry from the journey. Also, there was no telling what food they'd have on down the trail. Best eat while I can, he thought.

In the corner, he saw a body stirring and struggling to a stand. He hadn't noticed the form before. It was an old man, leaning on a long stick for a cane, and he was dressed in a dirty homespun shirt over a raggedy pair of britches. His face was indistinct. It seemed to recede into a cloud of gray whiskers and shocks of matching pale hair framing his cheeks. He saw the old man looking at him hard, eyes shining in the fireglow.

"Come over here, young'n," the man called to Joseph John. His voice was gravelly, but strong.

Joseph John ate all he could, then moved away from the rest of his family at the table. The old man had waited patiently for him, pulling up a chair and sitting down while the boy finished eating. He pulled another chair beside him.

When Joseph John approached, the old man tapped the second chair with his stick.

"Sit down, sit down."

He inquired about Joseph John and his family, asking where they were from.

"Abbeville Dist'ict? Why, I'm from there," said the old man. "Used to farm a homestead on Rocky Creek. Wha'd you say your pa's name is?"

"William Morgan, sir. His brother's here, too, he's Sam Morgan," Joseph John answered.

"Morgan...Morgan. I campaigned with a fella named Morgan. There was a mess of 'em around went by that name. Why, there was a Reverend Morgan that settled five hundred people from Ulster in that neck of the woods. Man I knew was—I know the man, I can see him, give an old man some time here—John...no, it was Joseph Morgan."

Joseph John's eyes grew big. "You knew my grandfather?"

"Well, I did if your grandfather was tall and kinda fierce-eyed. Man could shoot a longrifle farther than any person I knew. And he didn't wait for a fight. But he was a man a God, too. We took to calling him Preacher Morgan."

Joseph John sat quietly as the Revolutionary War patriot talked of the old days. The man's wrinkled face had brightened when he recalled the name of his fellow soldier. He looked past Joseph's head, deep in reverie. Red, weathered cheeks caught the firelight, and his blue eyes twinkled as he talked.

"I never knew your grandfather had two sons—I just knew about one. We were in the campaign to Cowpens together. Yeah, we were 'litia fellas, fightin' under Gen'ral Pickens. A course, we go back a lot further, to

'69, when we saddled our horses with rifles and rode down the Cherokee Path to Charles Town to demand a vote. The planters in the Low Country had denied us voting, even though we'd settled the back country to keep their huge plantations safe from Indians. D'you know there were seventy silversmiths in Charles Town turning out purties f' the planters big houses? An' here we were 300 miles away with no courts or schools or ministers. An' wha'd they do—they voted Charles Town ladies sixty thousand pounds for a ballroom! Now, which 'f old Joe Morgan's sons is your pa?"

"His name is William, sir—"

"William. That's the name. I remember when your granpa got word he was born. We were at Hobkirk's Hill when it happened an' he wept for joy on hearin' it."

The old man spat a wad of chew to his side, barely missing the fire.

"Oh, them wuz the days for fighting and scrabbling out a living up there in the back country. At first, there was the Indians. You know about the massacre at Long Cane Creek, prob'bly."

Joseph John watched the old man's eyes gaze beyond him and saw him relish the retelling of the details of life in the back country. It was almost like the man was talking to himself, as he showed little awareness of Joseph John's attempts to ask a question. Having learned the lesson of respect for his elders, Joseph John listened but didn't listen at the same time.

"Then there were the Indian traders stirring up the Indians against us. Thomas Brown, the Cunninghams—"

Joseph John started for a moment as he heard the familiar name.

"—Richard Pearis—he was the one who married an Indian woman and then had his half-breed son purchase land in the Indian territory then sell it back to him so's he owned most of the northwest corner of the state. These men were the friends of the Indians—an' all of 'em beholden to the British Crown."

Joseph John waited for the old man to say Cunningham's name again, but there was no more mention. The old fighter was talking so fast the boy knew he wouldn't be able to interrupt. He looked over at his family still at the table and hoped someone would call him over. He was too polite to just leave while the old patriot jabbered on.

"Well, when we settlers started comin' in with our grants of land, we just assumed we wuz supposed to plant and cultivate and grow families and everything else would just fall into place. Our second fight was with the lowland planters, and that's when we rode down to Charles Town to give those aristycrats a piece of our minds and the glint of our rifles."

Joseph John resigned himself, placing his chin in his hand and facing forward, waiting for the family's exit from the table to provide his way out.

"After a number of years, the pop'lation grew and with the lack of law and courts and no schools and ministers there got to be a lot of crime, so a bunch of us organized an appeal to go down to talk to the legislature. Pretty soon we had 300 men all saddled and heading down the path. Then no sooner was we out of range from our homesteads than Pearis had rounded up some of the Cherokees and some 'a these ne'er-do-well's who'd settled in our area, and they began attacking an' burning our homes. So all us back country settlers turned around an' lit out for home."

"Now all this was before the war, Son, and that was our third fight."

"Tell me more. Was Joseph a hero? Did he whup the Tories?"

The old man's eyes saddened. His voice lowered. His slightly reddened lower eyelids were suddenly wet.

"Son, they's eighteen hundred widows and orphans throughout all of Ninety-Six when it was all over, my wife Obedeime and my two sons Charles and Andrew died with 'em—all because of that war among the neighbors."

Now Joseph John wanted to hear more, but it was just at this point that the family got up to leave.

"I gotta go. My ma and pa will want me. Thanks for the story." He ran to join the others, excited to tell someone what he'd found out.

The family moved up the outside stairway, with tired younger sisters crying and their mother and Alice trying to shush them.

"Mommy—I tired," two-year-old Laura cried. "Want bed! Go home. Now!"

"Go on up the stairs, honey, your bed's at the top of the stairs."

In the hallway between the small rooms and the large one, Rebecca decided that she would sleep with the young girls and the baby in the large room. William and his brother Sam were already heading for the bed in one small room. Gideon and Joseph John headed for the second small room.

"Did you see the size of that Mr. Darden?" Gideon asked, as he snuggled under several quilts and blankets in the bed he shared with Joseph John. "You can tell he doesn't work a farm like us."

"He does look a mite big," said Joseph John. "But there's no telling what people will look like where we're going. If there are enough tavern keepers, maybe they'll all look like that. Maybe we'll be the odd ones.

"Y'know Ma's countin' on this new place to be like Washington," Joseph John said. "I gotta feelin' it's gonna be more like this place—kinda scarce of social graces."

"Well, you know women—always dreamin'," Gideon yawned.

"Guess you'd better get your dancin' shoes on—she's already thinking of you gettin' married!" Joseph John teased his brother.

"Only woman I'm interested in is one who's rich as a queen," Gideon said with a sneer in his voice. "She better have lots of money. No more of this yeoman farming for me—that's for fools. Gonna be rich and lazy when I get a chance!"

Joseph John was taken aback by Gideon's strong words. He certainly didn't sound like he favored Pa's way of life. Himself, he'd never given marriage much of a thought, much less tried to decide whether he preferred someone rich or poor or in-between.

"Wha'd that old man want?"

"He fought in the Revolutionary War—says he knew our granpa."

"Which one?"

"Joseph Morgan. Y'know he was telling me so much about the area we just came from—Indian attacks, neighbor killing neighbor during the war—I think we're lucky to be leaving there."

"Aw, that happened over 50 years ago—"

"Maybe,"Joseph John said, recalling that the old man had mentioned Cunninghams among the Tories. "Maybe it's still goin' on."

Despite the disturbing thought of Cunningham, Joseph John's eyes drooped with fatigue from the three days of difficult, hot travel. Deep in the old wooden bed next to Gideon, he slept dreamlessly through the night.

Chapter 2

DEKALB COUNTY

1826

The fragrance wafting from the woods was sweet, arresting the senses and causing Joseph John to put down the axe he was using to strip the pine log laying at his feet. Sweat streamed down his face, chest, arms, and legs. He decided to take a rest.

He walked toward the tall trees and wandered into the brush girdling the lofty pines, hickorys, and poplars. He spotted the wild honeysuckle bushes with their large white blossoms tinged with pink. He picked a double stem of the woody plant, counting eight bunches of fist-sized blossoms. Burying his nose in the frothy growth, he inhaled deeply, then let out his breath.

"Mama will like this," he said to himself.

He returned to his axe and log, and continued cutting away the limbs and bark of the long, once-tall longleaf pine. The strong smell of pine and rosin greeted his nose. He decided to keep at his work rather than take the blossoms to his mother, at least right away. Every minute away from his work meant the longer it would be until their log cabin home would be finished.

He looked beyond and saw the large canvas tent that was their temporary home. His mother was outside feeding Susannah, and two of his smaller sisters played at her feet. He envied them their idleness.

He pulled at some of the yellow jessamine vine that wound around a small bush brought in with the pine and now laying drying in the sun. As he held the blossom up, he wondered at the brilliant yellow of the trumpet flower attached to the vine. His eyes returned to the ground where he followed a trail of other blossoms that had fallen on the path from the woods that once held the pine and the wandering, climbing jessamine vine.

As his eyes lifted from the floor of the forest, he was startled to see a shimmering canopy of white blossoms up above the honeysuckle but far lower than the lofty pines and oaks. The canopy seemed to go on forever, changing to a thicker layer, then suddenly thinning as it extended deeper into the woods. Then Joseph John realized that it was not just one tree, but many, many trees bearing this unusual blossom, and they seemed to carry their series of lacy blossoms into infinity.

"A beauty of a spot," Joseph John told himself, then went back in earnest to finish the stripping and trimming.

He felt a firm hand clasp his shoulder, and turned toward his left side where he felt the hand.

"Looks good, Son," William Morgan said to Joseph John. "Be careful you don't hurt yourself with that axe. I sharpened it real good before we left home."

"Okay, Pa."

"Be sure you get all you can so we can add that to the other logs. Looks like we'll be finished before sunset—that is, getting all the logs ready. Got church on the morrow, and then Sam's leaving, so I want to get as much done as possible."

Joseph John nodded his head, acknowledging the inevitable loss of his uncle. He would return to Abbeville District, and it was unknown when they would see him again. This was common, Joseph John knew. Families broke apart regularly in order to find their own land, build a homestead, and provide for themselves. He guessed it had been going on for centuries, ever since that poor Scotsman left the cold hills of his land to try his luck in Ireland. Selling to the newcomer and moving on from the old homestead was a way of life.

After Sam returned to Abbeville District, William and his family would continue to build their cabin. They'd plant the summer garden so their first winter would find them with sufficient food. Livestock pens would be built, and they'd acquire breeding stock to restart the family's meat sources. With the loss of Sam's strong hands to help, Joseph John and Gideon would have to work even harder.

"Be sure you leave enough restin' time tonight so you can be there for the Lord tomorrow, Joseph John."

The youth noted the difficulty he was going to have with both directives from his father—one to get the logs finished, the other to rest—and then resumed raising the axe and striking the tree bark. He'd skillfully made sure some of the smaller pieces of bark fell on the blossoms of wild honeysuckle to hide them from his father while saving them for his mother.

The next morning William Morgan guided a farm wagon full of Morgans down the road that went in the direction of the old Creek village, Sandtown, on their way to the church meeting. Mockingbirds and bluejays were flushed up off the road and out of the bushes alongside by the sound of the horses' hooves and the rattle of the wheels. Warblers trilled and woodpeckers kept up a constant call across the woods they passed. Several times Joseph John saw a brilliant red male cardinal fly across the open spaces in the woods to either side of them. As they travelled south on the road, dense forest occasionally gave way to cleared fields; often a settler's log cabin could be seen.

Joseph John noted his father's determined set of jaw, and his mildly receding hairline that was the beginning of a head of fine, brown hair worn tucked behind the ears to keep it away from his eyes. He knew his father would help with the church service, as he was very anxious to assist the preacher and show his appreciation for his presence. Today the Reverend David Thurman would be preaching as a guest of Utoy Primitive Baptist Church. The term "church," Joseph John knew, was a kind way of referring to a few gathered faithful, as a log church for their congregation was just being started.

Trained as a Methodist minister, the Reverend Thurman could sometimes be prevailed upon to preach so that they could have a service more than once a month. The surrounding community here in the western part of DeKalb County, which only had about a dozen families, still lacked a regular Baptist minister.

As Joseph John regarded William, he saw the pride in his eyes and the way he held himself erect as he drove the horses. Joseph John realized for the first time that as the son of this man, he would have the same yearnings, the same tendencies to want to create something better than what he had before. He looked at the strong, moderately tall, intense man dressed in a black serge suit with a white starched shirt. The stiff collar strained under bulging neck muscles. The neck muscles, the sunburned skin, and his large, scratched hands that held the reins were the only clues to hours William spent in heavy labor, lifting and holding heavy iron tools, wagon wheels, and other equipment over hot coals in his forge. Joseph John remembered the ritual of his mother carefully putting that same stiff-collared and cuffed white shirt away each Sunday as soon as they returned from the meeting to make sure it didn't get dusty. Then his pa would return to his farmer's clothes, for the rest of Sunday, which was usually spent reading the Bible to his family or passing time down the road a ways at a neighbor's farm. On Monday, when it was time to work the forge, he'd don the big brown leather apron that protected him from sparks from the anvil he used to work metals.

Joseph John looked back at his mother, his five sisters, his older brother, and Uncle Sam riding in the back of the wagon. He knew this was part of it, the pride in family and belief in bringing into the world a flock of other believers who would continue the work and respect and love of those before them. Their religion and Scripture were as much a part of their lives as the farm tools, horses, or crops they raised. It was a daily interweaving of their work, their lives and The Word, not a Sunday-go-to-meeting kind of thinking. His father's and his mother's lives were interwoven with a consciousness of some other world to which they aspired and gently, persistently, and firmly urged their children toward.

Reverend Thurman wound down his sermon on this third Sunday in April, the first after Easter Sunday. Then, turning to the twenty or so attendees at his service, being held under great oaks near a clearing that held a rough field stone foundation for a church, he told them:

"My dear friends, our brother Samuel will undertake a great journey today. Samuel, will you please come forward for a blessing? And let us all bow our heads as we pray over Brother Samuel."

Samuel moved forward and Reverend Thurman placed his hands lightly on Sam's lowered head.

"It was Samuel who was the first prophet, the man who as a child was called by God. 'The Lord did let none of his words fall to the ground.' It was Samuel who led the the many who came after—Isaiah and Ezekial, Malachi and Micah, and hosts of others, warning of Yahweh's law, foretelling the Messiah who would come to redeem us.

"The Book of Samuel relates the story of David's greatest sorrow and the greatest threat to his kingdom, the denouncement by Absalom— Absalom, who decried David's concubines and set himself up as a rival king; Absalom, who became wise like David, but who was a chaste man, unlike David; Absalom, who made David flee Jerusalem and who later was slain by Joab when he hung himself in branches of a tree he traveled under; Absalom, whom David mourned and for whom David put away his concubines in atonement.

"Go in wisdom, Samuel Morgan. We all pray that you return safely to your family in former home, that you travel without affliction and in the Spirit of the Lord. Amen."

Reverend Thurman finished the service and dismissed the members of Utoy Primitive Baptist Church. They moved out from under the arbor into the open space where the adults visited together and the children broke into games of tag.

"Gotcha last!" David Thurman, Jr., called to Joseph John as he touched Joseph's arm and quickly ran away. Joseph John knew that his long legs would quickly outrun David's, as he was six years older, so he gave him a few moments' start.

"No you don't!" Joseph John yelled menacingly. He took off after David, then broke his run as he almost tumbled over two very small Thurman sisters all dressed up with ringlets of curls, wearing their best yellow and white striped cotton frocks. Four-year-old Lucy, holding two-year-old Jane's hand, continued on her path as though nothing had happened.

Immediately, Lavinia Mann Thurman grabbed her son by the collar and pulled him away from the other children, talking to him in a low, but still audible tone.

"David, don't start a game when so many of the smaller ones are around! I'll have your father speak to you."

David looked at Joseph John, then motioned with his head back to the arbor where the meeting had been held.

"Let's play another game where we won't run into my dumb little sisters," he said.

When they were under the enormous oak trees, he took a knife with a very sharp, pointed blade from his pocket.

"What're you going to do with that?" asked Joseph John.

"We're just going to see who can throw it the farthest and make it stick up in the ground."

"My papa won't let me play with knives."

"Aw, it'll be okay."

A shadow fell over the clay-packed open space that David was preparing to use for a knife-throwing range.

Joseph John glanced to his left to see who was watching their game. David looked up as well.

"What do you want?"

The other boy, his coarse black bangs falling forward into his face, said nothing. He looked at both of them with dark, silent eyes.

"Hey!" yelled David. "Are you an Indian?"

The boy, who was dressed in Sunday clothes, broke away from the two and started to run.

"Hey. Come back. We want you to play," Joseph John yelled. Faster than he could think, the boy was out of hearing distance and down the path where the families were greeting each other. He disappeared among skirts and bonnets and dark suits.

From that direction, Gideon approached the younger boys.

"Papa says to come on, we've got to go home so Sam can get on his way."

"Goodbye, goodbye!" The younger girls waved their aprons and the skirts of their Sunday dresses as they jumped around in the excitement of the wagon leaving the Morgan farm.

Each of the boys had a greeting for Sam's oldest boy, their cousin.

"Tell John to keep a watch out for snakes on the road! Tell 'im we'll save him some turkey to hunt if he comes this way!"

"Yeah, tell 'im to keep an eye out for the Indians!"

Joseph John, as he waved goodby to his uncle, thought about Old Man Cunningham and the musket he'd aimed at Joseph John's head. The boy wondered if his uncle would run into Cunningham as they had just as they'd begun the trip west. He thought for a moment about warning Sam, but how would that sound? He'd have to explain, and he didn't feel he could without looking foolish. Had his father warned Sam?

Again, Joseph John missed the familiar sounds and sights of the farm he'd helped his father build in South Carolina. He pictured the new owner running the mill, planting the summer crops in their fields, and working the smithy. How many tools and resources were there to work with! Here they had trees and wild animals and virtually no roads, only old Indian paths and trade routes among the dense forests. Except where the Morgans and a few other families had punctured the wilderness with clearings, cabins, pens for animals, and fields of crops, there was only nature as God created it.

After Sam left, the family gathered for dinner at a long table set under the trees. His mother had heated a pot of stew she'd put up back in

South Carolina, and they gave thanks for that and the corn cakes that she'd cooked over the fire outside their tent. They also gave thanks for the good weather. Most of the days had been fair, and the rain was just enough to water the crops they'd begun to put in, in addition to the expansive vegetable garden, the first to be planted.

Joseph John finished his meal and helped put away the leftover food. He walked about 200 feet from the tent, down a slight incline to a small spring. He placed the butter crock in the gently swirling water to keep it cold until the next use. He looked up across the spring and saw a boy, the same boy he'd seen after the church meeting, running through the woods in front of him.

"Hey! Where're you goin'?"

The boy looked back at Joseph John, stopping in mid-stride.

"Home."

"Where's that?"

"Across the hill—over yonder."

"Hey, come on over. I want to talk to you."

The boy, who was dressed in long pants, a white shirt, and brogans, turned and came toward Joseph John. His hair was cut short like Joseph John's, but a straight, dark hunk of it hung low near his eyes, which were darker than any Joseph John had seen. He was more slender than Joseph John and a little shorter, but he looked about the same age.

"What's your name?"

"A-Adam."

"My name's Joseph. I'm called Joseph John by my ma and pa. Where'd you say you live?"

"We live beyond the river. We come down here to sell corn. I'm out lookin' today."

"You Indian?"

"My mother's Cherokee, my father is a white man. Jessie McDaniel."

"Weren't you at the meetin' this mornin'?"

"We been churched, but my father wants us goin' more regular."

"Have you joined?" Joseph John had never seen an Indian or part-Indian at his church. He wondered if it would happen.

Adam shook his head quickly. "You want to play a game?"

"Sure. What can we play?"

He pulled a narrow bundle of cane sticks out of his back pocket. The cane had been split down the middle, cut in eight-inch lengths, and tied together with a piece of old cloth. Adam removed the tie, then held four sticks out to his new friend.

"What do I do?" Joseph John asked.

"We take turns. You throw them up. Then sticks fall down. You get the most points if all of 'em land cut side down. Few points if they land cut side up, or mixed up."

Joseph John threw the sticks into the air, making sure his arm was steady so they'd all rise and fall about the same distance. He figured that was the best way to make sure they landed face down. But the slight breeze around them caught two of the very light sticks and caused them to topple over and over, landing face up.

"Aah! You lose. Only two points for two up, two down."

"What do you mean?"

"If all facing down, you get ten points. Five points, all facing up. Three points, three face up, one face down. You get low points, two for two up and two down. Only worse is three down and one up.

"Well, I'm ready to play again. Your turn." Joseph John settled down in the open space where they were playing. "I'm going to keep track of the score."

He pulled up handfuls of grass and weeds, and created a small dirt space. He took a stick and wrote the number "2" in the dirt. He continued to tear away grass so he could make a larger space.

The wind continued to play havoc with the boys' game. Time after time they threw the four pieces of cane into the air. The breezes blew the sticks this way and that, making it difficult to call some results, as the sticks would land some distance away. Once when it was Adam's turn, one stick fell in the stream and was floating away until Adam grabbed it.

"It was down. I saw it. It was down."

Joseph John looked at the totals he'd kept on the dirt tablet.

"Well, that gives you twelve, and I've got five. What other games do you know?"

"Here's another one. First we have to find lots of sticks about the same size."

Joseph John and Adam searched the ground for sticks, and then picked branches off the nearby bushes, pulling off leaves until they had a pile of medium long branches.

"Need more," said Adam, so he and Joseph John crossed to the other side of the stream and pulled more branches, denuded them, then lay them on top of the others. There was a pile close to knee high when they were done. Adam immediately knelt and silently counted the branches and sticks. He then took a long stick and pulled a knife from a handsome, decorated leather holder attached to the rope holding up his pants. He whittled one end of the stick until it had a sharp point.

"Here." He handed the sharpened stick to Joseph John and urged him toward the pile of branches.

"What do we do?" Joseph John asked.

"Stick it in the pile. Pull branches to your side. If you have odd number of branches, you win. If you have even number of branches, you lose, you give me something that you own."

"Own. Well I don't have much that's mine. Maybe some clothes." Adam looked disappointed.

"Well, wait a minute, let me go see. Don't go away, I'll be back soon." Joseph John ran back to the family tent up on a slight rise above the spring. He moved to the back of the canvas home where there was a set of cots, his among them. He was bending down to find his favorite dominoes when his father appeared at the door to the tent.

"Son, what are you doing?"

"Doing? Oh, I'm playing with a new friend."

"Are you playing with that Indian boy?"

"He's part-Indian. His mother is Indian, but his pa's English. His name is Adam McDaniel. We're playing a game where you cut into a large number of branches and whoever gets the odd number wins—"

"So you're wagering with your dominoes?"

How does Pa know what I'm doing and I haven't even told him? Joseph John wondered.

"Joseph John, you've sinned against the Lord by attempting to wager, and even more grievous a wrong, you've about gambled away your one nice plaything." William's face grew red and he gestured with both his hands. "And you're doing it on the Lord's Day, an even greater shame!" He tried to speak again, but his words were choked.

"...No good half-breed..." He looked toward the front of the tent, then back at Joseph John. He frowned in exasperation.

"I ought to wear you out with a strap. You stay on your cot for the rest of the day and contemplate your sin!"

William disappeared for a moment, then came back with his large, worn Bible in his hands.

"I want you to start reading this," he said. "From the beginning, in the Old Testament. I don't want you lying idle. Just think of your sin as you read about the kings and David."

Joseph John sat on the cot for the rest of the afternoon, regretting he couldn't play outside in the beautiful spring weather. He stroked the cover and some of the first pages of the Bible, but he didn't read because the words were too big for him. There were lots of names of places he couldn't pronounce. Instead he thought about how he'd had to leave Adam by the spring, waiting for his return. How long would he wait there, sharpened stick in hand, before he returned to his own home?

Joseph John had lost his new playmate, and come tomorrow it would be work, work, work from breakfast 'til dark. His one day off was spent in punishment. He couldn't understand why his father had been so irate with him. It was a harmless game, and there was at least half a chance he'd have been able to win Adam's fine knife and leather holder.

And even if he were Indian, he wasn't very different from Joseph John.

He sure knew how to do sums and takeaways, he told himself.

Chapter 3

DEKALB COUNTY

1834

In his father's forge on a Saturday afternoon, Joseph was helping William hold a wheel frame he was molding to make a carriage wheel, a task that required a great deal of skill and concentration. As it was the latter part of August, sweat poured from Joseph's forehead as well as William's while they handled the hot iron. William looked intently at his work and swung a hammer to strike the outside edge of the wheel while Joseph held it steadily on the wide, heavy black anvil.

"Do you remember much about working silver?" Joseph asked.

William stopped his hammering and looked at his son in surprise. Joseph realized it had been a full eight years since even he'd thought about it. No telling when was the last time his father had thought of it.

"I remember everything," his father said. "Unfortunately, there's no call for it now. If there hadn't been a national bank started and folks still kept their assets in coin silver vases and platters then it would be very much in demand."

Joseph saw what he thought was a look of regret come across his father's face. William used his wrinkled, damp handkerchief to wipe his forehead. He didn't return to his work, and Joseph felt his father's gaze on him.

"Would you rather we not have the banks?" Joseph asked.

"No, I think it's far better to have the banks. The nation is growing, and it was time for that to happen. But even without the coin silver business, some areas can support a silversmith, even several silversmiths, but this is not one of those areas. It's too poor. Farmers subsist here, they don't acquire assets. They can't be prospering as long as there are threats like the Creeks to keep their minds off crops and land."

Joseph saw his father about to say something else, but his mouth suddenly closed, and he moved toward a jug of water. With a single swift movement, he reached one hand down and put his index finger through the small handle at the mouth of the gray jug, lifted it to his shoulder, then pointed it toward his mouth and guzzled generously. He wiped a trickle of water from his mouth with his other hand when he finished, and in one neat movement replaced the jug on the tall stump from which he'd taken it. He studied Joseph John silently for a moment. Joseph John saw his glistening face in the partial darkness and felt his steady gaze.

"You know now that you've reached your majority, it's time you had your own land and your own assets. Now that Gideon's got his land, it's time for you to have yours. Old Man Benjamin Thurman is needing some cash to help educate his five nephews and nieces, so I'm going to purchase some of the land left in Reverend Thurman's estate for you. It'll be yours to develop, live on if you want, or do whatever you wish."

Joseph had been waiting for him to mention his majority. It had been a month and a week since he became twenty-one years of age, so he had been patiently awaiting this talk since that time. It was a time of a lot of changes. The family had received a rare letter from Abbeville telling them his uncle Joseph had died back in Abbeville, so there was no need to distinguish him from the older man. As result, he was now simply "Joseph," the John name was retired. Even more exciting, William had given Gideon half a land lot. Gideon soon after sold it, married, and moved down to Griffin with his wife, Josephine. Now they had two boys. With his father's gift of land, Joseph would have prospects and could think about marrying and having a family.

"Thank you, Father, though I don't want to live on land away from you if you feel you want me here. With so many mouths to feed, I feel I can be a bigger help to you here."

"Well that's true Son, I do indeed need you. I didn't know the Lord was going to bless us with so many lovely but dependent females."

"Where is this land?"

"It's south of us here about a mile. It's a half a land lot—a hundred and one acres plus a fourth of an acre. Reverend Thurman was able to parlay his land into a substantial living for his family, even after his untimely death."

Joseph was pleased at the amount of land and its location. It would be close to his parents and to whatever development occurred in this area. Already there was talk of railroads crossing Georgia. One railroad had been chartered the year before to build a line from Augusta to Athens. Where the railroad would go after that was unknown, but surely DeKalb County would attract a branch.

"How did Reverend Thurman acquire the land in the first place?"

"He drew a lucky number in the 1821 lottery. While the lottery divided up the Creek lands east of the Chattahoochee and gave them to the whites, Reverend Thurman was able to win a hundred and sixty acres of Cherokee land just across the river. He swapped it for land on this side of the river. Then he bought more about the time we came over here from Abbeville. He worked the land hard and had a few slaves, so he was pretty well set up by standards in this area."

The sound of a horse's hooves hitting the hard-baked ground outside interrupted their conversation. As they looked out in the strong afternoon summer light, it was impossible to tell whose horse was outside, much less who the rider was.

"Whoa! Slow down, you bastard!" A young man's voice was heard barking at the horse. Joseph saw his father's eyes wince on hearing the crude rebuke.

As the man got down from the horse, his body lit from behind by the afternoon sun, he presented a silhouetted figure of indefinite proportions.

"Morgan here?" asked the man. When he emerged from direct sunlight into the smithy, he turned out to be of about medium height, gaunt, sharp-eyed, and black-haired. His hair lay matted and oily from lack of washing. His dusty clothes and the strong smell from his body indicated he'd been riding quite a while. The pack on his horse signified a traveller. He had a stoop in the shoulders, and his eyes darted about as he spoke, canvassing the shop.

He's almost evil-looking, Joseph thought. There was something familiar about his slouch.

"I'm William Morgan," Joseph's father said. "What is it you're needin'?"

"I need some shoes for my horse here. How much will that set me back?"

"Fifteen cents a hoof. I can do it for you if you can wait til I finish this wheel rim. I have to shape it before the iron cools."

"Waal, I don't know as I can wait. This horse shore is in bad need of new shoes."

"Suit yourself," Morgan said, and turned toward the wheel and anvil.

"Hey, you're not real respectful to a man who wants to buy a new rifle."

William looked closely at the man, who snorted and moved his head back as Morgan looked at him. The stranger's prominent Adam's apple moved in his throat.

"Got rough neighbors where you come from?"

"Naw, I jest heared you was the best gunsmith in this area. Need a trusty companion jest like any man does."

"Well, I'm the only gunsmith. What's your name?"

"Cunningham," said the dark-haired man. "Tom Cunningham." Joseph's heart sank when he heard the name. His slouch, sharp eyes, and emaciated body looked like those of the Thomas Cunningham they'd left behind in South Carolina. Could this be his son?

"You wouldn't by any chance be comin' from South C'lina?" William Morgan asked.

"Well, shore, I'm from up around Abbeville area."

William's eyes narrowed.

"Tell you what, Mr. Cunningham. I'm a peaceable man and if you're related to who I think you are, then we're not going to be able to do business."

"Wha'd'ya mean, not do business? I got the cash right here." Cunningham reached into an inside shirt pocket and withdrew several dirty bills of currency. "What's a man gotta pay for one of them longarms?"

"My price is normally thirty dollars for a walnut stocked piece, but for you there's no price. Like I tol' ya, I'm not dealing with no relative of the Thomas Cunningham I know."

"Hey, you don't know nothin'!" Cunningham shouted. He spat on the ground in front of them, then remounted his horse. "An' I'll tell you what, you and that young whipper-snapper son of yours. You'll live to regret this!" With that, he turned his horse and left, with his horse limping in an uneven walk.

"If that man darkens our doorway again, I want you to let me know," William said. "He means to do us harm, I've no doubt of it. I won't sell him a gun."

"What do you know about his father? How do you know it's the same Thomas Cunningham that you knew?" Joseph asked.

"There's no mistaking him," the elder Morgan said. "I'd know that man's progeny anyplace."

Joseph knew his father was slow to anger, but this man had lit a fuse quickly. He didn't understand why.

"What did his father do? You told me long time ago that he was one of the reasons we were leaving Abbeville District, but you didn't tell me why."

"You'll know soon enough, Son. Now I need to get this wheel done or we're going to have to make it all over again."

Later that afternoon, when the sun's heat had lost its smothering qualities and left just a hint of its previous humid weight, William and Joseph Morgan sat in the doorway of the blacksmith's shop, legs stretched in front of them, each leaning on a beam lining the entrance. They took turns drinking from the jug of water. The wagon wheel on which they'd worked so hard stood inside the smithy, cooling in the shade of the shop.

"You know, Joseph John," William started. Joseph sensed something major, probably negative, was coming, because his father rarely used his full name any more. He'd been called Joseph John all his days up to six years ago. He'd gotten the double name because his father's oldest brother was also named Joseph. Then one of the rare letters from relatives back in Abbeville District had arrived.

None of William's brothers or their wives wrote very well, so letters and news were infrequent, except to send news of deaths. The news of weddings and births had stopped long ago. This letter was about Uncle Joseph's death. From that time on, Joseph John was Joseph.

"I hope you're not still trying to be friends with that half-breed, Adam."

Joseph felt his skin flush at his father's suspicion. It had been many years since he and David Thurman and Adam had spent their time in the woods. After his father had punished him for playing with Adam the day he met him, Joseph and David, in defiance of William's order, had gone in search of the young Indian and found him on their side of the Chattahoochee.

"No, Pa, I don't see him," Joseph said with a mixture of anger and embarrassment. "Not since that day you found us."

"Good," William said. "Because the Sandtown Pony Club is getting more and more active over in the Indian settlements across the Chattahoochee, and I don't want you to get mixed up on either side of that."

Joseph had heard of these night-time raids on the Indian towns near where Adam lived. He knew they were meant to harass the Indians and get them to retaliate so the whites could declare war and send the militia to invade their territories. He also knew that he might be called up to do just that.

"That's where the good men of our county go and steal horses and generally harass the Indians?" asked Joseph. "That seems like mischief that's just bound to bring more violence. You've been a militia colonel," Joseph said to his father. "Now I'm liable to be mustered for any 'peacemaking' activity. I resent having to clean up the messes the whites make. Especially because it's done deliberately."

Joseph thought back to his days with Adam. He remembered how different he had been from what he expected an Indian to be. Adam was curious, not treacherous. He was an enthusiastic game player who hated to lose. He wore no war paint. He wasn't even red. Since then, Joseph had learned that the "redman" name came from red juice of the bloodroot plant that they mixed with clay and applied to their faces for ceremonial use— and, yes, as war paint. Adam's skin was brown with a hint of yellow, maybe, and smooth. Coppery was the best way to describe it. He'd seen Adam naked when they'd bathed in Utoy Creek near the Chattahoochee. His body was brown all over, not just his chest and arms.

Joseph had seen his father's skin turn dark after lots of exposure over fires in the smithy; he'd shed his shirt regularly if the weather was warm. But his father's skin would turn red as a beet first. Then it would become brown in the most exposed areas, like his arms, shoulders, neck, and chest. The areas where the heat of the forge wouldn't reach, like under his arms, or under his chest muscles, would be just as white as a baby's skin. And below his pants' waist, William and every other white man Joseph knew was white and bumpy with hair, like scratchy woolen underwear. Adam's skin was like poured copper, smooth and hairless. But not red.

Joseph had felt his fears about the Cherokees melt away further as he and David Thurman spent time with the young Indian. Sunday was the day he and Adam would meet by a large creek, near the Chattahoochee River a couple of miles west of their home. How Adam made it across the river, Joseph wasn't sure. His clothes were usually dry, so he couldn't have waded at a low point in the stream.

"I have canoe," Adam had told him, his eyes bright with excitement. "I hide it under a tree behind rocks. No one comes—very few people."

David accompanied Joseph each time he met Adam. That way, Joseph could truthfully tell his father that he was out playing with David. Those were innocent days, filled with ramblings and boys' games, Joseph recalled, before there was any substantial settlement in the area. Now road commissioners busied themselves with building projects to link the various portions of the county, especially roads to Decatur and to the mills on the Chattahoochee. But when he and David and Adam played, there was no one to see them, no one to tell his father.

Had he ever let William know he was consorting with Adam, he was sure he would strap him first, then lay down the law, never letting him see Adam again. His father feared people with the dark, honey-colored skin. It was uncanny the way he'd see his father's eyes go from sky blue to steel whenever the topic of Indians came up.

With their knives, they played mumblety-peg, which Adam usually won, as he was a better marksman with a blade. He could reach his arms around his head and still throw steady as a rock. The boys introduced him to marbles, which he had a harder time getting the knack of, until he realized he could keep the marbles he won. Then Adam became a successful player, putting many a clay ball in his pouch to take home.

They generally had the run of the woods and could shoot game with blow guns made from reeds and actually kill it. At the end of the day, David and Joseph reluctantly turned their quail and turkey over to Adam, so as not to give away their whereabouts on Sundays, almost drooling about the wonderful dinners they could have had. Instead, Joseph and David satisfied themselves with the thought that they'd make their own rifles someday, when they mastered all the difficult lessons in William's forge. Then they'd be able to shoot all the feathered stock in this part of Georgia, and bring it home, too.

Joseph could still remember the day three years after they'd met Adam when his father caught them at the river trapping fish. They used Adam's fish trap, a long triangular net made of hemp rope that they stretched between two boulders on the DeKalb County side. His father approached without a sound while the three boys lay on rocks on a sunny, early spring Sunday.

"Joseph John Morgan," he shouted. "Get over here to me in one minute or I'll blister your hide on the spot. You, too, David. If your father could see you now—"

The boys leapt up, running awkwardly across rocks to the banks. William was livid. Joseph remembered seeing David's dark eyes taking in his father's angry words. William was almost a father to David, and hurt and shock registered in those dark coins of eyes. William directed David to go home and tell his uncle what had happened. David's father had died under the feet of his rebellious horse the year before, when the horse threw the minister, then, in the confusion, kicked him in the head. David lived with his Uncle Benjamin and his large extended family of uncles, aunts, and cousins.

"If I catch you with that half-breed, I'll lock you in the shop and you'll never see the light of day again," William warned Joseph.

The required meeting in the shop as soon as Joseph reached home left fear and trembling in the boy for a long time. William thrashed his son's fifteen-year-old bare bottom and legs. Joseph, holding back shameful tears, thought he would never stop. After his father left, Joseph cried for what must have been an hour. He never knew who tattled, or even knew to tell.

That was the last time Joseph saw Adam. He sent a note by a trader who travelled that way regularly, and hoped that Adam would be able to read it.

He'd sat for an hour with a knife-sharpened lead pencil, trying to think of the words to use. How did one say, "Pap afraid of redskins"? How did he let go of a friend, not because he was moving, but because of someone else's fear and hatred?

Finally, he'd written:

Der Adam,
I won't be able to met yu at th rivr ennymore. Forever,
   Joseph

"Pa, when I knew Adam, he was more white than I am. He knew our language thoroughly, an' he even went to the missionary school."

"Joseph, the Cherokees are doomed. They are trying to fit into the white man's culture. They've intermarried with whites, the missionaries have built schools to teach them, an' they've even got plantations with slaves to rival the whites'. But the federal government plans to run 'em out of here before long. I don't see any wavering from that in what I see and hear.

"You are your own man now, and you must have your own opinions. But I hope you'll see the wisdom of what I say."

"Pa, it seems like the people we have to fear around here aren't the Indians. They take care of themselves, and except for wanting to keep the land that was theirs, they don't cause trouble."

He drew a breath. Even at twenty-one, he found in hard to differ with his father.

"Seems like who we have to fear are ones like Tom Cunningham. Now you won't tell me why he's a threat to us, but I've got a strong feeling about him. The man's as much as said we're marked in his book. What I want to know is, after travelling all this way, and pushing back the wilderness, and building a new home, a farm, and a new shop, why are we confronting the same scalawags as you and your father dealt with back in Abbeville? Are we that much better off here?"

William Morgan's face was red with anger.

"Joseph, that's enough! How do you think I'm going to provide a home for all these children? How do you think you're going to make your own living? The only way to make your way is to earn by the sweat of your brow and hands. That's how my father did it. That's how I did it. Selling that land, and the farm and the smithy and the mill to some people who wanted it badly is what's made it possible for me to provide for all of you. And that's how you're going to get your living: working in the forge, and then holding onto land that I give you to sell to the next feller—but at a higher price than what I'm going to pay."

He motioned with his hands toward their home and fields.

"This didn't just happen. We are much better off now than we were in Abbeville. Gideon has land, a farm, and a family. You'll have land that will allow you to think of settlin' down and starting a family. And if people continue to move here, then we'll have prospects for your sisters as well.

"You see, Son, a home is a relative thing. If you're scrapin' by with just enough to eat, then sometimes it's a good idea to move on to some other home."

"But the Cherokees—"

"Will be well paid for their lands. There's a survey about to start that will write down every house, barn, corn crib, fruit tree, livestock, and whatever the Indians own, and they'll be paid for it. They'll be paid handsomely. They can start a new life in Arkansas."

Joseph became quiet, contemplating all his father said. He knew there was no arguing with him. William didn't talk much, but when he did, what he said was not to be disputed.

"I'm going to see to that wagon wheel," William said, getting up and dusting himself off.

Joseph continued sitting in the doorway. He was determined to have a home that he wouldn't have to leave. He'd be different from his father—somehow—and make his living in DeKalb, right on that property his father was buying for him.

Joseph scraped the clay soil in front of him with a stick. He drew off a house and a small barn, with a shop on the side. He put paling around the front of the house. Above the shop door, he traced a sign: "J J MORGAN." Then he paused, drew in the dirt, and stood up. Next to the shop, a railroad track he'd traced in the red dust made its way toward his settlement from the sea.

The next day, Joseph rode out to the Chattahoochee on Selim, his horse. He was thinking about Adam and wanting to go see the creeks and ravines where they used to play. He spent the afternoon wandering among oaks, hickories, sweet gums, and pines. He brushed Selim up against numerous hollies as he descended into ravines so steep the horse almost toppled forward. He urged him through azalea and rhododendron thickets to find their old haunts by backwaters of the river.

He wandered back to his home, riding at a leisurely pace east on the Sandtown Road. At the point that the road continued farther east towards Covington, he turned on the rough trail north. Where he saw streams he stopped and allowed the horse to drink, then continued on in the heat of early afternoon.

Arriving at the homestead, he decided that instead of joining the family, he would go to the shop. He led Selim to the stables nearby, fed and watered him, and put him up for the day. He walked over to the large shed that served as the shop, and stepped inside. As usual, all was open to the outside, and Joseph looked around for a few minutes before he noticed that some tools were missing.

Two hammers, several small pieces of iron, a mallet, and wedge were missing from their places on the wall of the shop where his father and he religiously replaced them at the end of each day. He went to the house to ask his father about the tools. William returned with him to the shop to look for them.

"Somebody's taken 'em. There's no doubt," he said. They scanned the walls, then searched the dirt floor of the smithy.

"Father, look here. There's footprints in the dirt. It looks like a pretty slender boot print."

William inspected the prints, mixed in with Joseph's and his own. Joseph watched him as he moved outside the shop and looked up and down the fence rail that held the cattle next to the shop. Then he spotted the hoof prints. He bent down and placed his fingers around the tell-tale signs.

"Looks like Mr. Cunningham's our culprit," he said. "These hoof prints are very uneven, a dead giveaway for a limping horse.

"Do we need to close off the shop?" All their buildings were unlocked.

"No! I'm not going to try to outthink every n'er do well in the county. We'll catch Mr. Cunningham first, and save ourselves a lot of trouble." Joseph asked no more questions because he knew his father was planning a solution to the problem in his head.

That Sabbath afternoon William spent some time showing Joseph his treasured flintlock rifle as a way of teaching him the mechanics of riflemaking. Joseph, who'd been thoroughly schooled in blacksmithing, now was ready for gunmaking.

"This gun belonged to your grandfather, Joseph Morgan," William said. "I took it apart many, many times and put it back together again to figure out how it was made. That's how I learned to make a rifle like my father. That's how I'll start you learning."

Joseph lifted the rifle to his shoulder, pointed its long two-band barrel at an exterior wall, and looked down the gunsight. There wasn't a ripple or defect of any sort to interfere with his line of sight. He caressed the smooth, polished walnut stock and noted how easily it accommodated his fingers. It was a fine piece of workmanship.

As William explained how he worked with the brass to form a trigger-guard, Joseph reflected on how similar this work must have been to silversmithing. Noting the curved, decorated guard, the other brass trim, and the engraving on the rifle, he asked where the gun design came from.

"Your grandfather's family had been making guns for as long as he remembered. Probably brought the trade from Scotland or England. In Pennsylvania, many a gunsmith gave your ancestors an idea or two. That's where a lot of the longarms were crafted for frontier use. A backwoodsman and his longrifle were deadly at even three hundred to four hundred yards. The longrifle is like the sporting rifles used by the wealthy English before the Revolution, only much faster."

His father next took Joseph and the gun out to the shop, where he lay the rifle on a table in plain view.

"We're gonna see if Mr. Cunningham can resist that," he said. He sat down in the dirt in the doorway and motioned for Joseph to do the same.

"Tell me more about my grandfather and how you got to be born in Virginia," Joseph said as he seated himself.

"It's not somethin' I exactly remember—bein' born that is," William said with a hint of humor in his voice.

"I know, but they must have told you about them days—"

"—those days," William corrected him.

"—those days, then."

"My pa didn't talk much about that time. I mostly heard from my mother who'd tell me things when he wasn't around. I know that things in the rebellion broke out hot and heavy soon after Charleston finally fell. The British made the rebels prisoners on parole. Things got real quiet. But then the Brits made a very stupid mistake. They abolished the parole status of all the Charleston folks and started forcing the rebels to fight for the British. Naturally, that didn't sit well—they had to fight for the British or they had to go to war to keep from fighting for the Brits. Meantime, they were forced to put up British soldiers in their homes, where they rudely ate up all their foodstuffs and generally harassed the American sympathizers. They tried to make examples of leading citizens and hung a few for treason 'cause they wouldn't join the British forces.

"When they burned old Tom Sumter's plantation, that made him real mad, and he and others started gathering militia; that started a bunch of campaigns that put South Carolina in the war—there were battles every other day that year.

"We got d'rectly affected 'cause a lot of those fights were happening in our neck of the woods. Elijah Clarke brought five hundred Georgians into Augusta to dislodge that big Tory Tom Brown. They battled just this side of the Savannah River and the Liberty Boys unwisely left their wounded when they took off afterwards. The Tories chasin' 'em took 'em prisoner—all twelve—and brought 'em into Augusta. Brown had been shot in both legs during the fight and was holed up at Seymour's when they hauled in the twelve injured Liberty Boys. Brown had 'em strung up where he could see 'em hang."

Joseph felt sick to his stomach. His father was ranging free with details he'd never heard. Joseph guessed his pa figured he was grown now.

"So most of the settlers anywhere between the Savannah and the Saluda became concerned for their families' safety," William went on. "Your grandfather and his family and neighbors were stuck there between Tom Brown in Augusta and the strong Tories to the east across the Saluda River. If the Tories'd hang injured prisoners, there was no telling what they'd do. Your granpa got leave to come home, pack up my mother and brothers, and start off in a caravan with other families to get beyond the Blue Ridge, up to Augusta County in Virginia, whence he'd come nearly twenty years before. He and many others living there in the Long Canes had come from that part of Virginia originally, and most had kin there they could hole up with."

Joseph wondered about the more than three hundred miles of rough terrain north that were only horse paths, for the most part. No taverns, no inn—only high, blue mountains, deep woods, and maybe an occasional farm at which to camp. What if they were set upon by wolves or bears or bobcats?

"Mind you, they had to watch out for hostile Tory homesteads— and they had to stay clear of Patrick Ferguson's Tory troops that were parading around that area. One or two men rode out ahead of the caravan, scouting the countryside to make sure they were well away from Loyalist troops and homes. Because people's allegiances shifted from one side to the other, they stayed away from farms. At one point, they were within a half day's ride of Ferguson's North Carolina militia camped at Gilbert Town, but they were able to avoid the Irishman's troops. Instead, they came upon the forward group of the over-the-mountain men rushing to chase Ferguson out of Gilbert Town. They'd been travelling for five days straight and had just emerged from the snows of the highest mountains. Ferguson had made all the backwater Whigs real mad by sending a message he was going to kill 'em in their homes over the high mountains. They were comin' to get him.

"Your granpa wanted to join 'em of course, but he had to get his family north. They travelled on and endured straight up-and-down mountain trails where they sometimes hung out over cliffs too dangerous to look over, passed between lines of bloodthirsty militiamen on either side of the fight, and survived overgrown trails and stale vittles.

"After three weeks, they made it to Augusta County and safety."

Three weeks! Joseph thought about how hard he'd found the three-day trek west from Abbeville District ten years ago. Here his grandfather's family travelled for a almost a month—and with not even a farm to provide a roof!

"Did it rain?" he asked.

"I understand there was a deluge at one point. But they dried everything as they fled. They couldn't risk being caught by the snow in the mountains. They were at great peril if they stayed, as most of the Tory sympathizers back in C'lina lay just east of 'em between the Saluda and Catawba rivers."

When would his family stop having to move, Joseph wondered. Would they be safe in DeKalb County, or was this theft of the tools a sign of more trouble to come? A home is a place were a man hoped to be free of assaults and war and famine and drought. Could they be free of major threats here?

"Wha'd Cunningham do, Pa?"

William looked down on the ground. He didn't reply for a while.

"Your granpa got his family settled in Virginy," he said slowly. "Then he turned south and was able to return home in less than ten days. However, when he descended the path to the homestead, he found charred timbers. Cunningham and other ruffians had taken their revenge after King's Mountain and burned the homes of the rebels."

"What'd he do then? He had to be back in the war—did he just leave it all?"

"What else could a man do? He had to return to his unit. But I reckon he showed less mercy after that. It was long after Yorktown before he could return and get his rebel neighbors to help him and his sons rebuild. 'Course, I was just a litt'lun then, so I was no help." William smiled for the first time since they'd begun talking. The smile quickly vanished.

"So that's why old Cunningham would've been just as pleased to do me in on the road when we were leaving Abbeville," Joseph said. His father nodded, his face grim. Joseph's heart beat hard in his chest as he thought about Old Man Cunningham's son causing more mischief.

Joseph felt his heart grow heavy with sadness as he realized that the circle of vengeance and violence had rolled right over the Carolina hills and landed here in DeKalb County.

No wonder his pa never talked about Revolution. Hearing the stories of atrocities had made his blood boil. It was chilling to think of homesteads under attack by neighbors and of so many widows and orphans at the end of it all. Would the circle ever end? Could he and his family live in peace here?

Joseph and his father spent the night in the shop, taking turns keeping watch. Their plan was to hide themselves under the table if they heard Cunningham coming, to grab him and hold him, then take him to Decatur for justice.

Near dawn, they heard the horse approach and the crack of leather as a man dismounted, followed by the sound of soft footsteps outside. Joseph felt his heart beat faster, but he rose slowly, his back hugging a wall, and looked through a cloth drawn over an opening in the wall. He recognized Cunningham, although he was dressed in dark clothing and had a different horse.

While Cunningham approached the shop, the Morgans stole under the table.

Cunningham went right for the rifle. He strode toward the table, grabbed it up and turned on his heel. William and Joseph jumped up, but Joseph caught his shoe on the edge of the swage block and fell flat on his face. As he fell, Cunningham leapt back. William was too far away to catch him.

"No you don't, you good for nothing bastards!" Cunningham shouted, running out the door. Gripping Joseph's grandfather's rifle in one hand, he struggled onto his horse and took off towards the east, galloping down the Decatur Road.

"Ride," his father shouted. "Quick, to the Scotts' and the Johnsons', Joseph. We've got to stop that man and take care of him for good!"

Joseph ran to the stable next to the smithy and untied the reins of the horse he'd had ready in case Cunningham fled. He jumped on Star and pushed his boots against the horse's sides to get him to move quickly, gathering speed as he galloped down the road in the direction of the Johnsons' farm.

A few minutes later the young rider arrived at the Johnson homestead, where he leapt off the horse, tied him to a front hitching post, and went up to the door, rapping loudly.

"Eyeah?" he heard Old Man Johnson on the other side. The wood plank door opened, and the farmer stood with his Sunday shirt opened at the throat and the stiff high collar removed. He held a Bible in his hands with a thumb placed at his stopping point. "What's the trouble?"

"Come quick," Joseph said, breathless. "Tom Cunningham from Abbeville just ran off with my father's rifle, and we think he's stolen tools from the smithy. I'm running to the Scotts'—see if you can help us catch up to 'im. He headed down Decatur Road."

"I'll be right behind you."

With that, Johnson closed the door. At about the same moment Joseph was astride Star and turning in the roadway towards the Scott plantation. As he moved eastward to alert Patrick Scott, he saw his father trailing him down the road and motioned for him to follow. He sped ahead, stopped at the Scotts', gave the same message, and headed down the six-mile-long road to Decatur.

The four men rode at varying speeds with Scott, the oldest of the four, sometimes as far back as a quarter of a mile. Joseph maintained the lead, with his father close behind. Joseph spurred Star to a full gallop, then reached the ridge that formed the highest point between the Morgans' settlement and the town of Decatur.

At the ridgetop he looked down the road, hoping to see Cunningham. The sun was higher now, forcing Joseph to pull his hat down over his eyes to see through the brightness. There was no dust, no sign of a fleeing horseman. Rather than waste the men and horses in a haphazard search, Joseph waited for the others to catch up.

"Mr. Scott, you take the stagecoach road that goes to Covington for a couple of miles, then double back and meet us at the courthouse if you don't see 'im. Mr. Johnson, you take the north side of town. Pa and I will work the nearer sides. Talk to anyone you can to see if Cunningham has been here or if anyone knows where he might be stayin'."

"What if we find 'im?" Scott asked.

"Just keep your gun on 'im and bring 'im to the courthouse."

Scott and Johnson pulled away and made their way to town. Joseph and William moved on down the former Indian trail that approached Decatur from the southwest side of the settlement. At a knoll just west of the town, the two horsemen paused, and Joseph looked into Decatur's center. They saw the courthouse perched on top of a rise, then looked to the right and on down McDonough Road.

"You take McDonough Road, I'll circle around the smaller streets on the west," he told his father.

"Just be careful. If you find him, keep your gun on him. If you don't see the rifle, don't try to find it on 'im. Just bring 'im back and we'll get the sheriff to help find the rifle."

"I'll get it somehow!" Joseph stormed. "It's not right for the likes of Cunningham to have something valuable just by takin' it!"

"Heed my word," William said, the anger in his voice so heavy that Joseph sat up in his saddle. "Nothing's so important as to lose your life over it."

"All right, Father, I'll be careful," he promised in a more subdued voice. With that he pulled his horse out in front and sped down the lane, climbing the hill to the courthouse. At the two-story log structure he cut to the left and followed another road back west.

He saw a family walking away from him up ahead in the dusty road, apparently returning home from church. The man wore his Sunday black suit. His wife was pleasantly dressed in a soft blue chambray gown with white cotton trim. The two children, a boy and a girl, heard him first and turned, then excitedly interrupted their parents' conversation and motioned toward Joseph.

"Ma'am," Joseph said, doffing his hat to the lady and greeting her husband.

"Naw, can't say's I've seen anyone out t'day," the man replied after Joseph had inquired about Cunningham. "Even in church the attendance was 'way down. Must be the heat!"

Joseph thanked them, then travelled a few more small roads on the west side of the town, then returned to the courthouse area, seeking out the small churches located on different points of the square.

"'Mornin', sir," he said, greeting a well-dressed gentleman he stopped on the north side. "I'd be much obliged to you if you could tell me—I'm looking for a rather desperate-looking fellow travelling by horseback in this area. He would have been pretty dusty and dirty. He's taken my granpa's rifle."

"Oh, he has, has he?" said the man with obvious alarm. " A good rifle costs the same as a new house in this town, and goodness knows a gentleman needs one, just to ward off the unsavory in this area. No, I haven't seen such a man, but I'll be glad to look out for him. What's the name, and what's your name?"

Joseph gave the man the details and told him that he and the other pursuers would be at the courthouse should he have any news. He then turned and retraced his path, looking for his father and neighbors.

"Any luck?" he asked Scott upon the older man's return.

"Naw, and anyone I encountered said I'd just as well stop lookin' 'cause he sounded like a clever ne'er do well."

"You start goin' by what others say an' you won't last long around here. Folks don't show enough interest to look out for thieves like Cunningham, they're gonna be missing a lot of their property, too."

"Son, you do what you can," said a familiar voice behind Joseph. It was his father, drawing up beside him on his horse. "Most folks are discouraged because they thought they escaped the kind of stealin' and messin' around we had back in C'lina, but it doesn't look like it's goin' away."

"Well, the only way we'll combat it is by goin' after the beggars when we see 'em!" Joseph exclaimed. "We need to go knock on a bunch of doors right now and get everyone alerted. Who knows who he'll steal from next?"

"Joseph!" his father said sternly. "Calm down. We'll go to Sheriff Jones and tell 'im what's happened. If Cunningham continues to harass people in this area, Jones will know soon enough and he'll help us search for 'im. But we've done the best we can for the day. Unfortunately, he accomplished his work before folks around here came out of church, so most fresh trace of 'im's gone."

Reluctantly, Joseph agreed to follow his father to the sheriff's home, which they knew from previous visits. Frequently, they'd gathered there when trouble broke out in the community and the local men were enlisted for help, especially militia members. As expected, the sheriff was concerned about the theft. After leaving his house, the Morgans and their neighbors hitched their horses to posts at the courthouse and talked to townspeople nearby in an effort to find Cunningham's whereabouts. Although one man recognized the fugitive from his description, no one knew where he stayed.

"Well, we've got to be gettin' on home so we can keep what's left of the Lord's Day," William Morgan finally said, announcing their return to west DeKalb County.

The next morning Joseph rose before dawn to take goods to Decatur to sell—and to look for Tom Cunningham. He'd loaded the wares the evening before, filling the back of the farm wagon with axes, mauls, hammers, plows, and various other implements new settlers always needed. He'd thrown in several stacks of hay to feed the horse, as well as to provide seating for himself and any men who wanted to stop and gab. He hoped someone could give him information about Cunningham.

He proceeded east down the road he'd travelled the day before, only now it was early, and the sun just rising. He turned down the brim of his slouch hat to keep the sun out of his eyes. While the glare was an inconvenience, the young man was in awe of how the light-filled sky tinted the earth. The sun colored the dusty, rutted road with a pinkish-golden glow that made the road seem like it was made of a molten precious metal rather than red clay.

As he picked his way along the road, he reflected on the family's fortunes thus far. The loss of his grandfather's rifle to Tom Cunningham smarted, although it was a small one compared with those other settlers had suffered. Inexperience with the hard soil caused many farmers to lose crops; the sometimes heavy, sometimes very sparse rain patterns played havoc with everyone's livelihood. Crops often failed, ruining those who depended on them. Those families either sold their land and moved west or moved in with relatives only marginally better off than they. Joseph was grateful that his father had a trade—actually two or three trades when you counted blacksmithing, gunsmithing, and some woodworking—in addition to his farming. The gunsmithing was by far the most lucrative business and one for which his father was well-known, being the only gunsmith in the area. William Morgan was respected for his worksmanship, and there were always takers for his rifles. In fact, the demand was so great Joseph hadn't brought any guns to market; potential purchasers knew where to find his father.

Joseph knew that his father depended on him to help him make a living. As the only remaining son in a family full of female children, he had to contribute heavily towards the family's welfare. The girls helped out in the fields, but they couldn't run the forge like he could. It would be a while before he could think about striking out on his own.

He daydreamed of the home and shop he would have. He would have such a business in the smithy that he wouldn't need any but a kitchen garden to keep him and his family going. To spend so much time trying to raise every crop, when he could come to the square in Decatur and buy all the corn and greens he needed, not to mention cotton fabric, seemed senseless to Joseph. Of course, he never told his father that.

As the young man urged Selim along, he looked to both sides of the road for any signs of Cunningham. He knew he would recognize the horse— a pale brown mare, about three years old—anywhere. But maybe Cunningham had traded it, just as he had the old gimpy horse. Or stolen another, he told himself; that was more likely.

"Joseph, look who I've brought with me," young David Thurman called as he walked up to the wagon Joseph had parked near the square to display his wares. Joseph looked up from the wagon gate where he sat and saw David's younger sister, Jane, on David's arm. Just barely out of young girls' short dresses, she was a vision of coolness, wearing a pink chintz gown trimmed with black ruching on the sleeves, collar and skirt. Her bonnet was drawn close, attractively framing her oval face. Bright, twinkling eyes that matched her brother's snapping ones greeted him.

"It's nice to see you, Miss Thurman," Joseph said, jumping down, taking her hand and bowing slightly. "Have you come to market for anything special? I can tell you what the best bargains are."

"Why, no, nothing in particular, just what strikes my fancy," Jane said, laughing as she glanced about her. "I got tired of staying at Uncle Benjamin's and not having any decent society—no disrespect, of course, to my brothers and sisters and other relatives."

"Well, I'm not sure of the quality of the company, but there's lots more of it in Decatur, that's for sure," said Joseph.

"Well, so far, the society looks just fine," Jane said, then demurely looked away at his hammers and axes displayed on the bales of hay nearby.

What a saucy flirt, Joseph thought. She's probably advancing the long skirts by a year or two at least. But he was also amused.

"David, did you hear about our excitement yesterday mornin'?" Joseph asked.

"No, what happened?" his friend asked. Joseph told him about the initial theft of the hammer and other tools from the forge, followed by the encounter with Cunningham, and his escape with the rifle. His hands moved dramatically as he detailed all the efforts to find the Carolinian, and David's eyes grew large while Joseph retravelled the road to Decatur, then back.

"How will you make another one?" David asked.

"Same way's we make the ones we do now, one piece at a time, one part gathered from here, one from there, a lock ordered from Pennsylvania, a couple of brass bands converted from something that's already around."

"Can I help with this one? I think I can do a gun stock after all the practice you and I have had whittlin'!"

Joseph hesitated, as it was his father's forge and he still was under his tutelage.

"Sure," he said, remembering that he was, after all, a man now. He could make some decisions for his and his father's business. "C'mon over tomorrow."

The rustling of Jane Thurman's dress and a deep sigh interrupted their conversation. "Sakes alive, David, if you don't walk on down the road with me soon it'll be supper time before we're finished in Decatur!"

"Coming, Sister. You could go on to the next stall and it'll be all right, nobody will think you're unaccompanied. I'll be right behind you."

"Goodbye, Joseph, it was so nice to see you," Jane said, then curtsied and moved away before Joseph could respond to her discreet compliment. He watched her full skirt swirling around her slender young girl's body as she walked down the dusty road to the next merchant.

Boy, this is something I didn't anticipate, Joseph told himself after the Thurmans left. The four Thurman children, who had been left without a father at an early age, had moved with their mother to live with their uncle, one of three who came with the Reverend David Thurman from South Carolina to DeKalb County just before the Morgans removed to Georgia. Joseph, although a few years older than David, had spent a lot of time with him and hadn't seen his sister in some years. It seemed his last recollection of her was at maybe three or, possibly, five years of age. Surely he'd seen her since, but what had she been doing? What had she looked like? Why hadn't he noticed? Since their father's death, David had been over at the Morgan house a great deal. Mostly he was in the forge, watching Joseph and his father as they turned a gun barrel or hammered a lock. At mealtimes David was a regular guest who fit right into the large crowd around the table and was a welcome curiosity for the numerous Morgan sisters. Always entertaining company, he was never a bother to feed.

Joseph returned to his perch on the wagon's drop gate. With few prospects of customers, he took his whittling knife out of his pocket and picked up an unfinished knife handle from a box at the rear of the wagon. With heavy concentration, he focused on the handle, beginning his strokes easily to make his slices shallow and smooth.

Now that he was twenty-one, marriage entered into his thoughts now and then. He recalled his father's conversation with him as his age of majority approached. It had taken place a week before the talk about the land his father would give him.

"Y'gettin' older Joseph. Have you thought about gettin' married and settlin' down with a family? I don't want to compare you unfairly with your older brother, but he does seem pretty satisfied."

"Well, you know, Pa, it'll take someone pretty special for me to leave you and mother here without help in the forge and the farm."

"I know you're concerned about that, but we're more concerned for your happiness. Besides, who says we have to live in separate households? As long as we can make space you can always live with us."

Joseph had not considered living in the the same household with his parents. He felt he wouldn't mind, but what woman in a thousand could live with all his many family members? Seven women, maybe more, in the same house?

Another feeling, deep in his gut, overcame him any time he thought about marriage. He had a hard time figuring out what it was. But as he felt the silken knife handle with his fingers, he was reminded of the surface of a bowl, a silver bowl his family once had. His father had made the bowl when he was younger, living in Charleston and apprenticed to a silversmith. Now he remembered.

It was a dim memory that became clearer. He had only been in Georgia with his parents a short time, so he was probably twelve, no more than thirteen, certainly. He was sleeping in the tent, so it must have been early fall, because their cabin had been framed in with all but the mud chinking applied when they moved in at Thanksgiving.

In what seemed like the middle of the night, he'd awoken suddenly. Something was different. He saw Gideon sleeping in the next cot, and he could hear the sounds of his little sisters breathing as they slept. But someone else was in the room, moving ever so slightly in the dark, which was punctured by streams of moonlight coming through the tent opening. Across the tent where Joseph John's parents slept, he saw his mother sitting on the bed and sobbing quietly. He wondered where his father was.

As he watched her bent over her lap, with her head bowed down and a piece of cloth he thought was a handkerchief in her hand, he wondered what she was crying about. He'd never seen her cry, other than on the trip from Abbeville when she was recalling the Indian attacks on her family, and later in the dining room at Washington. She'd experienced a great deal of extra strain and hard work with this move, having to keep five little girls and two strapping boys fed regularly, not to mention his father, Uncle Sam, and the men he'd hired to help him build their homestead.

Just as Joseph was trying to guess what the problem was, his father stepped into the tent opening near where his mother sat. Through the dim moonlight, Joseph saw he had the old silver bowl in his hand, and a blown-out lantern in the other.

"I'm sorry, I couldn't fix it. The creases were just too deep," he told her quietly.

"If you just hadn't used something good to carry grain to the horses. I'm so regretful. Now I have nothing nice, and it's so sad because you made it with your own hands. It was special to me!" She continued sobbing.

"I had to feed Ol' Abner quickly, before it rained. I used the first thing I pulled out of the box by the door. Rebecca, I wish I could restore it for you. The horse suddenly stepped back. I hadn't secured the bowl and he stepped on it. There's no way I can put it back. I'm sorry."

"I just wanted to have one or two nice things. I feel like we'll never have a household where there's some dishware and cutlery we can serve company with. It's so crude here—crude people, crude ways!"

"Hush, my wife. You can't change what's been done. I'm sorry, I'll give you the things you want some day. You'll have the house you need, the finery you so well deserve." William sat down next to Rebecca and put an arm around her.

Eventually, she quieted down. The boy no longer heard her sobs. He lay back down. Soon, what he heard was a woman's sighs, and, later, something mumbled from his father. He did not look, as he was ashamed of having heard as much as he did—all that conversation meant just for the two of them, no one else.

Joseph felt bad for his mother. He recalled how genteel she was, always having the English creamware out for company, even when they lived in the tent. He remembered how lovingly she touched the fine chest of drawers, how she managed a spontaneous waltz at that inn at Washington during the trip west, and how she'd expressed the hope that their new settlement would be as refined.

He feared his mother would never get her wish, as this part of Georgia was quite different from the county where Washington was. He feared for his father, too. How helpless he must feel if he couldn't provide for his wife. That was a man's duty. He wondered if his father remembered this event. He looked for signs of it in his father's face when William talked to Rebecca. He couldn't tell from their conversation or facial expressions if the bowl was ever discussed again.

Several weeks after that night, Joseph's parents forsook their usual pattern of not telling any of the children about the impending birth of a sibling. Rebecca took Gideon and Joseph aside one Sunday morning and told them there would be a new baby in the spring.

Not too long after that, William Morgan took his second son out to the pasture one afternoon on the pretext of checking a heifer whose foot was lame. As he lifted the cow's right foot and inspected her hoof, he looked sideways at Joseph, who was intent on figuring out why the cow was lame.

"Son, do you know how the cows get their calves?" he asked.

"Of course, Father. Every spring, we get a bull from a neighbor, and the bull chases the heifer and pretty soon, there's a calf in her belly."

"Well, I don't know if you've seen the bull actually mount the female cow, but that's how it all happens. It's in a way similar to the way a man and woman are united and conceive a child. But you don't want to make the mistake of thinking it's the same. For one thing, it's done face to face, with the man on top. In the second place, it's done in a spirit of love. Man is better than the animals, Son. Don't you ever forget that. He doesn't act like the animals and follow instinct. He always has to be mindful that he is above the creatures and responsible for them, but not like them."

The young man heard his father's admonitions, but he knew there were likenesses in carrying a child. He'd seen his cows get skittish with the others once gestation began, and he knew they were tired and weighed down by their load, and especially in weather that was either very hot or very cold. Likewise, he reasoned, his mother may have been crying over the silver bowl that night because of her condition. Certainly he'd seen her suddenly overcome by heat in the summer weather. She'd stop whatever she was doing—churning butter or sewing a shirt—and take to her bed. She'd loosen her gown and get a rag with with cold water from the creek, holding it on her face while she rested.

Joseph John immediately resolved to work as hard as he could to make sure his mother had all the comforts she needed and wanted. If she was going to bring more children into the world, he felt surely it was because the ministers they heard at Utoy Primitive Baptist Church frequently quoted commands in the book of Genesis to "increase and multiply" as a way of making sure Christian people dominated the earth. It was true, there was so much sin and degradation, and so many sorry, no-account people in the world, that a decent person's only defense was to make sure there were more of you than them. But, still, Joseph John reflected, a woman who bears this burden should be cared for. She who so readily took on the yoke placed there by the Bible should receive some compensation.

The young man sitting on the back of a wagon on a sunny August Monday, waiting for customers, looked down at his whittled knife handle. The handle was expertly shaved, almost too generously. He was so deep in thought he'd scarcely noticed he'd almost whittled too deep to have a sturdy handle. Joseph looked up at the street where the Thurmans had walked.

If I want to marry, he thought, it will have to be when my circumstances allow it. I do not want a wife of mine to cry over small but important losses such as a nice silver bowl. If my mother had to worry about everything from Indian attacks to having her few pretties demolished, I want my wife to have all that she needs, and even some things she wants, even if she doesn't need them. Besides, he reasoned, if a girl like Miss Thurman were to some day, a long time down the road, consider me as a husband, I'd first have to find a way to get that fine French ruching for her dresses over here from Charleston. Not to mention being able to pay for a dressmaker.

"Hey, Morgan!" a man's voice broke the young man's daydreaming. Joseph looked up and saw a man he'd spoken with the previous day, the only one of those they met who'd even shown awareness of Cunningham. "I've got some news of your friend, Cunningham."

"Waal, he ain't my friend, but no difference. Wha'd you find out?"

"He's high-tailed it back to Abbeville County. Seems he told a friend of mine he couldn't make much of a living here, so that's where he's bound. Left in a real hurry, hoofs flying, pack on his horse. 'Bout the time he stole from you's the time my friend saw him."

Joseph nodded his thanks, then said, "Much obliged to ya. You know where I am—if you see that scallawag set foot in DeKalb County again, or anywhere here'bouts, I hope you'll let me know."

"Sure 'nuff," the middle aged man said, ambling on to the next stall. "We don't need those types 'round here."

"Amen, brother," the young Morgan said. He exhaled a long, deep breath, then turned to the back of the wagon where he'd stored a board with cut-out letters on it. He hung it on the end of the wagon in full view of passersby. WM MORGAN, GUNSMTH, it read.

Chapter 4

MARTHASVILLE

1839

Joseph walked out the door of the Morgan home and paused on the front porch. He adjusted his collar, pulled down on his unfamiliar black coat's sleeve to cover his starched shirt cuff, then turned to look at his mirrored reflection in the six-over-six paned glass window. He stooped to fold his pants legs and stuff them into his heavy leather boots, as the late April rains had left plenty of water in miniature lakes in the road. After checking the glass again and satisfied with what he saw, he eased down the stairs looking towards what the settlement's leaders said would soon be the Western and Atlantic Railroad.

He walked quickly, but carefully, through the puddle-spattered, rutted dirt road, making his way east to the Marietta Road. From there he would turn southeast on his way to the tavern on Whitehall Street where he was to meet Justice of the Peace Tom Perkerson. He was on his way to sell half a land lot to Mr. Jett. At twenty six, he was completing his first business transaction, the first of many he hoped would happen in this bustling settlement. This wasn't the best news, however. Miss Jane Thurman had accepted his proposal, and they were to be married in the fall.

As Joseph danced around the clay-colored water patches, he felt successful. He'd been a keen witness to many changes in the village and had watched as each house or store went up or was converted from some other use. He'd been part of the village from the beginning. Most townspeople knew him, and he felt good about that.

Joseph had seen humble houses fashioned of slab wood given away at Jonathan Norcross' mill as well as more substantial shelter made of planks from Norcross' general store and post office. He'd watched men working nailing roofs and hanging windows in the holes left in the walls on some of the more respectable homes. He'd seen mule-drawn drays without their wheels level the ground for the houses. And the man who drew the pencil sketches the owner went by was his brother-in-law David. He and his father had hand-forged the nails, hammers, crowbars, and many other implements to build each house around them. He felt connected to each building he passed because his labor and some of his heart has gone into each one.

Almost every structure began with the ever-present, soft pine wood. He pictured the rough wood and could almost feel the fuzzy surface raised with the saw's pass across the pine plank before it became the tall, hopeful frame that outlined the building. If a man had the money to hire a carpenter to dress the wood, a hand planer smoothed the surface and tamed the wild smell of piney woods and grasses that came with the rough-cut planks. After their humble cabin, the Morgans' next house was made of brick, the first in the area. William now rented it to newcomers.

They had an opportunity to buy the frame of a house left by a man more fond of Alabama; they built it out with dressed planks. It hadn't been painted or whitewashed, but he and his pa had told Rebecca they'd do it soon. One of these days when they didn't have to make tools for the shop or take care of neighbors' needs for nails and such.

It was good to have a home. Life had changed quickly in the past several months. First, the planned route of the W&A Railroad had been laid out from their settlement to Marietta, eventually to connect them by rail to Ross' Landing in Tennessee. Next, John Thrasher had won a huge contract to build a giant fill across a gully for a railroad from the south to join the W&A line. Then there was talk of the Georgia Railroad line from Augusta bypassing Athens and hooking up with the terminus of the W&A in the middle of this small community. The settlement now was called "the terminus," an apt reference to what it was: the end of the line. Only wilderness and the farms and plantations of Alabama lay to the west.

Joseph recalled how as a child he'd played in woods that surrounded his home and farm. It had been a horseback ride to the nearest neighbors. More settlers arrived, and his father's gunsmithing business grew to the point that he could sell their farmland to newcomers wanting homesteads and concentrate on the gunsmithing and blacksmithing. Yet that move had made them vulnerable to the dips in the price of cotton and other commodities—when the cotton price went down, they had fewer customers and had to scramble for other business during those fluctuations. The ups and downs were troublesome sometimes, and often their prospects seemed gloomy, but since last winter, they'd seemed to be on more solid ground financially.

The Creek Indians had been routed only three years before, after the brothers Calhoun had led infantry and cavalry groups against them along the lower Chattahoochee. His father had been spared the militia duty because of the need for him to repair guns supplied by the state arsenal in Milledgeville. The guns were found wanting for service, and militiamen joked that the rifles had seen their last good days in Revolutionary War skirmishes, so William and Joseph were hired to repair them.

The Creeks, seeing the futility of fighting the whites after years of intense pressure from the newcomers, finally left for Arkansas. Then the next year, thousands of Cherokees, including Adam, had been rounded up to be relocated out West, forced to leave their land under the guard of the federal army and Georgia militia.

His father had been spared that task, too, this time because of his toolmaking skill. But he relayed stories of his fellow militiamen going to the homesteads of Cherokee families and arresting them and transporting them in wagons to Fort Bluffington, up in Cherokee County.

"The federal soldiers surprised them in their homes, pulling bayonets on them," he said. "Many women and children were separated from their families, many men were just taken from the fields. Livestock were driven away, and some of our countrymen, I'm afraid, resorted to plunder."

"It must have been terrible," Joseph said.

"Most of the Indians encouraged their people to go in dignity. Others were crying, some trying to take knives to their own throats, some trying to run away," he told Joseph. "It was so senseless, it didn't have to be like that."

"Only because you think they should have been made to leave in the first place!" Joseph had retorted. Angry over the loss of his friend Adam, he'd not talked with his father about it since.

Joseph watched his feet as he maneuvered through the muddy holes in the road he was now walking towards Whitehall Street. He longed for boardwalks built above the mess so he could make his way to his business appointment with greater speed and less muss to his clothes. They'd seen such boardwalks in the little town of Washington years ago, but Terminus hadn't the resources to do anything—all those resources were allocated to the county seat, Decatur.

As Joseph looked at his feet, he thought of the intricate figures he'd learned at Mrs. Scogins' ball in Decatur last January. It was a holiday ball where he'd danced—at his mother's urging—with many young ladies of quality from the area. He remembered well his discomfort at the time—how difficult it was to perform the steps that were called and how ashamed he felt of his clumsy efforts. The figures were all so foreign, and he could barely keep up.

A small band of strings assembled for the occasion played reels, waltzes, quadrilles, and grand marches while everyone Joseph knew congregated in the Scogins' great hall. It had been a long year, and townsmen and settlers from throughout DeKalb County and beyond had gratefully accepted invitations to the dance.

His brother Gideon and his sister-in-law Josephine waltzed by, laughing. Joseph felt a twinge of jealousy as he watched the two of them. Visiting from their plantation in Griffin, they cut a handsome figure, Gideon in his black wool suit and she in swirling skirts of green brocade.

"How're things going?" his older brother asked him as his wife excused herself during a lull in the music.

"As well as could be expected with the business so poor," Joseph said, not daring to let on about his true feelings of longing to his older brother. "What's the latest you hear on cotton prices?"

Joseph knew his faked interest in cotton prices must be apparent to Gideon. He felt like his brother could easily pretend nonchalance—but Joseph was finding the charade here on the dance floor difficult to carry off. He felt so lonely. Somehow all the time he'd spent working in the smithy or on the farm seemed purposeless right now. Why didn't he have a wife?

Joseph watched Gideon's eyes for signs that he knew Joseph was talking cotton but feeling deprived.

"The London market's not helping." As Gideon spoke, Joseph realized his brother was more interested in his crop. "Got word the crop I just sold won't get but five cents a pound," Gideon continued. He looked worried. His brows knitted together over a perfectly aquiline nose. Gideon's features made him look every bit the planter; yet even those privileged farmers could have problems. Five cents a pound was nothing.

"Is that all?" Joseph asked, incredulous. "That's robbery. You've got more than that in it. You've got to pay the mortgage on your land, keep up your people—"

"You don't need to tell me, little brother," Gideon cut him short. Lifting his punch glass delicately to his mouth, he took a swallow, then continued. "Those are the risks. I'm stayin' in it, no matter what. I'm just going to try getting into livestock and other types of crops. How're you and Pa doing?"

There was the rub, Joseph thought. The family's income was suffering mightily because of sinking cotton prices.

"Not well," Joseph scowled. "Cotton used to go for twenty-three, twenty-four, even twenty-seven cents With these prices, farmers ain't buyin' tools and others aren't buying land. Nobody's buyin' guns for keeping critters off their land"

"Or keeping darkies at bay," Gideon said, a smirk on his face.

Joseph ignored the comment. He hated to think of some of the uses some rifles were put to in this area. While lashings were usual punishments for the field workers, no doubt rifles they made helped planters keep things in line.

"Well," Gideon grimaced, "they're callin' this the 'panic of '37,' but it's lasting much longer. I don't know when prices will go back up. We'll probably never see the likes of the prices you just mentioned.

"But," Gideon let out an empty laugh, "at least cotton's a lasting business."

"By the way, Joseph," his brother said with a wink and a mock punch to the younger man's shoulder. "When are you going to get in the marriage way? I've never seen anyone look so lingeringly as I've seen you looking at all the ladies tonight!"

"What prospects do I have?" Joseph answered, angry that Gideon saw what was on his mind. "Who wants to marry a blacksmith and gunsmith with no business? Who's going to be interested in me?"

"I've offered before to share land with you and perhaps loan you a little money for labor," Gideon said. Joseph felt his blood roil as Gideon began his familiar line about how he should take up cotton.

"If you'll get off your high horse and live as a planter. But you don't want to own slaves. What a pity. You could do well if you'd simply change your views about creating capital."

"It's not likely, Gideon," Joseph said. His blood had cooled. He felt able to stay calm and tell his brother off at the same time. "I don't like being in debt and depending on the labor of others for my income."

"Well, give the old matrimonial route a try. You never know. Maybe Miss Scogins has some money coming to her if her mother can put on a ball like this. Strikes me that's why she's holding it in the first place. A young lady of sixteen can quickly turn into an old maid before you know it, so she's probably anxious to marry her off."

Joseph later danced a quadrille with Letitia Jones, whose brother Edward had married David Thurman's eldest sister Lucy three years before. While Miss Jones' dress showed taste and she was ever so polite, Joseph formed an immediate opinion.

"Too gaunt," he told himself, noting her lack of bosoms and hips. His next partner was Miss Jane Thurman, and he remembered how the sparkling eyes had attracted him before. And she'd blossomed physically, a decided asset.

"How are you this evening, Joseph?" She asked as he held her hand aloft for the turn.

"Very well, and you, Miss Jane?" He felt his skin prickling and hoped she didn't notice.

They sashayed nicely down the middle of the two side couples, then returned to the square while their opposites did the step. As they balanced at each other's sides he thought how effortless the steps seemed with his best friend's sister. But then he'd always felt comfortable with her. While she was almost ten years younger than he, she had a grace about her that erased age differences. During the next seven intricate figures, she pressed her hand in his and otherwise made small signals to prompt him to the next step, which he tried hard to follow.

But when he was waltzing with Ella Scogins he felt a great need to stop and run. Her blond hair was pulled up in ringlets, with tiny tendrils hanging down softly framing her face, the upturned nose of which Joseph could scarcely resist. Her body was enveloped in a fragrance he could not identify, but it was musky, and very appealing. She showed her bosoms and small waist to advantage in a white chambray ballgown trimmed with blue satin folds and blond lace. As soon as he could, he excused himself and went outside into the cold night air on the front porch.

"'If you lust in your heart, you have sinned'," he quoted Scripture to himself. "But, Lord, why give me this temptation if you're not giving me a way to turn it aside? What am I to do? Fornication is a sin, yet you place this temptation in front of me!"

He heard someone opening the large plank door to the Scogins home, and coming out on the porch. It was his friend David.

"David, old friend, am I glad to see your face. You've grown a beard!"

"Yes, I must be preparing myself properly for the ministry. People won't take me seriously if I have such a baby's face!"

Joseph, reassured, took the young man into his confidence about the problem he faced.

"So, you want to do the proper thing and get married? But you don't have the finances. What about your land over past where the railroad's to be built?"

"I can't sell that," Joseph exclaimed, amazed his friend would not understand finances. "That's my only asset."

"The Lord says it's right for a man to leave father and mother and cleave unto woman. What would you do—stay a bachelor all your life? Look at some of these fine specimens of humanity around the village who choose not to enjoy the company of a fine woman. Do you want to be like them?"

"Well, who's going to buy land that won't pay off till who knows when? The W&A is creeping towards us from Tennessee. The railroad from Augusta is delayed. Besides, who knows what business can be generated from trains? They're ugly, foul-smelling, always breaking down. Can you see these folks here riding them in their finery? And you know they can only run during the day. How will they bring any more business than drovers and stagecoaches bring us now?"

David's dark eyes regarded Joseph quietly. His beard made him look older than his nineteen years. Joseph was aware David was deliberately silent to give his friend a chance to think.

"Have faith, my brother," David finally said. "The Lord will provide." He smiled benevolently, turned, and went inside.

Joseph also went inside, hoping the intermission would last a while longer before he'd have to attend to the next lady who had his name on her dance card. He saw Miss Scogins looking his way, and he felt his blood stop in his veins as he saw her lift her fan in a definite show of interest. Joseph quickly returned to the front porch.

After gazing at the stars for a while, Joseph went back inside. He remembered that Miss Jane Thurman was his next partner, and he hurried to be by her side before the music started.

While he stood next to her, Miss Thurman began a conversation Joseph had not expected.

"Tell me about your friend Adam," Jane said. "I understand you and David used to sneak off and play with him when you were younger."

"Well, he's gone, left last spring with the others, I heard through some folks visiting the shop from over near Marietta. I haven't heard anything about him, but I can only assume he's out west somewhere."

"Has there been any word about the trip?"

"The latest news is old news," he said, looking at Jane's dark eyes. Those dark orbs glowed with interest, so he kept talking.

"But apparently there was a drought last summer and the rivers, particularly up near Ross' Landing, all dried up and the boats had to be pulled through 'the suck,' where the river's real low. They ended up traveling by foot and wagon."

Joseph stopped, saddened. "There were a lot of casualties on the way."

"How horrible! I know you're concerned about him."

"I am." Joseph regarded Jane with interest. He found it easy to talk with her. Like her brother David, she was able to understand about Adam instead of castigating Joseph for his friendship with the Indian.

Jane motioned with her hand and looked beyond his shoulder.

"Here comes David. He looks like he's looking for you."

"Joseph!" David said, running up excitedly. "I've got a buyer for your property. I told you the Lord would provide." He turned to address a man following behind him. "Come, Mr. Jett, meet my good friend Mr. Joe Morgan!"

As Joseph made his way to Whitehall Street, he saw to his right the place where soon hordes of laborers would begin to build the massive Monroe Embankment, so called because it was the Monroe Railroad that was building a line from the town of Forsyth. The massive dirt pile would raise the land so the Monroe Railroad would join the W&A Railroad line being built from Tennessee. On past the Marietta Road and going along the Decatur Road was the route of a third prospective railroad line. The Georgia Railroad was extending its Augusta-to-Greensboro line to Terminus to join with the crucial W&A. The link with Tennessee would open up the West— the Ohio and Mississippi river valleys.

Joseph passed by an occasional log cabin as he walked down the Marietta Road toward the stores at the juncture of Whitehall and Peachtree. He counted five large pigs rooting about in the clay-packed streets, some wallowing in the mudholes.

Terminus had few named streets and lots of rutted paths that were not dignified with a name. These paths were worn into the landscape by the feet of large numbers of cattle, hogs, horses, and other livestock, driven through the village from long distances like Ohio and Tennessee. They were on their way to south Georgia markets, farms, and plantations. The road he was on was one in the village that sported a name, and he was heading for a couple more that had acquired names once taverns and nondescript stores had been constructed on them.

"Gee! Gee!" Joseph heard a wagon driver shouting at his mules, as he tried to move them to the left in front of Joseph. "Move, ye stricken ani-mules!" the man exclaimed. As Joseph approached with a scowl of displeasure on his face, the man began cursing anew.

"Blast ye, y'dumb good-for-nothing bastard children of the devil. If you don't move and move fast, I'll blast ye to kingdom come."

Joseph realized the mule driver was drunk. Financially enriched by his delivery of produce to Macon south of this settlement, he was returning with cotton loaded on his wagon for sale in the northern and western settlements. He'd probably spent the night in the drover's hotel near Whitehall Street. His pay in his belly, he was squalling and yelling in a way Joseph despised. But how could he do anything about it? The settlement had no law enforcement, only the appeal of reason—or guns—for a weapon. And reason in this part of the country said that the driver should not be denied his only comforts because of the many, many miles of treacherous territory he would cover, all in the name of commerce.

Joseph's mission with Perkerson was to sell the land—more than a hundred acres west of the Monroe Embankment site—that had been given to him by his father. Now that he had a buyer for his land, he'd decided it was time to marry.

Joseph had speculated on what his life would be like trying to satisfy the worldly expectations of the voluptuous Ella Scogins and had compared her with the relatively easygoing Miss Thurman. He thought about how very attracted he was to Ella, and weighed this against the fact he felt attracted to Jane, and enjoyed her company as well. As in most of his dealings, Joseph thought things out fairly carefully, and sought his parents' guidance.

"She'd be an excellent wife," William Morgan had told his son when he raised the possibility of courting of Jane Thurman. "She's talented, I know she's been schooled in readin' and writin'. She's as fine a Christian woman as her father, God rest his soul, was a Christian minister. And there aren't too many Christian women around in these parts."

"She also knows music, painting, and embroidery," said Rebecca Morgan, looking up from the needlework she was doing by candlelight at their large eating table. "You'd make us very happy with the choice of Miss Jane."

"I hope I can be worthy of her," Joseph said. "She's so fine, and my work is so rough. My prospects aren't quite the equal of hers."

"Her prospects are not so great if she's a spinster," William Morgan pointed out. "She'd not be allowed to own any property unless she were married. Then you'd be the one to take care of the property. If she didn't marry, any assets would be managed for her, remember."

"I realize that, but I still hesitate to throw our fortunes together when my earnings are not so plentiful right now."

"Keep in mind, Joseph, that your father has been a father for young David, and that's been appreciated by the Thurmans," said his mother. "And you and David have been friends for so long that they feel that you are almost his brother. Don't forget the strength of family relationships in helping make a marriage successful."

Joseph had prayed about the decision. One morning when he was in the stable saddling a horse to ride to Decatur for some supplies, he recalled the conversation with Jane about Adam and the Cherokees and how close he had felt to her at that moment. And what a coincidence that on that very night David would find a buyer for his land.

That wasn't coincidence—that was Divine Intervention, he decided.

He had wooed Jane Thurman quietly at Sunday School suppers, and then, at the beginning of the year, appealed to her Uncle Benjamin and her mother Lavinia Mann Thurman to let him call at their home on Huff Road.

His father and he proceeded to plan for a joint household, where, if Joseph were successful in winning the hand of Miss Jane Thurman, they would live with the elder Morgans and share household tasks and expenses. In the meantime, Joseph would be able to build up assets through sharing more in the income from the gunsmithy.

"It's worth it to us, Son, for your marrying well and prospering will assist me in making good marriages for your sisters," William confided to him. "With your brother Gideon now a planter in Griffin, I need the help in the smithy so I can help support the ones remaining!"

Now that he'd been successful in his suit, Joseph reflected, it was a bit daunting. He didn't mind selling the land, but what if all those grandiose plans for railroads didn't happen? What would he do to increase their future prospects? Suppose Macon eclipsed the efforts of the promoters in Terminus to make this a big junction and all the commerce from the north and west went to Macon? He was still thinking about this when he reached the frame building serving as a tavern in the middle of Terminus.

"Hallo, Joseph!" Tom Perkerson greeted him at a small table with chairs whose legs were crooked and unsubstantial-looking. "Sit down. Let me buy you a drink. Fine day for a young man like yourself, making your first land sale."

"No thank you, I don't drink," Joseph said, a bit of nervousness overtaking him. He didn't like drink, and he didn't like being around imbibers.

"Best thing you'll ever decide for yourself," said John Jett, pulling up a chair alongside them. "I like a man with principle!"

"Mr. Jett, you've made a life of principle, just make sure you're supplying the principal and not borrowing it!" Perkerson laughed at his own joke, then was quiet as he saw the two other men were only slightly amused.

"Well, I'll witness the papers presently," Perkerson said. "But first let me share some news I picked up from the *Southern Recorder*." He pulled out a piece of paper, a thin sheet of newsprint from Milledgeville. He handed it to Joseph and John, then stepped away to get another drink at the bar.

Marietta, April 15, 1839
Messrs. Grieve & Orme:
   Gentlemen:-It may be interesting to some of your readers to be informed of a horrid murder committed in this county on the night of the 6th inst., on the road leading from Marietta to Montgomery's Ferry on the Chattahoochee River; the circumstances are as follows: Twenty-one Irish workmen from Savannah, going to Allatoony [sic] with their carts and plunder, to work on the Railroad, they struck camp near the house of a Mr. Brumley, and about 10 o'clock went to rest, and at 1 or 2 o'clock in the morning, were awakened by the fire of a gun, and next followed about seventy of the Irishmen who were engaged with Mr. Thomas on the Railroad, near the place where they encamped, with picks, spades, knives and sticks, killed two of the

*females dead on the spot, and severely wounded eight
more, and did not stop at that—*

Joseph felt his hand shaking as he held the paper. His eyes rushed
ahead to read the signature. It was unsigned.

*they next broke open their trunks and plundered them
of everything valuable. On the next day citizens raised
in arms and went and arrested sixty-four of the
supposed murderers, and thirty-four of that number
were identified to be the murdering clan and committed
to jail to await their trial. If you should think any part
of this will be interesting, it is at your service.*

Joseph felt a gagging in his throat and the taste of bile. He put the
paper down, his hand still shaking, and looked at Jett. "I can't believe this
goes on, and people don't know about it."

Jett, a tall, well dressed man with bushy eyebrows and graying
temples, looked at the young man and reached out his arm to touch Joseph's
shoulder.

"Only a bunch of poor, unfortunate Irishmen beating up on one
another," he said. "It looks like you have fine sensibilities, Joseph, but you
need to get used to this sort of thing. There's going to be more. It's one of
the costs of the railroad coming through. There'll be roughs and toughs,
and you won't be able to do much about it."

"Seems that God-fearing people should do something about it!"
Joseph exclaimed. He pulled his arm away and straightened his cravat.

"One of the bright developments that comes with the roughs and
toughs is a whole cadre of sisters and widows and what nots," said Jett, his
lecturing tone turning to one that seemed to anticipate pleasure. "There's
already a swelling in the number of unspoken-for women in these parts.
You know, a young man like yourself has the pick of more than one woman
here in this village. Don't you think you ought to test some of the
merchandise?"

"What do you mean?"

"Why, do I have to paint you a picture? Have a good time—sow a
few wild oats—" he winked. "Find out for sure if you really want to marry
Miss Thurman. Or get yourself some ladies to see when it's that
'inconvenient' time for your new wife."

Joseph felt his neck grow warm. He was extremely uncomfortable and felt like Jett had been reading his mind. How was it possible to be devoted to one person for God knew how many years? What was it like? What if Jane was revolted by the Experience? He'd heard of women who were so affected by it that they got pregnant once and then never again, leaving their husbands to look elsewhere to satisfy their needs. Or what if he caused her to suffer with his lack of experience?

Then Joseph noticed how pleased Jett was at his discomfort and decided to take on the older man whose dreams of his younger years, Joseph surmised, were just that—dreams.

"Well, Mr. Jett," he said. "Perhaps you could introduce me to a few of these young ladies, since you seem to know so much about them."

Jett began to gag on his drink, coughed loudly, sputtered into his handkerchief, and belatedly gained control of his throat. Then he laughed heartily.

"Now, you know, too much consorting with the young ladies we've talked about might lead to a man turning papist, and we couldn't have that in this village!" he exclaimed "Quite a match you've made with Miss Thurman. Her old man did right by those children, picking up property before any of the rest of us got here. Too bad he had to die before he got to see how he'd prospered through his land."

"I've no doubt," said Joseph, "that he knows the good he's done. As for your true question, sir, no, there's not a substantial dowry. Reverend Thurman was more a minister than a lawyer, so his old lottery claims are confused right now. But his daughter is very refined, and I'm pleased she's agreed to marry a young tradesman. She will bring into the marriage a valued family servant, Miriam, and for that I am extremely grateful to her father."

Joseph's only consideration on accepting Miriam was that he knew it would make Jane's life easier. Jane was young, and, if the example of his mother was any sign, she'd be producing many young ones right away, so they'd need Miriam's help. In fact, Lavinia Thurman had insisted that Jane have her, as her father had provided in his will. Miriam was close to fifty, Joseph figured, and was a widow with few known blood relatives. She'd need a stable home, and he was sure he could provide that.

"Well, that's the wealth of the planters, my Son," said Perkerson, laughing and picking up on the conversation as he returned. "You won't find many a planter with $200 in his safebox. It's all tied up in his land and slaves. And no money to even think of buying any of those northern machines, even if we could get them down here."

Joseph had winced at the term "slaves." His brother owned them, but that was his choice. If Gideon was to farm acreage, field hands were the only feasible way. Joseph, personally, would rather not have the responsibility.

For a moment Joseph debated whether he wanted to do business with these men with whom he had so little in common. While he'd been busy laboring to make tools for the building of this village, he'd not been in a place to pass idle chatter with many of them. It was a good thing he didn't have to put up with their coarse talk for any more time than it took to transfer this land.

Drawing in his breath, he looked at the paper detailing his sale of "the south half of Land Lot 116 in the 14th District of originally Henry, now DeKalb County" for $150. More than a hundred acres were to be conveyed to Jett with the stroke of a pen. He picked up the pen beside the sheet of paper, dipped the point in an open ink bottle, looked at the other two, and said, "Gentlemen?"

With the crisp bank notes rewarding him for his land laying close to his breast, Joseph walked out onto the front porch of the tavern and looked down the mud-puddle filled street called Whitehall. As it was a weekday and he was not expected home right away, he decided to walk around the settlement to see what was new.

His eye was caught by a thirtyish-looking Irishwoman walking towards the tavern, looking like she was going to enter the building. Her grey skirt draped across curved hips and a fullsome body and then hung just over the top of boots. Hers, like his, were spattered with the ever-present mud. Above her waist, large breasts ballooned inside a white blouse that hung irregularly from hunched shoulders. A wool shawl was pulled close around her waist but framed her shapely bosom as if protecting it from the cold was not so important. She mounted the porch from the wet clay street below and walked straight towards him.

"Hello," the woman said with a strong Irish brogue. Her eyes locked on his. They were pale green, and her brown hair was tousled, uncovered except for a shiny silver-like comb holding her hair to one side of her face. She stood provocatively with one hand on her hip, allowing her breasts to rise from the rest of her body, clearly enticing him. Joseph sensed her coyness and knew from her addressing him so directly that this was a woman such as Jett had talked about, one of the women hanging about the village unattached to any male.

"What's your name, dear-o?" she asked in a low voice. Joseph said nothing.

"Well, to be sure, you have a name," the woman said, her eyes sparkling and connecting with Joseph's. "And, to be sure, you wouldn't mind buying a lady a drink!"

Joseph stood, still not speaking. It was as though that other Terminus he'd heard about had revealed itself. What he thought was an older woman was actually one of about eighteen or so. Her skin was soft, not wrinkled around the eyes. He felt himself almost reaching out to touch her face. He wanted to run. Despite the wet and cold, he felt his face and his lower torso warming, and he thought about Jett's bawdy suggestion. He was conscious of wanting very badly to extend his hand and touch her breasts.

"I-I don't have time," he lied.

"Aw, it wouldn't take long, just a teensy-weensy part of an hour. I know you'd enjoy it," she winked at him.

"Mary McCree, what are you doing talking to that heap of horse droppings?" a scratchy male voice said behind her. Tom Cunningham reached her side, then put his arm around her and pulled her close to him.

"Well, Mr. Cunningham," she said laughing and looking up at him with those twinkling green eyes. "You were late and I was about to make the acquaintance of this nice young man. Had you been a few minutes later you wouldn't have found me waiting for you at all."

"Ha! You would've still been standing here, love, because this 'young man' of yours doesn't even know how to take off his pants without his mama present. C'mon, you little colleen, I'm thirsty!" With that, Cunningham pulled the young Irishwoman into the tavern and slammed the door in Joseph's face. He heard Cunningham's roar of greeting to the other patrons of the establishment.

His face burning, Joseph turned and ran off the porch onto the street. Cunningham was here. How long had he been here? What was he doing? Where was he staying? He felt heat all over his body and realized how close he'd come to succumbing to the physical charms of Mary McCree. How he wanted to touch her! How lovely was the lilt of her Irish brogue as she enticed him! What a blasphemy that he'd even consider it, especially when she was a favorite of Cunningham. She had him so bamboozzled, he'd lost the opportunity to take Cunningham and get the rifle back. He felt confused and frustrated. How little experience he had with women—none! How could some women be as tawdry yet appealing as Mary, and others be as modest and wholesome as Jane? Would he be disappointed with Jane if he could be so easily tempted by Mary?

Joseph ran down Marietta Road toward home, ignoring the mud on his suit, not sure how much of the day's events he would relate to his father.

Chapter 5

THE WEDDING

1839

The rain on the roof drummed louder as waves of water ran across it and over the hard packed clay yard out front of the Morgan home. A cold November wind wafted across from the west, blowing the drops straight into the faces of Terminus residents mounting the wooden stairs to the long porch that ran the length of the house. Joseph held a large umbrella over the heads of ladies who made their way from carriages stopping at the front picket fence and then struggled against the wetness as they went up the path to the front porch.

Inside, candles glowed in each of the receiving rooms, giving off warmth that complemented the welcoming fires in three hearths. Magnolia leaves and ivy vines festooned the mantels and the dining table. William Morgan and his family were preparing for Joseph's wedding to Miss Jane Thurman.

"Why, Mr. Morgan," chatted one elderly lady whose long, black wool cape covered her finest brown silk dress. "This is just lovely. Miss Thurman is lucky to be welcomed into such a nice home."

"Why, thank you, Mrs. Addison," Joseph said. "I hope you'll favor us with a call once we're settled in."

"Believe me, when the month is up, we'll be among the first," Mrs. Addison said, and smiled broadly at him as she passed from Joseph's arm into the main parlor. The young bridegroom returned to the road and to the carriage stoop where more guests were alighting.

It had been seven months since Miss Jane had agreed to wed. In the meantime, Joseph had worked almost feverishly trying to put their household together. There was furniture to make, and rooms in the Morgan home to complete so that they could have privacy. They'd finally settled on making the two rooms on the right side of the top floor their bedroom and sitting room, and Joseph had immediately begun building a large rope bed with a good-sized trundle. May as well make it now as later, he figured.

Then he'd made a hunt board and china press that would occupy the sitting room for now, which would be a place to store and display some of their wedding gifts. Joseph made these from the wood of the large wild cherry trees he'd cut and dried the year before. The two pieces now shone with the lustrous finish of a fine cabinetmaker. While Joseph had plenty of experience working with fine woods, as he used them for rifle stocks, he wanted Miss Jane's furnishings to have the touch of the German cabinetmaker, Mr. Rucker. He'd paid Mr. Rucker to come on successive Saturdays and help him out in the blacksmith's shop, where he'd hidden the pieces until the night before when he'd brought them up to the house.

"Miss Jane is so pleased with the furniture, Joseph," Alice, his older sister, had told him this morning. Of course he hadn't been able to see Jane this morning, as it was bad luck to see her before they went before the minister.

"How do you know?" Joseph had asked.

"She told me. She's told me lots."

At first, Joseph was jealous that his sister got to hear his new bride's thoughts. Then he decided it was customary for the women of a family to share a lot of secrets. At least Jane was getting along well with Alice. His fear was that she'd be overwhelmed by the sheer numbers of his womenfolk.

The only time he'd questioned his decision to marry Jane Thurman was on the porch of the tavern back in April when he'd encountered Mary McCree. He hadn't seen Mary McCree since then, nor had he crossed paths with Tom Cunningham. On asking, he'd found that Cunningham was occasionally in the area, usually selling whiskey at the tavern. He'd reported seeing him to Sheriff Jones in Decatur, but, without the sheriff being in Terminus, it was difficult for Jones to track Cunningham and arrest him. It had been so many years since the rifle had been lifted that the sheriff discouraged the Morgans from trying too hard to get it back.

"Like as not, the man's traded it long time ago," he said.

Joseph saw his sister looking at him as if waiting. He remembered his previous high curiosity about Jane.

"Well, what else did Miss Jane say?" he asked. The nervousness about the marriage returned, causing his voice to raise slightly. He hoped Alice didn't notice.

"She was very happy that we're friends. She was concerned that we wouldn't accept her since there were so many of us Morgan women. But she's happy that I'm there to watch over her and guide her like my other young sisters."

Joseph thought about the age difference in the two: Alice, who would soon see the underside of thirty, and Jane, a young sixteen growing into adulthood. It was clear Alice would remain unmarried, since she'd gone past twenty-one and had never shown much interest in the young beaus who sought her company.

"My life here is far too interesting to consider going with any of them," she'd laugh. Anne, the next daughter, had a lot more beaus. Nevertheless, Alice did seem to relish her position as assistant mother in the Morgan household.

Joseph thought that a less fulfilling life awaited Alice if she continued to decline the attentions of suitors in Terminus. On the other hand, what would be her future if she did accept someone like Miss Jane's cousin, young Billy Mann? Billy's father was constantly being criticized for letting his pigs run in the streets. They tore down picket fences, ran up on the porches of neighbors, and caused all sorts of mischief in the settlement. Old Billy Mann acted as though he was back in South Carolina where free range was the rule. It hadn't been outlawed, as there was no law in the new settlement, but whether a man let his animals range freely seemed to distinguish the common people from the fine. If a man didn't have the sensibilities to keep his animals penned, it was like he didn't have consideration for his neighbors—wasn't civilized. So these people were Alice's prospects?

What trade would young Billy have to support his sister? Maybe he'd be a storekeeper like his father. But Joseph knew it would be a hard life, whether it was here or wherever Billy might move—Alabama or Mississippi—to improve his fortunes. Maybe it was better that Alice hadn't married. At least at home she was surrounded by those who loved her. And she'd never be destitute like Mary McCree, consorting with the likes of Cunningham.

Joseph straightened his black frock coat and checked his cravat in the hallway looking glass. In his pocket was a band of Dahlonega gold he'd made from a nugget he'd taken in trade for a rifle.

"You look very handsome," said Rebecca Morgan as she placed her hand in the crook of her son's left arm and gently tugged. "Now it's time to gather by the preacher. Are you all right, Son?" The gray-haired woman peered at her son.

"I'm all right, Mama. I just hope I'll be able to make Jane happy. We're looking to maybe fifty years together. Is it possible to be happy for that long?"

"Well, I know Lavinia Thurman has prepared her eldest daughter well for her responsibilities. You stick to making the living, and Jane will be in charge of the cooking and keeping house and loving and caring and smoothing over your rough edges. That's what women do, Joseph. All these years with all these females around and you've wondered what was their use. Son, you're about to find out."

Joseph turned back to the mirror and regarded himself with his mother at his left side. His eyes were intent, his brown hair already receding from his forehead. He recalled what he'd overheard one of the men in town say of him: "He looks like he means business."

"It's hot in here," he said, then turned with his mother to the parlor, the preacher, the guests, and his new wife.

Reverend Parker, an older, short, bald man with wisps of gray hair standing out from above his ears, stood at the end of the parlor near the fireplace, his order of service clutched under his arm.

Joseph strode forward and stood in front of the preacher, making sure he and his bride would be positioned with the floor planks coming straight from the preacher, to ensure good luck. He heard a small murmur and the rustling of silk skirts as wedding guests turned behind him. He moved his own tall body around just in time to see Jane descending the staircase, looking as beautiful as an angel.

The small figure wore a flowing white gown with a veil hiding her face. Friends and family moved aside as though they were the Red Sea parted by Moses, letting his bride walk through them and to his left side. Her hair was caught up in ringlets and braids, and intertwined with a circlet of netting decorated with white camelias. Jane's eyes shone like buttons. She was smiling shyly.

What a peaceful, miraculous moment, Joseph thought. For a moment, he remembered his friend Adam and the Cherokees assaulted by militiamen. He thought about the attacks on the Irish railroad workers up near Marietta and the women dying under blows from picks and shovels.

His mind flashed to the evil face of Old Thomas Cunningham and his thieving son Tom. These were violent times. Could they trust the future? Would they and their children be safe? The whole country was still feeling the effects of the Panic. Joseph had been able to take the proceeds from the sale of his land and, with his father, invested in a piece of land down near where the Georgia railroad would join the W&A.

He looked at Jane and decided to let go the worry. The Indian conflicts were over. The Morgans and their kin were much better off than the Irish workers fighting each other for the railroad work. They at least had their land, their businesses, and a good home. He blessed his good fortune as he glanced at Jane at his side, her hand tucked in his elbow. He breathed a prayer of thanksgiving for his gifts, especially Jane.

The minister read a short passage from Scripture, then turned to the two of them.

"Jane, will you have this man to be your husband, to live together in the covenant of marriage?" the minister read. Joseph watched her face. She was so young! "Will you love him, comfort him, honor and keep him, in sickness and in health?"

What kind of sickness lay ahead?

"—forsaking all others, be faithful to him as long as you both shall live?"

"I will," Jane said softly, but with conviction.

Joseph made his response with equal conviction and was glad to see his young bride smile as he spoke. Would they have children? Would they prosper and see their grandchildren?

The minister joined their right hands and led them in their vows.

"—till death do us part," Jane said quietly.

"—till death do us part," Joseph said strongly.

Joseph placed the band of Dahlonega gold on Jane's left hand.

"What God hath joined together, let no man put asunder," the minister read.

"Hurrah! Hurrah!" Gideon led those gathered in a cheer for the couple after the ceremony ended. Gideon, ever the dapper gentleman in his black suit and jauntily tied cravat, guided the guests to a table loaded with a wide choice of food: venison and pheasant that Joseph had hunted the days before, pork roasts, apple pies, squash vegetables, breads, and potatoes. The infare, a customary dinner provided by the groom's parents in honor of the couple, began.

Jane Thurman brushed her hair by candlelight and regarded the letter laying on her dresser. She had been given the parchment paper by her mother earlier that day as she dressed for her wedding. The letter from her father had been a surprise, and her mother had handed it to her with tears in her eyes. Her father would have had to compose the letter for Lavinia to write even as he was dying.

Jane had wept, too, as she read the letter in front of her mother and imagined her father's voice saying the caring words:

To my dear daughter,

You are now at the age when you will be anticipating possible marriage to your companion for life. With God's help, I would like to instruct you in your duty to your husband and family.

The man to whom you will be betrothed is to always merit your respect and love. When your will and that of your husband shall conflict it is his will that must prevail, as Holy Scriptures tell us that is your duty. You must ever show him affection and tenderness and never demonstrate your differences in the company of others.

He should always be proud of your well-bred behaviors. He should arrive home from his day's labors to a house you have filled with smiles. No matter how disagreeable your day, you must lighten his load.

You promise to love and obey and to HONOR your husband. Always hold him as the first object of your esteem. And should you at any time discover any defects in his manners or infirmities in his nature, you should never treat these with bitterness and mockery. If you find your views in opposition, never let yours overcome his, as to do so will cause his character to lose much of its force and vigor, and he will become unable to accomplish his endeavors and become weak willed. He will lose all self-confidence and will diminish in importance in the world.

If he should fall on hard times, that is when you must support him the most, foregoing criticisms and avoiding the temptation to remonstrate. This is the time he needs you the most.

From my long and most satisfying life with your mother, I can tell you that those who accept the gifts the Lord gives them in the form of children are, indeed, blessed, and shall be rewarded in Heaven. To bear the fruits of your husband's love willingly and without complaint is the greatest gift you can return to Him in Heaven.

My blessings are with you, my dear one, as you embark on your new life.

Your loving father,
David Thurman

Jane's wedding day had been one of excitement and nervousness. There were lots of people's names to remember and lots of manners to keep in mind. Hardly more than a girl, she had been preparing for this day—and night—for many months.

So here's the man you cocked your hat for, she'd told herself as the time to descend the stairs approached. The moment had arrived. She'd schemed with David, getting him to place Joseph on her dance card at Ella Scogins' ball. And she'd worked to be here or there so their paths would cross. Now she faced the consequences of all her scheming. How would she know what to do tonight?

"Remember that Joseph may be nervous, too, dear," Lavinia Thurman had told Jane as she dressed for the wedding earlier. "If he's not, then you've a lot to worry about. If he is, then he's been true to you, and I would expect this of your young man, as he's also your brother's closest friend and a man of fine Christian upbringing.

"Observe him and respond in kind. If he's nervous, take his hand and let him know you are his friend. Whatever happens, don't be alarmed. Let him take the lead. What happens can be wonderful or it can be not so comfortable, but you must never make him feel foolish or show anger."

When Lavinia said that, Jane decided she'd just put aside her worries and let come naturally what apparently had been going on for generations in her family without undue alarm.

Jane, looking in the mirror, finished brushing her hair. If her mama wasn't worried, then she certainly didn't need to be. Now the wedding celebration was over. All the guests had left the house, and the elder Morgans had retired below. Even the girls, who slept in two rooms downstairs, had quieted down. She awaited the signal they had agreed upon. Joseph was to knock and stand in the hallway until she answered that all was ready.

In the looking glass over her new dresser, she viewed her long brown hair cascading over her shoulders and glancing across the white cotton nightgown. Its high collar was embroidered with white flowers. The French tucks across the front were a luxurious touch added by the Charleston dressmaker from whom she'd purchased the gown for her wedding night.

Joseph's knock at the door nearly made her jump. So soon! She carried her candle and placed it on a stand next to what she had decided would be her side of the bed.

She quickly turned down the "best quilt," appliqued with large Whig roses, atop the large four-poster rope bed and slipped between embroidered sheets, underneath several lesser quilts piled on for warmth.

"Come in," she said. There was no response. She cleared her throat, then replied a little louder. "Please come in, my husband."

He entered the room carrying a candle and wearing a thick woven white nightshirt. The opening at the neck showed thick hair on his chest, and Jane felt a tightening in the area between her legs. His eyes were fully on her as she sat up in bed holding the dense covers open for him.

Joseph removed his night shoes, placed his large fists on the sheets, and lifted himself into the bed. He moved his body until it was in full contact with hers, and pulled the sheets and bedding over both of them.

"It's been a long day," he said, breathing into her hair.

"I know."

"Are you afraid?"

"Yes."

"Well, so am I."

Joseph slowly stroked Jane's gown-clad body, gradually moving his arms completely around her. Cradling Jane in his arms, then reaching down her body, he hugged her to his chest and legs. He kissed her forehead and her lips, and placed his hand on her breast. Jane had never felt such sensation as he stroked her and kissed her softly. She wondered if his lack of hesitation meant he'd had a woman before her. But she forgot her question as he, in what seemed like one motion, moved on top of her, lifted her nightgown, and entered her for the first time.

PART TWO

ABBEVILLE FAREWELL

Much the larger part of the infant city, or rather the city in prospect, was a forest. The young timber had been cut out for wood, and the pines for lumber, and the beautiful oaks formed a great park.

On the left was Murrell's Row, where every house was a groggery and gambling house, except a few small stores, till Ivy street was reached.

Rev. George G. Smith
"Recollections of an Atlanta Boy"
Atlanta Journal, 1909

Chapter 6

MARTHASVILLE

December 1842

Jane ran her hand over the oak mantle above the fireplace in the parlor of her home to make sure it had been dusted recently. When she satisfied herself it had been done properly, she placed a magnolia bough and holly stems on the mantle and went to the table to gather more.

She wanted lots of greenery for Christmas. She thought about how her mother-in-law had decorated the parlor for her wedding three years before. Now, two boy babies later, she had more responsibilities in the household she'd joined back then. While Absalom was entertained by his aunts and Will napped, she'd gone out to the yard and adjoining land to gather the Christmas decorations.

She placed more greens around the candelabra on the reading table, a polished piece of furniture stationed between two chairs near the fireplace. Red berries from a prickly bush contrasted with the deep green of the effusive holly and the shiny-leafed magnolia.

It was a welcome relief to Jane to be able to do something not connected to small mouths opening like those of hungry little birds in a nest, the growling of her husband's stomach, or cleanliness of house or clothes. There was so much heavy work to be done just to keep the household going that she and the other women didn't get a chance for pleasurable pasttimes, like laying the greenery to prepare for Christmas.

Jane picked up a long rope of pine boughs lying on the floor alongside the stairway. She mounted the hallway stairs, and began winding the rope around the stair railing. Gradually, she moved down to the bottom step, tied an end to the newel post, then moved back to admire her handiwork.

"What an elegant touch," her mother-in-law Rebecca said behind her.

"Oh, Mother," Jane blanched, embarrassed. "I didn't know you were catching me in my childish pride. I should be ashamed."

"What on earth for, Jane?" Rebecca said, smiling. "Your festoon adds such a nice touch."

Jane felt a slight warming of her cheeks as she explained the decorations.

"You don't object to the pine garland, do you?"

"Of course not, dear," Rebecca said, her blue eyes admiring the new look of her house. "You'll turn us into quality people for sure."

"Well, of course we're people of quality," Jane said. "After all, the Morgans are very well respected in the community."

Rebecca put her hand on Jane's shoulder. "We don't see ourselves as particularly standing out, but your charms add greatly to what we have."

Jane felt her skin return to its normal warmth. Mother Morgan had a way of making her feel comfortable. Jane decided her indulgence wasn't childish after all.

"My father wouldn't have approved, nor David, I'm afraid," she said. "It's something I wanted to do all the time as a child in my Uncle Benjamin's household, but didn't get to because David considered it papist. If I'd done anything like that, he'd probably have seen to it I was punished severely."

She laughed as though thinking of the rebellious act and confronting her brother.

"I guess Mr. Wesley was very clear that there should be none of the excesses of the traditional church when he started the Methodism. Of course, David follows everything Mr. Wesley said," Jane added.

Jane considered her mother-in-law as one of her greatest blessings. She viewed Rebecca as a woman with a lot of common sense, a quick wit, and a good judge of people. She'd never enjoyed such ease in talking to someone—even to her own mother—as she did with Rebecca. She felt Rebecca was willing to overlook her girlish mistakes, to give her a second chance if she erred in her efforts to be a good wife to Joseph. Yet her own sixth sense told her something was on Rebecca's mind.

"We need to talk about our labors here around the house," Rebecca stated. "William is getting on up in years, and he's developed a terrible cough. I know you've heard him."

"Yes, I'm sorry about that," said Jane, wondering what kind of changes Rebecca was talking about.

"It's customary when a young woman comes to the house of an older one, that they work out their roles," Rebecca continued. "It doesn't do to have two women battling it out for mistress of the house. I've watched you learning how to cook the meals alongside Miriam, and I've seen the laundry you've done for Joseph..."

Jane half heard Rebecca as the older woman described her observations about the chores Jane normally did. How could she want her to be mistress of the household? She was too young and green as a spring corn sprout to do that.

"—so I'd like you to take charge," Rebecca was saying.

"But Mother Morgan, I couldn't," Jane protested. How on earth could she run a household of a dozen people? And what about the arguments that might spring up among the women and girls? With several sisters-in-law, and her husband's parents, and her own husband and sons, there was bound to be a hullabaloo just about any day.

Jane was amazed at the power being a wife brought. It was as though putting on the wedding ring of a Morgan male brought a passel of traditions and roles that she didn't know if she'd be able to fulfill. Alice could probably beat her in any contest of domestic accomplishments with one arm tied behind her back, yet she would defer to the younger, less experienced Jane. It still was awkward. She could just hear the talk in the beds upstairs under the eaves if she didn't do rightly!

"I know you're worried about my daughters," Rebecca said, reading her mind. "All I can tell you is that the girls are human and there may be some tender feelings. But it'll save them the pain of resenting each other if one of them were to become the boss.

"But don't get the idea you'll have to do lots more work. You've seen us pitch in around here. You'll have the kitchen and the larder, and you'll oversee the laundry, which I think Anne and Becka should keep doing. I'll help out with the children, as will all the girls. We'll see how it goes, and you can ask me for help any time you're feeling put upon. After all, I'd not want the house falling down around us for want of a nail that needs tending to."

Jane's eyes filled with wetness brought on by fear.

"I'll need your advice on just managing!" she cried.

Rebecca brought her face close to Jane's and stroked her chin.

"Don't cry, Jane, you'll do fine," Rebecca said, her blue eyes twinkling. "You'll do Joseph proud!"

"Father," Joseph said, as he placed a log on the fire after dinner on an evening a week later. "Have you heard the news? They're bringing in the first train on the W&A Railroad!"

He addressed William, whose lower half was wrapped in a quilt while he sat by the fire in an oak rocking chair.

Jane and Rebecca occupied the two chairs by the reading table. Each was bent over her handwork.

"Where's it to be?" William asked with a voice that showed the strain of speaking.

"Down by State Square, where the railroad buildings are being erected."

"Nice to see something's come of all this surveyin' and diggin' and everlastin' noise. When're they sayin' the railroad's supposed to come, have y'heard?"

Jane picked up her basting and listened attentively as the men discussed the train's coming to the settlement. It had been planned for years. Joseph told her their family's lives would be changed for the good, and their prospects for business would improve greatly when the train was built to Marthasville.

"They're thinking later this year they're going to bring in a big engine from the Central of Georgia Railroad and run it up to Marietta from here."

"How're they going to get an engine here—fly it on wings?" his father asked, laughing weakly.

"Why, no, they've built a huge wagon and they're going to put it on the wagon and pull it overland from Madison!" Joseph excitedly used his hands to demonstrate the placing of the locomotive on a wagon and it moving along. "Seems they couldn't wait for tracks to be laid for the last section from Greensboro. But it won't be long 'til both railroads are in place."

"For goodness' sake," Rebecca broke in. "When that happens, pigs will fly!"

"Mother, just wait. I'll take you down to see it. The most advanced form of transportation you've seen is the stagecoach coming in and leaving, and you've not even seen that very often, much as we get down to the roads."

Rebecca continued her sewing, her strokes twinned with Jane's, and sighed.

"Well, I know, ever since you were a boy you never failed to tell me each time you saw one," she laughed.

"Folks," Joseph said. "Remember it wasn't too long ago they were calling this 'Terminus.' Before that it was called 'Thrasherville,' after Old Man John Thrasher, the one that built all those shanties for his Irish diggers. Now it's Marthasville, named after the governor's daughter. If changing names is any sign of the growth of a metropolis, then this town is bound to be big!"

"Son," William said, pulling the quilt tighter around his legs. "I know you have high hopes for this village, and I hope you're not disappointed, but from what I hear, even the engineer hired to lay out the track for the W&A had so little faith in the town's prospects, he turned down an offer to buy land in this area. Then he chose Marietta for his headquarters!"

William was now showing more energy, enjoying his recall of facts of coming and goings in the local commerce.

"Then that Mr. Thrasher—the one that brought in all those Irish to build the Monroe Embankment—he got so disgusted when the W&A moved their line east and ruined the Monroe Railroad junction, he sold all that land for half what he paid for it and went back to Griffin."

"Yes, Father, but did you notice a grocery store has opened up in one of those old shanties along Marietta Road? The couple that started it had to evict a cow before they could begin living and commercing there, but at least it's a start."

Jane continued basting the dress for Miriam, pulling threads that contrasted with the pale blue calico fabric. Pretty soon she'd be able to see how the two pieces of the bodice would fit together. As in most of these after supper discussions, she said nothing and listened only to the parts she found interesting. Otherwise she made plans in her head for the children's clothes or her next bodice and skirt combination. It had been some time since she'd had a dress from Charleston, and she eagerly substituted the works of her own hands rather than completely desert fashion.

Jane watched Joseph, whose eyes lit up everytime he talked about Marthasville. She recalled how unsure he had been about his prospects when they'd married—unsure that this town would be the place to make their home. Yet, with the birth of their children, he'd mellowed and watched with intense interest as the W&A was completed from the Etowah River, through Marietta, and now to Marthasville.

"What I think a lot of it is," Jane's attention suddenly returned to her husband's voice in the room, "—is that those senators and congressmen and presidents, they don't trust us common folk. And that's after more men than ever before in American history voted 'em into office."

"What has me concerned," her father-in-law said, "is to see the numbers flooding into these new territories and pretty soon the South will be outvoted in Congress. If Texas is annexed and isn't a slave state..."

The young mother silently said a prayer of thanks for her many blessings.

Now Absalom was attempting to climb everything in the house and expressing himself with cute phrases like "Me mama's"weetheart" and "Me papa's li' man!" And did he ever follow after Miriam! "Mirum" is what Absalom called her. His mammy was ever watchful, making sure the toddler didn't get in his mama's way, and taking care to feed him before she put everyone else's dinner or supper on.

"What's Mr. Morgan's pleasure today, ma'am?" Miriam would ask in her deep, musical voice at the beginning of their day after breakfast dishes were cleared away from the table. Their breakfasts often consisted of eggs and ham with soda biscuits and butter and milk from their cow, along with the treasured coffee from Brazil. Jane ate sparingly. Joseph wolfed down everything in sight. It embarrassed Jane to see his lack of manners—her brother David was smoother—but she took care not to criticize him. After all, his work was hard and he needed the food to work the blacksmith and gunsmith shops.

Miriam ate after them in the kitchen, but asked about their needs for dinner first.

"Well, he usually is pretty hungry by one o'clock," Jane said of Joseph. "Maybe some ham and peas. I'll see if we've any greens from the garden. And if you can do your miracle with the cornbread, I'm sure that will be appreciated."

Jane, as part of her new housemistress' duties, would go to the smokehouse to retrieve the ham, first unlocking the heavy padlock, and making sure it was locked after her. She'd next go to the locked storeroom off the kitchen to retrieve the field peas. The root cellar was her next stop, where she'd sort through the harvested vegetables for the greens. Always, always, she had to lock behind her, and she would after each locking replace the ring of heavy keys on the chatelaine hanging from her waist.

This was her daily routine since taking the housemistress role: get up before dawn, go downstairs to the warming kitchen to where Miriam had built the first fire, get water warming to take back up for her and Joseph's washing, perform her toilettte, put on her successive layers of clothes, including pantaloons, chemise, petticoat, and day dress. She would then attach her chatelaine, which she removed only when dressing for bed.

Jane recalled the first night she'd forgotten to lock the smokehouse. She awoke in the night with the realization, then nudged her husband to get him to go lock it. She was shocked when, instead, Joseph became angry with her.

"You'll have to get up and go out and lock it."

"But, Joseph, it's cold out there, and I'm not dressed for it."

"You'll have to go out and lock it. I give you total responsibility for the household. If you fail to take care of it, you've got to set things right."

She'd realized she couldn't argue with him. She rose, dressed as best she could for the December cold, and went outside to lock the smokehouse door.

He was asleep when she returned.

Later he'd lectured her, kindly but very firmly, about the realities of keeping the household fed and clothed, with security of their possessions being one of the most important concerns.

"We never know who will try to steal, even from within our own household," he said. It didn't seem to matter to him that there'd never been an incident, and that Miriam was the last who'd pilfer their food.

Jane pulled a final stitch in her basting there in the family parlor, and tied off a knot. She picked up a sock from her repair basket that sported gaping holes in the toe and heel, and shook her head. Then she rethreaded her large needle and began darning with an expert stroke.

Without help from other members of the household, she knew she would find this a very hard life. If she had no help from Miriam, it would be impossible. She often counted the number of big heavy iron pots and skillets Miriam would have going at one time and it astounded her. Five was the average, what with needing to boil water for Absalom's gruel, making cornbread in advance, and then cooking the peas, meats and greens that would be on the table at one that afternoon—not to mention keeping the fire going with firewood brought in from the back porch. At least Miriam didn't have to gather that from the woods—that was something Joseph always did—but the constant feeding of the kitchen fire was a job in itself.

"Mama, mama!" Jane's reverie was interrupted by Absalom, dark-haired and lively, padding towards her in his night clothes, followed by the large, slow-stepped Miriam.

"Come, young man, let me see you!" said Jane as she put down her sewing. She leaned over to the toddler, and put her arms around him. "Give me a kiss before you go to sleep!"

Absalom pushed his round face towards her cheek and made a sloppy smacking sound. She hugged him closer and then rubbed his mop of hair.

"Come here, little man," Joseph stood up from the chair he'd occupied for his fireside talk. He swooped his long frame down toward the youngster, lifted him in his arms, and with one step covered the distance to the table.

"Now this is for you," he said as he removed the sugar bowl lid from the bowl, then lifted the bowl toward the child. "Have some sweetening!"

Jane said nothing, remembering her advice from her late father's letter not to object to her husband in front of others. But she was concerned he would spoil Absalom and start bad habits at the table.

Absalom obediently put his fist into the bowl of thick,brown crystals and then into his mouth, savored the sugar and then smiled widely at his father.

"Do it again, Papa!" he said. His grandmother and grandfather laughed.

"No, you don't, young'n," Miriam teased in a semi-scolding voice while she took the youngster from Joseph's arms. "It's up to bed for you— right now!"

Joseph's blood quickened as he heard the rumble of still another farmwagon out on the road not far from the shops on the Morgan farmstead. He listened and heard the rest in the convoy following after the first one. Not stopping to go out and look, he estimated this party to have five wagons.

For two days now he had heard them with increasing frequency. At first it was a single wagon. Now there were lengthy wagon trains coming in from the western and northwestern areas, through what had been Cherokee country. Farmers and planters had come from as far away as Alabama to see the big event. Now, on the morrow, the historic occasion would take place: the initial run of the W&A Railroad from Marthasville to Marietta.

After five years of planning, and many stops in the work, the track was finally ready. There'd been a national recession, the suspension of all work, then work resumed, but only on the part of the line from Marthasville to below the Etowah River; to do that short section, the state had resorted to convict labor.

Joseph concentrated as best he could on the tools he was assembling for their new shop near the railroad. But he couldn't help thinking about his excitement at seeing the *Florida* for the first time.

Ka-pow!

Joseph jumped when he heard a report of the rifle not a hundred feet away. He strode to the front of the shop and saw a couple of men walking out on the road and away from his frontage on the road. Both carried their rifles as though hunting game. One was wiping his firearm as he walked and spat on the ground. In the bright December light, he thought he saw Tom Cunningham's hunched back hobbling away!

Grabbing his pistol from below the worktable, he quickly primed and loaded it. He stuck it underneath his leather apron and ran towards the men, who were laughing and talking as though in a state of inebriation.

"Hallo!" he called. His heart stopped for a moment as the two turned around at his summons.

The man was not Cunningham, but he looked just as unsavory and apparently was not taking kindly to Joseph.

"I'd be much obliged if you didn't shoot that thing around a man's family," he said, calmly and nonthreateningly.

"Waal, din't know we was a-botherin'," drawled the man who had shot. He regarded Joseph as though waiting for a quick movement, which Joseph carefully avoided.

Joseph waved his arm. "Y'all have a good time watchin' the locomotive. I'm sure it'll be somethin' to be proud of," he said, familiarly.

"Yer right as rain about that!" the man said. He spat on the ground once again as he and his cohort continued on up the road toward the Marietta Road.

After he watched them leave, Joseph reflected on what he would have done if one of the men had been Cunningham. It would be up to him, he realized, if the varmint were ever to be brought to justice. He'd have to encounter him in a place where there were few others who could get hurt, pull a gun on him, and somehow deliver him to the sheriff six miles away. That was the way the law went in this area, still. If a man wanted to evade the law, it was easy enough to go stay in the woods during the day and return home to family and food at night. After awhile, the urgency of the search would blow over, and the victim of the crime often would give up, due to the difficulty of prosecuting. Which was why there was an occasional shootout to even up scores.

Perhaps it was fortunate Joseph had not seen Cunningham since that day three years ago when he'd seen him with Mary McCree, the day he'd sold his hundred acres. Joseph hadn't accosted Cunningham then because he wasn't wearing a gun, and he didn't fancy trying to take him in a tavern full of patrons in various states of intoxication.

The crime and general lack of respect for authority were constant problems around them. Joseph and his father had given up paying taxes that were levied for their area, because no one else in that section of DeKalb was paying theirs.

The rowdiness of the citizenry worried Joseph greatly now that he was responsible for so many family members. His father was gradually letting go of the new shops because of his health. Old William had problems breathing and could no longer spend a whole day working. Joseph had assured him that he could handle today's work and sent him home to rest up for the coming of the *Florida*.

Joseph had watched William in the shops with growing sadness. It was hard for his father to operate the bellows, and he required assistance when lifting implements that he formerly handled almost effortlessly. As he followed his father with his eyes, Joseph thought about his own life. Would it be reduced so abruptly? Would Absalom or William Henry some day have to help him lift a plow and hold it on the anvil, as he now helped his father? He hoped that day would never come. I'll go out fightin', he told himself. He had come to suspect there was a connection between the amount of time spent over the forge and William's breathing problems. There was so much dust in the air; no doubt it settled in his lungs. Joseph decided he had to find other businesses to keep from being tied to the anvil and the forge to supplement what the forge brought in.

"Look, Absalom! The locomotive's coming! The train's coming! Here come the mules!" Joseph was ecstatic as he spotted the locomotive on its amazing cradle. Sixteen mules pulled a heavy cart bearing the iron monstrosity down Decatur Street toward the depot. The family stood in front of the Morgans' shops on Decatur Street.

"What, Papa? What? 'Momo?'"

"No. LO-CO-MO-TIVE!"

"MO-TIV!"

"That's right, Son," Joseph beamed as he held his son close in his arms. "LO-CO-MO-TIVE!"

"Oh, Joseph, this is so exciting," said Jane, who stood next to him. She placed her gloved hand over his forearm and snuggled close. Miriam carried little William Henry, just four months old, draped with a blanket over his face to protect him from the Christmas Eve cold. William and Rebecca Morgan stood bundled up on the other side of Joseph. Behind them stood Joseph's brother Gideon and his wife Josephine and two young sons, visiting from Griffin for the unprecedented run of the *Florida*.

All along the route, young boys rushed into the path of the oncoming cargo, trying to see how long they could stay in front of it before being pulled back by mothers or fathers or shooed away by railroad personnel.

Shouts of welcome competed with firearms being discharged into the air all the way along the line. Joseph had never seen so many people in one place! Suddenly, he envisioned the town that would grow up along these railroad tracks. The iron rails would eventually, like vines intersecting on the ground, connect and intertwine with each other, opening up the western lands of the Ohio and Tennessee valleys to north Georgia. Then products from all those areas could be traded to the world through Savannah and Charleston.

"Can you believe your eyes, Father?" Joseph shouted above the din, as he leaned over to his father.

"It's amazing!" the grizzled man, sporting a heavy wrap around his head, shouted back. "What about the other parts of the train? Where are they?"

"They're over by the depot. If you look hard, you'll see a side rail, and the freight car and the passenger car that'll be used for the first load! They were both made in Milledgeville at the state prison. All of it's been pulled here by mules on a wagon."

"Too bad you couldn't have been among those riding," his father said.

"You know I would have given a lot for it, maybe even my wife!" Joseph teased. Jane's twinkling eyes met his, and she smiled. "Of course, that would be unthinkable," Joseph said, pulling her arm closer.

"I don't know, " said Gideon behind them, "I might think of it myself!"

"Oh, yes, and how long do you think you would be able to get along with out your better halves?" rejoined Rebecca, pointing a finger at both of her sons.

The Morgans watched in fascination as the long chain of mules finally pulled past them. The beasts strained at leather harnessing, snorted puffs of steam from their nostrils, and struggled to put one foot in front of the other. The burden the beasts pulled, a three-ton monster perched on a low, specially constructed wagon, was strung up with endless ropes and chains. It was as though the Lilliputians had expected the great Lemuel Gulliver to slip his bonds and escape to freedom!

"Oh, look!" Jane said, once the engine had passed. She leaned over in front of the crowd, peering down the Decatur Road at the entourage following. "Look at the barouches! I've never seen such elegance!"

The oncoming line of carriages carried the state's and Decatur's leading citizens as they arrived to board the passenger car hooked to the engine. There was former Governor Lumpkin, who oversaw construction of the W&A and whose daughter, Martha, became the namesake of the town.

"I recognize him from the Whig rallies over in Decatur," Joseph volunteered.

The other dignitaries and their families passed in a kind of review as they followed the engine to its destination at the southestern terminus of the rail, there south of the Decatur Road.

"I understand that we're about to call this Decatur Street since they did that survey," Gideon said.

"That's right, and they've laid out city lots all over this area," Joseph said. "It's about time. One of these days when business gets better, I'm going to buy some, maybe even get some land beside the depot."

"I suppose there aren't any dignitaries from Marthasville on the train," Rebecca commented, almost sadly.

"Well, remember, Decatur is where the county leadership—and the money—are," William said. "We're just a little sprout of a town. Barely even got a name 'til recently."

"Oh, there's a gentleman with one of those new silk hats," Jane exclaimed. "They are so handsome—and so much more sensible than beaver hats."

"Well, it's a time of great change—in more ways than one!" William Morgan laughed.

As the engine was placed on the W&A Railroad for the first time, train engineers and others took turns clanging a huge bell from its cab. *Clang! Clang! Clang!*

The engine slowly began moving up the track towards Marietta with its distinguished passengers bound for an all night ball in the northwestern town. There was much shouting and shooting of rifles and pistols. *Clang! Clang! Clang! Kapow! Kapow! Kapow! Kapow!*

"What excitement," Jane said.

"Papa—bang!" said Absalom, and closed his chubby hands over his ears.

Layers of black powder smoke fell over the crowd, but no one seemed to mind.

Joseph said nothing, but pressed his wife and son closer to him. As he looked at the departing train, he saw the mountains to the north of them, the farms in between, and pictured the rolling surf of the Georgia coast. He'd only seen it in books, but it was soon to be as easy reach as Marietta.

He felt prickles under his chest skin as he thought about the changes that were bound to come. Little matter if the tracks weren't in yet—his town would never be the same when they were. He knew he'd found the permanent home he'd been seeking for his family.

Chapter 7

ATLANTA

April 1848

Jane Morgan straightened her bonnet in the hallway mirror, then pulled out the loops of the bow that she tied to the side of her face to form a becoming poof. The rose cotton trim made her look more youthful and added flesh to her thin face, she thought. She'd borne three children since her marriage eight years before, and another might be on the way. She'd done well for a matron of twenty four, she thought, as she inventoried her looks. She felt her body and her face were showing the wear of children coming so fast. Her eyes looked more dull than sparkling, and she was tired a lot of the time. Attractive colors and clever attention to little details of grooming would no doubt help hide some of nature's incursions.

Jane planned to surprise her husband and her brother at their shops. Since the trains had come, Joseph's business had grown quickly, and the year before he'd built brick shops to take care of the increased business. The railroads and the stagecoach lines were always in need of new kinds of tools and repairs to wheels, brake poles, and carriage parts. Tradesmen, shopkeepers, planters, and farmers in the area kept him busy with their requests for implements to build houses and stores. An ongoing business was fixing plows, singletrees, axes, and chisels. And everyone wanted horses shod.

Several years before, Joseph and his father had paid Lemuel Grant sixty dollars for the triangle-shaped lot. Butler Street ran to the side and Decatur Street bordered it to the rear. It was a good-sized parcel located at the end of Atlanta's business district with enough room for testing rifles across the undeveloped land to the east. Joseph had bought the bricks from her Uncle Benjamin Thurman and supervised one of the town's brickmasons as he built the set of buildings there near the railroad.

Inspecting the construction, Jane had felt herself bursting with pride as she looked above the wide doorway. It was tall and wide enough to allow the carriages and even stagecoaches Joseph worked on to be brought into the shop. On a large brass plate bolted to the space above the door was her husband's name: JJ MORGAN.

But Joseph was not alone in the enterprise. He had so much business, he'd persuaded David, Jane's brother, to join him in it. While David was a minister, he didn't have a church, and so the arrangement worked out well. William also worked in the smithies, but at sixty-seven years of age, he was slowing down dramatically.

Jane turned from the mirror ready to start her journey.

"We'll have dinner, just like when the shop was at home," she told herself. She'd been so busy with her babies and the home that she coudn't recall if it was last year or this year when she'd been to the newer brick shops last. "They'll be so surprised!"

As she turned around, she saw Laura, her sister-in-law, drawing Jane's daughter Susan Ann into the hallway towards Jane.

"What's that on your face, young lady?" Jane asked her.

"Got honey, Mama!" the three-year-old exclaimed.

"Well, that's just fine. Mama's about to step out, and you're already into treats. I think your Aunt Laura's going to spoil you yet!"

"Don't worry about a thing, Jane, we'll take care of her and the two young men, too," Laura said. "Just go have a wonderful picnic."

"So much has happened in the last few years with all your sisters getting married and the forge moving to Decatur Street," Jane said. "It's not like it used to be, when the men would come in from work and we'd have the big meal of the day. We'd all gather around the table, and the talk would be lively. I miss that. Seems I never see my husband now. And with David working with him, I rarely get to visit with him either."

"Well, you still have four sisters-in-law at home—as well as Mother and Miriam—and that's plenty to take care of three children," Laura, a delicate blond, told Jane. "Just be careful driving the carriage. I'm not sure the men driving some of the rigs out there have the respect they should for a lady. Is Miriam ready to leave?"

"She's still getting ready for Gideon and Josephine's visit. Would you please go and see if you can spell her? We've pulled every treasured food out of the larder for them, because they are used to fine foods and relishes and fruits. Not to disparage your brother, Laura, but it is indeed a large endeavor to entertain them."

"I know," her slight relative said. "I almost wish they didn't have to come to Atlanta for supplies. They wear poor Miriam out, demanding this and that and treating her so badly. They don't realize we're all servants, in a way. I've got the kitchen garden, Alice milks the cows—we all have chores."

"Well, you know Gideon calls Joseph a 'slave spoiler,'" Jane said. "But they've no right to treat our Miriam like one of their plantation workers," Jane said. "Shouldn't be treating their help the way they do, anyway. Nevertheless, they're family, and we need to be respectful. No doubt, if I showed my true feelings, your mother and father would rebuke *me*, not them!"

The sun shone on small craters of water left in the street outside. The April rains had come in force, then disappeared, leaving a glorious day. Jane was glad she had broken the household routine to take Joseph dinner. The spring day rivaled any Jane could remember.

Or is it just that I've been too busy to notice the other years? she asked herself.

Miriam, standing on the curb with the horse's reins in hand, helped Jane off the carriage stoop and up into the carriage. Jane pulled Miriam into the buggy and settled both of them on the driver's seat. The carriage rolled off, travelling east towards Marietta Street. They stopped at the W&A railroad tracks to look for trains, then carefully crossed.

"Lordy," Miriam breathed out."Glad we got past without one o' them big trains coming! "I'm feared the horse will bolt and land us under those big wheels!"

They reached Marietta Street, then turned southeast to follow it to the center of Atlanta. Jane knew that the entire journey to Joseph's business was not more than a mile, but she was concerned about travelling to the east side of town.

"The west and east sides are quite different," Joseph had said. He hadn't ever told her she couldn't ride to that other side. Actually, it had never come up in their conversation, probably because Joseph observed her being tied to her chores from dawn to dusk and even around the fireplace at night, when she was busy with the needlework she hadn't gotten to during the day. Jane rarely went out.

Atlanta—that was the name the railroad gave the town when the Georgia Railroad reached the W&A terminus—consisted mostly of thick stands of giant oaks punctuated here and there by a log cabin home or store or, occasionally, a large homestead. Marietta Street and Peachtree Street were wagon roads, but there were still intense green trees, grasses, and vines growing along them. The pines, sweet gums, and walnuts had been winnowed out and the undergrowth had been cut, but wild honeysuckle grew in myriad colors of orange, light pink, and scarlet, along with lacy white dogwoods, red woodbine, and the bounteous yellow jasmine. Paths off the main roads led to small farms nestled in the city, which now included an area one mile in either direction from the railroad depot.

Along the road to town, Jane and Miriam heard the music of cardinals, brown thrashers, and other songbirds mixed with the sound of metal striking metal, of men working on the railroad lines. A third railroad had joined the other two. This one, the Macon & Western, was close to the homestead, and frequently the Morgan home rang with the sound of hammers landing on the iron rails. "That's the sound of our livelihood, dear," Joseph had reminded her when she objected.

The biggest change in the past two years was the *who-oo-wee* of the wood-fired engines as they pulled out of the Atanta depot en route to Chattanooga or Macon or Augusta or announced their arrival from those points. She knew their schedules by heart because the whistles would be followed by five-year-old Will's cries to "go see the trains, Mama!" She'd allow him a look only once a day; there wasn't time to show him each one. Such trips slowed the work at home while someone accompanied him. The household knew the sound of the train was the time to locate Brother Will and make sure he wasn't heading down the road to the track.

Jane and Miriam came to Peachtree Street, where Jonathan Norcross ran a general store and post office. Jane pictured her brother-in-law Gideon inside negotiating with Norcross—as he would be soon—trading cotton proceeds from his plantation for tools and fabric. They waited for farm wagon traffic along Peachtree to pass before moving across.

When they had passed the post office and the road changed names to Decatur Street, they began hearing loud voices. Up ahead she could see drovers in the street, shouting and cursing. Suddenly she realized: Murrell's Row! Joseph had fussed to her about it one night weeks ago, and she'd forgotten! It was on the left, across Decatur Street from the depot and railroad yards—taverns combined with gambling houses, one after the other, for practically an entire block. There were even bordellos, with vile women.

A lady, even an accompanied lady, could scarce go near there, he'd said. And she'd forgotten!

Jane picked up the whip and urged her horse along with a strong tap. "Come on, Jason!" she yelled at the horse. "Giddyup!"

Jason kept plodding and didn't respond, but continued to lurch forward at his normal speed.

"C'mon, Jason," Jane repeated, landing the whip smartly on his back.

Ca-thunk! Jane felt the right side of the carriage sink and looked down. The wheel was stuck in a mud puddle. She hadn't been watching, startled as she was about entering Murrell's Row.

"Miriam, take the reins," she yelled, then nimbly jumped down from her side on the left. She carefully walked around the rear of the carriage to inspect the problem. Dismayed, she looked at the right wheel.

"Well, well, if it isn't Mrs. Morgan—smart Mrs. Morgan—stuck in the mud. My, my, I didn't know such things happened to refined ladies!"

Jane looked up into the sneering face of a man in flannel shirt and heavy jean pants. From where she stood, bending from the waist to look at the wheel, she could smell his foul whiskey breath. Clinging to his left arm was a heavily rouged blond woman wearing a bright green silk dress with a matching bonnet. Jane immediately saw the social contrast and blanched at her lack of shame, walking about in midday. The woman pulled at the man's arm.

"Just who are you?" Jane asked the dark-haired man.

"Friend of the family, ma'am," he said, pretending to doff a hat. "Tom Cunningham's the name."

"C'mon, Tom, let's go," whined the woman.

Jane suddenly felt her legs weaken under her. Tom Cunningham. That was the man who stole Mr. Morgan's rifle. Her menfolk had been hunting him for years!

"Woman, leave me be!" Cunningham shouted. He pushed the woman to the ground, into the same large puddle that trapped the wheel.

"You bastard!" she sputtered as her bonnetted head hit the water. Her bright green shoulders and chest were drenched with mud the color of cattails.

Cunningham turned to Jane and grabbed her arms just above the elbows. She struggled to pull away, but he held tight. She deliberately relaxed, thinking she could outsmart Cunningham by pretending to give up. She let the arm go limp, praying he'd let go. What was she to do? Two women without defenses against this strong, sinewy ruffian? And one a slave?

The tactic worked. When the man lightened his grip, she whirled herself away from his long hands and ran around to the street side of the carriage.

Whack!

"Wha—?"

Whack! Whack!

Miriam stood up in the carriage driver's seat and smacked the buggy whip down onto Cunningham's head and shoulders. The blows came so fast and hard he didn't have a chance to recover from one before another landed.

"Stop!" he cried.

Jane ran to a small shop between two taverns along the row. Before entering, she looked back at Miriam and saw Cunningham run from the carriage to one of the grog shops. The woman in green had disappeared. Jane turned into the doorway of the shop—a tailor's—and asked the owner for help.

"That man attacked us," she gasped. "We're all right, but, please, come help me get my buggy free!" A well-dressed gentleman customer and the tailor rushed out to the street with her.

"What's the problem?" the customer asked.

"I've been accosted by a drunken drover or ne'er do well of some sort. He tried to grab me! I'm on my way to my husband's right now, and the wheel of our carriage is stuck!"

The two rocked the wheel and rig back and forth several times, and soon the buggy was free.

"Lady, be careful!" said the tailor, as he helped her back up on the rig. "Are you sure you know where you're going?"

"My husband is Mr. Morgan," she said. "The gunsmith. His business is just down the street. I'll be all right." Jane, with Miriam panting heavily beside her, started off once again.

"Oh, Miriam, you saved me from that despicable man," Jane said as she took over the reins from the other woman. "Are you all right? That was brave of you to start whacking on his head."

"Brave or crazy," Miriam mumbled. "Thought about it, mightn't've lambed him so hard. Could get killed for that in Charleston, but couldn't have 'm messing with my family," Miriam said, her heavy breaths now further apart. She placed her hands in the lap of her skirt. "But I's afraid some white man might come along and beat me with the whip instead!"

"Don't you worry. Mr. Morgan would never stand for that."

"Fine for you to say, Miss Jane, but Master Morgan wasn't there to save old Miriam's black hide!" the servant said, not smiling.

With her hands firmly gripping the reins and her eyes on the road ahead, Jane pressed Jason hard, and drove the carriage down the middle of the street to avoid any other puddles. When they passed Slabtown, blocks of houses made from pine slabwood from Mr. Norcross' mill, she relaxed a little, knowing they were within sight of the gunsmith's shop.

When Joseph heard her choked account of what happened, his face changed from deep curiosity to anger. His eyes narrowed in fear.

"Are you all right? Whatever..." Then his eyes blazed. "Whatever gave you the idea to come down here in the first place?" he exploded. "You might have been killed."

"I wanted to surprise you—"

"Wait here. I'll return only after I've found that scoundrel. I may be a while."

Joseph grabbed a rifle from the wall of the shop. He stormed off to the rear of the shop where he freed his horse, mounted him, and cantered away. Jane turned to David.

"I only wanted to surprise all of you," she said in a small voice, beginning to cry. "I thought you'd enjoy a dinner from home."

David put down the gunstock he had been polishing and went over to his sister. He put his arm around her shoulder. She was still shaking.

"Don't cry. You scared Joseph. He'll be back. Hopefully Cunningham will have sense enough to disappear. I'd hate to see what Joseph might do if he finds him. It's one thing to take his grandfather's rifle, but he's really mad now. He loves you, and he's scared of you being hurt."

Jane wiped her tears away with a handkerchief drawn from the folds of her large skirt, then returned to the carriage with David to help Miriam down and to retrieve the basket. Less than a half-hour later, while she and David were spreading the meal on the blanket on the ground in a sunny part of the doorway, Joseph returned.

Jane stood up to greet him. He pulled her off the blanket and quickly drew her to him, lacing his arms around her. She felt him shaking.

"When I went back to Murrell's Row, he was gone. I don't know where he went, and neither did anyone I met. They must be protecting him." He held her out to look at her, and his eyes softened, tears rimming them.

"The whole time I was riding, I was thinking of you, my darling, and how I love you in my arms at night, and how it was to hold our children just after they'd been born. I don't know what I'd do without you! Don't take such chances!"

She pulled close to him and felt his large chest against hers.

"I'm sorry, Joseph. I'll be more careful. But that man is a menace. He frightened me to death! Except for Miriam, I could have been badly hurt."

"I found out Cunningham's been in town for a while now, working at Murrell's Row in one of those tipsy parlors," he said. "It's bad enough the man can't make a living doing anything but pouring whiskey, but he's got to go beating on another man's wife. I'll sure give him a whipping when I see him."

She saw the window curtains moving—first slightly, then more forcefully. The white of the curtains flashed bright, almost blinding her, as they snapped quickly as though in a breeze. But the air in the room was still—Jane wondered how the drapes could flap in the calm air.

Then a hand appeared on the sill. It was a man's hand, dark, sinewy and covered with dirt, the fingernails edged in black.

Then another hand, and then his head, long and slender, topped with thick black hair, and below it, the man's chest. His upper body emerged, wearing a dusty indigo flannel shirt. His face was contorted with the strain of pulling his lanky body over the sill.

Jane screamed. Silence. A household of in-laws, and not one to come to her rescue. Joseph, beside her, lay fast asleep.

Where is everyone? What can I do? she asked. There was no escape. The white walls of the room closed in around her, squeezing out her breath.

The dark-haired, skeleton-like man with a large Adam's apple moved his body forward across the window sill. He pulled his arm through, pointing at Jane. The shiny blade of large bowie knife flashed in her eyes. She screamed again. She could not move. She was paralyzed. She tried moving her arm, then her leg, but nothing happened.Her heart was pounding so hard in her chest she could hear it. She watched, frozen, as Cunningham moved nearer.

Then movement returned to her hands, her arms, her legs. She threw her body out of the bed. She hit the floor and lay there immobilized while Cunningham continued to pull the rest of his body through the window.

She moved to stand up. He knocked her down with a blow to her middle.

He was on top of her with one hand around her neck. He was choking her, piercing her skin with the tip of the knife.

She pushed against his chest with her hands. She couldn't get him to stop. Suddenly she gave her body a swift jerk to the left and escaped. He reached for her leg. Jane felt his hand tightening around her ankle, and snatched it free.

She ran through the door to the next room, into the hallway, and then out the front door. She'd run to the neighbors, beat on their doors if necessary.

When would Joseph wake up?

Jane woke with a start. She didn't know where she was. The sun streaming through the curtains on the pine plank floor told her it was late. She looked down at her bed and touched her hands to the red appliqued rose of her wedding quilt. She realized she was in her bed. Joseph's side was empty.

She felt confused. Joseph had been there a moment ago, and now he was gone. Then it came to her: It was a nightmare! A feeling of relief swept over her chest and arms.

"Morning, Miss Jane!" said a cheerful Miriam. "Rise and shine. It's getting late."

"Oh, Miriam, I just had the most horrible dream. Thomas Cunningham was chasing me and Joseph was asleep and—and—" She felt herself shiver, and looked up into sympathetic eyes. Then she thought of her chores.

"Miriam, why didn't you wake me? I've never slept this late—at least not since I was a girl! I've got to be up to help get ready for the company coming."

"Master Joseph, he came and told me you didn't need to be bothered this morning, you needed your rest. So I let you sleep. Ain't nothing I can't get to without you. You may think you're the whole show, but you ain't, you know. Old Miriam takes good care of you."

Jane frowned at being reminded of her essential dependence on her black woman. It would always be so. As long as she lived, Miriam would take care of her and her family.

Miriam moved toward her and drew a small leather pouch from her skirts. A conspiratorial look came over her face."Look what Master Joseph gave me!" she said, a smile wrapped across her face. She opened the pouch and emptied several gleaming coins into her brown hands. "Seven silver dollars. 'That's your reward for saving my precious wife,' Master Joseph said. I was shocked. You know niggahs don't usually get money. White folks's 'fraid of us having anything nice. Know what I think? I tells you, Master Joseph really thinks you're something special."

Jane's eyes teared up as she thought of her husband making such a gift to Miriam. Seven silver dollars! That he would give this to a slave was a sign that he regarded Miriam as a person. Giving a slave money was also illegal, Jane knew. Why that was so was another mystery Jane preferred not to try to understand. There were just so many things about their way of life that caused her to think the abolitionists were right. Why should blacks not own property at all?

Miriam was not like a white person, able to make her own way in the world, Jane believed. So it was reasonable not to give her a full wage. Miriam was—in a way, perhaps, but not exactly—like a white spinster without an inheritance, dependent on her male family members for support. She was their charge.

It felt good to Jane that Joseph had these sensibilities and that he didn't fear the punishment he could incur for giving Miriam money. Miriam was part of their family and an indispensable aid to Jane. Still, it would be better if others didn't know of the gift, for fear of what could happen.

"We'll just keep the whole business quiet," Jane winked at Miriam. "You are my rescuer, but I guess we'd better not let the town know how you were rewarded for braining Tom Cunningham."

"What are you doing?" William Morgan asked Joseph as he saw his son bring a single-shot pistol out from a locked cabinet in the gunsmith's shop. It was Friday, the day after the assault on Jane. Joseph squinted his eyes in concentration as he loaded the gun with black powder and placed a percussion cap in his pocket.

"I'm going to find Cunningham," Joseph said.

"That's dangerous. You know there are all kinds of toughs around where he works."

"I can't help that. It'll be worse tomorrow when all the farmers and planters come to town. There'll be wagons loaded with folks buying equipment and seed and what all clogging the streets, and there'll be more fights and drunkenness along Murrell's Row than usual."

"I'll have to go with you. You can't hope to take him to jail in Decatur yourself. Have you checked to see if the justice of peace is in town?"

"Father, I know I can take him and I'll get Old Man Norcross to hold him in a storeroom if I have to. I'll get the drop on him, he won't be expecting me because he thinks I'm afraid of him. Well, I'm not chicken, I'm just careful, and I mean to carefully sneak up on him today and take him in. And I don't want you involved. I don't want you to get hurt."

William shook his head. "I know I'm not the steady shot I used to be, but I'm still a very good shot, better than you, probably. You're not going by yourself."

"Suit yourself," Joseph shrugged. "But I'm going." He cleaned the pistol barrel and loaded it into a holster attached to a belt around his waist. He looked into his father's pale blue eyes, where he saw concern and fear. "I really could use a backup. You never know how these betsies are going to fire."

As Joseph and his father strode the three long blocks to Murrell's Row, Joseph thought back to the time when he and his family left Abbeville District and encountered Old Man Cunningham, who'd leveled the rifle barrel at Joseph's head. Who could have guessed the menace of that day would lead to this? Rather than leave the fractious war behind in South Carolina, it had followed them here. And that conflict was now nearly seventy years old!

He didn't know which tavern he would start with first, but he would find Cunningham today and be done with this. Joseph was grateful his father wanted to accompany him. At this moment he realized that he counted on his parents' faith in him even as he made his own life. They'd been a source of strength to him. He felt very close to his father.

Joseph's body felt very light. He was frightened. He knew Cunningham had struck something close to bedrock when he hit Jane. He'd threatened Joseph's entire life.

Fear drove him down Decatur Street toward the dram shops where he knew he'd find Cunningham. What would he do first? How could he accost Cunningham without making him dangerous? What if the man resisted, refused to be taken in? Joseph had never killed or wounded a man, and he didn't want to kill Cunningham. But he knew if he didn't prepare to shoot the man, he might die himself.

He breathed a prayer that nothing would happen to either him or his father. "Lord, you made us Morgan folks," he said quietly to himself. "We're a good and gentle people. Protect all of us, and let Your righteousnous prevail!" The prayer calmed Joseph's nerves. As he walked with his father, some of the burning fear left him.

As they drew closer to Murrell's Row, Joseph saw a brawl in progress in the middle of Decatur Street. Men were shouting and pushing each other around. One had apparently thrown the others out of a saloon. Then one of those evicted drew a gun and shot the man standing near the barroom entrance. The man went down, his body sprawled in front of the establishment. Joseph and William ran towards the barroom while the assailant took off down the street.

"Stop!" Joseph yelled, but the man had a good twenty-foot jump on Joseph and ran faster. Rather than pursue him, Joseph sped up to the man on the ground. His heart leapt into his throat and left him speechless. It was Tom Cunningham.

"Someone go get Doc Gilbert!" yelled one man.

"It's too late," said another. "He's a goner."

Near Cunningham's hand lay a pistol, unfired. The wound had pierced the heart. Blood drained from his chest, soaking the dirt and painting a dark circle on the red clay underneath him. His cheeks were sunken even more than Joseph remembered, and his black hair was as oily as before. Joseph stared at the body, stunned. The crimson flow stopped. The blood feud was over.

"What happened?" he turned to others.

"He got real hostile," said an oafish man with sandy hair and a large stomach who wore the rough clothes of a drover. "Tried to throw us out for just being smart with 'im. Wasn't no call to do that. Don't know what touched him off. Anyway, he pulled that pistol and marched us out here. Didn't know my friend Mac there's from Kentucky, and he c'n drive a cross at a hundred yards," he said, nodding in the direction of Peachtree Street.

William appeared beside Joseph and looked at Cunningham's body.

"What is it the Bible says? You live by the sword, you die by the sword," Joseph said.

"It was bound to happen," William Morgan said. "His father cast his fate when he warred on our families back in South C'lina." William looked sadly at the body. "It's hard to live among your father's enemies when they became a whole nation of believers."

Joseph shivered. Cunningham was dead, and his end had come at the hand of another.

"Thank you, Lord," he said quietly. "Thank you for letting the fatal shot not be mine!"

Rebecca let herself out the front gate, running to greet the arriving carriage. William, noticeably slower, trailed her by several feet.

"Hi, folks!" Gideon lifted his straw hat to his mother and sisters as he climbed down from his carriage. He turned and offered a hand to Josephine and to their sons, James and Neil. Rebecca Morgan watched as the youngsters jumped down onto the ground. It had been six months since she'd seen her grandsons, and they looked like they had two years' growth since.

"Gideon and Josephine, I scarcely recognize my boys, they've grown so!" she said. Rebecca saw Absalom and Brother Will carefully regarding their older cousins from her side. Neither smiled, but each seemed to be sizing up the other two boys.

"What's for dinner?" the ebullient Gideon asked, clapping his father on the back and hugging his mother. "I'm starved."

"How're you doing, Son?" asked the gray-haired Morgan, as he stood holding the horses' reins.

"Fine, Father. Hope you don't mind us taking up a bed or two here."

"Never, Son, just make yourself at home. Of course it's mostly Joseph and Jane you'll be troubling. You know they've been master and mistress of our household for some time."

Gideon leaned near his father's ear, but Rebecca heard his words clearly. "I'll be the perfect guest, as long as he lets me drink my Madeira after dinner—a libation I have to provide, mind you!"

William Morgan handed the horses to Miriam and Laura, and they walked to the house. Gideon and his family had travelled from their plantation near Griffin, about forty miles south of Atlanta. They had spent the previous night at a friend's plantation. While Josephine went to refresh herself, Gideon walked with his father and mother to the parlor.

"Where're Joseph and my sweet sister-in-law Jane?" he asked.

"They're burying a man who died here yesterday," said Rebecca, hoping the subject could be dropped.

"Someone I'd know?"

"I'm sure you've heard the name Tom Cunningham," said William.

"Well, sure, he's the one that stole Granpa Morgan's rifle and got away with it."

"He was killed in a shootout on Decatur Street—he had been pouring whiskey at a saloon."

"Well, good riddance to him. He wasn't worth saying a prayer over in my book. Why're they going to his burying?"

"David Thurman offered to say some words. They needed some mourners."

"So my swell brother and his dear wife went. I declare, Joseph would nourish a snake in his bosom if it needed warmth."

A small commotion arose from outside.

"Wait! Young men, stand apart. Don't you go hitting at each other!" Josephine's voice carried in from the open hallway. She was yelling at the four young boys who'd taken over the front porch.

"Well, don't let James hit me first, then," cried six-year-old Absalom. "Tell him to keep his fists to himself and off my neck. He gave me a punch when I had my back turned."

"Boys, boys," said Josephine.

Gideon looked nervously towards the front porch, then announced: "Well, I'm going upstairs to clean up. Better be in shape to bargain with old Jonathan Norcross. He might try to take advantage if I'm dusty and dirty."

"Gideon, don't you think you ought to help Josephine?" asked Rebecca.

"No, she'll handle it. I give her complete authority when it comes to the boys." He turned and left the room.

Rebecca and William looked at each other. Both arched their eyebrows.

"I don't like what I'm hearing outside," Rebecca said, turning to go to the front porch.

"Father," Rebecca said later to William, "I worry about our elder son."

"What do you mean?" They were both bent over the eating table, sorting okra seeds for the spring planting.

"Well, he seems to treat Josephine like a servant. His leaving her to handle that row with the boys seemed to me like shirking his responsibilities. And he seems not very sensitive—like the way he made fun of Tom Cunningham's death."

"Now, don't go worrying your head about that, Mama. He probably was tired from the trip and had his mind on business. You never know what cotton prices are going to be, and he won't know until he's gotten a price from Norcross."

"Do you agree, my husband, that our son has changed? I remember him as sweet and so responsible."

"I agree," William said, reluctance showing in his voice. "Gideon's operating in a completely different world on that plantation. I wouldn't be surprised if the idea of being a big boss didn't go to his head. I've been around planters, and they are indeed a puffed up bunch!"

"Well, you've seen firsthand the trouble they cause, and I thought you'd be the first to argue against him becoming a planter in the first place."

"The ones I had a grievance with were the larger ones—"

"I know, but they're all the same underneath. It's just a matter of degree. And Gideon is becoming more that way. You remember, I'm sure—"

"Now, hush, Rebecca, let's get back to our seeds. If we worry about our offspring, we'll start interfering where we oughtn't. Let's let our children make their own mistakes. The situation's different here. Gideon's smart. He'll grow tired of trying to feed and clothe his people and come to his senses. He'll appreciate his old man and be asking to be part of the smithy one of these days. Just you wait!"

Rebecca split a brown, dried pod down the middle and emptied out the seeds on the table. Her mind was not settled, but she decided to drop the discussion rather than be in conflict with her husband.

"Well, I was just wondering what you thought," she sighed. Then a bit of mischief took over her mind.

"Watch out," she said, playfully flipping an okra seed off the table onto William's chest. He recovered, then grabbed her hand and held it, enjoying its warmth and looking deep into her eyes.

"We've a lot to be thankful for," he said. "Especially each other."

"Well, we can talk about that later," she smiled, and tilted her head to the side like a coquette.

"You know, sometimes you make me think you're a young girl again!" he said.

"Well, this creaking gate's hanging long on its hinges," she said, laughing.

Joseph stood on a platform behind a large iron steam engine, traveling fast above the small shacks and woodframe buildings on either side of him along the railroad track. He could feel the wind moving past his exposed ears, flipping his shirt collar tabs, and whooshing through his opened vest. The blast of the steam inside the boiler and the screech of eight wheels barrelling down their steel tracks rang through his heart, creating fear and exhilaration at the same time. Joseph's nostrils inhaled burning oak and poplar, the fuel for the genius steam boiler laid on its side, straight out in front of him. He thought about the many versions of engines there'd been since one of the country's first trains left Charleston. One engine sported a boiler behind the engineer until someone saw the folly of trying to watch a fire in the boiler behind and the track up ahead at the same time. There'd even been a double engine hinged together so the train could make mountain curves. That was before a Yankee invented the separated truck with wheels that turned with the curves—showing the British train designers a thing or two.

Blinking woodsmoke out of his eyes, Joseph looked through his tears down the track and saw the town of Atlanta rising up in front of him out of a forest of thick hardwoods extending to the horizon. He marvelled at the iron monster he stood astride. Its voluminous dark stack rose like a "v" over the engine, then ballooned out at the top as though to catch the very sky. He stood next to the engineer for the Georgia Railroad engine *Kentucky* enjoying the ride of his life, approaching the depot near Decatur Street. He'd boarded in Decatur, then rode with the engineer to Atlanta to test the brake pole he'd just repaired over the coals of his forge.

The engineer squinted, wrinkling up the leathery, sun-browned skin around his eyes, seeming not to mind the sparks and heavy smoke that blew back at him from the huge chimney. Occasionally, the engineer disappeared from Joseph in a flume of black, soot-filled smoke. Then a sudden lurch of the engine to the left or right, or a dip over a depression in the track, cleared the cloud for a moment, and Joseph caught another look at him.

"Reverse engine!" the engineer called. Joseph held his breath as the fireman and another man on the rear car both thrust the Johnson lever back and pulled with all their strength. The engine shook and vibrated, causing Joseph's body to shake. High-pitched squeals invaded his ears. Foul-smelling black smoke assailed his nostrils.

Who-oo-ee! Who-oo-ee! blasted the train's whistle.

Scree-ee-eech! The wheels let out terrifying screams.

Joseph felt the mass of black iron shudder underneath him and wondered if it would stop in time. He was travelling at a speed faster than five miles an hour, he was sure. Finally, after several minutes, the engine lost speed and gradually came to rest just beyond where it was supposed to stop. Joseph talked with the engineer and another man, shook the engineer's hand, walked to the rear of the engine near the wood car, then jumped to the ground.

"Hello, brother," Gideon hailed him. "That's some horse you're riding today."

Joseph looked down at the grandly dressed man standing near the loading platform. He was pleased his brother had found him. He acknowledged a little rivalry between them. No little victory to have Gideon watch him climb down from the most famous citizen of the area.

"Glad to see you here, Gideon. Is the family back at home?"

"Sure is," he said as they walked back to the main entrance to the depot. "I came down here after transacting my business to see if you actually do any work on your premises."

"Well, let's walk down there, and I'll show you," Joseph said, giving his brother a mock-punch on the shoulder.

"So you're working on the train engine?"

"They call in a blacksmith for something unusual, like this brake," Joseph said. "The railroad has its own workers and they handle most of the repairs, but I get called on every once in a while when something commences to fall apart."

Joseph motioned to the street they'd take to the shops, and Gideon turned with him.

"The railroad's coming means nothing but good things for our shops. All their railroad employees moving to town means they need horseshoes and hammers and pots for their own homes, so we've got lots of business.

"In fact, as you can see, the whole town's prospering. Year before last the Georgia Railroad ran the first locomotive in, and it changed everything. People are laying out streets, surveying and selling land—seems like the sound of the train whistles just announced to the world that here was a town with a future."

Gideon said nothing. Joseph couldn't tell what effect his boasting was having on him.

"Of course," he continued, "the war with Mexico doesn't hurt business. Peters' stagecoaches run a regular business through here carrying soldiers and supplies to Texas. I'd love to have just one of those contracts. I do get some gun business from those folks, as they need security for the trip out.

"But look to your right. See that hotel? It's brick, a full two stories, and that veranda goes all the way across. There's another wooden hotel over behind it. Remember when it was all forest when we first moved here? The area's really grown since then."

"What's this I hear about Jane being attacked?" Gideon asked, as they entered the blacksmith and gunsmith shops.

Joseph's face clouded. "It was the scariest moment of my life. She's so precious to me, and when she came tearing in here breathless from her escape, I wanted to go shoot Cunningham immediately. If I'd found him he probably would have died by my hands, not someone else's."

"Naturally, it wasn't discussed openly at home. I just picked up on the conversation and asked Father."

"Well, it's a long story that's finally come to an end, and I'm thankful to God it's all over."

"Brother, don't you think you owe it to her and your gloriously burgeoning family to get into a more civil part of the world. My plantation, for instance?"

"What, and leave all this?" Joseph asked, his arm sweeping the dark interior of the shops. "With my trade, I'd starve on a plantation."

"You could change trades. Become a planter. Then you wouldn't have to contend with the likes of Cunningham and the man that shot him. I look at these toughs walking along the streets and I wouldn't want my wife or sons to be near them. Their frontier ways would just rub off on them. I want my family to be fine and cultured. You don't seem to care about yours!"

"Now, just hold on a minute—"

"Mr. Morgan," a man's voice called. "I'm looking for Old Man Joe Morgan!"

"That's me, sir. What can I do for you?"

"I'm looking for a rifle to carry with me on the stage," said a man in frontier clothes. He walked in out of the sunfilled doorway. "Man at the hotel said you're the best gunsmith in town."

"Don't believe everything you hear," laughed Joseph.

"Well I need a gun bad, because those Mexicans don't cotton to us invading their area too much. Man's got to defend himself."

Joseph took the man over to his padlocked shop cabinet, opened it, and pulled out a couple of samples. After discussing stock wood, caliber, and price, the man selected a walnut-stocked two band rifle with the smooth lines of an English hunting rifle.

"This is a fine piece," the man said, admiring the brass trim and engraved plates.

"Shoots good, too," said Joseph. "If you won't take my word for it, try it out back there. Nothing out beyond our property so you won't hit nothing. It'll hit your target at a hundred and fifty yards."

"Good enough for me. You look like a man that means what you say."

"That's a true statement, sir. I try to do no man wrong."

"How much is it?" the man asked.

"Seventy dollars silver, sir," Joseph said. "That may seem a lot, but that's the going rate, I'm afraid."

"Don't mind paying for a gun that shoots straight. Never know when it's gonna increase your years on this earth."

"Now that's a fact!" said Joseph, slapping the man on the back.

After the man had left, Joseph stood for a moment in the middle of the shops looking out the door towards the railroad track, which lay not spitting distance away. He held some of the man's money in one hand; the other hand hung at his side. With his free hand, he opened and closed his fingers, as was his habit when he was looking around at the shops for his next task. He remembered that he had been about to argue with Gideon when the stagecoach driver came in.

"You know, Gideon," he said, turning back to his brother. "It's hard for you to understand, but I'm good at what I do here," he said, some of the excitement of the sale still in his eyes. "I put in real long days. Father works hard. David works with us when he's not off preaching. What you don't seem to realize is that I like working with my hands and seeing a gun I can touch. I like making money, too, but I don't want to make it off the backs of poor, ignorant slaves. You are what you are because of their sweat and labor. I don't want to depend on others like that."

"Well, I'm making land bloom that otherwise would lie fallow!" Gideon exploded. His face was red, and he shook a white hand at his brother. "I'm keeping Southern manhood and womanhood protected and in their rightful place, above the sub-human races."

Joseph felt his blood beginning to simmer, like a pot of water on the back of the fireplace. Gideon was full of airs and pretense. He found himself wanting to give his brother a piece of his mind. But Gideon appeared just as eager to do the same.

"Look at what happened to the French," Gideon railed, "after they did away with their aristocracy—it was a bloodletting, dehumanizing rather than enobling us all. The only hope is to have an aristocracy in power. Look at the Greeks, the Romans—every great civilization has been built on the backs of slavery."

As Gideon spoke, Joseph's skin began to feel even warmer. Gideon's delusion rankled Joseph and tore at his insides. His brother, with his narrow, aquiline nose and imperious manner, struck him as the the image of a Roman ruler.

"The Egyptians had the Hebrews, the Romans had everyone as their slaves—"

"Stop it!" yelled Joseph, suddenly boiling over with rage. "I won't hear you talking like that. You've got a patch of land God gave you to raise up the fruits and vegetables for your family. You got six slaves bending over acres of cotton, and they're ill-clothed and mistreated. It ain't like it's a blooming kingdom you've got down there."

Joseph shivered from the anger in his chest. His blood ran hot through his veins. Why did they have to fight? He was sad about the gulf that appeared between them. "I don't want to talk about it. We're brothers, we're supposed to get along. I don't want you to be mad at me, nor I at you. Let me show you the rest of the shops, then let's go home to supper."

On Monday following Gideon's visit, Joseph and William and David began work on the rifle for the stagecoach driver. While his father built the fire in the forge, Joseph selected a tall three-inch wide strip of wrought iron from their stock. Normally all business when he'd begin a new project, Joseph found himself distracted. He felt there was something lurking in the corners of the shop, but he couldn't put his finger on it.

As he pulled the iron from an upright stack of long metal strips, a chain of images chased through his mind: He saw Tom Cunningham's still body on the ground. He saw his brother contentedly smoking his after-dinner Havana cigar while pontificating to the rest of the family about his plantation. He remembered the drovers and farmers pressed around Cunningham's body.

Joseph inspected the long metal ribbon, looking for flaws. The black bar showed no unevenness of color or flecks of trash in its smooth surface.

Pictures of Cunningham lying dead, then his brother pouring Madeira, then his mother looking at Gideon with a worried look ran across his thoughts. He shuddered, his body cold. He returned his mind to the metal.

The edges were straight, thanks to an English-made precision cutting machine. His barrel would likely turn out true, driving the cross when he tested it out in back. There he'd rigged a target by charring a large plank of wood over a fire until it turned black and scoring a cross in the top of one end, using his Barlow knife. In the middle of the cross, he attached a small diamond of paper which he trimmed so that it would accomodate only one bullet. He set this upended plank with its paper bull's eye on the firing range on vacant railroad land a hundred yards from the shop. They'd anchored the board so it wouldn't flip upon impact, and then tested their rifles, trying to score on the first attempt.

"Ready with the fire," William called from the forge. "Are you ready for us?"

"Yes, directly," Joseph called. He propped the bar against a bench and went over to a second, lower bench which held the swage block. He looked at the huge block he and his father had struggled to load onto their wagon back in Abbeville District. He moved tools from that bench to a shelf so that there was room around the swage block to allow two men free range to strike the end of the iron bar after it was placed in the block. Joseph then selected several hammers, a mallet, and a round-tipped chisel and placed them on the bench on either side of the block. The semicircular indentation on the block was used first, to shape a rounded tube. Next to this mold were three angular indentations that would give the long Kentucky-style barrel its distinctive octagon shape. Each of the four hammers Joseph placed near the swage block had a concave head that was the exact reverse of the impressions in the swage block.

William and David gathered nearby, and, in a ritual familiar to them all, Joseph signalled David to stand opposite him on the other side of the swage block. Joseph handed the metal strip to William, who stood at the top of the bench, near the forge. William placed the end of the iron ribbon in the fire, and the three of them stood motionless, like dancers in position on a stage.

Joseph watched as the fire colored the rod a dull red, then a cherry red. His heart beat faster as he saw the tip of the bar turn a glassy red and start to turn yellow.

"Now!" he called to his father.

William used one smooth motion to swing the iron bar onto the block. Joseph then stepped forward and picked up the hammer and the blunted chisel point and struck the chisel to the bar, giving off a *whanngg* sound. The iron caved inward under the weight of the chisel hammer, filling the rounded indentation in the block. Again and again William pushed the bar forward and Joseph struck it at higher points along the bar as William pushed it forward. David inspected the bar after each stroke and signalled to William. Half of the bar now looked like the beginning of a barrel.

Joseph's thoughts returned to Tom Cunningham lying in the street. He'd never seen a man die of a gunshot wound before.

In all these years of making rifles and an occasional gun, Joseph had imagined the destined victim of his craft to be a fox, a bear, or maybe an Indian to be frightened into submission. He had never seen a man killed by a gun. He realized now that he sometimes lived apart from reality. The effect of the gun's use on a man was so bloody, so final. Cunningham's wound had been a large one, expertly delivered to the heart.

Joseph remembered William telling him stories about 15th century England, when the "hand gonne" was not in widespread use. The British, whose military superiority rested in their famous longbows, were slow in adapting to the "gonne" because it regularly malfunctioned and often killed the shooter. Most at that time believed its wound killed because it was poisonous, and as such could not be cured. What poison had spread to Cunningham's limbs, head, and trunk, stilling them forever, quieting that hard-edged voice, the voice that had terrorized his family?

It wasn't a bullet that killed Cunningham, he told himself. It was the man's hatred of anything that was good and decent. He poisoned himself.

Joseph landed the mallet on the chisel with surprising force. He saw the iron almost soften under the weight of the blow. He realized it was Cunningham he was striking, and that the crease was in his old enemy's skull, not the iron. His anger rose as he struck the metal again and again.

Why couldn't Cunningham's father have left the Carolinas like the other crown lovers, boarded a boat for the Bahamas or Nova Scotia? Joseph asked himself. No—he stayed around Abbeville, where no one would give him work or trade with him, to raise his son. Then the son Tom dragged himself over to Georgia to infect their lives, to menace them.

Joseph struck another shattering blow. When this area was just a settlement in the wilderness of DeKalb County, Cunningham was there, stealing their tools and his grandfather's rifle. When it was Terminus, he was carousing with Mary McCree, threatening Joseph on the saloonkeeper's porch. And then—Joseph hit the iron again, feeling tears of rage burning his eyes—Atlanta wasn't half a year old before Cunningham attacked his wife. He was always in the shadows, like a snake under a log, waiting to strike.

Joseph remembered helping to bury Cunningham on Saturday. God forgive me, that was no act of Christian charity, he thought to himself. Jane might have gone to display such sentiments, but he went to make sure the man was deep in the ground. He delighted in putting him under, the sorry no-account!

"How does it look?" William's question to Joseph startled him.

"Uh, very well. This part shouldn't take too long."

"We don't want to rush things, but remember, David is leaving this evening for Walker County. We'd hoped to weld the barrel before he has to go."

"I'm not forgetting."

"Now, Mr. Morgan, I don't want to be the cause of a job not done," said David. "But it will please me and my wife if we can leave as planned."

Joseph waited while William compressed the huge leather-and-wood bellows, aided by the mechanical advantage of a lever. The bellows heaved and sighed loudly and the flame in the fire leaped higher. William put the tip of the long half-curved barrel in the fire and stirred coals around it. After a few moments, the now red-yellow section of iron was placed in the three-sided groove of the swage anvil to shape the flat sides of the barrel. Joseph and David picked up hammers with concave shapes to match the impression from the swage block.

Now Joseph shifted his position. He was still opposite David but more at the head of the block. William once again heated the bar, handed it to Joseph, and moved past Joseph below the other two. He inserted a long, rounded, and tapered iron rod into the long curve of the iron and signalled the others to begin hammering. Joseph struck first, then David. Joseph struck again, and the two moved in a steady rhythm accompanied by *whanngg, whanngg*. The metal edges of the iron moved to join while

William twisted the mandrel insert to keep the barrel straight. A fine seamless joint emerged under their hammers.

Joseph aimed his blows carefully, as he knew the hammering, if well done, would increase the sturdiness of the barrel. He was unwilling to have a gun leave the shop that would not last a man's lifetime and more, so he helped guide his brother-in-law's strokes on the metal, just as his father had once tutored him.

"Brother Dave," Joseph said between strokes. "I'm glad you could be with us t'day so we could get this gun made. Pa tells me you're headed north this ev'n'ng."

"Ah, and it's a fair place I'm goin'," David said, his eyes lighting. He laid his stroke where Joseph's hammer hit. "You should go with me sometime. The country is wilderness and beautiful and the people very hospitable."

Joseph motioned around the shop with his hammer. "And who would get this work done?"

"Maybe you'll have the chance to go someday. There are long, green mountains with wide valleys in between. And the people are so anxious for the word."

Joseph smiled at his friend and kinsman. "Well, I'm glad you're having a chance to preach to a grateful people. Lord knows we need more appreciation of His word around here."

"There are good people here," David said, continuing to follow Joseph's strokes. "We just need more of the good to outweigh the bad. That means the righteous have to work harder."

"I don't know if I can work much harder than I do. Father and I labor sunup to sundown to feed this household as it is."

The two younger men took up hammers with a reverse pattern that would give the final octagon shape to the muzzle of the welded barrel. Joseph moved the barrel to the last slot in the swage block and proceeded to strike the barrel surface, while William twisted the mandrel inside the barrel.

Gideon was right. Atlanta had grown, especially since the railroads connected them with Savannah and Augusta and soon with Chattanooga. The only block to getting to the Tennessee River lay at a long ridge twenty miles this side of Chattanooga. All the west would soon be within easy travelling and transporting distance. With stagecoaches taking soldiers to the war in Texas and the gold rush further north in Auraria and Dahlonega, business had quadrupled. The town had become a magnet for all kinds of undesirables. There was a cockiness and godlessness about the manner of a gold miner. He'd heard men murdered each other over disputed claims up there in the mountains where the shiny flecks and nuggets had first been discovered. Yet he benefited from the orders for axes, saws, adzes and augers he filled for building the federal mint that turned out gold coins.

As drovers spilled into town from Kentucky and Tennessee, herding pigs, cows, and horses to the plantations in middle and south Georgia before them, they brought with them a thirst for gambling, drinking and whoring. One had taken Cunningham's life. What was to stop another from harming a family member, or even Joseph or William or David? What about that Slabtown, the collection of shanties memorializing Old Man Norcross' sawmill giveaways there just west of their shops? Ends of pine logs had become makeshift siding for blocks of small, rickety-looking houses clustered near the old sawmill site. What if one of the poor shanty residents decided he wanted Joseph's horse?

Atlanta was rough and dangerous. Like Gideon said, it was a frontier town, and it lacked cultural amenities. They didn't have regular schools. Occasionally a teacher would raise subscriptions to teach the older children, but he would soon be discouraged by the lack of attendance, or get the itch to move on.

Joseph recalled sitting after dinner in the parlor and coughing through a stream of smoke from Gideon's fine cigar while his eldest brother held forth about aspects of life on a Griffin plantation—darkies who avoided work, the price of cotton, his children's tutor trained by the famous Moses Wadell himself. Certainly Joseph's children could be offered none of the polish of the tutors and the dance master shared by several plantation owners near Griffin that Gideon's children enjoyed.

Joseph returned his thoughts to the barrel in front of him as he and David reached the end of the welding. All three men stood back as Joseph lifted the barrel from the swage block and admired the well-formed long, straight barrel shaped under their hammers.

"David, you get working on the rifle stock. And I apologize if I sound impatient with your traveling. I just wish you could get some work nearby so you'd be more available to work here."

"If I could get pulpits here, I'd sure be preaching here," David said. "I'm still studying to preach, and I have to go where my sponsors can find me willing hearers."

"I don't mean to be faultin' you. Just keep our families prayed over, that's all I ask," said Joseph.

"Who in our family do you think needs praying over now, Joseph?" William asked as the two of them moved the barrel to the boring bench. At the bench, they secured the ends of the rifle barrel in two clamps and mounted a boring rod that they carefully drilled down the center of the barrel.

As he watched the rod disappearing into the barrel, Joseph wondered at his grandfather's craftsmanship—the steady hand and mechanic's mind that went into making the boring rod and the rifling bench. His father had inherited both implements and many other tools, just as Joseph would receive them from him. No other gunsmiths had set up shop in these parts.

He realized he had a great investment in machinery and expertise. They had hit their own gold strike, a bonanza of all the work they wanted making new types of plows and wagons and tools for locomotives, finding ways to produce things faster for the people pouring into Atlanta every day by train, stagecoach, and horse-drawn carriage.

"You haven't answered my question, Joseph," William said after the rough boring was complete. "About the prayers for the family."

"Oh, I don't have anything specific in mind," Joseph said, looking at William's thoroughly gray head and allowing himself the lie. "We can always use some prayers, don't you think, Pa?"

Chapter 8

JANE'S WORK

November 1848

"Here's your meal!"

David Thurman struggled out of the autumn cold and into the warm cook house, grappling with a heavy bushel basket of ground corn.

"Can't say I haven't done something for my little sister and her large family!"

"Thank you, David," Jane said, smoothing her cotton apron over her large stomach. She was sure she looked as huge as the mountain of granite that rose dramatically out of the land east of Decatur. She slowly moved aside to allow her brother to make his way to the grain bin in the corner. "And my large family thanks you. I'll get Joseph to bring you the money tomorrow."

She dusted off hands covered with flour and used the back of her hand to press her hair, which was swept back into a bun, to make sure it was still in place. She glanced at his slender, tall body dressed in a dark broadcloth coat and pants. He sported the beard he'd worn starting as soon as the dark hairs would lie down together, making him look older than his years. Here they were in their twenties, she thought, and she still relished having her big brother do things for her.

"No bother. I'll get it from him. Next time he asks me to go out and get change for a ten dollar piece, I'll just keep a dollar of it." David laughed. "Of course, I'll tell him what it's about so he won't think I'm shortchangin' 'im!"

"That's all right!" Joseph said, entering the cook house. David wheeled, smiled, and thrust his hand forward to shake Joseph's. Joseph returned the greeting and playfully chucked his brother-in-law on the shoulder with his free hand. "After all these years, I ought to trust you. Can't trust a man of God who's kin, cain't trust no man!"

David smiled again. Jane knew how much David basked in his brother-in-law's attentions. Joseph was like a brother to David, and David was proud Joseph took notice of his being an intinerant preacher.

"We've been blessed with the Lord's power this week," he said. "Many mourners at the altar each time we gather for services. Even at Bethel, we're receiving two and three in each Sunday. You both ought to attend to see what you're missing."

"Well, I've been fetched up to go by the Baptist way of doin' things," Joseph said. "And I'm sure you'll appreciate it'd be pretty hard for your sister to attend anything these days."

Jane blushed and moved toward the door to excuse herself from any discussion of her approaching confinement. Joseph's frank way of speaking about her condition, even in front of family, embarrassed her.

"Don't go, Jane," Joseph said, reaching out for her hand. "I'll say nothing else disagreeable. David, what's goin' on in the city? You get out and about more than any man I know."

"Lots of activity, no doubt about it," David said. "I've been busier than a cat in a room full of rocking chairs, trying to answer letters asking the cost of beef from up Hall and Walker counties, puttin' to writing some property I'm buying, pencilling for several people building new homes. Can't seem to stop this flow of new people into town. The rents I'm able to get astound even me. I'm getting fifteen dollars a month for the house I lived in before I bought your old homeplace."

Jane admired her brother's industry in renting out the house to supplement the small amounts he made as a minister and gunstocker. The house he now lived in was the brick home the Morgans built, there on the site of the log cabin Joseph helped raise when the family first came to the settlement. As with the materials used for the shops, the bricks came from Jane's Uncle Benjamin's brickyard out on the Chattahoochee.

"Pa probably should have held onto it," Joseph smiled, "at sixty-two dollars, you got a good price. Course, you've got a good lick of work to do."

"True, the chimney was gone, and it needs shoring up around the supports, but I'll have it liveable soon. I've put up some paling already. Makes it look right smart."

David thrust a dark hat on his head and moved for the door.

"Well, you all have a good evening. I've got to get home with the rest of my purchases—I've got chickens, pork, and beef out there in the buggy, got 'em at real good prices. We're having guests we know for dinner tonight and, doubtless, some we don't know."

David turned at the door.

"You want me to pick up some walnut planks in case we get more rifle orders? Rushton's likely to give 'em to me for forty cents or less."

"Might as well," Joseph replied. "We've got more business than we can shake a stick at—or a gun stock, for that mattter."

David laughed. "Well, that's good news. See you at the shops. I'll be preaching at Sardis again Sunday, then I'm off again to Walker County for one more round of preaching before year's end."

Joseph and Jane waved to David as he departed. Joseph then turned to Jane.

"Thank the trains for bringing us the English gunbarrels from Savannah," he said. "If we had to keep making our own like we used to, we'd never be able to keep up with the demand."

Jane smiled. She enjoyed hearing Joseph talk about the shops. It was the way she learned about how things were changing about her. She appreciated that the trains had brought a whole new way of doing business.

"Here, sit down, don't wear yourself out." He offered her a chair. Jane perched on the old ladderback used mostly by Miriam, trying not to sit so far back in the chair it would be hard to get up.

"Are you feeling all right?" Joseph asked. His voice shifted from the loud tones he used with David to softer, more tender sounds. Each time he saw his wife so clearly with child he grew concerned, aware of how many wives had a hard time in childbirth.

"Except for the sick stomach that's returned," Jane said, "I've no complaints. A bit of biscuit in the morning takes care of the queasiness. What was that about the English gunbarrels?"

"We're able to import barrels, and for the first time don't have to make our own. The English have machines that turn them out much faster than we can—like in half a day. For us to do one takes a week, sometimes longer. So we're doing away with the rifling and boring. What a relief, not to have to do that long labor any more. Now we put more work into stocking and fitting locks and other metalwork. I can decorate the brass pieces on the sides. And be freed up to do more toolwork and repairs generally."

Jane nodded, encouraging Joseph.

"Do you remember two years ago when Will got hit by that army wagon? Liked to have scared us witless. It was during the Mexican War—those wagons were rumbling through here loaded with rifles. There are factories in Springfield up in Massachusetts and in Harper's Ferry, Virginia, that make hundreds of rifles in one day to supply the army. What a pitiful comparison we make, doin' em by hand!"

Joseph stroked Jane's cheek. He thought about the child they were expecting. Getting babies past the first two years was a trial. It was like planting a crop of corn and not knowing if all the shoots would make it enough to feed the family. Some would go limp for lack of water and sun, others would barely survive. Watching for signs of weakness, Joseph always held his breath during those first years, enduring each cold and episode of croup with the fear it would turn feverish, and that the child might die. The trains had done away with their total dependence on their own corn crop—the iron horses hauled in huge quantities of meal and bran and most other staples a household needed. Yet a child's health was as fragile as always.

"I'm really glad you're doing well. We've been blessed with three healthy children already."

Jane looked up at Joseph and smiled. "If the past is any sign—and we womenfolk are believers in those—this one should go well, too."

Joseph walked to the fireplace, where he poked at the fire that had dwindled while they talked. He put on another log to keep the fire going for its next use, warming supper for the large family.

"We really have been blessed. In your family as well as mine. As far as I know, there haven't been any stillborn among my mother's brood, although there was one who died young."

"You never told me, Joseph," Jane said. "Pull up a chair if you can spare the time."

Joseph plopped down on an oak split stool next to her and put his arm in what was left of Jane's lap.

"Was it a boy or girl?" Jane asked.

"A girl, Nancy—she was named for my grandmother, Rebecca's mother," he related. "I don't remember much about her, as I was four when she died, and she was two."

He related how he and his mother had talked about the baby's death during their trek west to Georgia. He related how he stood at the door with his brother, listening to the little girl's choked breaths. The retelling thrust up again in Joseph's chest a tightness and a choking sensation.

"We all know it's likely a baby might not make it to one year," Joseph said.

"None of the folks we know talk about their children pow'rfully or fuss over 'em too much. One reason is we don't want to spoil 'em, but, heck, I don't have to tell you all this. You know how the womenfolk feel, I can just tell you the menfolk's view."

He looked at Jane tenderly, then spoke quickly.

"If we're not too attached to 'em, we can't be hurt as deeply if somethin' happpens to 'em."

Joseph related to Jane how once, in the shops, he'd asked David about his diary. David had begun it as part of his following John Wesley, as the reverend had encouraged all his followers to keep such a record. David wrote while at the shops and at home, when he had time. He'd light up his pipe and prop his feet up for a few minutes in between jobs and dip his pen in a bottle of ink they kept at the shop for the customers who insisted on a written receipt. He'd scratch for a while, then put his journal down and get back to work.

David was proud of his role as scribe for the village, so he willingly showed the book to Joseph. Joseph told Jane he happened to open it at the section that detailed events at about the time David and Margaret lost a child, Sally. Joseph was startled to see, among the mentions of the price of firewood, grains, beef, and chickens, David's church activities, and other events, but one line concerning his daughter's death.

"There it was," Joseph told Jane, "among the mentions of each day's activities—gardening, teaching, making a wheelbarrow. On that Sunday he wrote 'funeral of my daughter and T.L. Thomas preached today by J.H. Smith.' The days before and after were full of news about the price of pork and wheat."

Jane looked down at her hands.

"I know," Jane said. "He *was* sad. And we draped the mirrors in black."

"I don't wonder that he didn't talk about it," Joseph said. "It's just too painful a subject. I guess I shouldn't have been surprised at the small mention he made of it in that black notebook.

"I'm not unlike David," Joseph said. "I'm constantly worrying about the children, but I show it by fussing over you in your delicate state or making sure my sisters keep up with the little ones."

They talked about how Rebecca had borne up under the baby Nancy's death so remarkably.

"I know we're supposed to take willingly what trials the Lord gives us," Jane said. "But if it happened, I would be as distraught as Margaret was. It would be hard for me to say, 'It's the Lord's will' if we lost a child. I'm just thankful that up to this time, we haven't had to face that."

"We are indeed, blessed," Joseph agreed. Jane was holding Joseph's hand, her arm entwined with his on her lap.

"So that's why you're so solicitous of me when the new one's on the way," she said softly. She touched his hair with her free hand. "You know, you're an amazing husband—involved with life's hard labor here and in the shops, harsh to the point of getting your poor new wife up in the middle of the night to lock the smokehouse door, and yet soft as uncooked biscuit when it comes to your children."

Jane saw Joseph's face become solemn. He was worrying about the baby, she could tell. She pulled his arm closer to her belly so he could feel the baby's movements. She placed her head on his shoulder, brushing the side of his face with her hair.

"We'll be fine," she said. "I feel it in my bones. It'll be all right."

Jane lay on the bed, exhausted and unable to move. Her stomach loomed large in front of her as she looked down towards her feet. She turned on her left side so that she faced the window in her bedroom. She pulled folded quilts under her bent legs and under her shoulder, creating a kind of well for her stomach. She sighed in satisfaction at having found a position she could bear. Outside, an overcast November sky showed through gold and red leaves on the hardwoods in the front yard, and birdcalls filled the morning air. The family rooster crowed loudly as though calling his hens to a party, the shrill sound covering the more delicate songbirds' calls.

A fire built in the brick fireplace earlier by Miriam gave some warmth to the room, but rather than struggle to rise and tend it to get more heat, Jane decided to get another cover. She slowly and awkwardly reached down to the end of the bed for another quilt and unfolded it halfway across her bulging body, snuggling under the heavy weight as a protection against the chill.

Jane studied the irregular lines of the bricks in the fireplace. Her Uncle Benjamin's slaves had made them at his brickmaking company on the banks of the Chattahoochee. The bricks that were used indoors were much better formed than the outside ones, where wind and weather had softened and curved their edges. Still, each inside brick seemed to have a shape of its own, as little chinks of the baked clay had crumbled and fallen to the plank floor below. To take her mind off her tiredness, she focused on naming a brick for each of family member. There were her immediate kin, her mother, two sisters, and a younger brother and their families. And of course, David, her older brother, and his wife and three children. That took a couple of courses of bricks. And there were the relatives she lived with: the elder Morgans, William and Rebecca; Alice, the maiden sister who'd wiped the noses of all the rest of the girls. Those four girls—Anne, Becka, Laura and Susannah—were now married. Then, of course, there was Miriam, the black woman who came with her when she married. And Joseph and their three children. Almost ten people under one roof, and more to come. That took another couple of courses of bricks, each one extending long arms for the ones next to it.

Jane grew tired of naming bricks. Her unsettled mind went from one concern to another as she lay resting with the weight of the new child falling towards the feather mattress. Their house was bulging at the seams. She must speak to Joseph about building their own home, she fretted. But when would she talk to him?

Joseph was working so many hours, she scarcely saw him any more. When he was finally at home he ate a supper that had been warmed over just for him because the rest of the family had finished eating long before he got home. Then he was so tired when he came to bed that husbandly duties seemed out of the question.

Not that she minded, she told herself. If she'd had another baby last year, it would have been difficult. With each child it was harder and harder to carry the weight around. Sometimes, when walking through the house, she could hardly find a chair fast enough to sit down and get herself together. Since she was not allowed out because of her condition, she didn't have to bother about reciprocating social invitations. But she did miss the news of the city.

God would probably punish her for this, she thought. She hoped she hadn't offended Him, but she had needed to keep Susan on the breast as long as possible. If the child had refused her milk, then she would have had to find a wet nurse for her. Then Jane would've been with child again in no time. As it was, the baby had the croup for so long and needed to keep nursing longer than the others.

Jane knew it was scandalous for Susan to be nursing long after she was walking and talking, but she was sickly. And Jane needed her to nurse. She just couldn't have another baby. There was barely a year and a half between Absalom and Will, two years before Susan came along, and now nearly four years between Susan and the one kicking in her belly. People at church probably were talking about those age differences—not that it was any of their business.

"I am so ashamed and I feel so guilty," she told the window. "Maybe God will make this child backward or ungainly, or even deformed because I've interfered with Him."

A sharp, twisting pain filled her body. The suddenness and the timing intensified her fears.

"See here, Jane!" she scolded herself. "You're bringing on your baby with those thoughts." She held herself still to see if more pangs would come. The pain left as quickly as it came.

She didn't need to be thinking those thoughts. A mother was supposed to keep a happy countenance and bright frame of mind when carrying a child. As far as creating a little breathing room between children, a woman did what she had to do.

Maybe she would talk to David about this. Usually he was sensible about problems. No, on the other hand, maybe she wouldn't. Men just didn't understand what it was like to carry this bundle around. It was different from preaching or working in the shop.

She rested a moment, breathing easier now that it seemed the pains had subsided.

Their work may be prolonged, she told herself about the menfolk, but it was over within a reasonable amount of time. What if they had to carry around a chest full of Bibles or a load of rifles all the time, as they tried to do all their other chores? Jane giggled to herself at the thought of her brother bearing a load of Bibles or of Joseph shifting a rack of rifles on his back. If they had to carry their work with them for nine months, and plant the garden, raise the food, cook the vittles, tend to the children, and clothe the entire family, and yet always be careful to make sure nothing happened to themselves or the child, they'd not stand for it, she thought. Only a woman is strong enough to carry these burdens!

Jane smiled to herself and snuggled down into the quilts that held her like her body held her child inside—protected and warm.

Was it possible that a woman was actually stronger than a man? Jane thought about the newest fashions—ball gowns that showed so much as to be indecent, and sleeves that actually forced a woman's arms to her sides with no room to move around. Why, a woman was helpless to reach out to grasp a stairway bannister! A gentleman had to guide her down the stairs with his arm around her waist, as though she would fall if he weren't holding her up. And she probably would!

You'd never see her in one of those, Jane told herself. Not that she'd have the opportunity—each new child erased that waspish waist she once claimed.

Wearing such dresses seems to confirm women's helplessness, Jane thought. But really, women are actually more resilient than men, she mused. Could that be? Then why did Christ place man at the head of woman, as Saint Paul says?

Jane recalled a story she'd heard from a visiting Decatur woman who'd heard it from her husband who sold machinery to the gold mines in Dahlonega. It seems that when white men heard the Cherokees had discovered gold, they couldn't wait to run up there to Indian country to start their own hunting. They went up there, built cabins, using rough split logs for beds and tables and chairs, and set about looking for the gold.

One night a group of miners was working in a deep pit, when a very large half-naked Cherokee woman screamed and jumped down into the pit. She starting hitting the men in the head with a hickory knee bludgeon. She screamed and slammed into them, knocking the men down and scaring them badly. They lit out, not to return for a long time. Other miners in the area named a nearby stream Amazon Creek in her honor.

And what of the Amazons? Jane wondered. Were they the only physically strong women in history?

Another pang hit her body, this one much stronger and longer than the other. She must call Mother Morgan soon, she told herself. She felt the refreshing absence of pain after the second twisting sensation left her body. She'd want someone to go for her own mother, too, in time for the baby's coming. Should she call for her now?

Jane Thurman Morgan, she told herself sternly, you've got to stop this carrying on about women's strength. You're going to turn this child into an Amazon if it's a girl, and a useless cipher of a man if it's a boy, the way you're going on. Another pain slammed her body, causing her to double up her legs around the baby in her womb.

"Mother Morgan!" she shouted, then reached for a cornshuck broom leaning against the wall near her bed. She grasped the handle, turned it upside down with one motion, and hit the end of the broom on the floor, summoning help.

It was July and the windows were open, admitting heat that rose in drifts from the hard-packed Georgia clay in front of the house. Jane was walking through the parlor of the Morgan home when she heard a woman's muffled cry. She stopped, trying to figure out who was calling so urgently.

"Jane!" It was Alice. Jane flung open the door and ran across the porch to the front stairs. She saw her sister-in-law struggling towards the house, her shoulders bent, holding the motionless body of five-year-old Will. Blood was spattered down the front of Alice's tan cotton day dress.

"Oh, my God, what happened?"

"Send Anne for Joseph and Doc Gilbert. I think he's injured very badly." Jane turned inside and called for Anne to come quickly.

"Go get Joseph and Doc Gilbert. Will's been hurt, he's not moving!"

Anne fled to the rear of the house where the barn sheltered a horse and carriage. While Jane held the door, Alice crossed the threshold, entered the wide hall and turned to the living room, Will's limbs dangling like white stockings below her arms.

"Army men are coming behind me," she explained breathlessly. "They were travelling with a big cargo wagon down the Marietta Road when all of a sudden they felt a jolt and saw Will's body behind them on the road. They stopped the wagon right away and called to me. I was just coming from the Huffs' house when I saw them. It had just happened. I grabbed him up and came running home."

"What was he doing out on Marietta Road? Wasn't anybody watching him?"

"Absalom was with him, but Will ran too close to the wagon, and he got caught by a wheel and was knocked down. Thank God he wasn't caught under a wheel, because it's a large wagon carrying guns down to Texas, and he would surely be dead now."

"Where's Absalom?"

"The soldiers are bringing him."

Jane looked at Will's pale face and cried, "Miriam, bring rags and some cold spring water. Quick!"

She helped Alice lay Will on the settee in the parlor and placed cloths under his head to absorb the blood that seeped from the back of his head. There were scratches across the rest of his face, and his light brown hair lay everywhere but straight across his head. His small arms showed other scrapes, also bleeding.

"I should have someone with the boys at every moment. I had no idea he could wander to the road like that. Will! Will! Can you hear me?"

Will's eyes, with their light brush of lashes across his fair cheeks, remained closed. Jane bent to his chest to listen to his heartbeat, which seemed strong. She then touched his forehead softly. His head was hot. She rose and met Miriam in the hallway, coming with the rags and water. Miriam carried an old bowl with water from the springhouse that she kept in a crock in the coolest corner of the hallway.

"Here you are," Miriam said. "My poor baby Will. I'll go fetch some more out by the well."

"Thank you, Miriam—please bring more cloths, quickly, please." Jane placed the rags in the bowl and soaked them, then applied the folded cloths to Will's forehead. She used one to gently wipe a tear in his skin and pressed the flap of flesh lightly to his temple. The rag quickly soaked through with blood.

"I don't know what I'm going to do," she told Alice. "I can't lose this child!"

They heard the loud jingle of horse's harness outside, and the women looked out through the open windows to see a pair of horses ridden by men in dark blue uniforms and heavy boots. They pulled to a stop outside the door and dismounted, then tied up the horses. The two riders came up the steps.

"I'm very sorry, ma'am," Jane heard one of them say when Alice opened the door to them. "We've hurt your little boy. We didn't know he was there alongside the road."

Alice invited the men in, and they entered the room where Will lay. They quickly bowed their heads to Jane and apologized once again. Jane saw that Absalom was with them.

"What happened, Son?" Jane asked.

"I don't know, Mama, we were walking and then—then—Brother Will was down." The six-year-old's eyes were red with tears. "We didn't mean to get hurt, Mama, the wagon just came along and hit Will."

"Son, I find that hard to believe. You were chasing the wagon, weren't you?"

Absalom turned his head into Alice's skirts and began crying afresh.

"I'm not faulting you for doing that, Absalom, but I want you to tell me the truth. Will was trying to get closer to the wheels so he could see how they were made, isn't that right?"

"Yes, Mama," Absalom mumbled from behind his aunt's skirts. "Brother Will likes wheels. I promise we won't do it again."

Jane turned to the unconscious Will and said in an even tone, "Alice, please take Absalom upstairs and tend to him. I need to stay by his brother."

Absalom moved toward Jane and put his arms around her. "I'm sorry, Mama. Is Will all right?"

"Just say some prayers, honey. Pray for Brother Will."

Jane saw Dr. Joshua Gilbert's head hovering over her body when she looked up. She was sweating and felt a hot glow in her face.

"What have you been hollering about?" he asked, teasing.

"What do you mean?"

"You've been yelling my name to help Will. Will's your oldest, isn't he?"

"No, Will's my second boy. And you helped revive him when he was hit by an army wagon train years ago. I must have been reliving that. Everytime I have a baby, I get scared. I could lose it. I'm so frightened."

"Your baby's coming, just hold on. Don't push yet. Keep holding on. When I say 'push,' give it all you've got, Mrs. Morgan."

Jane held her legs together, praying the child would not come until Doc Gilbert gave her the word. She shivered, thinking about her dream about Will. He'd been so taken with the sight of the massive rolling Army wagons. It was so like him, always into things that moved. Thank goodness the accident was so long ago and Will barely showed signs of it now.

"PUSH! NOW!"

Jane pushed with all her strength, pushing down. Nothing happened. She despaired, thinking she had held back too long. She pushed again, hoping this time the baby would fullly crown. She tried several more pushes. Then she felt an overwhelming pressure at the opening of her womb. She felt like there was a huge overgrown pumpkin from the garden in her backside, and she was expelling it. It was turning her inside out as it went. She opened her legs wide and slid forward in the bed. A long, deep moan rose from her throat. At the same time she felt excruciating pressure at her opening. She sensed the doctor probing for the baby's head. Within a few seconds, a moving mass of blue, red and white flesh was pulled out. Held upside down in the doctor's two hands, it gasped for air and let out a flat, high cry. He passed the baby to Jane's mother, who was waiting to receive it.

"What is it?" she shrieked.

"You've got a girl," Doc Gilbert said, smiling down at her. "Now hold on. I'm going to cut her cord."

"I don't believe it. What happened?"

"We almost lost her, and maybe you, too. There was a long delay in her descending into the birth canal, and I think it's because her back was to your back. But she turned herself around. You're okay. She's fine. Five fingers each hand, same for the toes."

"It all happened so quickly. One minute I was resting and..."

"I know," Doc Gilbert said. "Your mother-in-law sent for me as soon as she saw you."

He looked at her and spoke cheerfully. "You're fine now, just rest. The baby's fine, too. She'll need to nurse in just a minute. See if you can get your strength a little bit, and we'll give her to you."

"If she'd been stuck in there, would we have both died?" Jane asked. "Or is there anything a doctor can do?"

"Don't worry about it," Doc Gilbert said quickly, sliding his forceps into a black cloth wrapping. He also wrapped a large knife in the cloth. He placed his hand on her forehead. "Now we'll just keep an eye on you for the next several hours and hope that you stay warm, but not hot. I'll go speak to your husband."

Doc Gilbert walked over to the washstand, where he dove for a bar of lye soap, washed his hands, and rolled down his sleeves. Then he donned his black coat and went out into the hallway. Lavinia Thurman brought Jane's baby to her for the first time, wrapped in a cotton sheet. Jane looked at her, amazed.

"She's just absolutely beautiful," she said. "My second lovely, little girl!"

Jane opened her gown and placed the red-faced, wrinkled mass to her breast, urging her to the nipple.

"Remember, she doesn't know how to do this," Lavinia reminded her gently. "Give her time."

The baby girl nuzzled the breast, sucked a little but didn't seize upon it as though she were hungry. A yellowish fluid ran down Jane's lower breast. The child began to cry, and Jane rocked her gently and talked to her while Lavinia watched.

"She'll be hungry in time, they always are," Lavinia said, smiling in relief.

"Where's my baby girl?" Joseph asked loudly as he strode through the door. Both his mother and his mother-in-law shushed him as he drew near his wife and baby. Wisps of wet, blond hair graced his new baby's head, and she looked up with puzzled blue eyes as he appeared over her, speaking only a little quieter than before.

"She's beautiful, Jane," he said, kissing his wife on the forehead.

"And healthy, my husband," she said, rubbing his shoulder with her head. She held the little girl out from her body so he could see her full length.

"And you, my dear, just survived a very difficult birth. Doc Gilbert said it was what they call 'back labor.' I'm glad Lavinia sent for him. It could have been very close."

"All I know is that it hurt a lot, more than any of the others."

"What'll we name her? If she'd been a boy, I'd have named him after Doc Gilbert."

"How about Alice?" Jane said. "Your sister has been so sweet to me the whole time I've known her. And we couldn't have done without her when our first two came so close together."

"That's fair. Susan got your sister's name, this one gets my sister's. But I want her also to be named Jane."

"Well, how about Alice Jane?"

Joseph grabbed the hand of the little bundle in Jane's arms and put his large finger into its fist.

"Hello, Miss Alice Jane," he said warmly, leaning close to his wife as he held the infant's tiny hand.

Chapter 9

ATLANTA

1853

Plates clattered and cutlery hit bowls as Jane cleared the table. Miriam followed, picking up serving utensils and dropped napkins. The rise and fall of deep voices filled the room as the menfolk talked quietly. Jane saw her brother David looking intently, his eyebrows drawn, with dark eyes fastened on his brother-in-law Joseph. It was early October, and David's first visit back to Atlanta after moving his family to Walker County in northwest Georgia.

"It's gotten busier since you left," Joseph was telling David. "Atlanta's the jumping off point for so many points west—Alabama, Mississippi, Texas—"

"Too many people," William broke in with a weak voice. "Tryin' to move through here like bandits—an' there's a lot of that, too."

"The town is full of speculators," Joseph went on. "People without any real money, just dreams of turning whatever they have—a dray, a small dry goods store, a distillery—into a bundle. Everyone's after a fortune, but they haven't taken care of necessities, like having a decent house to live in, or food on the table. They run around like they've had breakfast, but they don't know where lunch is coming from!" Joseph quipped.

David pushed his chair back from the table, satisfied from the big meal, and laughed with Joseph. William Morgan, sitting in a wooden wheelchair at the head of the table, sputtered and coughed as he laughed with the others. Then he went into a fit of coughing. Jane held her breath, wondering if this coughing spell would ever end. She was afraid her father-in-law would choke. Gradually the hacking subsided.

"Father, are you all right?" Joseph asked, his heavy eyebrows wrinkling as he looked at William.

"Um, just give me a moment," William squeezed a response out of his congested throat.

Joseph, keeping an eye on his father, waited until William cleared his throat and settled back in his chair. Then the younger man continued regaling David with his stories of Atlanta.

"I had a man come in with his wife to look at a rifle the other day. He wanted a gun for running off the bears up near him. She talked him out of it, saying there wouldn't be enough money for that and her new dishware, too!"

"So maybe she could show the bears the plates and saucers and scare them off that way," joked David.

Jane listened as best she could while going back and forth to the warming room. She was glad to see David laughing, despite his cares. And she wanted to find out what Joseph was planning.

It was October now, and for three months Joseph had been subdued. Jane first noticed it after Gideon's last visit, one of several he'd made to Atlanta since moving to Whitfield County. Gideon had bought the most fertile land in that area, several hundred acres lying in a large bend of the Conasauga River. Was Joseph envious of his brother?

Joseph talked about that land a lot, how it flooded each spring, producing soil so black a crop of cotton would be ashamed not to grow there. Jane gleaned from Joseph's talk that Gideon was becoming fabulously wealthy, or at least he was leaving Joseph behind in some heavy trail dust, prosperity-wise. But then Gideon didn't have six children, Jane thought to herself. Anyone could be more wealthy than Joseph when there were only two children to support, and it looks like that's all there will be.

Jane had been so busy with her newest child, Catherine, that at first she did not notice Joseph's withdrawal. But it occurred to her one night after the baby was no longer sleeping in their bed that it had been a while since Joseph had desired her, and that was unusual. After each of the other children, Joseph had practically counted the days until he could lay again in Jane's arms.

During that time when a newborn slept with them all night, Jane would feel torn as she woke with the baby in bed between them. She loved feeling the baby's nuzzling, then feeding the child and dropping back to sleep as the little one's tugs at her breast became light and intermittent. But at the same time, Jane would look at Joseph's long body in bed with his back turned to them and long for his caresses. The two-week confinement when a baby was born, followed by several weeks of having the tiny one sleep with them all night, left Joseph, and sometimes Jane, feeling cranky and argumentative.

Jane thought about Joseph's lack of interest and recalled he'd been quieter recently. At first she blamed herself. But her only failing could be having another child, and she knew that Joseph loved his offspring too much to consider that a fault. The way he tossed his fifth child, Gilbert, into the air and took pride in naming him after old Doc Gilbert told Jane that having more was not the problem. Perhaps it was Gideon's success.

Jane was sure that Joseph was grappling with some sort of plan, as he'd been bent over his desk at home for several nights in a row. She'd asked what was going on, but he had motioned her away.

"Nothing to worry your pretty female head," he said.

"But Joseph, I'm your wife, and I need to know what you have in store for us."

"Don't worry, you'll know in time."

Now, as the family sat around the eating table, a warm sweet smell filled the entire downstairs.

Back in the warming room, Rebecca was pulling out a steaming peach cobbler, unwrapping cloths from around the hot pan. She smiled at Jane as she walked past her in the dining room.

William Morgan's face lit as he saw Rebecca draw nearer.

"My favorite!" he said.

"I know it is." Rebecca placed the cobbler in front of William. "You deserve a treat."

He closed his eyes and drank in the spicy fragrance. He placed his hands over the pan, taking in the warmth.

"Makes an old man's hands feel much better," he said. Jane winced as she thought of the pain swelling William's diseased joints and the incessant coughing racking his body.

"Here, let me serve you," Jane said, taking a stuffed pad and pulling the pan towards her as she stood at William's side. "Those other men are so busy, they don't even know what's under their noses."

"Aw, now, Sis, I do know when there's cobbler around," David protested.

"And my wife wouldn't let a good thing escape me, I'm sure," Joseph said as she cut into the cobbler and began dishing a full crusted serving. Steam rose and ribbons of sugared juice ran out as she lifted the section of cobbler, dripping with peaches, into a waiting bowl. Jane smiled and served up bowls for all, then the Morgan women resumed their places at the table.

"I'm glad you all appreciate the work," Jane said. "Miriam and Mother Morgan worked hard to dry the peaches after last summer's harvest."

"How are things up in Walker County, David?" Rebecca asked, changing the subject and shifting attention from herself.

"They're going quite well, thank you, Mrs. Morgan," David replied. "Margaret has settled into the house, William Melville and Benjamin like the countryside to play in, and Nancy is mixing well socially with her Boyles cousins. We're expecting, as you know, in early November."

"Yes, we were hoping to have Margaret here, too, but she wrote about her delicate condition. Please give her all our good wishes."

"I will, and we appreciate your concern."

Jane was glad the baby would be born before winter. She knew too well that David was thinking the same thing. The Thurmans had lost two children in one year in Atlanta. Both were born during the bitterest cold in January. An infant boy, named John, barely survived birth and died nine hours later in January of 1850. Then little Sarah, who'd survived for two years but was always sickly, died the next January. The families breathed a sigh of relief when David Clark, born in the month of August, recently reached two years of age and showed signs of doing well.

"I say prayers for you and Margaret every day, hoping you'll have the healthiest baby ever," Jane said.

"God willing, that's what we'll have," David said, without smiling.

"What do you think of the land in Whitfield County around where Gideon lives?" Joseph asked David later when both were sitting in the parlor. "When we sold land up there that was left in your father's estate, we got less than $2 an acre."

David leaned forward on the dark brocade covered settee and lit a pipe, then settled back and turned to answer Joseph. One eye closed to smoke, David recalled the transaction. Joseph and the husband of David's other sister, Lucy, were heirs to the elder David Thurman's land as a result of marriage. The men and Lavinia had sold the Northwest Georgia land in 1850.

"That's still about what you'll pay," David said, "for land without a lot of water. Prices haven't changed that much in three years. I know because I write letters for Mr. Blalock and others responding to inquiries about land. Yet I can see the growth—you know, I travel through that valley several times a year. It'll be worth a pretty penny in the future."

"Well, I don't anticipate making any moves any time soon. However, Father continues to weaken, and when he passes on there'll be an opportunity to sell what we have here and go buy land where it's cheap."

"But why would you want to leave Atlanta? Your business is excellent, and you're settled here, being a deacon and all at your church."

"It's just grown so much. You and I can remember when there were vines and trees and fox and turkey to hunt—that's all gone now. Newcomers move in every day from up north and all points beyond. They've taken down the trees and built roads every which a way. They talk fast, they walk fast, they're rude, and I don't like being around them. I can't secure the shops enough to keep thieves out. And, every day on Decatur Street, it seems like there's some kind of uproar or shootout."

"Ah, yes," David said. "It seems, when we first moved here, this was indeed the land of milk and honey," David said. "The promised land that we'd been intended to find." He looked at the pipe with disgust in his face as his fire went out.

"It's pretty much a den of theives pitted against the honest folk," Joseph said. "God knows, I've tried to make a decent life here. And I give thanks for it everyday. But I can't see having my family exposed to the violence and licentiousness in this area."

"That was on my mind when I moved to Walker County," David said, lighting his pipe a second time. He drew on the stem, making a light popping sound as he resurrected the fire."The children were becoming used to all the attractions of the shops and picking up very selfish ideas from their friends. And with the death of our two small ones..." David didn't finish.

Joseph waited, sensitive to his brother-in-law's loss. "Moses kept moving the Israelites until he found the Promised Land," he said. "I wonder if we just have to keep moving until we find the place where He intends for us to prosper?"

"Land is abundant where we are," David said, dragging again on his pipe. "We're able to grow all our own food, and then some, for market. And cotton grows fast, with large, soft bolls in land that's never seen the plant before, it's so unspoiled."

"Maybe that's what I need to do," Joseph said, hunching down in the parlor settee, excited by the thought. "If I wait much longer, my boys will never know how to provide for themselves. We're so dependent on city goods now that they don't remember what it was like to make or grow everything. We grew cotton for shirts and made horseshoes from every piece of scrap iron we found. If I move in the near future, I can help my three sons learn all the old skills before they go off on their own." Joseph's eyes were alive with energy as he talked. "Then maybe I can acquire some land and store up some goods to help 'em make a life for themselves. And of course I can't forget my girls; they'll need the usual things to attract good husbands."

"I can't advise you," David said. "But as your brother-in-law and dear friend, I can tell you that since we have moved we have overcome some of our sorrow about Sarah and Baby John. David Clark's thriving has been a sign to us that we did the right thing. And the people around us are good people, willing to go to church and abide by the Word. God has been good enough to show us a new way."

"There's so much uproar going on here. Remember the fire at Old Man Wheat's? Wiped him out of store, warehouse, horses, livery—everything."

"Sure, I remember. The church bells kept ringing and ringing to get us all out. You worked on the bucket brigade as I recall. Old Man Wheat left town very soon after that—sold his bare lot and went to Campbell County to farm."

"Well, you maybe never heard the real story. It was arson, a fire set to draw attention away from a robbery at the Georgia Railroad that same night."

"The audacity!" David closed one eye as the pipe bowl plumed in smoke. He exhaled slowly.

"But, Joseph, do you think it's this area of town? Decatur Street has had Murrell's Row and Slabtown all these years. Maybe if you moved to another part of town—"

"It wouldn't make much difference. Besides, there is no more Slabtown."

"What do you mean?"

Joseph told David of the local citizens' desperate attempt to clean up Slabtown and other areas.

Joseph stood outside the abandoned building on Whitehall Road, his heart pounding in his chest at such a rate that he thought it would explode through his skin. He looked at the men gathered in front of him. Some wore slouch hats—those were obviously workmen or tradesmen—while others who usually wore the fashionable silk hats of a gentlemen went hatless. One of the workers, a local mechanic like Joseph, spat nervously onto the ground and kept a lookout while the others gathered closer to hear the leader of the group, Ezekiel Smith.

As he looked at them, Joseph thought: All these people are ready to take justice into their own hands, to destroy property to achieve peace in this neighborhood. There's a justice of the peace, a lawyer, a physician, a wheelwright, a grocer and some store helpers. They are not mindless toughs, but upstanding citizens who are sick and tired of the rowdies and their ilk.

Smith pulled his white flour sack with two slits for his eyes over his head.

"Let's go!" he shouted to the twenty or so men around him.

Joseph held his cotton sack in his hand. He'd made the slits for his eyes. Should he join them? How could he not? He couldn't turn back now, or everyone in the Moral Party would soon know that he'd declined to join the raiders.

He fingered the rough cotton cloth. He remembered how Jane looked, breathless after her escape from Tom Cunningham. Her agitated eyes had sought him out, looking for his protection. He recalled how frightened he was as he took down his pistol to look for Cunningham.

William had insisted Joseph attend a mass meeting earlier to nominate Jonathan Norcross for mayor as the candidate of the Moral Party.

Then the opposing Free and Rowdy party—full of Atlanta undesirables—had nominated its own candidate. When they couldn't stop Norcross that way, they managed to have a Bowie-knife wielding rowdy arrested. The man tried to murder Norcross while he presided over police court. He didn't succeed.

Then the party stole the old Revolutionary War cannon from the Decatur court house square and trained it on Norcross' store at Peachtree and Marietta. They blasted the store with sand and gravel, but did little damage. They left the cannon and a threatening note for Norcross and disappeared.

"This despicable act will be punished," Norcross told a secret meeting of the Atlanta City Council. As a result, Joseph and about a hundred others had been called to City Hall to hear a proclamation summoning men to form a volunteer police force.

"We need a vigilance committee," a grizzled man standing next to Joseph complained.

"This is it!" Joseph said, and stepped forward to join.

All day, the newly created police force patrolled the Crossings in front of Norcross' store. The dust lay practically undisturbed, and cows and pigs wandered by while the men stood at the ready. The silent cannon looked increasingly out of place as no crew came to shoot it. Not a Rowdy appeared all day.

After the sun went down, Joseph and a strong band moved east on Decatur to Ivy Street, to the Rowdy Party headquarters. The Rowdies were said to be arming themselves and holing up in the building on the northeast corner of the intersection.

Joseph knew the building well. The Morgan home was on the west side of town and each day Joseph passed this building, which stood on the very western edge of Murrell's Row, on his way to work.

As the large squad of volunteer police moved toward the headquarters, more squads approached other Rowdy holdouts around the town. Joseph's group drew their guns and pistols. They climbed single file up the rickety wooden stairs outside the building. They heard shouting as the Rowdies ran out the door and jumped to the ground from the upstairs veranda. One after the other leaped from the end furthest away from the new policemen and scattered into the night.

"Quick, men, we've got them on the run, let's get the others," cried the Moral Party's leader as they lunged the rest of the way to the second floor entrance. There they found about fifteen Rowdy ringleaders. When the Rowdies realized their disadvantage, they put their firearms on the table and surrendered.

Within two days they were tried and convicted, and most put in the new, secure jail.

Now Joseph stood, the mask in hand, debating whether he should join in on the second part of the plan to rid the area of its lawless element. The city limits ran in each direction a short distance from the Crossings, and the toughs had found homes in an area just outside where they could elude the law. Further on out Whitehall Road on the west side of town was an area called Snake Nation. It was the target of their raid. They also were going to attack Slabtown, a poverty stricken row of shacks on the east side, that got its name from their pine slab building material.

Joseph had heard stories of routine assaults, several murders, and men carrying on with known prostitutes in broad daylight in Snake Nation.

"If the truth be known, most of Atlanta's mayors have been glad that area's outside the city," Smith, the leader, had said earlier. "No one has the manpower to go down in that cesspool and clean it out."

But cleaning it out was what they were bound for tonight. Each man in the group pledged to deny being there or seeing others there. Protected by the night and their hoods, they'd take up torches and sticks and framing boards to roust the remaining Rowdies.

"C'mon, Morgan, get a move on," Smith yelled at him. "Let's go!"

Joseph quickly weighed his choices. Either clean out this mess and rid the town of filth, be forever subjected to it, or move. He could not move away from the railroad, as it supported him and his family. He would not subject his many children, wife, and elderly parents to the lawlessness. He felt he had but one choice.

"Lead the way!" he shouted to Smith, as he pulled the sack over his head, grabbed a lit pine torch, and fell in with the other men. They ran quickly down the road to a shanty on the left, its porch full of derelicts. One of them looked up in surprise as he lifted his head from the railing, wiping puke from his mouth.

"Ee-yah! Get! They're coming after us!" the man shouted. Joseph and the others swung at them with sticks and boards, knocking teeth out of one man's mouth and knocking the others to the ground. When they tried to crawl away, they were battered again. The only sounds from the raiders were the grunts delivered with solid blows to the men below them. Women screamed inside the house. Joseph ran inside towards them, grabbing the first one he saw just above the elbow.

"Let me go!" the woman yelled at Joseph. "Don't you touch me!" Her loose dress gaped to show a very deep cleavage, and Joseph stared, taken aback at the display. She struck at him with a shawl covered hand. He quickly deflected it away from him, sensing the bottle underneath the shawl. He pinned her arms behind her back, and found himself pressed hard into Mary McCree's expansive bosom. He freed one hand, circled her while he held her two wrists together, and called for help.

"Give me a hand here," he called. "Get the women outside. We'll have to load them up and take them away." He pushed Mary McCree in front of him out to the porch.

Ezekiel Smith was standing over several men lying prone on the front porch. "Get out of town—now! If I ever see you in here again you'll get worse. You can claim your women out on Decatur Road—way out!" One of the men rose, and Smith struck him again with a long oak bludgeon. "Now get along!" he cried, prodding the man to rise again. This time he let him run.

Joseph heard Mary McCree weeping as he firmly guided her down the steps. Her long, gray-streaked brown hair, which had been loosely pinned, now fell unevenly to her waist. Joseph marched her up to the man guarding the wagon. How close he had once come to being tempted by her. What a debauched life she led! Could she be the same gender as his precious wife, Jane?

Then he went to retrieve the other women in the shack. His body shook as he approached the house. He was sad about the hardship he and the others were inflicting on the women, shocked to see the conditions in which they lived, and angry that the lawlessness had forced him to become an outlaw. As he looked down Whitehall Road, he saw fires lighting the night, fed by the wooden homes all along the road. Against the backdrop of red and yellow flames roaring to the skies, white-hooded assault squad members mingled with the Rowdies bursting out of the shacks and running south. Snake Nation was in ruins.

At last, Joseph told himself, it is finished.

As he ended his tale, Joseph saw that David was very quiet. He had put down his pipe and was regarding Joseph with lively brown eyes.

"I was so ashamed of myself that night," Joseph said. "I knew better. I'd been raised to know better. Pa asked me about it the next morning, and I told him I was out collecting on bills. I told him I did see the goings on, but I didn't get mixed up in it. Of course, he knew what was going on. He could see the flames from Slabtown from the window where he sits in his wheelchair. I know he heard the hollering and commotion.

"When he asked me about it, his clear sky blue eyes held me like he'd grip an iron bar on the anvil—unrelenting and fierce. And I lied. I lied with the innocence of a young boy in church with the minister looking down on him. Pa probably figured it out. But he didn't say anything. He just looked down at his lap as he sat there in his chair, and his shoulders dropped. Maybe he knew that, if he was me, he'd have to burn the trash out like I did."

David's eyes were downcast. Joseph found himself wanting to talk more. He was restless.

"Should I stay or should I go? This place isn't safe. But I'm doing well—very well. Do I trade that success for the unknown? I remember vowing to myself many years ago that I would not move from this place like Pa took us from Abbeville. Even if there is a bad element, even though I can get a great price for my land, I feel bound by that pledge. When I think about leaving, it feels like I'm letting someone down. It's not just myself. I think about old Joseph Morgan back in Abbeville District, settling the land and telling himself he'd finally found a home, and then Pa having to break that home apart and move it west. I'd like us to have a place finally and for good."

Joseph was quiet for a moment. He continued, "I think about Joseph settling an area where black bears regularly invaded cabins for victuals and there were Indian raids and buffalo so thick you couldn't stir 'em with a stick. And my granpa making guns with only the sun for light—and that only through a shed doorway, they had no glass windows. What powerful urge made him join the other associationists—even though taxes on glass and paper affected them not a whit. It was the idea of a despot they hated—a powdery-wigged tyrant who used men laboring and sweating far away in the colonies to line his own pockets."

Joseph paused, opening and closing his fists as they lay on his knees. David waited.

"I guess my *father* found the despot is other people, and if they won't leave you alone, you have to go where they will. I've got to face the same thing—where can you make a living to raise your family, and make a life where people are decent and lawabiding and godfearing?

"I've already told Gideon to look out for some land for me. I never thought I would say this, but I'm actually looking forward to living near my brother. My sisters are almost all married off and starting their own families. Father's nearing his end. When he's gone, if you and Gideon are up in the northwest, I'd rather be there as well." Joseph sighed and said, "Atlanta's a sinful and bawdy town. I'd like to be rid of her."

David nodded slowly, in agreement. Joseph imagined him as an ancient wise man, giving his blessing.

Joseph moved past Jane, three of his sisters, and his oldest daughter Susan. They were gathered in the hall talking quietly, some of them dabbing handkerchiefs to their eyes. He carried an armload of firewood for the hearth in his father's room. Alice pushed open the wooden door. With his available hand, Joseph quietly opened the door wider and moved into the room.

William, bedridden for two weeks, looked up at Joseph from a narrow bed piled with quilts. A cold November chill stood about the room despite a roaring fire in the fireplace. Joseph dropped the logs on the hearth and moved next to his father.

"Do you remember the persimmons that used to grow in Abbeville?" Willliam asked.

"Pa, I don't know if I remember them or not." Lately, Joseph had taken to calling William "Pa," a name Joseph hadn't used since he was thirteen years old.

"I really would give a king's ransom to see one of those again." He sighed, then his eyes brightened with hope. "Can you get me one?" Before Joseph could respond, William travelled on. "There just aren't any here like there were back home," William said, a sadness drawing down the edges of his mouth. His fair skin was paler now than Joseph ever remembered. His lips, which always had a dark tinge, were now definitely blue.

Joseph hung his head, listening with sadness as his father went on about his childhood.

"Yeah, those McAllister boys were always after the persimmons. Only time I saw them except at church meetings once in a great while was out there in the fields shaving those trees of their red gold," William said. His voice was raspy, his breathing forced.

Joseph wiped his eyes with his fingers, then pulled a bandana from his workshirt and pulled it across his forehead. Despite the chill in the room, he was suddenly warm.

"Get me a persimmon, will you, Son? I really would like that. They should be ripe by now."

Joseph knew his father was not himself. He never asked for anything for himself, and would never put anyone out with a request that was hard to fill. "I'll see what I can do, Pa," he said, gently laying his hand on his father's forehead. "You seem a little warm. I'm going to put this cloth back on your head here." He reached for a wet cloth in a bowl beside William's head.

William moved his head and looked up at Joseph. "Thanks, Son."

"That's just a small thing I can do for you after all you've done for me," Joseph said, tears catching in his throat.

"Do you remember after the war," William continued, "how many orphans and widows there were in Abbeville? I remember Widow Davis and Widow Jones and Mrs. Gallaspie—there were so many. They had their children cull the persimmons from the trees all over the county, and I remember I couldn't spy a tree but the fruit would be clean picked off. I couldn't get a persimmon after the war ended. Scarcely during the war, either. I was so small then I didn't know a persimmon from a muscadine."

Joseph waited, amazed at his father's detailed memory.

"My playmates' fathers were killed in the murdering that went on during that war. Miz Susanna McAllister—her man John was strung up by the Tories. Her boys Michael and John were always having to do chores, like we all did, but they were always working, and working those persimmon trees. Muscadine vines, too. Miz McAllister always had the best pies and preserves from persimmons and muscadines, persimmons and muscadines..."

William drifted off in a kind of sleep, his mouth working as though tasting the favored fruit. Joseph watched his father's face relax and wondered if the old man would see another sunrise. He wept quietly.

Later that day William's breathing became labored. Sitting at supper in the other part of the house, Joseph could hear his tortured attempts to get air. It was like the bellows in the shops *whooshing, whooshing* in and out. He couldn't bear it, and went out in the back yard on the pretense of inspecting Miriam's milk cow. The red cow with white splotches in her face regarded him with her large brown eyes, and Joseph stroked her head.

His mother came to the door, urging him to come to his father's room.

"He's getting worse," she cried softly as she took Joseph's arm. He placed his arms around his mother and held her close. He wiped a tear from her cheek, something he'd never done before. It was always she who was comforting him, and not too often since he'd become a man. He'd never consoled her before now. He remembered that time in Washington, Georgia, in the dining room of that inn when he told her about old Thomas Cunningham. She'd cried a little then, but it was all over when she began waltzing. He had seen Jane hold his mother, and Rebecca doing the same for Jane. At a time like this, it seemed embracing might ease the pain of William's slipping away from them, and he squeezed his mother in his arms once more.

Joseph sat near his father's head. Rebecca stood on the other side. William was barely conscious. Joseph took his father's hand and pressed it between the two of his. He looked at how his large hands dwarfed his father's shrunken palm. Joseph remembered how huge his father's hands had looked when he was a young boy helping out in the forge. When his father pulled an iron bar out of the forge and it was all red and sparking he seemed as powerful as the Almighty. And then when he struck the iron with his hammer! It was awe-inspiring.

"Be sure you watch over Gideon," William said, his eyes still closed "I'm afraid of his ways." William paused to get his breath. Joseph waited, wordless. His mother sat weeping quietly. "I'm afraid for his soul."

Joseph knew he could say nothing. His brother's slaveholding ways had always been a concern to William, who'd used the labor of his own hands for seventy years, never that of another man, unless he paid him.

"Joseph, son of Abraham," William strained to talk. "You are a favored one. We are a favored people. Almost all of our children survived, and all of yours grow larger and more healthy every day. God has indeed blessed us."

William opened his eyes to look at Joseph. Those pools of blue were weaker now as they looked into Joseph's eyes. "Keep the family together. Family is all you've got." Then William closed his eyes.

"I will Pa," he said. "I will, Pa." He squeezed William's hand slightly. The wheezing got louder and louder. There was a rattling noise from deep in his chest. William's throat gave a loud, guttural sound. Then there was silence. William released his hold on Joseph's large hands. The son looked at the slack hand in his, unable to believe it held no life.

"He's gone," he said, turning to his mother. "Call the others in."

Joseph felt the sharp jolt when the carriage hit a rut in Whitehall Road. As the high wheels hit the bump, his body lifted out of the leather seat, throwing him up against his wife's hoop skirts. He looked at Jane squeezed next to him on the right and saw her grimace through the film of her black veil. His older sons, across from him in the open carriage, smiled and laughed quietly at each other as they jostled with the bumps from their half-standing position. Absalom, thirteen, and Will, twelve, grabbed the edges of their seat and stiffened their legs as they waited for the next sharp drop, looking at each other seriously to see who would smile first.

Joseph became absorbed in their pantomime. He knew Will would smile first, because Absalom was a better actor and could keep a stern face as long as need be. Will was quiet, vulnerable. He'd likely give in and lose in the facemaking contest. Joseph restrained an impulse to squelch the game. It was not fitting for a funeral procession, but William's long illness had strained the family, and the boys' fun didn't seem too disruptive.

Rebecca, sitting to the right of the boys, was entertained by their antics. The widow's head was draped in a crepe veil falling from her bonnet, which like everything else she wore, including a long wool cape, was dull black. Despite the heavy cover, Joseph could see the beginning of a smile across her face. As they all shuddered with the uneven ride, the boys began playing a game of rock, scissors, and paper. Absalom would call "Go!" in a voice just above a whisper, and the two would each jut out one hand, in the shape of a fist for a rock, an extended palm for a sheet of paper, or two fingers in the shape of a "v" for scissors. Scissors beat paper, rock beat scissors, paper covered rock. The two boys lunged in unison side to side with the motion of the carriage, intent on their game.

"Mother, make them stop!" Nine-year-old Susan whispered as she leaned toward Jane from his wife's other side. "It's disrespectful to Granpa!"

Joseph watched Absalom scowl at Susan and decided to intervene.

"That's enough boys," he said.

"But, Pa!" Absalom objected. "Granpa used to play this with us."

"I'm glad you want to honor your Granpa, but it's customary to do without games and other pleasures on the day of burial."

Absalom's frown was matched by Will's.

"Brother Will, maybe you could tell us your favorite story about Granpa," said Jane. Joseph wondered at how his wife could turn a difficult moment into an opportunity. Will appeared to think about the request.

"Well, what I want to know is why did Pa put wood shavings in Granpa's coffin?" Will blurted out. "I tried to clean up behind him, and he wouldn't let me."

Joseph was taken aback by his son's question. Hadn't he explained? Then he remembered that with all the activity two days before he'd not taken the time to answer questions from the ever inquisitive Will. While he worked on William's coffin, Joseph thought about his father and his simple burial request, made a year ago. He'd wanted to be laid to rest at their church at Utoy, and he insisted that there be no elaborate gravestone, only a rough fieldstone of the kind that marked most graves in their area. Joseph had told him that a more fitting stone could be obtained from Charleston, a fine work from a stonecutter's hand, delivered by the railroad.

"The money you would give for that is far better spent on the living," William had said, placing his hand on Joseph's. William went on. "When I was growing up in Abbeville District I heard of a man, a very substantial citizen, who was a slaveholder over near Old French Town. This planter had a dozen slaves, and after he died and his slaves subsequently died, he had them buried standing up on either side of him, as Romans had their slaves buried, as though they were to serve him in the afterlife as well as this life." William frowned and clasped Joseph's hand harder. "Whatever you do, make mine a simple resting place and a plain burial. I want this family to be known for its service to man and its humility before God, not for its audacity."

Joseph had thought of his those words as he planed the cover of the box that William's cold body would lie in. He also thought about how fine David Thurman would have made his father's coffin—David, the master woodworker and gunstocker.

As he sat facing his sons and mother in the carriage, Joseph longed for his friend and wished to share the sadness of his father's passing with his brother-in-law. But David was in Walker County this Sunday to serve his chapels, and William was being buried, as was the custom, as soon as possible. Winter rain had delayed the burial by a day. William had been dead two days, and now enough family and local citizens created a procession that stretched back as far as Joseph could see.

Joseph returned to Will's question. "I saved the scraps of poplar when I made the coffin and put them in the box so that you would not touch them. If you did, it's thought you'd be the next to be visited by death, and we don't want that to happen."

"Really, Pa?" Will asked. "How can you believe that? That's not true, is it, Granma? How could shavings cause death?" Will was incredulous. As usual, he wanted the details of how things worked.

"Will, there are lots of things we do that we don't understand," Rebecca said. "We just do them to make sure we honor the dead and don't invite the spirits to come take more of us."

Will fell into silence, watching the countryside.

The procession turned west on Sandtown Road going toward Utoy Primitive Baptist Church. Joseph remembered another bumpy ride to church when David's father had preached under the brush arbor. Joseph had been Absalom's age, and the Morgans had only recently come to DeKalb County. He remembered looking around at his family then as he did now, and thinking what a force for good they were. There was hope then for the future. But what would the future bring for Absalom and Will and Susan, and Alice Jane, Gilbert, and infant Catherine? For generations the Morgans had sought a permanent home. Would these Morgans find one? Would he live to see them grow up?

Joseph looked back at the other carriages. Behind them was the very elaborate one carrying Gideon, Josephine, and their two boys so close in age to Joseph's boys. Gideon's slaveholding, plus the fact that he'd moved away from Atlanta, had caused a shift in the positions of the two brothers. Without a word being spoken, Joseph had assumed the role of the oldest son. Now that their father was dead, Joseph had become the family patriarch, even though Gideon was older.

After Gideon's carriage, there followed several of Joseph's sisters with their husbands and children. Joseph knew they looked to him to lead the family. The Morgans were spread all over northwest Georgia and Texas now. Three sisters were married, had children and were living in Texas and Atlanta. It was a large and potentially influential family. What would he lead them to?

Joseph, now forty, looked over his wife's shoulder, past the driver of their own hired carriage. He gazed at the coffin being pulled ahead of them on a dray. His father's box was almost six feet long, thirty inches wide at the shoulder, a foot deep. He heard the bronze bell in Utoy Primitive Baptist Church begin to peel, slowly sounding out a ring for each of William's seventy-two years.

"Pa, I can't believe you've passed on," Joseph said quietly. "What do I do now?"

At the grave, the minister prayed over the coffin. Six men held heavy ropes that balanced the coffin over the grave, then lowered William's body into the ground of his adopted home. Joseph placed the first shovelful of damp, heavy red clay on top of the box. He was followed by Gideon, and then by their brothers-in-law and the male members of the Thurman family. A bitter, cold wind from the northeast swept across the graveyard, and the women and some of the men and children wept.

William's body lay in its unevenly dug hole, and the rain began anew, making dollar-sized stains on his coffin. Joseph felt a vast empty space next to him where his father had stood for so many years. Now instead there was thin, damp air gusting at his side. Sad and alone, he turned to join the others. William and his companions in the earth faced east, awaiting the sunrise of Resurrection Day.

Two days later Joseph gathered his brother and sisters and their spouses together after breakfast. Jane sat while Joseph stood in the parlor of their home, with nearly twenty others in the room or pressed in from the wide hallway.

"We are moving to Whitfield County to be near Gideon and to buy more land," Joseph said quickly. "Mother and Alice will move with us, of course."

Joseph heard Jane let out small gasp and hoped the others did not hear her. He hadn't told her, but he felt it was the right move.

"Each of you will receive some cash from father's estate— unbeknownst to us, he'd been saving it up so he could assist each of you, and his executor will see that you get that as soon as possible. He left me his interest in the blacksmith and gunsmith shops, and I intend to continue his trade once we are settled.

"Let us keep the family together though distances separate us. We are Morgans—" Joseph's voice broke, and then he recovered. "Don't ever forget that. It is a wondrous legacy."

The gray and black figures moved about like birds on a bush, embracing, crying, talking quietly, building memories that would keep them until the next gathering.

"Joseph, my husband, I can't believe my ears," Jane said when they were alone. Her dark eyes were livid. "Why didn't you tell me?" Joseph saw both hurt and anger in her eyes, and he felt warm around his stiff collar, despite the cold weather. They had seen their last guests depart and the house was quiet. The children were with Miriam, and Jane and Joseph stood in the parlor.

"I'm sorry, Jane. Gideon just brought me the writings on a large parcel of land. I didn't want to discuss it with the burying of my father and all."

"But, Joseph, I'm your wife, and I need to know these things. You expect me to uproot our family that's been here since before Atlanta was even thought about, and you act as though we're going for a walk down Broad Street. I don't understand."

"What you don't understand, Jane, is that the hard part has been done. I put quite a bit of thought into the purchase of this land. I've also been buying other land lots—"

"Land lots. Why they're a hundred sixty acres apiece. At least I know that much. I'm not a simple girl, Joseph. Exactly how much land have you bought—and where?"

Joseph explained that he'd bought a hundred acres near Gideon's rich bottomland. In addition, he'd bought one land lot and parts of four others and had hopes of buying more. "When the price is right, I'll buy land on the railroad, just like we have here, and that'll enable us to have a blacksmith shop and gunsmith shop just where the railroaders will need it."

Jane looked at him with sad eyes. "Joseph, I know that as your wife I don't own these things, you own them. However, I would like you to have discussed them with me. Now I know why you've been so preoccupied. But I want to be your helpmate, and I can't do that if you won't tell me what you're thinking about."

Joseph put his arm around her shoulder and pulled her to his side. "I know. I should have. But this is an important move. Once I'd made my mind up, I had to go through with it without your questions. I'm sorry." For the first time, he wondered if he'd made a mistake by excluding Jane. But he felt he couldn't do it any other way.

"You get to take your mother with us. Mine will be here, and I'll be many miles away," Jane sniffed, tears falling from her cheeks.

Joseph pulled Jane to him and held her in his arms. "I'm sorry. It will all work out, I promise." He felt her soft breasts next to his lower chest, but her back was rigid.

PART THREE

ABBEVILLE FAREWELL

For the Lord thy God bringeth thee into a good land, a land of brooks of water, of fountains and depths that spring out of the valleys and hills;

A land of wheat and barley, and vines, and fig trees, and pomegranates; a land of olive oil and honey;

A land wherein thou shalt eat bread without scarceness, thou shalt not lack anything in it; a land whose stones are iron and out of whose hills thou mayest dig brass.

Deuteronomy 8, 7-9

Mine eyes shall be upon the faithful of the land,
*   that they may dwell with me;*
*   he that walketh in a perfect way,*
*   he shall serve me.*
He that worketh deceit shall not dwell within my house:
*   he that telleth lies shall not tarry in my sight.*
I will early destroy all the wicked of the land;
*   that I may cut off all wicked doers from the city of the Lord.*

Psalm 101

Wherefore, seeing we also are compassed about with so great a cloud of witnesses, let us lay aside every weight, and the sin which doth so easily beset us, and let us run with patience the race that is set before us.

Hebrews 12:1

Chapter 10

TILTON, GEORGIA

December 1855

On the way back from Dalton, Joseph got down from his horse to give him water from a spring tumbling from the side of a hill not far from the road. Local farmers had trapped the spring with rows of fieldstone, creating a large pool. Joseph could see the bottom of the pool and see the shelf of limestone rock forming the bottom.

He cupped his hands and drank, enjoying the cool sweetness. Then he let the horse drink. While the *whzzzz* of the horse inhaling water reached his ears, his mind dwelled on the tingling sensation he'd felt earlier that morning as he returned his holdings for the year at the Dalton tax office. He felt a thrill spreading from his chest to his arms when he filled out the form showing his land.

He claimed two hundred-ninety acres, including close to a hundred acres of Conasauga River bottomland, not too far from Gideon's eight hundred acres. Like Gideon's, his river land was flooded several times each winter. The slowly receding river left the loamy soil rich with minerals, decaying vegetation, and topsoil from the Cohutta Mountains above them. Such land sold for three times the price of ordinary cleared land.

Joseph had invested in that large parcel several years ago, speculating the land would only increase in value. After the Rowdies had attempted their coup, and Snake Nation and Slabtown were torched, Joseph started thinking for the first time about moving.

Atlanta and Columbus had become jumping off points for the great westward movement of thousands of immigrants, many of whom had only a few years before left Virginia and the Carolinas to move to Georgia. But Joseph hadn't been interested in the West. He watched as Irish workers with enough money to leave their railroad building jobs started small wheelwright and carpenter businesses in the new counties carved out of Cherokee County, which occupied most of the northwest part of the state. As soon as the long railroad tube had been blasted through the mountain at Tunnel Hill and the railroad had been connected to Chattanooga and the Ohio Valley, the movement north had been continuous. Because of wildly appreciated land values in Atlanta, William's property—left to his children in his will—gave them a huge windfall, making it possible to acquire more land. Joseph, remembering with sadness his own determination not to move around as his parents had, decided to give up on Atlanta and throw in with the settlers moving north along the railroad.

Now, nearly three years later, and he owned significant timberland holdings and his prize: an inn next to the railroad tracks in Tilton.

Did he fancy his inn on the new railroad stop to be the Tilton version of the White Hall, that once-famous hotel owned by his neighbor Charner Humphries in Atlanta? Humphries' inn, which had been built in the 1830s across the only stagecoach route crossing that part of the state, had done a brisk business, Joseph allowed. It was the center of all the activity, including militia musters, when he was young. With eight boarders' rooms, a magnificent veranda supported by six large columns, great hallways, and inside stairwells, it was an awe-inspiring building.

Joseph's inn at Tilton was small by comparison—a two-story, weather-boarded affair, with a stairway leading from the front porch to the upper level so guests could reach the rooms and not disturb the family. Not that heavy, rough boots tramping up those stairs at all hours contributed to domestic peace. His four boarding rooms were small compared to Humphries' place. And the White Hall sported real white paint, making it a noteworthy building for miles around. Joseph's inn was as yet unpainted. There'd be time for that once the business was more substantial.

Humphries' place had given Joseph the idea for his own establishment. Humphries had staked out the area for the inn about the same time the militia had been called up in the Columbus campaign to fight the Creeks. Joseph pitched in with the returning militiamen and other neighbors to roll logs to the site and knock supports together to raise the structure. The White Hall lost business after the train tracks were laid a couple of miles to the north, where Atlanta was born six years later. The White Hall's business slackened and eventually died.

After watching trains ruin the stagecoach traffic, Joseph had decided an inn right on a railroad would be a much better prospect for providing for the ten members of his large family. In Tilton he'd found a large deep river as well, bordering the eastern edge of the town in one of its many loops and bends through the wide valley. Now that he'd moved the family to Tilton, they were farming on the ninety-acre tract just across the Conasauga and north of town.

Joseph was feeling successful. Owning the inn and land lot on the west side of the railroad tracks assured him plenty of room to expand his business. He could sell off parts that would become more valuable as more people came to town. But there'd never be huge crowds like in Atlanta, he told himself. When he'd arrived in DeKalb County in 1826, Decatur was the bustling county seat, and their neighborhood six miles west was literally the wilds. The town that grew up to be Atlanta sprang to life around the stockmen pushing their animals through the area on the way south. Businesses blossomed to serve them and to supply the settlers building farms around the forested village.

The building of three railroad lines was a slow process, but their joining catapulted Atlanta into a boomtown. He remembered sitting on his front porch and reading in the paper about the 1850 census count as dozens of people walked by on the road in front of his house, something that was a fairly rare occurrence before the railroads came. This simply reinforced the newspaper story: The town was bursting with new residents. In 1849, just two years after incorporating, Atlanta counted 2,000 people. By contrast, Decatur had only 600. By 1853, when Joseph was feeling the pinch of all the loud-talking, fast-walking newcomers, Atlanta had tripled in size to 6,000, and its exuberant city fathers encouraged the birthing of a new county— Fulton—from part of mother DeKalb. Atlanta became the county's seat.

Joseph had seen sweaty, muscular Irish gangs lay shining ribbons for the iron horses that noisily steamed into Atlanta. Like Aladdin's lamp, the huge boilers belched out curls of smoke that revealed a sizeable genie working magic in the pockets of eager businessmen. Joseph was sure he wanted to have a piece of the pie when railroads worked their sorcery in his new home. But, if his life depended on it, he'd see that the growth here was orderly, not like growth had been in Atlanta.

Joseph had learned that control of the land was everything, and, with his holdings here in Whitfield County, he felt he had more control than he ever did in Atlanta. He felt like he was on the edge of something great for the first time, a man freed from shackles about to make a new life. Or perhaps a man ascending to an unreachable place high on a mountain. It took work and perseverance and dirt ground into a man's hands, face, and body. Joseph felt stronger than Gideon—after all, Gideon made his money on the whipped shoulders and backs of helpless blacks. Joseph was succeeding with the help of the iron horse, as well as countless hours of work.

It was April, two years ago, almost three, when his family arrived in Whitfield County. How could it be that long ago? It seemed like only last week.

After William died, Joseph moved quickly to relocate the household. It took several hurried trips following poorly traveled horse trails north to locate the land and begin setting up his shop. There were long separations from Jane and the family. Once, he took his sons with him over a summer week when their teacher was not holding classes. The last trip north was a long two-wagon ride with his six children, wife, mother, Miriam, and sister Alice, and it reminded Joseph of the one he and Alice took as children from Abbeville thirty years before.

Now Alice was accompanying Joseph and their mother and his large family to Whitfield County. She very skillfully assisted Jane and Miriam with the four younger children as they made the trek north. Alice would continue to live with them—that had been decided long ago, even before Alice and Joseph's father had died.

They crossed the Chattahoochee River by ferry and followed the Marietta Road to that city, passing homestead after homestead—hundreds of thousands of acres cleared of most of their significant trees.

"Feeds the railroad," Joseph explained. In fact, the bohemeths required a full tender of mostly hardwood fuel every thirty miles. With three to four trains a day, they created a yawning gape of need for wood. Joseph noticed that, rather than the dense, exquisite forests he remembered from his boyhood, there were huge tracts totally stripped of trees. Other neighborhoods they passed had timber felled and waiting to be cut up and hauled to the nearest wood station, or a passel of men working the trees that still stood.

Wood was cheap, selling for fifty cents a cord in town. The railroads paid even less. Yet, because there were so many trees, and because a man could always make some money cutting them, logging was ever present activity—girdling the trees, cutting the tall sentinels, and hauling them to the nearest market.

The railroad paralleled the wagon road, so there was ample opportunity to be doused with smoke and cinders from the engines that passed beside them four times a day. Will seemed particularly chagrined that they were not traveling by the faster means, but Joseph humored him with stories of how lonesome and sick their cattle and horses would be in the boxcars. They rode in two of the wagons the family used for the journey from South Carolina, and Joseph saw no reason to forego them for train accommodations. Most of the family was just as content, reluctant to trust their safety to the speeding, loud monsters.

Leaving Marietta, their horse-drawn train passed through the valley between Kennesaw Mountain and Brushy Mountain. As they turned east, they could see Lost Mountain up ahead and Pine Mountain to their right. They turned north again, and passed Pine Mountain on their left. The road veered away from the Western & Atlantic tracks, joined the Tennessee-Sandtown Road, and took them through the village of Acworth, where their route again started to parallel the railroad. As they drew near Allatoona, they prepared for a stop at an inn located in the middle of the bustling iron foundry town. Joseph hoped he could visit some mills in the area and discover sources for iron that would be a short railroad trip away from his new home in Tilton.

The two wagons had a hard time making the incline up the ridge to Allatoona Pass. This slowed the journey, and made Joseph wonder if they would make Allatoona that night. The roads climbed higher, and the horses strained harder and harder to pull the heavy loads up the rutted, clay road. As they approached the Allatoona Range, the road gradually began to curve to the east, seeking a way around the tall mountains.

Gradually, they climbed to a point where they could see a mountain shaped like a large, deep blue Chinaman's hat, and Joseph wondered if they'd been misled. They drew nearer, and the mountain stayed in their path. At the same time, Joseph started seeing signs of heavy settlement around Allatoona—mill workers' shacks and small stores. The town had sprung up because of traffic pouring through the pass from two directions—drovers from Tennessee and Kentucky pushing down the Sandtown Road to the Georgia and South Carolina coasts and the settlers beating their way west from the Carolinas and Georgia into Alabama, Texas, and lands west.

Allatoona had toppled into fame when a vein of gold was rumored to run through the area, and discovery of a dozen minerals and valuable iron ore caused it and the surrounding towns of Emerson and Etowah to feed the dreams of investors from near and far.

Night fell as they approached Allatoona. They stopped at the inn and settled down for the night. Joseph was so excited about seeing working mills in the area that he could hardly sleep that night.

The next morning he and the boys explored the marvel of the neighborhood, a huge hole in the mountain near the town that had been blasted to allow the railroad to pass at level grade through three hundred-sixty feet of rock. As they followed the W&A tracks through the pass, Will looked back and forth again and again, watching for a train that would squeeze them out of the pass.

Walls of rock, pressed in thin layers and dripping with water, climbed up on either side of them, blackened from soot from trains' engines. Green ferns with no memory of winter displayed their fronds, perched on watery rock formations shooting up from the floor of the pass, like so many walls shoved up with the force of gigantic underground blasts. Marks left from huge drills used to dislodge the granite scarred the remaining rock. Joseph explained to the boys that weeks and weeks of work had gone into cutting the pass for the railroad line, with hundreds of workers removing tons of material in tedious runs of wheelbarrows and work carts.

"You walk through this pass so neatly now," he said. "If you were on the work crew you would have wondered if you would ever get all the dirt and rock out of here."

The next morning they pulled onto the Tennessee Road and found that the Alabama Road at that point joined the northbound road for the pass through the mountains. The road climbed up a steep hill. The wagons lumbered, wheels squeaking. The children walked beside the caravan to lighten the load. The hills on either side of their pass were even steeper than the grade they traveled; crossing them without the road would have required even more effort.

At last they rose to the saddle of a ridge, then began the descent. Joseph noticed that on the left side the ridge passed near his shoulder as he walked the mules. But on the other side of the wagon, the ground rose to at least fifteen feet. Years of traffic from cattle and hog drovers as well as settlers and traders passing from north to south had worn a wedge of a roadbed into the sharp slope of hill that at one time was impassable by wheels.

What trees remained on the hills boasted their first greenery, and tufts of green grasses and vines stuck out of a cover of leaves dressed in the browns and grays of winter. As they descended to the Etowah River, they could hear the clamor of mills, and the air was gray with debris. As they drew closer to the river, the skies were filled with every kind of smoke. Soot and dirt filled the air, occasionally dropping bits on the travelers. Cacophonous sounds of wheels grinding, water rushing, and men yelling mixed together as they reached the low, marshy areas of the riverbank. Roads stretched in front of them on either side of the river.

At this point, the river was the color of unfired bricks, and a powerful current pulled it west toward Alabama. To the east, a tremendous dam was built across the river, causing a sheet of ponderous water to fall, powering several mills, including a five-story building Joseph heard was a flour mill. On a ridge across the river, a railroad line climbed gradually to the east in the direction of the falls. On the line, a small engine with a large chimney chugged backwards, pushing a short load of cars. One car carried great chunks of limestone, another carried charcoal.

As the train neared the top of its run, Joseph saw it dump its load at the top of a tall, rock furnace, built just underneath the end of the rail line. At the top of the furnace, black men surrounded the cars and, together, tipped the cars over into the top of the furnace. At the bottom of the furnace, other black men, working under a white overseer, stood where the ore from the furnace had been unplugged. They'd let the black mass run into a trench. Joseph knew the trench was built with smaller trenches on each side where the iron cooled and solidified. In its final form, the ingot would resemble a black mother pig suckling, giving it the name "pig iron." Large, muscled men would load the ingot on a hay wagon pulled by six mules. The wagon, with mules dropping their long-eared heads groundward, stood at the ready by the riverside. From there, Joseph knew it would make its way to the rolling mill, where it would be made into bars and sheets for plows and skillets and gun parts.

Everywhere there were men pushing wheelbarrows, horses dragging sleds, and teamsters urging their horses to pull large wagons—all of them loaded with chunks of iron ore. Joseph knew the men would pour the iron ore into the top of the furnace, which had already received loads of limestone and charcoal, to produce the dark, flowing, liquid iron.

Many of the men had the close-eyed features and pugged faces of the shanty Irish, breakaways from the railroad building that had brought so many poor Catholics to the area. Near Tilton, there was a town with so many Irish immigrants it was called Dublin. There were also the light and dark-haired men of English-Scots-Irish ancestry who'd come in waves from Northern Ireland and England—good Protestants all. They pushed their barrows and sleds with equal fervor, Joseph noted. Occasionally, he'd see a freedman pushing a wheelbarrow.

All of them were looking for a home, Joseph told himself, just like he was. They were all starting homes and trying to make their fortunes in a new land. The men might have come from Ireland or South Carolina or Africa. He wondered if any of their longings were as keen as his own.

The family crossed the Etowah River below the mills on a rickety ferry handling the Tennessee Road traffic, and then followed a road along the edge of the river back towards the mills. Upriver from the pig iron works there rose several huge buildings: a rolling mill and nail factory, a blast furnace and foundry, the five-story high merchant flour mill, two corn mills, and two saw mills.

"Gracious me," Jane gasped as she saw the buildings rising up ahead alongside the river. "It's liked they plunked Atlanta down in these hills. They just knocked over a few trees and built a town."

Joseph grinned, thinking how he was going to enjoy buying his materials from a location near their new home.

"Even better than Atlanta," he said. "Atlanta didn't have this kind of industry. No sources for pig iron, no homemade sources for skillets and ovens and iron to make railroad ties and tools for the smithy. Everything we worked with in Atlanta we had to get from New York or England through Charleston or Savannah. This'll just be a short lick down the railroad line. I couldn't be happier."

"Pa," Will broke in from the back of the wagon. "Can I go with you when you talk to the mill folks? Can I, please? I want to see the inside of a mill. Oh, please!"

"Look over there," Joseph showed Will. "There's a spur railroad line. That's a switching engine that's carrying coal over to the furnace. I bet they bring their coal from up above Chattanooga to smelt the iron, unless there's some in the mountains around."

"I wonder if Ab is getting to see what we're seeing," Will said.

"He's probably got his hands full just guiding the wagon," Joseph said. "You can fill him in on the details when we stop."

"Which one can we see, Pa? Which one? There's so many!"

"We'll go to the rolling mill. They've got iron bars and nails, the sorts of materials we'll use in the smithy."

Joseph and the family's two wagons moved along the riverbank's north side. Workmen wearing clay-stained clothes and pushing carts of every description heaped high with moist, red dirt moved alongside them at about the same pace. They drew nearer the greatest concentration of industry any of the family had ever seen. The air was smoky with soot from the cold and hot blast furnaces lining the creek that ran alongside Cooper's furnace, the large rock furnace fed by the train engine.

Magnificent fires could be seen coming from the chimneys of the furnaces; they seemed to march up a steep hill just above Cooper's. Wood smoke from the little engine fouled the air even more.

"I can't believe how filthy this is, Joseph," Jane said from her seat just behind him. She flicked ashes from her dress and from those of the girls riding with her. "Might we catch on fire from all this ash?"

"I think the fire's out by the time it hits the air," Joseph said. "But it is a bit dirty, isn't it?"

At the rolling mill, while the women and girls stayed in the wagon, Joseph and his sons went inside and inspected the goods at the mill store. They peered inside the mill, where drums pressed heated pig iron made molten again by tremendous fires and shaped the iron into plates and bars. Joseph priced bars and picked up lists of other goods from the mills in the area that he could use in his shops in Tilton.

When they arrived back outside, Jane had gotten herself and the girls down off their wagon perches and was vigorously dusting flour and ash from the girls' bonnets, skirts, and bodices.

"I do hope our new place won't have any of this," she exclaimed. Joseph knew it wasn't friendly banter. Things had been cool between them lately, and it was better to ignore her complaint. He pulled onto the wagon buck seat, waited until all the family members had taken their places, and then shouted at the horses to move on back to the Tennessee Road.

After the river, more hills, many of them gashed with ore mines, returned to challenge the wagon wheels. Then they diminished again as they neared the turnoff to the old Cherokee Indian capital.

When they reached the crossing, Joseph thought of his childhood friend Adam. He was sure that nothing remained of the town, but twenty years before it had been a gathering point for the Cherokee removal. He was sure whites had long ago taken over the buildings, plowed under the Indian's fields, and run off anyone who had even a near ancestor who was Cherokee. Yet Joseph longed to find traces of the young half-breed. Did he make it to the Indian Country? Joseph was sure he'd never know. He pictured Adam—if he survived the deadly removal West—with his own family and bits of gray hair like his.

For the next part of the trip to Tilton they managed small hills in the valley, and then the long ledge of Taylor's Ridge appeared at left. First they saw shorter, rounded mountains forming in wishbone fashion on its southern edge. Then, near Dalton, the ridge spread itself northward, spinning off John's Mountain, Horn Mountain, and Rocky Face, like so much spare cartilage from a backbone. The long ridge, a looming presence alongside the wide valley thrusting toward Tennessee, would stretch all the way to Chattanooga.

The family continued their journey in the valley, while up on the ridge light green-and-brown trees springing new leaves sparkled among dark green pines. There were rows upon rows of light brown, flowering oak trees. Occasionally, there appeared darker green trees that were shorter than the pines, but feathery and cone-shaped. Joseph hadn't seen cedars like these growing since his days in Abbeville District, and he wondered what made the soil here and in his old home give nurture to the ancient trees, while denying them life in Atlanta. Soon he drew his family's attention to a new set of mountains, the Cohuttas, off to the right, far in the distance.

"Fort Mountain," Joseph said to the others, lifting his hands with reins laced through them in the direction of the Cohuttas. A bluff on the western edge of the mountains seemed to be guarding the rest of the hills. "It's said that there are remains there of an ancient fort, but no one knows who built it. They were there before the Cherokees."

As the Morgans approached their destination, the southern end of Whitfield County and the town of Tilton, the blue-gray Cohuttas drew a little nearer. Turning west toward Tilton, Joseph saw the land flatten out again into a broad valley, making easy crossing of a bridge over the Oostenaula River.

"Pa, why do these rivers have such strange names?" Will asked as they crossed. He'd been particularly taken with the Etowah when they'd crossed it back in Bartow County.

"They're names the Cherokees gave to the rivers. I know I've told you about their removal—it was back before you were born."

"You mean this is where they lived? And we're going through their land? Maybe there are some left and they'll come after us!"

Joseph waited to respond to his son's alarm, reminded of his own worries of thirty years ago. "Before you get too excited, Brother Will, remember that the Cherokees inhabited many of the homesteads you've seen on the way up here, and they were very much like white men in their ways. They farmed, raised pigs and cattle, and even grew corn for market as well as for their tables."

"Then why were they sent away?"

"That's a long story, one I'll have to tell you when I don't have to keep an eye on these rutted roads. The whites who forced them to leave belatedly decided to honor them by using the names the Indians gave the land—Ross' Landing became Chattanooga, Hightower became the Etowah once again."

"So that's why it's the Oostenaula River," Will commented. "And Cohutta Mountains, and Coahulla Creek, and Ocoee River, and Tallulah Falls and—"

"Whoa!" Joseph laughed at Will's recitations. "You don't have to list all of them. We know you have a mind for facts."

Will looked at him with the quiet satisfaction of a boy who's mastered a lesson. He probably covered the Cherokee and Creek removals in school, Joseph reflected. He just wanted to see what an old timer like his pa had to say about it.

Another thing Joseph noticed during their long journey north was Jane's silence. She'd lost her mother's and her sister's company as a result of the move, and Joseph knew this made her sad. Her quietness was not stoicism so much as torpor. She took care of the children and her household, but days would go by without her eyes meeting his. As he thought about it, Joseph felt a chill in his body.

Joseph told himself that the move was hardest on Jane, and the adjustment was still going on. They hardly were acting like man and wife, and it was about to drive him to distraction. Once in a while she'd let him near her, but most of the time she was tired. Joseph did not press. She had born him six healthy, bright children in Atlanta, and she deserved a rest. How long a rest, he was not sure. It had been more than two years since the move. It was time to talk to her.

Joseph's mother had warned him not to be too urgent with his needs. Rebecca had cautioned him to give Jane a rest. "Many a man has worn out a good woman," Rebecca had said, listing some of their friends who'd lost wives and mothers due to weaknesses begun with pregnancy and childbirth. In fact, several women they knew in their old city of Atlanta had succumbed during confinement. Even the new doctors—recent graduates of the medical college in Augusta—were helpless when childbed fever or convulsions took over.

"Give Jane time to get used to this change," Rebecca advised. "You know, when you married you were twenty-six—you were a man. Jane was only sixteen, barely a woman and still a girl in many ways. Now you've pulled her away from all her family. A woman relies on her mother all her life for help and friendship—you men folk don't know what a precious tie that is."

"But she's got you and me and all this family—what more does she need?" To Joseph, Jane's needs were inefficient. If what a person required was close at hand, why go looking in distant corners for something more?

Rebecca had given Joseph a look he knew not to argue with, and he said no more. Women are a peculiar lot, he thought, and thick as thieves when they band together. Nevertheless, not to take care of one's wife was like not taking care of one's horse. They were very difficult to replace, so it would not hurt to give her some consideration.

Thus Joseph had decided that his wife's health was more important than his needs. He'd used hard work and constant activity to alleviate his discomfort. As a result, he built a successful business in Tilton, and he was fairly certain he would eventually be able to sell all his holdings in Atlanta—the ten acres downtown, the blacksmith/gunsmith works, and the other parcels. Here in Whitfield County, he was already a large landholder, especially for one who had no field slaves. His industry and prosperity more than compensated for his unfortunate relations with his wife. In fact, at night as he lay next to Jane, he'd learned to calculate in his head the per-lot profits he was making in Atlanta to keep his mind off his needs.

Most men would be proud just to work a trade, Joseph told himself, "and I've got several trades—blacksmithing, guns, woodworking—plus a good deal of land. I've been blessed. Maybe this is the land of milk and honey after all." It thrilled Joseph to think that they may have found their final home. Maybe the questions he'd had when he buried his father would go away. Surely, there was so much opportunity here that no one could fail to do well, unless he didn't want to work. There was fertile land drained by powerful rivers. The terrain was flat in some places, wild and rolling in others, providing great bounties of game.

The railroad brought in new people and goods from the West and from the coast. Their frequency caused the table at his inn to swell with visitors, each of whom paid by the night and by the meal. Travelers by road paid not only for their board, but for boarding their horses as well. He'd rented his father's brick home when they'd lived in Atlanta and had found it a fair way to supplement a living. Keeping the inn here was a splendid occupation for his younger daughters. Everybody who was able worked from an early age in the Morgan family, and that pleased Joseph immensely.

Now, still watering his horse at the spring by the Dalton road, Joseph gazed at the water splashing down the side of the hill. It wound down to the pool in a crooked path broken by rocks and worn, soft boulders. The obstacles forced the stream to detour back and forth, crashing into moss-covered, smooth river rock, then ricocheting to the other side, where it encountered large, angled pieces of limestone, then splashed back.

Like a shining ribbon jostled by hunchbacked men in a gauntlet, it zigzagged, sending up fine sprays of water that misted the delicate ferns tucked into rocks. The ferns' fronds were an intense light green against the dark rocks, and they fell in larger and larger layers like a lady's hair undone.

How much of this life-giving water ran down hills and through broad fields here in the mountains! It reminded Joseph of the passage in Exodus when Moses led the Israelites out of Egypt and into the desert. The Jews were grumbling in discontent, yearning for their former home. God ordered Moses to use his rod to strike a big rock, and a great stream of water came gushing forth. Moses named the place Massah and Meribah to commemorate the Israelites' doubt of their god.

He hadn't seen anyone smite a rock, yet there were cascades all over the valley, feeding into the Conasauga, or the Oostenaula, or the Etowah, all large rivers less than a short day's horse ride from his home. He imagined when the first whites had arrived here they thought the same as he, that this was the wellspring of all the rivers in three states.

How many baptisms had taken place in these rivers? Not enough, Joseph was sure. The sinfulness that drove them from Atlanta also existed here.

"Whosoever drinketh of the water that I shall give him shall never thirst; but the water that I shall give him shall be in him a well of water springing up into everlasting life." That passage from John's gospel describing Jesus' encounter with the Samaritan woman at the well. She was so amazed at Christ's knowledge of her five former husbands and current one that she went to tell others of the Messiah's presence at the well. He promised her that those who believed in Him would have water forever. What better sign was there for Joseph that his and his family's faith had been justified than the home they had found? There was fertile land to farm, so they didn't go hungry. The railroad brought enough travelers to the inn to provide for his family. And the valley and its surrounding mountains were filled with rocks and rills of water, each gaining more speed as they plummeted down toward the deep rivers. Along the way, they supplied plenteous water for the forge, as well as for animals and fields.

Rains filled the valley frequently in the spring, falling down from low clouds whose weight could almost be felt. The rains soaked the fields, filtering down to enormous beds of water that underlay much of the land.

Wherever wells were dug, they yielded more of the wet vitality. To the northwest, the mountains near Chattanooga and the Alabama border were riddled with limestone caves with huge waterfalls, the result of water filtering through the mountains. If there were deserts out west, Joseph felt sure he could supply them all with just a spring rain's yield in the valley here between the mountains. The pure, sweet, rock-kissed water tasted as the wine must have tasted to the wedding guests at Cana.

Here was the proof of the home they have been looking for. The children were thriving, the four oldest attending school. They would be better off with tutors like Gideon's boys, perhaps, but they were smart enough. Ab at fifteen—almost a man—was astounding all with his love of the classics and could easily learn Latin if he had a teacher. Will, who seemed to have been born with a hammer in his hand, grew more helpful in the forge every day, picking up the mechanics as though—Joseph smiled here—he were born to it. Susan and Alice Jane, at twelve and eight, were helpful assistants at the table in the inn. They were learning skills they'd need to manage a useful household. Before long, it would be time to begin considering some suitable mates for them. Gilbert and Catherine were too young to be much help, but Alice Jane was giving her little brother some lessons in hog slopping. He might be slight, but he was going to be sharp, once he got the hang of the pigpen.

Joseph bent down beside his horse and took another drink of the delicious water and nudged his horse to drink before they got back on the Dalton Road. Was there a better sign that God was pleased with his family than the health they enjoyed? All normal births, assisted by a doctor? Here, without such help, it would be more difficult to guarantee a healthy birth, but Jane had borne so many she'd proved her ability to withstand the dangers of childbirth. And, praise God, Rebecca was enjoying a long life and looked as though she might assist in a few more Morgans coming into the world. She'd just passed the three-quarters of a century mark and looked like she might go on for still many more years.

Joseph got back on his horse and urged his mount towards Tilton. If long life, good health, and moderate prosperity were signs of God working in their lives, he mused, then they were on the right path.

There was a grayish-blue haze lying over the land, a land that dipped and rose, then dipped and rose again around creeks and rivulets forcing their way down brown hills, following deep creeks carved out of the countryside. Joseph drove the carriage and his wife snuggled into a large bearskin robe, hiding from the cold December air. His oldest two boys grabbed the edges of the skin over themselves, but finding it not enough to cover them, stuffed their hands deep into the pockets of their homespun jackets and huddled low, with Will next to his mother. The carriage approached the high ridge that formed the crest of a high peninsula above the two lengths of river that bent like a hairpin around Gideon's lands. As they mounted the ridge, they turned right in the direction of the bend, which lay two miles farther down the peninsula.

The bare trees along the road to Gideon's plantation stood in black-laced contrast to the wall of gray winter skies rising up on either side of them. It was Christmas Day, and they were on their way to the celebration that was becoming an annual tradition in the area, the day when Gideon entertained in his large home, enjoying the envy of neighbors, as well as that of his brother.

The land on either side of them fell gracefully away towards the river. The swift, deep green Conasauga was hidden by hardwoods and cedars that lined the riverbanks. Dark, black-soiled fields stretched down to the trees by the river, announcing rich yields of corn and cotton, valuable bounties that fell into the owner's hands with the mere planting of seed in soil.

Joseph passed a barn on the left side of the road, flanked by two slave cabins that faced towards the barn. Every time he saw the rough cabins, Joseph thought back to when Gideon began acquiring slaves. He'd bought the blacks from the Boston slaver who'd taken up near the Huff house in Atlanta. Gideon had actually bragged about how big his men were and how long he could keep the women working in the fields up to childbirth and how he had them back in the fields not long after.

When Gideon moved to his Conasauga River land, Joseph reckoned that having Carter's Quarters across the river for a neighbor dazzled Gideon into thinking he was a big timer like Farish Carter. The man had a couple thousand slaves on his place down in Milledgeville, a number unheard of in north Georgia. He kept three hundred on his land here, which stretched from the Conasauga River to the Coosawattee—a huge plantation covering twenty-five square miles. Steamboats carried his many products from the landing there at the beginning of the Coosawattee, down to where it joined the Conasauga to form the Oostenaula River, clear to the Gulf, by way of Rome and Montgomery and Selma. So Gideon got to hobnob with the finest here, at least during the summers when Farish and his chattel escaped the malarial miasma of South Georgia.

Dusk became dark as they traveled a short distance, then turned left down a rough lane that ended in an open gate at Gideon's plantation house. The house rose up out of a small forest, its entry lit with lamps on the exterior and with light from nine-over-nine windows within. Oil lamps in abundance made a daylight brightness that filled the rooms and fell on the driveway outside, where a few carriages and many farm wagons pulled by horses stood.

An impressive structure that imitated Greek style with white lapped boarding and black shutters at the sides of the large windows greeted the visitors. Medium sized cedars, transplanted to ward off mosquitoes in summer, flanked either side of the front entrance. The house was coated, not with the lowly whitewash that was the greatest improvement most folks in this area aspired to, but with pigment paint. Four sparkling white cylindrical columns completed the effect.

It was the grandest house in three counties, Joseph thought. Only the mansion at Spring Place and the big house at Carter's Quarters could claim greater notice. He acknowledged a flash of envy that had taken hold in his stomach and now seemed about to consume him.

A high roof with windows on either end signaled a second floor. Gideon's boys, James and Neil, each had half of the upper floor for their own. Joseph couldn't imagine such luxury. He'd grown up sleeping in the same bed with Gideon during his younger years. His sisters doubled up in beds, several to a room, for most of their lives. Even now, five of his children were spread between two rooms on the first floor of the inn, so paying guests could sleep in the upper four rooms. The sixth slept in a trundle at the foot of their bed.

But at least his family always had food to eat and a roof over its head, Joseph thought, in the face of his brother's obvious riches. He continued looking at the house, which he'd seen on previous visits, but not in such holiday dress.

Joseph snorted as he saw the elaborately trimmed front doorway festooned with pine ropes and topped by a wreath with fruit stuck in the greens. "Christmas decorations worthy of an English lord," he said to no one in particular. "I can remember when folks wouldn't of been caught dead celebrating Christmas like the pope," Joseph growled. "What d'you suppose happened to people's just quietly visiting abroad on Christmas Day and wishing each other goodwill?"

"Times have changed," Jane said through the fur of the bear blanket brushing her face. "Folks are following the new English custom. Queen Victoria—"

"The Queen and her German husband," snorted Joseph. "I think our own customs of keeping the back stick burning and observing the day with feasting and visiting are celebration enough. Next you know we'll all be worshipping trees with candles on 'em and burning down houses with the lighting of one taper."

"I didn't know you were a seer, husband," Jane teased him lightly. "Indeed, I've heard some of the more splendid plantation homes along the Mississippi do feature a decorated tree."

"Humph," said Joseph.

"Now, dear, don't be getting into a foul temper at Christmas—this of all times! We're supposed to have a Christian spirit of charity." Jane quickly sat up, letting the animal skin robe fall from her. "Oh, look," she cried. "There're our neighbors—the Brewsters and the Hogans. Joseph, let's do be bright. It will be so good to see them."

While Jane was speaking, Joseph was bothered by a sound Ab was making, mumbling to his brother. Now Ab let out a loud snicker. Joseph started to correct his son, but decided to let the gesture go unremarked. No doubt the excitement of seeing his cousins brought on a fit of the giggles, he thought.

As they stepped down from the carriage, a black servant shivering in a black broadcloth coat with threadbare elbows took the reins of their horses and guided the horses and carriage to the side of the crowded drive. They joined their neighbors, some of whom they knew, some not, and approached the large house. They exchanged greetings with the Brewsters and Hogans—John Hogan was the stationmaster in Tilton—and went inside.

They entered a large hallway with shiny heart pine floors, above which rose a winding staircase featuring a fancy newel post and an elaborate walnut railing. Before it turned back on itself up to the second floor, the stairway gave way to a wide landing that held a quartet of musicians—fiddles and flutes—that was providing lilting tunes.

On the left, a parlor held many guests, including several men dressed in black suits and more countrified men in homespun coats. Standing separate from the men in small clusters, the ladies wore everything from silk to plaid cotton dresses, and most had brought out their widest crinolines and hoops. Children, under the partial watch of elders, slipped through the hallways and sometimes behind bell-shaped skirts, playing surreptitious games of tag.

"Oh, my goodness, Joseph," Jane said, placing her hand in the crook of his arm. "Look at the feast of food!"

On the right, double doors opened into a dining room where they saw a table large enough to seat a dozen people displaying a bank of browned fowls—turkey, pigeon, and quail—as well as roasts of bear, venison, beef, and pork. A monstrous ham was the centerpiece, and interspersed around it were dishes of mashed squashes and pumpkins, field peas, sauerkraut, and white turnips, as well as several plates of pickles.

On the wall farthest from them, a large oval mirror with a gilt frame doubled the visual effect of the bounty in front of them. A hunt board beneath the mirror held roasted pumpkin halves drizzled with butter, a large pot of honey, and pies with crusts that rose half a foot high. Yellow-brown Indian corncakes and pale biscuits decorated the rest of the board. The house smelled of apples and cinnamon, pumpkin, turkey, and ham.

"My, those apple pies," Jane said. "Josephine must have had to lay out as many sheets as we have beds to dry those apples. We must find our hosts to congratulate them on this feast! Boys—"

She turned around to find Ab and Will, but they were long gone.

"Well, I guess we'll see them about the time we leave," Jane laughed.

"Let's try the parlor," Joseph said. "No doubt they're serving the syllabub there."

They moved to the parlor and found Gideon ladling the frothy syllabub into stemmed earthenware goblets.

"Greetings, folks," he called.

Joseph took a cup and grabbed his brother's hand in response to Gideon's welcome. He turned to Jane to offer her one, but saw her staring across the room at Josephine.

"What're you lookin' at?" he asked.

Jane turned back.

"Oh, nothing. Let me have a sip of that sinful concoction so I can say I've tasted it, at least."

"Well, just don't taste it," Gideon boomed. "You'll want a lot more once you've had it."

"This is a real swell occasion," Joseph said. "You've laid a feast the county will talk about for months."

"Just one of the benefits of doing well, my brother. Just one of the benefits." He turned to another guest, dismissing Joseph and Jane.

"What were you staring at, Jane?" Joseph asked when they were by themselves in a corner. "You're usually more polite."

"I am shocked. Look how thin Josephine is. She's dropped weight since I saw her a fortnight ago. And her eyes look odd."

"I'm sure you're imagining things. I swan, you women spy on each other to make these uncharitable comparisons."

"Let's go talk to her, Joseph," Jane said, ignoring his comment. "I'd like to see her more closely, and we must pay our respects."

They moved to where Josephine was talking to their relations, the Carrolls.

"Hello, sister!" Joseph greeted his sister, Anne. His sister had married Franklin Carroll and moved to Dalton after he and Jane married.

"Brother!" Anne, looking lovely in a dark blue silk dress with a lace trimmed collar, hugged Joseph. "It's been so long. It's so good to see you both, and so good to have you near us. Where are your boys? Have they discovered ours yet? They're close in age, not too much older than yours, so they're probably following each other around."

"I'm sure we'll catch up to them all eventually," Jane said, hugging her sister-in-law. "We'll make sure they greet you. You're looking fetching. Motherhood definitely agrees with you, I think."

Jane turned to greet Josephine, who stood waiting for the exchanges to end. She stiffly hugged Josephine, who wore a pale pink silk ball gown, the color of which was almost indistinguishable from that of her drawn skin. Joseph briefly hugged her also and saw why Jane thought her eyes looked odd. She had applied a thin layer of wax underneath her eyes and covered that with cornstarch.

"Thank you for your invitation, Josephine," Joseph told his sister-in-law politely. Inside, he felt uncomfortable. What was she hiding?

"You're most welcome, Brother Joe," Josephine said. Joseph thought she sounded nervous.

The quartet on the landing in the stairway struck up a waltz. Joseph noticed couples dancing in the hallway and saw a chance to escape from present company, as well as to hold his wife close. He bent and formally took her gloved hand.

"May I have this dance, madam?" he asked. Jane looked at him, her eyes friendly.

"Of course, you may," she said, with an edge of coquetry in her voice. "We'll gather up all our boys and make sure you see them in just a few minutes," she said over her shoulder to Anne. Joseph led her to the hallway.

Joseph held Jane in his arms and smelled the fragrance of lilacs coming from her hair. As he stepped so carefully, trying to remember the count of the step he hadn't done for many years, he remembered their first dance. That night she surprised him with the way she'd grown and changed, and with her sympathetic comments about his friend Adam, so uncharacteristic for a young girl of the time.

So much had happened in the years since they met, back before Atlanta was a town. They'd courted, married, had the two boys, then Susan, finally escaped Tom Cunningham, and soon after had Alice Jane. Then they'd had Gilbert and Catherine, and buried his father. Now they'd moved to Whitfield County. After nearly three years, Jane was still angry with him.

Tonight she was friendlier. There was a lightness in her manner, a waning of the stiffness he often experienced with her in the time since the move. Maybe it was the Christmas spirit. She was actually delightful this evening.

He pressed her to him, almost succeeding in pressing her breasts to his lower chest, but she gently resisted. Her back was still rigid. How he wanted her to unfreeze!

"Careful, Mr. Morgan," she said with a slight smile. "You'll be causing a scandal here if you pull me too close."

"Sorry, ma'am, I was just recalling some wonderful moments we had with musicians playing—and some not set to music as well—"

Joseph guided Jane past the front door in the enormous front hallway. As he did so, a loud noise arose outside. He heard Ab's excited voice and those of James and Neil together out on the entrance drive. He heard carriage wheels rumbling and the protests of a black servant.

"Let's step outside," he said to Jane. Then looking at her small figure, he said, "No, maybe you'd best stay back so you won't get cold."

He opened the door to pandemonium. The servant was trying to pull a team of horses towards him to stop a large, shiny barouche driven by James and carrying Neil, Ab, and Richard, his Carroll cousin.

"Aw, Cicero," James cried. "Leave us be. We're just trying it out for a ride. No one cares."

"Naw, Mast'," Cicero objected, shaking his head and looking down. "That there cherot's in my charge, an' I'm not lettin' you ride like a fury and risk bustin' a wheel—"

"James!" Joseph called. "Y'all come on down from there. That's not your carriage, and no one's given you permission to take it. Do what Cicero says."

James glowered at Joseph.

"You don't tell me what to do!" he exploded. "That nigger don't tell me what to do! I'm in charge here. I've got the horses under control."

One of the horses whinnied and tried to pull away from Cicero. Joseph walked over, grabbed the reins, and yanked them out of James' hands.

"Now, stop. What you're doing is unsafe. We'll go ask your father if it's all right if you take away a guest's carriage. Come on down."

James climbed down in a huff, Neil after him. Ab was quiet, looking down at his feet. Richard also sat silently. Joseph tried to gather his composure and think of what to say to his son and nephew. Taking the carriage was the height of tomfoolery, and Joseph was at a loss. What had gotten into these boys? Ab, he could see, was giving him a sidelong glance. Richard, too, was waiting for chastisement.

"You're still not too big, Ab, for me to take a strap to you," Joseph said, recalling his own father's administration of punishment in the blacksmith's shop when he was fifteen. "And, Richard, I know your father would be very upset to see you right now." Both sets of eyes looked at him, widening.

"But I'm going to consider that you've probably had time to think over your folly. I'd like to know what you're going to do next time your cousins tempt you with something you know is wrong."

Richard was first to speak. "I'm sorry, Uncle Joe, they told us the owners had approved—they said they were free to take it for a ride," the young man raced his words.

"Yeah, they were given permission, they said," Ab jumped in. "They lied to us. We can't help that, Pa!"

"Young man," Joseph said hotly, angry that they were taking advantage of his leniency. Had it been William, he would have had him over his knee without a moment's hesitation, letting the lesson be taught the old fashioned way. "I want you to answer for your own transgressions, not your cousins'! What are you going to do next time your cousins want to do something that might not be right?"

Ab sunk back in his seat some more.

"I'll ask more questions," he said quietly.

"That's better. Now the two of you go on. Try to stay clear of those other two and their trouble."

That spring, Joseph, Ab and Will tramped through bramble up to their knees as they climbed the hill above a flat expanse of land bordering the Conasauga River. There were blackberry bushes sporting white blossoms and fragrant clusters of pink wild honeysuckle growing among the riot of dense greenery that grabbed at their legs. Robins, vireos, and mockingbirds in full song gloried in the April air in the ridges above the deep river. The *thonk-thonk-thonkthonkthonkthonk* of a grouse beating its wings in a prayer for a mate resounded through the lower lands near the water. At that point the Conasauga flowed straight west, returning from one of its many bends around the green hills. Stands of hickory trees with trunks as wide as wheels grew in the flats near the water, but the attention of the Morgan men was clearly on the hill above them.

"Where are the fattest squirrels and rabbits?" Ab asked his father.

"Anywhere up here near the crest of the hill," Joseph answered.

"Why do we have to go so far?" asked Will.

"Because," Joseph stopped and leaned on his rifle, glad to have a moment to recover from the steep climb. "Miriam said she wants something other than pork. She said that if we made the move all the way up here from Atlanta, and then I bought the old inn, giving her even more mouths to feed, then we ought to be able to give her something other than fowl or pig for her skillet," explained Joseph. "So we're going to find her the biggest rabbits and squirrels and maybe even a turkey or two, and she'll not complain again about having the same foods to fix."

"Well, back home in Atlanta we could hunt without having to climb so many hills," observed his second son.

"You're right, but the hunting's better here. You'll see."

Joseph was delighting in the spring air, so welcome after a rainy winter that seemed never to end. He knew a cold snap would probably come before true spring, but the gloriousness of the day was all that was on his mind today. That and the fact that he was finally getting to hunt with his sons as he'd pictured them—combing the hills above the river on a day like today, him showing them hunting skills, using small game as targets. And of course bringing home some excellent eating.

On this cool morning, he was anticipating coaching his boys in the art of shooting straight and sure. They were trampling up a hill on Joseph's property on the west and north side of the Conasauga, the original hundred acres he'd put together for their move from Atlanta. Gideon's eight hundred fertile acres were just east of where they walked.

On a ridge to their right rose a huge tree that dwarfed all the others with its girth and expansive halo of long limbs, many the width of a man's trunk. He could almost feel the rough, fissured bark that ran in long rivulets down the tremendous length of the tree. Other trees seemed to keep their distance, letting this one have its way. Joseph figured its crown must reach eighty feet across, and its trunk was probably twenty feet around. If he, Ab, and Will ringed themselves around it, they couldn't touch hands.

Joseph lusted after the magnificent tree. He judged its height to be thirty or forty feet, and its butt cut to be at least twenty. The wood would have such a fine, smooth surface when cut that it would yield lumber that scarcely needed dressing. The finished lumber would make furniture that would last a lifetime, and, for the lucky man able to work enough trees down to make a homestead, a secure fortress for himself, his son, and his son's son and their families.

Joseph knew that the fruit would lie on the ground less plentifully than acorns or hickory nuts. They'd have to tread watchfully to locate the pods, for to fall on one would be like encountering a small porcupine. But the surprise of finding several nuts in a single burst of the prickly needle-bearing pod would be worth tearing through the outer shell.

The father wanted to show his sons the magnificent chestnut tree. He knew Will wouldn't stop until he'd stuffed his coat and game sack with the pods and then grilled his old man about the wood and what he could and could not make with it. But that would delay their hunting for meat, and they'd best not dilly-dally. Besides, the nuts on the ground –if the deer and bears had left any from the previous fall's orgy of eating—would be rotted now. Better to wait until September, just after summer and just before time to don shoes again. It would still be warm enough for going barefoot in early September, but it wasn't smart to do it around a chestnut. There was no hollering like a youngster landing an unclad foot on a chestnut spike.

Fifteen-year-old Ab broke his father's reverie by striding past him on his long legs, taking the lead. Then he stopped suddenly, almost making Joseph run into him. The youth pulled out a primer cap to put in his rifle. He held up his hand to the others and mouthed the warning, "Don't move."

Joseph watched closely as Ab, in one sure motion, brought up his rifle and aimed it for a large oak tree just above them on the hill. Several squirrels, excited by the crop of young buds, were running about the tree, including one that headed down the massive trunk. Ab sighted and shot it.

"I got him!" Ab whooped.

"Well done, Ab," said his father. "I didn't even have to caution you to take your time with your aim. You did well, Son. Go see what you got."

Ab pushed ahead through the dense brush, arriving moments later to hold up a very fat squirrel.

"Good for you, Ab," shouted Will. "I'll get the next one!"

Joseph's felt a warmth on his cheeks as he watched his son take giant steps through the bramble towards them, holding his prize high over his head. Heat spread across his face and he belatedly recognized a feeling of pride welling in his body for his son's skill.

Joseph looked down at the ground. His sons continued to talk as they followed behind him, but Joseph stopped abruptly and looked closer. There in the groundcover of blackberry bushes, thick grasses, and oak flowers was a deep depression, like the trace of a man's foot in the heavy brush. He saw more openings in the thick bramble further up and signs of two legs dragging over the ground in between the holes. Next to these, on the right, the grass lay down like a companion of the larger animal had parted it. Joseph knew they were upon a bear and her cubs.

Then he saw her. She was pushing a young cub up a shaggy-barked hickory tree just up the hill from them, about twenty yards away. Ab's rifle shot and their noisy celebration had interrupted her outing, and she'd sprung into action to protect them. She probably has another cub, Joseph thought, but he couldn't see it for the bramble. He knew he had to act quickly to protect the boys and himself.

"Quick!" he whispered, holding up his hand. "It's a bear, and she'll turn on us in a flash—run for the nearest tree! Hold onto your rifles and prepare to fire!" He urged Ab and Will toward two tall pines with low limbs, near enough on the left for them to reach quickly. Between the pines and the hickory, Joseph spied a black locust, also on the left.

Each boy climbed a pine tree and disappeared. Joseph climbed his own slender, towering hardwood, praying for safety, hoping they would all escape the bear's reach. The boys' trees would provide a lofty refuge. The bear would avoid trying to scale such a tall, narrow trunk. Joseph thought himself as safe as could be in his own perch, though he knew he was a better target than the boys.

A sharp pain pierced his chest, and, for what seemed like minutes, he could not breathe. He let out a soft moan to get relief. Joseph recalled having the sharp, vise-like catch in his chest before and reminded himself not to fight it, but to take very slow breaths. Each time he pulled in air,

Joseph feared the pain would return. During the first few breaths, the cutting pain gripped his left side, and then came no more.

With the pain gone, Joseph thought again about his sons. He'd coached them to never make a sound when trying to escape a wild animal, so he knew they would remain quiet and not draw the bear's attention. He wanted to spare them the fright they must be experiencing now, but he could do nothing. Peering through the thin limbs of the tree, about ten yards from the mother bear, he saw her urge the second cub into the hickory tree with its sibling. Here we are, both trying to protect our young from each other, Joseph thought. The similarity of his and the bear's quests struck Joseph, and for a moment he imagined talking to the bear as he'd heard wild mountain men could do. Some fancy dream, he told himself. What would he do if the bear came closer?

While straddling a high limb in the locust, Joseph pulled on the strap holding his rifle and moved it to his hands. He slowly loaded a charge, rammed it in, then placed a cap on the nipple. He took careful aim as he placed his finger on the trigger. He wanted to be ready if the bear should attack.

He heard scratching and bark falling to the ground next to him. Was another bear climbing the tree? Then he saw that it was Will shifting his body in the next tree that caused the noise. Joseph hoped the bear didn't hear. He'd seen bears climb trees before, quick as lighting in a late summer storm. Joseph estimated this one was at least three years old, and she was the biggest he'd ever seen, probably about three hundred pounds.

Now her cubs were up off the ground, and she was coming toward his tree! The mother loped scrambled to the tree, reaching the ground beneath him in no time. Joseph was frozen. He had to shoot her. If he didn't, and she climbed the tree, she could tear his throat out. If he shot her and missed, she'd take him out, and then she'd go after the boys.

Birds shouted their alarm all around Joseph, blue jays changing their songs to screams. *Skeer! Skeer!* Loud calls from the others filled the trees. Joseph felt the peril in his stomach, which tried to throw up his heavy breakfast of biscuits and bacon.

The bear was clawing the bark of the locust. Joseph could see splinters falling away from her mighty paws, but he couldn't see well enough to get good aim. He'd told himself the bear wouldn't try to climb such a thin tree—it was only a couple feet wide and hardly bore his own weight.

Then he thought of a plan. If it was going to work, his boys would have to hear him and do what he said immediately, or they would lose precious time, moments the she-bear could put to advantage.

"Ab! Get set to throw the squirrel as far as you can—up the hill away from us. See if she goes for the bait. Then get down out of the tree." Sweat poured down Joseph's face.

"Will, get to the lowest limb right now and if she runs for the bait, jump down the hill and run for your life towards the river. I'll follow and cover."

Ab wound up his throwing arm and hurled the carcass a good fifty feet up the hill. The bear, following her fine sense of smell, ran in the direction of the bait before it hit the ground. Joseph slid down the tree so fast he felt his chest skin burning. He followed Ab and Will as they lit out for the hickory flats near the river. Joseph kept turning back to make sure the bear was staying behind and urged his boys on.

"Hurry!" he yelled. "I'll keep and eye on her, you just run!"

Joseph reached the wagon just after his boys. They jumped inside. Joseph unhitched the horse from a log, then jumped into the seat. He hollered at the mare to move, thrashing her with the reins. He felt his heart's throbbing beats in his bark-burned chest as they pulled out and fled down the road towards home.

"What's happened to you?" Jane asked, looking into Ab's face as they entered the back hallway at the inn. Ab was exactly her height now and Will a little shorter, but they quickly came to attention as she stopped them. Both were sweating heavily, and their cheeks burned from excitement.

"We came upon a bear and her cubs out on our hunt," Joseph said, coming up behind them after tying up the wagon.

"We had to climb trees to get away from her," exclaimed Ab, his blue eyes excited. "She was after us because she thought we wanted to get her cubs!"

"Ab threw her a squirrel he shot, and we got clean away!" Will said. "Pa covered us and we ran like blazes."

Jane looked briefly at Joseph, who stood with his rifle pointed down in the crook of his elbow, then reached up to brush Ab's sandy hair back from his face.

"Well, I'm glad you're all right. You gave me a scare the way you both looked so tuckered out. Go on and wash up for dinner. Miriam will have it on very soon."

"Miriam'll be mad we didn't bring her a turkey," Will jabbered excitedly. "But we had this bear after us!" Will's blue eyes were wide from the thrill.

"I'm sure she'll understand if you tell her what happened," Jane said. Despite her light response to Will, she looked worried.

"Rebecca's in the parlor quilting, else we could go in there and talk quietly," Jane said to Joseph, her lower tones a sharp contrast to her son's voices. "But I'd like to know what happened. Why did you let the boys get so close to a she-bear? You know how dangerous that is!"

Joseph felt his back stiffen at being scolded by his wife. Since the party at Gideon's he'd thought there'd been a thaw in the frost. Now, he wasn't so sure.

"I didn't let them get close on purpose," he said with quiet anger. "I was leading them up the hill near Hickory Flats Road and I saw her tracks. It was just after Ab had shot a squirrel. She hurried away with her babies like she didn't want to be any closer to us than we did to her. So I got the boys into separate trees and they were well away from her. I was covering them, but I was scared, too."

"What did you do?"

"She came for me." Joseph saw Jane's eyes grow large, so he knew he had her attention. He decided to give her more detail. Was she worried about him? Did Jane still love him?

"She was clawing at the tree and I was about to shoot her," he related, "but I couldn't see her clearly enough. So I yelled at Ab to throw his prize away up the hill, and that attracted the bear. She took off and then we did, too, in the opposite direction. Fortunately, Ab threw the squirrel far enough that we had time to escape. Thank God for that boy's throwing arm."

Jane was all excited, he could tell. Was it possible she still cared for him like she used to? Could they pierce the bitterness that had invaded their marriage like a troublesome boil? Was it possible he'd have her back in his arms soon? There was but one thing that kept this move from being the fulfillment of his dreams. He missed his wife.

Tears lined Jane's eyes. "All of you could have been killed or hurt, especially you, Joseph." She went to him. He grabbed her to him with one arm and laid down his rifle on a hallway table with the other.

Both his arms encircled her thin shoulders and held on tight. He said nothing for a while. It felt good just to have her in his arms, fully there for the first time in a long time. Jane's chest shuddered with sobs, and Joseph hugged her closer.

"I've missed you," he said hoarsely. "And I'm glad nothing happened out there.

"When I die," he said pulling away from her and lifting her chin so he could see her better, "I want you with me, I don't want to die in the wilds at the hands of some crazed she-bear who thinks I'm after her babies!"

Jane sniffed tears back and nodded her head.

He smiled at her. "I'm learning not to make a woman mad," he joked. "They can make it real rough on you if you do."

"Joseph, I'm sorry," Jane said, looking up at him, tears making a path down her face. "I've been under so much strain. The thought of having another child really frightened me. I just didn't think I could handle another. Please forgive me."

So that was it. After a while, he'd guessed that was the reason for the long, cold spell. But it was over.

Joseph stood with his wife in his arms and thought about holding her at night. He sighed deeply. He felt calm for the first time that day.

"Dinner's on!" Daughter Susan appeared in the doorway to the dining room, a long white apron over her blue chambray dress. Jane pulled out a handkerchief she kept tucked up her under sleeve and dried her cheeks. Her eyes showed relief and their characteristic sparkle. She placed her small hand under Joseph's left forearm.

Joseph still felt the warmth and the touch of Jane's body pressed into his lower chest as he moved with her into the dining room. She had aroused in him an old feeling, a delicious freshet of power. But it was more than physical. He felt joy as he thought about a physical and spiritual reunion with his wife, a return to the delights and satisfactions among the bedclothes, and the many points of every day where their lives overlaid each other like the cedar shingles on the roof. He missed the soft touches to his shoulder as she passed his chair at dinner. And he wanted to roam these majestic hills with her—just the two of them. Take her in the wagon down to the steep banks of the Conasauga where the ridges full of thick hardwoods suddenly dropped to the river, that wide and swift expanse of gray, brown, and green water. In his mind he held her tightly by the waist as they climbed along the river bank, wondering together at the swift, high water coursing down the channel from the mountains and covering the limbs and trunks of trees growing on its steep sides.

Each time Joseph crossed the old bridge over the Conasauga, he was reminded of stories Adam had told him about how the mountains were formed. The Cherokees said that the Great Eagle flew over the land, and where it dipped its wings, mountains were formed from the impact. Joseph decided this land attracted a host of eagles, and they must have dropped their wings sharply because the ridges all around were so steep.

Now, as he entered the dining room with Jane on his arm, Joseph smelled the fulsome odor of lima beans and squash. He saw bowls filled with their buttery green and yellow mass in front of his place at the head of the table, their steam rising like the locomotive's exhaust standing trackside at the Tilton Depot. A large plate of ham was balanced with two bowls of biscuits.

He guided Jane to her seat on his left. Ranged around the table were an assortment of train passengers, engine workmen, Joseph's two older sons, his mother, and a couple of road travelers. Joseph guessed they were journeying by wagon or horse, judging by the light film of clay dust settled in the folds of the men's flannel shirts. Those from the train had a thin layer of soot on their garments. All had fresh-washed faces from cleaning up before dinner.

Joseph heard bits of phrases that were the telltale sign of a foreigner, probably one of the railroad passengers. It was an Irish brogue, a sound not frequently heard in these parts now that the railroad construction gangs had moved on. There were Irishmen who remained in the area—Joseph knew of at least two blacksmiths. Their accents quickly softened as they sought to blend their native up and down rhythms with the flat broad tones of the neighborhood. Joseph liked listening to their brogue, difficult as it was to understand, because it reminded him of music. It was closer to song than speech, Joseph thought.

"It's truly a pot about to boil over," the Irishman was saying to the train conductor. "The whole bloody place—full of shanty Irish and the streets teemin' with their children and kin. Can't find lodgings like this, where you can have all the people at dinner at once and not have folks standin' up eatin' in the hallway and such."

"Are you referrin' to your countrymen?" Joseph asked as he pulled out his chair and sat down.

"Yes, sir. I'm talkin' about the ones in New York and Boston an' every other city in the North. Now I've nothin' against my fellow countrymen. There's just so many of 'em. And they're the wrong sort—papists, you know. And poor farmers who don't know their way around a privy."

"Goodness," Rebecca gasped at the end of the table. "Could we please talk about more pleasant things?"

"Beg your pardon, Mum," the Irishman gushed. "Hope I didn't offend. But what I was saying was these folks have come over on boats by the thousands and it's unsettling to a lot of decent folks such as myself."

"There's no question the numbers are swelling the cities of the north," Joseph responded. "In fact they're pouring into factories and providing the manpower for manufacturing such as the world has never seen."

"Right you are, sir," said the visitor, proud of his knowledge. "It's the American system of manufacture—we had demonstrations of it in London, sir, at the opening of the Crystal Palace, and it was most impressive! But there's so much squalor—fathers and mothers working twelve to fourteen hours a day in those factories. Children left with no one to mind 'em. And the tragedies—one mick last week got his head blown off by a boiler on a steamship, another was horribly crippled by machinery at a woolen mills, then there was another son of Erin drowned in a bleach vat at a paper mill. Of course, each leaves a houseful of children."

"It sounds like it's worse for the Irish than for our people," said Ab, pointing the tip of his fork at the visitor. "Northerners claim they're abused and held captive,"

"Ahem. Well, yes, it 'tis—it's probably the same," the Irishman said, glancing around nervously to see if Miriam was in earshot.

"That's okay, you can talk," said Ab. "We do it all the time." Joseph looked up, surprised at his son's glib tongue.

"I-I don't know much about your business," the Irishman said, sounding like he wanted to get out of the conversation he'd led with such enthusiasm. He pushed his arm out to grab the lima beans.

"We're glad to talk about it," said Ab. "My uncle has a plantation full of slaves." Joseph felt his face flush in anger. Owning slaves was one thing. Being proud of it was another.

"Our housekeeper is a slave," Ab went on. "She's a lot different. Miriam's smart. Gideon's slaves are stupid."

Joseph was appalled. Where had he been getting these notions? "Ab!" Joseph hit his knife handle hard on the table. "That's enough!"

There was quiet at the table after Joseph's burst of anger, and Ab looked down at his plate and quietly lifted his fork to pick at his vegetables. Joseph felt rage melt from his face and sought a way to put peace back in the conversation. What was the world coming to that he'd get so angry that he'd lash out at Ab in front of a dozen people?

"Who's been kind enough to leave us the *New York Tribune* on the hall table?" Joseph asked, trying to renew the conversation. "We do appreciate getting it."

"I did that," said the train conductor, whom Joseph knew as Banks. "Thought you might like to see what's going on in the big metropolis. I'm able to pick it up in Atlanta off the train from Savannah. It's a might bigger than the papers we have."

"Indeed," said Joseph. "And it carries a heap more news from Washington and the North. This Horace Greeley person really is settin' the woods on fire with his scribblings!" Joseph grabbed at anything to take his and his guests' mind off his outburst and the conversation that brought it on. He knew that mentioning New York papers would get everyone talking because they were always full of half-truths, outlandish statements, and livid prose very clearly pointing fingers at a dozing South, out of step with the rest of the country.

The Southerners at the table roughly dismissed any news from a Northern newspaper, and affirmed the South's right to its own way of life, and expressed amazement at the gall of a New York editor telling a far-off region, one which actually more closely embodied the ideals of the American Revolution, how to run its business.

Joseph, meanwhile, decided he would talk with Ab as soon as possible after the meal. Where could Ab have been getting such ideas about Gideon's slaves? What other ideas was he getting and from whom? In his home, he tried to show respect for Miriam and other blacks. But his son was coming out with outrageous statements in front of strangers! He tried to think back to events that might explain this new Ab, but all that came to mind were the boy's quick spurt of growth that had him approaching Joseph's own height and his recent tendency not to talk much. Seemed like Ab was always excusing himself from the table, not lingering, not staying to talk like he used to.

After dinner, Joseph stood in the eating room looking out the window at the hogs and cows, trying to decide how to confront Ab. Already he'd let Ab leave the table and go about his chores. Joseph determined that he would find Ab now so he could talk with him before the incident grew cold.

Alice Jane and Gilbert were carrying swill in tin buckets. They picked their way among the deeply churned red dirt and puddles of mud that were the mainstay of the pigpen, even in dry weather. Alice Jane talked animatedly as she, an eight-year-old, instructed her five-year-old brother in the task of slopping pigs. Bending over near the hogs, she first emptied her larger pail and then the smaller pail her brother held. Slighter than his older brothers had been at that age, Gilbert squatted down near a sow's head and watched her in fascination as she inhaled the table scraps and milk. Her deep grunts between slurps did little to dissuade Gilbert from his task of watching the pig's every move.

Joseph saw Ab near the barn, putting a horse up after unhitching, brushing and feeding her. Joseph was rehearsing to himself the talk he was planning to have as he started out of the house.

"I want to know where you are picking up these notions about slaves like you showed at dinner," he'd say. "That's not what you've been taught in this house." He pictured Ab's response, probably the pout he was prone to show his elders these days. As he stepped out of the house, Joseph saw his nephew James walk briskly towards Ab, look all around as though to make sure they were alone, and follow him into the barn.

That boy's up to no good, I know it like I know my own name, Joseph said to himself. He needed to see what seventeen-year-old James was up to, but he needed to do it discreetly. He strode down the stairs and crossed the yard, stopping to commend Alice Jane and Gilbert on their work in a very low voice. He moved past the pens and around to the side of the barn where the horse stall was located. He held his head near the rough-cut lumber wall, hoping he could hear their talk.

"...You've gotta try it. It's so intoxicating. You'll think you been imbibin' in whiskey, but there'll be none on your breath. Believe me—"

Joseph heard a low murmur on the other side.

"Don't be silly. She'll never tell. She'd be whipped or maybe worse if she did and she knows it. C'mon, I can watch out for you. You'll have the time of your life, I promise. You'll be so excited, you'll thank me for lettin' you in on it.

"Well, look here, have you ever seen anything like this?" A pause, and then Ab raised his voice on the other side of the wall, showing more excitement. Joseph was afraid of what was coming. Ab had always paid attention to James, compared himself with him, wanted to be like him.

"A piece of lace trim from her pantaloons," James was saying. Joseph's heart fell. He was detailing an exploit with a servant, no doubt. "She didn't exactly want me at first, so I forced her. But then—was she ever sweet! You've got to try it now I've done it. I can show you how so you won't wonder what to do."

James was talking rapidly trying to convince Ab.

"Um-mm, let me tell you! It was some experience! Don't you want to know what to do with your bride someday? A man needs to be experienced before he goes to his wedding bed. You don't want to fumble and frighten her. You want to know how to ease her into it. My father says that loving on the side makes the marriage bed that much better."

Ab's voice in return was asking questions. Joseph tried to make out the questions, but could hear nothing from his son. His own ears were warm. His worst fears about his brother's slaves were confirmed. He listened for more about Gideon.

"You know that pretty nigger Sarah? He's her father—he told me. And he's done it with the other house slaves—even keeps them in his and my mother's bedroom. They have to sleep there on the floor anyway—always have—but my mother keeps begging him to move them. She doesn't like it. I think he does it with them when she's asleep. He's done it lots. He says it's his right because he owns them."

Joseph had had enough. He didn't care what Gideon did, but his filth was not going to infect his family. He clenched and unclenched his fists, thought of James' size, and decided he couldn't let fear of repercussions stop him. He left his post by the barn wall, ready to thrash James, but his daughter's voice stopped him.

"Papa," she cried, "come get Gilbert!" Her frightened blue eyes filled half her face as she ran to him. "He fell in the mud! I can't get his foot free!"

Joseph turned, saw his son covered in mud, and struggling to free his leg from the red-brown muck. He was on one knee with his other lower leg deep in the mud. Joseph ran to the pigpen.

"Hold it, Gilbert," he called. "Don't try to pull it out or you'll fall back in deeper. I'll get you out."

"Hurry, Papa, he's hurt!" Alice Jane's tears coursed down her face and pasted stray wisps of blond hair to her cheeks as she followed her father. Her blue flower-print dress, apron, stockings, and boots were splattered with mud from the yard.

Joseph grabbed Gilbert from behind, pulling him up while grasping his shin. He yanked Gilbert sharply—twice—the boy's leg sprang free. Joseph stood him up on firmer ground and then led him across the pen to the gate. Gilbert let his mud-slathered leg drag behind as he walked.

"Let Alice Jane take you in to Miriam," he said, placing his son's hand in the girl's. "Miriam'll clean you up. And you tell her you're going to be more careful next time." Alice Jane pulled the young boy toward the stairs.

Two rescues in a day! Joseph muttered to himself. And it looks like one young man is going to need to be rescued twice, so it'll be three in all, he said, heading once again for the barn.

He entered the darkness and let his eyes adjust. On the right, he saw Ab in the stall with the horse, brushing her coat. James was nowhere in sight. A piece of white, frilly cotton that was clearly out of place hung from Ab's work coat pocket.

"Hello, Son," Joseph let himself in the stall and greeted Ab, who looked surprised.

"Hello, Papa," Ab said in a dull voice, his eyes back on the horse's side coat.

"Son, I want to talk with you—" Joseph stopped as Ab reached for his coat jacket. "What is that?"

"Nothing, just a handkerchief Momma gave me."

"Let me see it."

"It's just a handkerchief, like I said!" Ab's voice was hot.

"I think I know what it is," Joseph said. "I heard James talking to you. I can't believe that you'd entertain such a vile idea."

"I'm not doing anything," Ab said forcefully.

"Well, then, what are you hiding? Son, I'm ashamed and shocked at what I heard—"

Ab dropped his brush and turned to leave.

"Wait!" Joseph said, his voice loud with anger. Ab stopped, giving his father a wrathful look.

Joseph grabbed his son by his coat collar and looked straight into his eyes. "I'll not have this disrespect. Is James trying to get you to do what he and his despicable father are doing? Tell me!"

Ab's eyes got bigger, but he said nothing. Joseph released him and grabbed the piece of linen from his son's pocket.

"I'm ashamed and sick," Joseph said, his voice choking as he held up the piece of lace pantaloon ruffle. "Why would you even allow your cousin to speak of these outrageous acts?"

"Well, why would you allow your brother to carry them out?" Ab, finding his voice, yelled. "It's not me who's sinning—it's Gideon, my own uncle—your brother!"

Joseph started to yell back. He calmed himself and looked into Ab's eyes. The youth was pressed against the barn wall.

"I must talk with you about this, Son. Let's sit down." Ab didn't move for a moment after Joseph sat down in the hay. Then he folded his long legs and sat a few feet from his father.

"This has been coming on for a long time," Joseph said slowly, trying to pick his words carefully. "I've never acknowledged Gideon's slave children. It was a dark place in my heart that I didn't want to open up. One only has to look at Sarah and John to see the likeness and their light skin. I tried to convince myself at first that a winsome, calculating slave enticed him, but I don't believe that now.

"Ab, we are infested through slavery with a sin that is wrong. The system has been with us for centuries, and I don't know how as one man I can stop it. I don't see Miriam as our slave. Our servant, yes, and one who is not free to go. But we provide for her. I was unwilling to say at the time of our marriage that we could not accept her. She was your mother's gift from her father's estate. I felt obligated to take care of her."

Ab had grown quiet as he listened to his father. Now he spoke without the anger he'd shown before.

"I respect what you're sayin', Pa, but I think there's a big difference between Miriam and Gideon's slaves. Miriam's got her wits about her—"

"Now, that's what got me riled at dinner. Where you have gotten these ideas about Gideon's slaves, I don't know." Joseph felt himself getting hot again as he had at dinner. He breathed slower to stay on top of his anger.

"But it's true," Ab protested. "Gideon's bucks dally and delay until his overseer practically has to take a whip to 'em to get 'em goin' in the morning. Then they make stupid mistakes like dumping entire bags of cotton so there's time lost packing bales. They laze around waiting for every single instruction, impudent as you please. You can't tell me they're not stupid. Why, James has told me when they first bought Cicero he tried to cut himself to death after the boss whipped him. What kind of sense does that make? They don't know Adam from an off ox."

"You've got a long ways to go, Ab," Joseph said slowly, "before you understand this situation entirely. Not long ago a group of slaves drowned off the Georgia island. They couldn't face living in those godforsaken mosquito-infested rice bogs, so they just walked out in the sea, holding hands. They were probably doing the only thing they knew how when faced with sure eventual death on those rice fields. Cicero probably had the same idea."

"If it's so bad, why don't you become an abolitionist, Papa? Then we'd really be the talk of the countryside!" Ab's sarcasm hit Joseph hard.

"Because," Joseph said, "to be an abolitionist in this state is a death warrant," Joseph said. "You know that. I'm not an abolitionist," he told his son. "I believe that you are entitled to what's gained by the sweat of your own brow, and that money earned from the labor of slaves is filthy lucre that will cause you to lose your soul, just as your uncle is losing his." He caught his breath and then went on.

"I excuse my ownership of Miriam because it's against the law in this state to free her. And she has nowhere else to go; having brought her or her parents or grandparents here, we have the obligation to care for her or return her to Africa, something we cannot do. So the choice is to care for her and to have her earn her keep through her labor."

"Well, I don't see where you got these ideas, Pa. Not a planter in these parts feels that way. They see slaves as useful and that's it."

"Look, here, Son," Joseph said, looking into Ab's eyes. "You carry around a leather-bound book in your back pocket. You love the classics. You read well, you learn quickly. You've been able to grasp your book learning quickly.

"That was a gift," Joseph said, "a gift God gave you. Circumstances allowed you to be born into a family that values your learnin'. I wish I'd had the same ability. I do pretty fair for a mechanic. I can write and cipher and figure what I need to know. And I can read and understand much of the Lord's word and the newspaper.

"That's much more than can be said for many a man," he continued. "Including some planters. And I got that because my father and his father were able to git their learnin'—but only after riding miles on horseback and doubling up on their chores to meet with a tutor—in the South Carolina backcountry where they grew up. They valued being able to read and write and to follow the Lord's word. So you see we come from moderate stock, religious folks who prize using all one's talents for the greater glory of God."

Ab looked away and down. "Pa, things are different now. And you know that there's never been a great civilization without slavery! It's right here in the Greeks—" He reached for his back pocket.

Joseph stood up. "I don't have time for your arguments straight from the degraded mouth of Gideon, Ab. You love to debate, and you've a fine mind for it. But you've got to listen to a basic lesson, and that is God's love. If we are not righteous and upstanding, we will be lost in hell. You are to ignore whatever James told you, and you certainly are not to follow in his vices. Do I have your word?"

Ab looked up as his father stood over him. Joseph could see him squint his eyes. If he sassed his father, he could be in line for a solid thrashing. If he disobeyed Joseph, he might bring on more severe punishment. Joseph watched the fires of rebellion in Ab's eyes and thought of his own anger when his pa chastised him for being friends with Adam. He knew he would never quell Ab's fire, only temper it.

Ab shifted his eyes to the ground in front of him.

"Yes, Papa," he said, slowly.

Joseph doubted his son's word, but decided it was just like his father's trying to change his mind about Adam; if he couldn't stop the rebelliousness, he could still curb it.

"If I hear of you even getting near one of Gideon's blacks, I'll tan your hide like you've never seen, believe me. I love you, and I want what's best for you. But I'll not abide any of this fooling around. It's a disgrace!" Ab sat with his head down.

Joseph unlatched the horse's stall door and walked out to the smithy, where Will was building a fire in the forge for the afternoon's work. While Will went to get more wood for the fire, Joseph pulled from his pocket the piece of lace he'd taken from Ab. Threads hung from the jagged edge where it had been torn from a pantaloon.

The lace openwork probably had belonged to a house slave or her daughter, as house slaves received the mistress' hand-me-downs. Joseph closed his eyes trying to bring up the faces of the servants in Gideon's large household. He was unable to picture any of them.

The bright white fabric lying limp across the flesh of his right fist formed a dramatic contrast to his weather-tanned skin, crisscrossed with prominent veins. Trembling from the knowledge of his brother's and nephew's sins, he placed the torn lace on the fire and watched it burn. If he could only put such an end to the disgraceful custom so easily. A heavy weight sat astride his chest.

Joseph lay in bed under the covers, one of them a new quilt made from pieces of their old clothing. The night had turned chilly. It was still April, and in the mountain valley, cold crept in quickly after the sun went down. Joseph had had a good supper of leftover lima beans and corn succotash and cornbread.

The candle by his bed gave a shadowy light. The room was an even square with walls of dressed whitewashed wood. Curtains of white broadcloth trimmed in blue skirted two six-over-six windows that showed only black emptiness outside.

Joseph was deep in thought, still dwelling on James' revelations. He let his thoughts turn to Jane and to the welcome she had given him at noon. Like a man who'd gone without water for days in the desert, his skin had started calling out for her; he ached for her touch and looked forward to their reunion.

He heard Jane open the wide plank door to their room. He watched her every move as Jane went to Catherine, three years old, who was sleeping below in the trundle, placing her candle on the floor while tending the child.

Jane was dressed in a nightgown Joseph had not seen in a long time. When was it last? Was it way back in Atlanta? It had an open throat. She must be cold, he thought. Jane was usually very attentive to staying warm. If she became ill, the house would be bedlam. Her lack of caution impressed Joseph, and he hoped it was for him she had dressed in such an uncustomary way. Lacework across the top of her chest let penny-sized views of her fair skin peek through, and the curves of her bare breasts were revealed as she bent over Catherine.

Jane, suddenly aware of him, quickly grabbed her gown to her waist as she adjusted a quilt over Catherine. Then Jane approached their high bed. She smiled at Joseph as she placed her candle on the bedside table next to the Bible. He noticed the skin of her hands was cracked from constant work in water, and he watched as she applied ointment from a jar. Little things were important to him tonight. He recalled how in the past two years every time she came to bed he had wondered what the result would be if he had tried to do more than touch her shoulder or stroke her hair.

So many times Joseph had felt the throbbing discomfort of his restraint—the manly brake on his instincts that his brother and nephew had forgotten. Now, he felt a rise of excitement. He decided that Jane's message today was a clear one—it was the first time she'd told him what had been on her mind in the days since they'd left Atlanta. A woman missed her women kin most, he thought. Her brother David was generally too busy making the circuit to spend much time in Tilton, so she didn't even have that family.

His wife lifted herself onto the feather bed and sat with her back to him for a moment as she rubbed more ointment into her hands. With a piece of flannel—actually a piece from a child's worn pajamas, Joseph recognized—she carefully removed the excess and stood beside the bed to lay the cloth on the bedside table. Then she turned the covers on her side of the bed, placed her knuckles on the bedding, and climbed in to lie down next to him in bed. She didn't pull up covers, as she usually did to hide her body.

The candle silhouetted her slender body and Joseph felt his manhood stirring. She took her long hair in her hand and moved it so it fell down one side of her chest. Joseph was enthralled. He wanted so badly to caress her dark, soft hair. She smiled as though she could read his thoughts, and Joseph felt lighthearted, like a bird diving and playing in the spring air. He wanted to play with her, to touch her all over and feel his body next to hers.

"Ab certainly angered you at the dinner table," Jane said, touching his shoulder. "Did the two of you talk afterwards?"

"I don't want to talk about that just yet," Joseph said, drawing her to him. "I want you."

Jane returned his kisses with a fervor he hadn't felt in years. He could barely restrain himself as he felt her arms, her breasts, her legs around him, and tasted her shoulders under the cotton gown.

He lifted her gown around her hips and then raised himself up to pull his nightshirt off his body. Jane looked with interest at his bared chest, without her usual modesty. He looked into her eyes and her dark eyes widened, but she made no objection as he reached for her gown and lifted her loose garment from around her upper arms and head. He ran his hand softly over her breasts. He pulled her to him and placed his fingers down below. She was wet, and felt silky like the cloth of her best dress.

"M-mm," he said in pleasure as he moved on top of her and pressed inside. For the first time Joseph could remember, Jane grabbed his back with her hands and held on hard while he thrust powerfully. He felt the new sensation of her naked breasts against bare chest and torso. All the stress of the day, from the bear's assault to the shock of James' revelations, came rushing to mind and all the fear and anger he felt burst forth, tearing through his body into hers.

Joseph thought of the lonely nights he'd spent next to Jane, the arduous preparations and journey north, leaving Atlanta, the many days packing and packing and deciding what to take, what to leave. The past rushed forward in his mind as he thrust deeper into his wife. He was angry, hurt, tired, lonely, and anxious. He thrust harder, angry that she'd kept herself from him all that time, but at the same time wanting to love her, love her totally.

He heard Jane gasping softly and he thought for a moment about their child below the bed, then placed his hand on her mouth with a loving touch, and held his finger to his lips to warn her about sounds. Jane's eyes were totally on him, in him, all around him. He wanted her so much. Thoughts of his nephew James sprang to mind and he pushed further into Jane, hoping to expel the whole memory.

When Joseph released inside Jane, he could think of nothing but his ecstasy. Then he heard Jane burst into tears. Joseph was scared. After all this time apart, he'd ruined things.

"I'm all right," she whispered. "Don't worry, dear, I'm just so happy—" He covered her mouth with kisses and felt her with his own body, sensing warmth and a silken stream beneath him.

Joseph came inside her again, the first time he'd done that in quick order since he was a young man. He was young again, responding to the freshness of spring outside and the resurrection of old feelings. He felt splendid, like he did when he was sixteen and he learned the power of making his first tool in the forge. Everything was new. He felt trembly all over, like a calf fresh from his mother's womb trying to stand up on wobbly legs in the barn and falling, then getting up again from the hay.

They lay without speaking for a long time, content to feel each other's nakedness under the covers, unable to bring themselves to put their nightdresses back on.

"I'll talk to you about Ab some other time," Joseph said, kissing the top of his wife's head and reaching his arm around her body to pull her closer. "This is too glorious to tarnish with domestic matters."

Chapter 11

THE SMITHY

Outside, on Monday morning, Joseph could see the spring rain falling in the gray mist just outside the wagon-sized doorway to the blacksmith and gunsmith shop. He loved the clean smell of April rains. Was it because they meant less worry about water for his food crops? That might be. When the early rains arrived and brought the smell of water hitting clay, he inhaled the moisture-laden air deeply and temporarily forgot the large, messy puddles that surely would follow.

The shop was on the side of the livestock barn that faced away from the inn. This way, Joseph could be close to the home and not risk having the smaller children wander into the dark, dust-filled smithy. The dark helped Joseph see the color of the metal he was firing—too much light, and a metal heated to red-orange could look gray and under fired, and he'd miss his opportunity to hammer and mold. Working in the dark, Joseph could judge the color best and avoid having to rework his weld or other repair—useless efforts that wasted his time.

Today Joseph and Cicero, Gideon's black, were working on a wagon wheel, for a set his neighbor James Hudson had ordered. Joseph had built a charcoal fire inside a ring of stones near the door where the smoke could escape easily. He'd cut the iron piece to a length just shy of the wooden wheel's circumference and then heated the metal over his forge in the chimney. Next, he'd hammered the strip, then fired and beat it again until it formed a circular tire. He'd wrestled the waist-high tire—it weighed as much as he did—over to the forge in the chimney. He heated the ends of the heavy C-shaped iron bar and prepared to lap the ends to form a smooth seam.

From his place at the forge, Joseph observed Cicero squatting over the fire in the ring of stones, warming his very large hands. Gideon had offered to hire Cicero to Joseph during the April rains. There was no outside work for him when the fields were wet, and Joseph, with a heavy load of work to get out, had accepted. He judged Cicero to be about thirty-five years old, but he wasn't sure. Cicero could not recall how old he was when Gideon had purchased him in Atlanta.

Since Saturday, Joseph realized he had been paying more attention to the black folks in his world. James' discussion in the barn with Ab had turned his world upside down, and his distracted mind continued to dwell on what his nephew said.

Yesterday, while waiting to give a testimonial from the pulpit of the Primitive Baptist Church, he'd found himself looking at the near-dozen slaves Gideon paraded into the church, trying to fit the whole sordid picture together.

Matilda entered first—Joseph judged her to be about thirty—her two children in front of her. Ahead was six-year-old Sarah, whose features suggested Gideon and who had light skin. Her companion, four-year-old John, had the same complexion. They were dressed in hand-me-downs and made-over clothes from Gideon's wife and sons. Joseph felt ill at his stomach. He knew Cicero, Matilda's husband, would not be allowed to sit with his wife and children, as he would huddle with four other male adult slaves on the last row.

Beatrice, a statuesque, older woman whose features were set today in a fierce gaze bearing the unmistakable veil of anger and resentment, shoved her daughters, Nicely and Prudence, into the pew before her. Nicely, slender and expansive in her movements, looked around her brightly with large brown eyes, smoothing the close-fitting waist of her red print full-skirted dress. She filed into the pew slowly, ignoring her mother's push.

Was this the child James had taken? Was she self-conscious of her movements due to the attention of the master's son?

Twelve-year-old Prudence, just showing small breasts above a loosely fitted waist, looked back at her mother with fear in her eyes, then quickly followed her sister. Joseph realized one of his relatives may have raped this child as well. He wasn't sure which of the wenches James had violated, but it almost didn't matter. Whoever had not been a victim would likely soon be.

Next, leading the men filing into the last pew was Jason. Jason was probably the mate of Beatrice, although not the father of her two maturing girls. Jason had a previous wife in Griffin, but Gideon had sold the woman to another planter to raise cash, so the two had been separated.

Jason's son, Homer, fifteen at the time, had been allowed to come north. He now was a sturdy field hand like his father on Gideon's plantation. With the other men were Ulysses, an older man like Cicero and Jason, and Samson, a young buck about the age of Homer.

As he prepared to open the church service, Joseph reflected on the irony of Gideon giving his slaves classical or Biblical names. He perpetuated the myth shared by many planters that they followed the tradition of the Greeks and Romans. Their ideal was the Republic, where the classes were distinct, forever separated. They believed themselves to be heirs to the classical civilizations, which had as their cornerstone the enslavement of whole nations. Joseph had had many an after-dinner row with Gideon over his brother's defense of the "Scriptural basis" of slavery.

Cicero, unaware he was being watched as he hunched down over the fire, reached his dark hand over the crimson coals and touched them.

"Doesn't that burn to get that close, Cicero?" Joseph asked, amazed at the slave's tolerance.

"No, suh!" Cicero started and then looked up. Joseph wondered what he thought of Matilda's children's parentage.

"It's all right," Joseph said, focusing again on the black man's hand on the coals. "I've just never been able to put my hand on coals like that. I'd get burned."

Cicero said nothing and stood near the ring.

"Yes, suh. What you want me to be doin' now, suh?"

Joseph wondered at the physical difference that enabled him to endure touching fire where he, Joseph, a man with a lifetime of experience in the forge, would have watched his hand crisp and smoke. Was it true that blacks were more physically endowed but not as mentally capable? Was it possible for them to accomplish the same as their masters, given equal chances?

"Help me with the bellows here," Joseph said. The black man walked over and placed himself next to the forge and grabbed the bellows lever invented by Joseph's father. *WhooshwhooshWHOOSH.* The bellows burst air onto the fire. Cicero slowly worked the lever until it kicked the fire up to a healthy, red glow. Then he accelerated his speed. The fire inside the pyramid of coals grew hotter.

"Keep goin'," Joseph encouraged. He watched as the metal ends perched in the coal fire glowed first red, then orange.

"Keep goin'," he said. Cicero's forced breaths matched the wheezing of the bellows.

Then Joseph danced away from the forge, grasping the tire with his large hands and placed the open end of it on the anvil horn. Joseph struck the iron strip with his hammer, gradually lengthening first one and then the other of the ribbon ends.

"Hold this," he said, motioning Cicero to leave the bellows and hold the tire so he could concentrate on the weld.

Cicero was always compliant. Slave lashings were frequent, as masters, including Gideon, complained that their dark workers had to be punished to get them to work. Joseph found it hard to imagine that Cicero was that way. He could endure the greatest of slights and never flinch.

Some weeks ago, James Willow, a farmer whom Gideon allowed to accompany him to local turkey shoots, was having Joseph reattach a hoe handle. While he watched Joseph work, he told second-hand stories about Gideon's slaves, using curse words to describe how lazy they were, until Joseph called a halt to the cursing. Cicero never winced. Instead, he continued putting up the tools, never taking his eyes off the wall.

"Dangdest thing I ever saw," Willow had said. "That so-and-so darky had that mule workin' so hard. All he had to do was stop and water the mule. Never lifted a finger, though the mule that pulled that plow was dying from thirst. Never gave 'im water, never stopped the work. That mule just keeled over from exhaustion and lack of water, right there in that Georgia field!"

Such talk in front of blacks was not unusual. What Joseph found unusual was their impassive response that never showed comprehension, much less a reaction.

Folks like Willow assumed the silence was from lack of brains, and it just fed the whites' idea that the blacks couldn't understand what was going on around them. Blacks understood plenty, Joseph knew. They were smart enough not to let on how much they knew, so as not to be punished for being too uppity.

Joseph returned to Cicero and the wheel he held. Joseph continued feathering the ends of the tire, scarfing them and laying them across each other so that they overlapped about an inch. In one quick motion he took the tire from Cicero and returned it to the forge fire.

"Flux."

Cicero stepped over to a pile of river sand in a wooden box near the fire and grasped less than a handful of sand in a fist. He threw it on the fire, right where the two ends joined. The weld glowed red and the fire around it turned yellow.

"Great. We've got yellow fire," Joseph commented. He swung the tire back to the anvil and flung it down on the point again, picked up the hammer and began beating the welded joint. Within minutes, the red iron was brown, and the weld finished so smoothly it was hard to detect. Joseph was pleased.

"Once we're done with this," he told the dark man, "then we're about finished for the day. But I do have a message I want you to take to Mr. Morgan. Once I finish the wheel, I'll write it down for you."

Joseph put down the hammer, and he and Cicero rolled the wheel against a sawhorse in the shop. Later, he would heat the tire by laying it over the cooler fire by the door and stretch the rim to fit over the wooden wheelbase, then pour cold water over it to shrink the metal. The result would be a fit so tight the wheel would last until the wooden fellows broke or rotted out after years of stress.

Joseph walked over to the doorway where a slant top desk was placed to take advantage of light. He picked up a pencil, opened the desktop, and pulled out a piece of paper. He wrote on the paper, then folded it and handed it to Cicero.

"Give this to Mr. Morgan," he told the laborer. He wished there was something he could say to relieve the vacant look in Cicero's eyes.

By paying Gideon for Cicero's labor, Joseph was partaking in a system he abhorred. He'd never agreed with the system, but he was benefiting from it, gaining the services of a well-trained blacksmith's assistant for little money. Wasn't he guilty of the system's offenses as well? Why was he comfortably working side by side with a colored man? Couldn't the man's anger spill out into an attack on Joseph? Didn't he avoid hiring Gideon's younger workers on that account? Cicero could turn on him one day and hit him over the head with a heavy tool. Could, Joseph thought, but probably wouldn't.

There had been slave revolts—one in South Carolina had almost succeeded, he'd heard. Many years ago, slaves in Virginia had rebelled, killing sixty whites. The certain death that followed insurrections had cooled the slaves' desire for open revolt. At least Joseph hoped that was the case.

Leaving Cicero in the shops, Joseph went around to the barn at the front and brought a horse to pull the wagon. After he and Cicero mounted the buckboard, Joseph glanced again at the man beside him, wondering what was going on in that sad, black head. The two of them moved on down the Tilton Road toward Gideon's plantation, getting thoroughly soaked in the spring rain. Gideon would be off in Dalton again, so he wouldn't respond to his note from Joseph for a day or so.

Gideon appeared at the smithy the next day. He pulled his new hat from his head and bowed with a flourish. "You look like you have your enterprise in good shape, for a man who has to do all his own work."

Joseph grimaced. He hated that his brother kept reminding him of the vast differences in their fortunes. What had happened to their father's instruction not to live off the sweat of another man's labor? Joseph realized that it had been many years since Gideon had remembered that injunction, if in fact he ever heard it.

Gideon struck a proud pose as he stood in the door of the shops in a late afternoon sun. "I received your missive yesterday, and I am here at your beck and call."

Joseph looked up at Gideon from the second tire he'd been preparing to weld. He hadn't gone for Cicero today because he'd thought Gideon would show up, and he had been right.

"Thank you for coming, brother." He stopped, took the tire off the anvil, and laid his hammer on a tree stump. "Have a seat," he said, motioning to a table nearby. Gideon looked around with a scowl, obviously concerned about dirtying his cream-colored duster. Joseph enjoyed his brother's quandary. Why should he have to provide a clean place for Gideon to sit, the peacock!

"If you're concerned about soiling your clothes, then maybe we'd best go up to the house and find a chair there," Joseph said. "But I didn't ask you here for a cup of tea." He sucked in his breath. He looked squarely at Gideon and jumped into the fray.

"Why do you bring your bastard children to church with you on Sunday?"

"Wh-what did you say?"

"You heard me. I'm offended, and my whole family is offended, that you bring your bastard children to church with you on Sunday. I'm disgusted at your behavior in siring those children. You're a disgrace, a blatant sinner braying in the face of all that is good and decent in my family, and I want you to stop."

"I don't know what you're talking about!" Gideon protested, standing with hands on his hips.

"You know exactly what I'm talking about. Sarah—your eyes, your nose. John—skin the same color as hers. Not only are you corrupting your slaves, the ones you're supposed to watch over and take care of, you're corrupting your son, and he's trying to entice mine! I'm not having it!"

"You've been sucking in this smoke too long, brother. You don't know anything about these affairs. If you had a bunch of blacks of your own, you'd see it differently—"

"Differently, hah! I'd see it with blinders on, as you do now. If you don't think the rest of the town doesn't know what you've been up to with Matilda, then it's you that's been inhaling too much smoke. My God, man, where do you stop? Don't you see that your behavior is vile? Your son, too! And attempting to corrupt my son!" Joseph found himself involuntarily opening and closing his hands. Gideon was closed to his own perfidy!

"Y-you don't know what's going on. Besides, those people are my property, I can do with them as I want. The law says I can. I have total control over their lives—"

"The law!" Joseph thundered. "What law allows such depraved ways of doing? Why can't you rein in your animal instincts?"

"You don't know what you're talking—"

"Gideon, if you do not curtail your son and show some difference in your behavior, I will refuse to have anything to do with you. If your son comes near Ab, I will order him off my land. I mean it!"

"Now, wait just a minute. You don't have any right to shame my son. He is, after all, your nephew."

"I don't care. Anyone sinking into such sin is not my relative. You are not my relative as long as you refuse to change your whoring ways—"

"Now, just a minute," Gideon said, picking up Joseph's hammer from the tree trunk. He backed away from Joseph, taunting him.

"Maybe you need to be getting a little more loving yourself, Joseph." Gideon continued to back up, gripping the hammer tighter. "After all, you haven't had a baby in several years. Are things all right with Jane? Maybe one of my wenches is what you need."

Joseph was immediately upon him, knocking him to the dirt floor. He struggled with Gideon for the hammer, and squeezed Gideon's wrist so hard he dropped it quickly.

"H-h-h—" Gideon gasped as Joseph grabbed his throat with both of his huge hands. Joseph felt the vulnerable flesh around his brother's windpipe. What was he doing? He released his hands, jumped up, and stood over Gideon.

"Get out of here!" he said, hoarse with fear. "Get out of here, and don't you or your son cross my doorsill until you've repented!'

Gideon rose awkwardly, swept the clay dust off his coat, and shook his fist under Joseph's nose.

"You ant! You can't touch me!" Gideon yelled. He stumbled from the shop, continuing to brush dirt from the back of his coat. He turned around, his face twisted grotesquely. He almost spoke but turned instead, punched his hat on his head, and mounted his horse. The animal's finely brushed coat shone in the sun. The horse shuddered under Gideon's weight. With a vicious kick to the mare, Gideon galloped away.

Joseph watched him from the doorway, leaning against the doorframe for support. He could feel his heart thump in his chest. The sounds of birds harboring in the trees above him were muffled. What kept them from killing each other? Only God's grace, Joseph decided. This roiling fight had to stop before it ended in tragedy.

His chest heaved as he tried to catch his breath. His body quivered, not quite able to move. He wanted to push his hand out in front of his face, just to see if it was bloody or not, but his hand would not move. He felt weak, and not able to stand, so he sat on a log stump, letting his body fall heavily on the sawed-off end. He sighed deeply—a long, drawn-out sigh— as he tried to calm himself.

He pictured Gideon in happier times walking down a road back in Abbeville and himself running to catch up to his older brother, chasing him so he could join in climbing trees and gathering apples in the orchard at the old home. Gideon would let him carry the biggest load, which made Joseph proud.

Then he saw an older Gideon as he was just now, his face grimacing and seething, his cheeks showing none of the diagonal creases that went with his charming grin. The fire in Gideon's eyes churned Joseph's stomach.

All over his body, Joseph felt the shock of knowing his brother truly hated him, hated him with a venomous rage. He hated him now and may have loathed him for a long time.

Joseph shoved his feet forward and felt the ground under his feet, first with his left foot, then with his right.

It felt firm enough. Yet Joseph still felt the ground was shaking. Maybe his body still quavered, not the clay soil. Gideon loathed him—and he never knew, never suspected. Gideon had eight hundred acres, slaves, cotton—wealth enough to hobnob with Farish Carter, the owner of thousands of acres in the next county. Joseph felt betrayed. He felt taken and foolish for heaping on Gideon his unquestioning love and respect. True, he hadn't always agreed with his brother and was a bit envious of him, but he never hated him. Joseph felt a hole in his chest where his love for his brother had been.

Rebecca looked up quickly when Joseph—exhausted, hair mussed, covered with dirt, and still wearing his leather apron—entered the kitchen. She put aside the dough she was preparing for biscuits.

"What on earth has been going on?" she asked. "Where did Gideon go in such a hurry? Miriam was on her way out to invite him to supper, but she said he took off like fire was lickin' at his heels."

Joseph took off his leather apron, shedding clay dust on the floor. He laid it on a chair near the fire, then sat down facing his mother, leaning his arms forward on his knees. "I need to talk to you, but I don't want Miriam to hear."

Rebecca immediately rose. Taking a broom from a nail, she went out in the hallway and spoke to Miriam. Joseph heard her softly ask the servant to sweep the front porch and yard. She returned to the kitchen.

"What?" Rebecca asked again. Her blue eyes were drawn, and her face had more lines than Joseph remembered. Her pure-white hair was pulled back in a bun.

Joseph pulled at his vest. He picked up a wooden stirring spoon from the table and fiddled with it.

"I've just had a fight with Gideon," he said. "I mean a fight like we haven't had since we were youngsters."

"What about?" Rebecca face was filled with fear. It was the same fear he saw in her eyes the day they'd left Abbeville.

"Mother, Gideon is corrupting his slaves. It's so far advanced that now even his boy James is doing it!"

"My word, Joseph, what a charge! Whatever made you think that?"

"Mother, I don't want to upset you and offend you. But I have no one else to talk to about it, and it's crazing me." Joseph drew in a breath. It had never occurred to him that his mother wouldn't believe him.

"I came upon James in the barn the other day, trying to persuade Ab to do what he's been doing, messing with Gideon's slaves."

Rebecca's blue eyes flashed at him as they used to when he was a small boy caught in the wrong. Would he convince her?

"I don't believe it, Joseph. How could that be?"

"Mother, can you look at Gideon's Matilda and not see a resemblance to him in her children?"

Rebecca held her silence. Then, frowning, she said: "The kind of contact you're talking about is a vicious slander against your brother. Are you sure?"

Joseph moved to his mother's side and put his hands on top of hers.

"Mother, I would give anything not to bother you with this. But I believe my brother will burn for what he's doing. I want to help him, but he will not acknowledge his sin. The least I can do is keep him from infecting my son. I've forbidden him or James from coming here until they repent."

Rebecca's eyes filled with tears that fell in large drops on their entwined hands. Joseph said nothing, nor did she.

"I knew it would come to this, I just knew," she sobbed. "Your father saw it coming. He would be so outraged." She continued crying, and Joseph said nothing, letting the tears come without comment. She cried some more, pulled a handkerchief from her skirt, and wiped her eyes. "If there was anything your father hated," she said, "it was planters. I shuddered when Gideon took up the cash crops. Your father wanted Gideon to be successful, but he didn't want it in that way. He was deeply ashamed of Gideon."

"Ma, I never knew," said Joseph. "I know he ridiculed the large planters, called them a 'puffed up bunch' and thought them lazy for not making a living with their own hands. I remember a number of Pa's sayings about slavery, but I figured Pa just envied the planters."

"No, he hated them," Rebecca sobbed. Tears continued to drip down on her hands. Joseph took out his handkerchief. With a free hand, he wiped her face.

"What you don't know," Rebecca said, "is that your father was run out of Abbeville because he took a stand against the planters."

"Ma, what do you mean?"

"You don't know—" Her tears flowed again.

"Don't know what?"

"Don't know what he went through. It was a disgrace to him and me and all our relations. It caused a rift that has never healed."

Joseph waited patiently, white linen in hand, until she had gathered herself.

"Do-do you remember the day we left Abbeville? You were only a young lad, just getting your growth, so you may not recall—"

"Of course, I remember, Ma. You had Susannah in your arms. And you were concerned about Indians. That's what I recall. You wanted Pa to have his guns at hand."

Rebecca looked down at her hands, and then up at Joseph, her blue eyes intense. There was more color than usual in her cheeks, and Joseph thought she looked beautiful, even though distraught.

"Yes, there were Indians to be concerned about," she said. The tears had now subsided. "And there were the loyalists, like Tom Cunningham's father."

Joseph felt the old fear. He suddenly found himself hoping the old codger had died a painful death like his son did in the streets of Atlanta.

"But the greatest threat came from the neighbors who disagreed with your father's views on slavery," Rebecca said. "There was a campaign to convert the non-believers to slavery. It split whole churches, and high feelings caused many to leave the area. Your father wouldn't bend." She paused and sighed. Joseph waited.

"So they ran him off.

"That's why we left. Your father had no more customers. For months, they tried every trick, every kind of mischief, to make your father go along with the slavers in the neighborhood."

Joseph listened as though struck by a bolt of lightening. What was all this about? He sensed his mother reaching back in her memory to a distant and wrenching moment. Her eyes seemed to look far away as she touched her eyes with a white ball of cloth.

"I won't mislead you. Your pa felt slavery was wrong, but he didn't believe the slaves around us should be freed. There was too much history for that. He just didn't want to be in the way when their fury was unleashed, when they threw off the bonds and murdered and pillaged as they tried to do in Charleston and in Virginia. He had you and Gideon to work with him, but having so many daughters burdened him. Much as they might work in the fields, they still would not be able to produce the work of a houseful of sons."

"So we left Abbeville?"

"Your father was being pressured. People in the area were shunning his business. They were irate because he got up in the church meeting and urged people to plant other crops so that they could make it without slaves. They didn't want to hear it. Their response was swift."

William Morgan sat at a slant-top desk in the back of his shop, using winter light to go over the scraps of paper he'd collected as debits for work. As a man would come for his sharpened plow or repaired wagon wheel, he would scribble a note in front of the person, or else he and the man would forget the deed and the cost. Later, with cleaner hands, he would list the cost on the man's account, which he kept running for a year until they settled up around Christmas. He looked at the ledger sheet for a man whose tatters of paper had been entered:

Account of John Armstrong:

January 29	*Sharpen plow*	*03 cents*
March 5	*Turn plow*	*20 cents*
March 14	*Fixing chain*	*03 cents*
March 20	*"Small" bolt*	*05 cents*

Yes, that was a small bolt, William thought. Armstrong had asked for a price before he did the work, and then it turned out he needed an eight-inch monster. Should have been 10 cents.

Was he ever going to collect? William mused as he went over each page. Reading each name, William grew more doubtful. Since his speech at the church four days ago, there had been a sharp drop in business. It had seemed unfair, since he had tolerated the wild speeches of others throughout the meeting and had held his peace. Listening to others was usually as natural to William as day exiting to night in a splendid winter sunset. Quiet as he was, that day he found he could no longer keep silent.

Things had changed so much from the time he was a boy. Then people made their livings mostly from farming and livestock and their trades. They made most everything they needed, swapped with others for what they didn't. Old Man Holcombe down the way made the best spirits, so folks didn't try to duplicate his skill. In the settlements near the sand hills, William traded tools and implements he made for pottery and crocks.

William remembered the excitement over the new mechanical gin, and the changes that came. He'd hear about a neighbor buying slaves who used to work his own farm. More and more, folks wanted to farm just one crop.

"Cotton's your crop for cash," farmers told each other. Families trickling in from Virginia and from the Low Country brought slaves to the upcountry hills—crowds of dark, sullen, ill-clad Africans, not just a few. And families who owned no slaves traveled down to Charleston to buy them. Their numbers were stronger than a raging river current.

William could count a peck of families with more than 20 slaves within five miles of where he stood. Even more plantations lined the banks of the Savannah, growing crops that filled the long Petersburg boats making their way through treacherous shoals to Augusta and then by steamboat to Savannah for export.

The night before he made his speech at the meeting, William sought Rebecca's counsel, and she read Scripture to him by the light of a candle late in the night in their bed. They turned the fragile pages to Matthew VI, and Rebecca's soft voice called out the words he would use to still his own heart and to stir the hearts of others.

When the call at the meeting came for matters to be placed before the members, he rose.

"Brothers," he said. The men, some in elegant frock coats and wide-brimmed hats, turned to him. He felt a chill. He was a yeoman farmer and tradesman. They were wealthy planters. He was not educated beyond the sparse lessons of his backcountry childhood. Some of these men had more books in their homes than he'd seen in a lifetime. At least one of them had been educated in Europe.

"For some time my heart has been weighed down like river rocks as I think about recent affairs in our neighborhood and in our section of the country."

William could see the surprise on their faces that he was speaking at all.

"My hope is that we can avoid the rancor that divided our brothers at the Presbyterian Church over in Due West when they lost a sizable portion of their congregation. As we all know, a quarter of their members removed to Ohio. Many of them now lead the Abolitionists."

William saw faces turn from surprise to intense curiosity.

"By now, you know whereof I speak," the blacksmith said quietly. "Most of you know that I am not given to words, but I can no longer be at peace unless I tell you what concerns me. Most of you know the value of reading the skies, the rainfall, and soil to determine crop-planting time. Now I think it is time we read the threats to our way of life."

"Hear, hear," one man said. William realized the man thought he would deliver a different message, one that supported the slavers.

"My concern is about the failed revolt in Charleston," he said, watching the men's faces. Several were turning red. But he had to continue before he lost his nerve. "We were told at first that all those responsible had been caught—thirty-five were hanged, more than that banished. But now we read that there may have been thousands of slaves involved in the insurrection. We are no longer safe, especially those of us who do not own slaves."

Two men grew florid, rose, and walked quickly to spit tobacco out the door. They returned to their chairs, walking heavily and slowly.

"It's been three years now. It has become clear that those Negroes whom we assumed saw the positive good of their positions harbor murderous rage. Many of us have chosen not to own them—"

"Or cain't afford to!" one man blurted out.

"Order!" called Deacon Brown, who led the meeting.

"For three years now," William continued, undisturbed, "we have watched as more simple farmers have purchased slaves. We are surrounded more and more by those whose livelihoods depend on the sweat of those who might just as likely slit our throats.

"Gentlemen, those slaves in Charleston made and hid 300 bayonets. They had swords and pistols at the ready. We know that they deliberately struck when the planters were away for the summer, so the families whose hands were clean could have died instead of those whose hands were sullied with slavery.

"They hung the slaves who led it, including Denmark Vesey. We've passed laws against teaching slaves to read and write and against importing slaves. In Charleston, they're building the Citadel to provide sanctuary in case of another insurrection. We are afraid. We have erected a prison around the plantation. We sit not so many hundreds of miles from a black republic that Vesey tried to have land on our shores. I beg you, think of the path you are on! We need to diversify our economy—"

"So, what would you do—turn back time to when they were good slaves?"

"Order!" Deacon Brown yelled. His voice was shrill. "Brother Wilson, you are out of turn."

"Brothers, the word of our Lord in Matthew Six tells us he will provide for us." William's Bible lay open in his raised palm. His other hand nervously stroked the edge of the leather cover, softened with age and use. "'Therefore take no thought, saying, what shall we eat? Or, What shall we drink? Or Wherewithal shall we be clothed? For your heavenly Father knoweth that ye have need of all these things. But seek ye first the kingdom of God and his righteousness; and all these things shall be added unto you.' We must first think of the right thing to do. "'The light of the body is the eye: if therefore thine eye be single, thy whole body shall be full of light. But if thine eye be evil, thy whole body shall be full of darkness,'" William read on.

"Brother Brown! Brother Brown!" shouted Brother Wilson. "Ask Brother Morgan if he yields the floor!"

"I yield the floor, brothers, but only so long as needed to hear your response," said William, sitting down.

"Brother Morgan," said Wilson, turning to face the others and with his back to William. "That same verse you quoted continues," he said, flourishing his open Bible. "'No man can serve two masters: for either he will hate the one and love the other, or else he will hold to the one and despise the other.'

"And then," Wilson ceremoniously turned his Bible page to a new section marked with a piece of scarlet ribbon, "He says, 'Servants, be obedient to them that are your masters according to the flesh, with fear and trembling, in the singleness of your heart.' Now," he paused, a smile spreading across his broad, corpulent, red face. "If God had not meant our Negroes to be enslaved, why in tarnation would he have used that example in his Divine Revelation, handed down from God, guaranteed to be our guide for life? I rest my case." Wilson sat down, grinning as his neighbors applauded.

The arguing went on, and William did not reseek the floor. At the end of the meeting, no one spoke to him or looked at him. Despite the cramped quarters of the meeting room, no one came closer than five feet from him as they grasped hands, laughing and talking gregariously. He left the meeting feeling the weight of the stones in his heart.

Now, days after the meeting, William was spending his days repairing the chair Rebecca had wanted fixed for months and finishing the dozens of other tasks that he had put off because they didn't bring in income. Now there was no excuse. And no income.

He and the other small farmers and tradesmen were being squeezed out. The large plantations had their own smithies now and the owners hired out their blacksmiths when their needs were met. He could hardly compete with slave labor. Mr. Jefferson's idea of equality among all men and the sense of threat posed by a moneyed aristocracy was lost. Status was more important. Gone was the ideal of each man having the right to as much say as the next man. Now the number of slaves a man owned measured his value. A man who owned five slaves had much more status than a man who owned one, and so on.

William heard a horse approaching at a gallop. He rose to greet the customer when an orange glow sailed through the open doorway.

A torch!

He dodged the flame, only to hear the crack of a musket. He smelled the sulfur from the shot and his nostrils burned slightly from the exploded black powder. He heard a thud as the lead bullet slammed into the thick log above his head. Then he ran out the front of the building, yelling. He saw a tall rider in a leather mountain man's coat leaning far over the saddle, rifle in his right hand, spurring on his horse.

"Hey!" William hollered uselessly.

He ran back into the shop in time to see flames reaching from his tinderbox, reaching high to the walls, spreading quickly to a pile of lumber he'd stacked near the wall. He grabbed burlap bags from the doorway and ran to the creek.

"Fire! Fire!" he yelled, hoping his young sons would hear. He plunged several bags in the cold water and ran back to the shop, beating the wet bags up against the wall. One after another, he pulled them down, hoping he'd extinguished the flames for good. He returned to the creek with more bags, ran back, and covered more area, wondering if his sons had heard him.

Finally, the fire was out. William's legs were wobbly beneath him.

The damage could have been worse. The shop was singed with fire, and wood that he planned to use for a new eating table was charred and ruined. It would be days before he could get everything dry and get back to work. He ran his fingers through his hair, then wiped them on his apron, disgusted and angry. He looked at his soot-encrusted hands and thought of leaving Abbeville.

"I never knew the shop was torched," Joseph said forlornly. "Father said he caused the fire."

"He didn't want to worry you. He probably didn't tell you about being visited by men with rifles and guns the next night. They told him he'd better clear out, or they were going to run him out."

"He probably made half the guns they carried, if they were from around there," said Joseph, bowing his head. His father's road talk about moving west to provide for his children and trusting God's providence was true, but it was inspired by backwoods-revenge arson.

"So the talk about guns as we left wasn't just idle talk."

"Your father rarely talked without purpose," Rebecca half-smiled.

"And the Indians? Were they Indians or our own white neighbors you feared?"

Rebecca smiled and touched Joseph's head. She then squeezed his hand.

"Both, Son," she said. "Both were problems back then. It was the Indians at first. For years and years there were fights between those settlers living close to the bone, barely subsisting and stealing horses to trade to the Indians, and the aspiring planters who wanted control. A regulator movement tried and punished the wrongdoers because there were no courts, thanks to the wealthy Charleston government.

"When the revolution broke out there was violence and retribution back and forth. I was just born then, but growing up, I heard stories about homes being burned out and sympathizers to the King or the Liberty Boys being shot or hung for being on the wrong side. That last fight with the slavers hit us the hardest. Your father lost his business. He had to go to Georgia. But don't blame us for not telling you right out," she said, her voice tired. "We were trying to protect you."

Joseph stood and caressed his mother's white head. The struggle that divided him and his brother seemed impossibly deep, a split that went back many years, even generations. Like a stubborn tree trunk in the way of his plow in a new field, his problem was not going to be removed easily.

Was it any wonder that he and his brother were at odds? Gideon was entrapped in his way of life—buy or beget more slaves to till and tend and harvest his single crop to pay back the bank loan based on a certain, bountiful yield. It was like a one-way train ticket to Tennessee—the plantation system allowed no turning around.

Could Joseph claim no fault in this system? He didn't lash Miriam. In fact, he felt he and his family and his boarding house business were more in her charge than the other way around, but she could not leave and he could not free her except in his will. Even then, if she were to gain her freedom, it would take an act of the legislature and enough money in his estate to transport her to a non-slave state.

For a moment, but only a moment, Joseph felt compassion for his brother. He could almost forgive him.

Still, Joseph needed to see Gideon gone, even though it would make his mother sad if Gideon left. It was no wonder she and Pa had hidden the strife that led to their leaving South Carolina. It hurt to talk about chasms between neighbors and friends.

"I don't blame you, Mother," he said sadly, bending down and pulling her frail head to him. "I don't blame you at all."

Jane and Joseph sat in the driver's seat of their farm wagon as it jostled and swayed, traveling over a road only recently cleared of rain.

Joseph sat on Jane's right, pulling on the reins and occasionally talking to the horse that pulled them. It was a light load: the two of them, a basket of dinner fixings, and a quilt to sit on for their picnic. They drove east, crossed the Western & Atlantic Railroad track, and headed for the bridge over the Conasauga River.

Jane looked around at nearby woods like she'd never seen them before—fluffy crabapple blossoms in hues the color of a child's blush decorating staunch limbs of dark, wet trees. Thickets of wild plum trees that wore lush white blossoms and light green dressings along black, thin arms. Stolid brown and gray oaks with wide crowns filled with naked, arthritic limbs and countless tentacles swept the sky. A small, squat chickadee pecked the limb of a tree for food, only to be chased away by a bossy blue jay, crying *scree, scree* over its domain. A bothersome crow took up the call to scare the jay away, leaving only his unnecessary *caw* for a calling card.

Just as the luscious crabapple blossoms covered up the gnarled limbs of a tree, so the spring air brought a new dress to Jane's mood. Winter meant long nights and early bedtimes to escape the cold. The days in the household turned around filling the iron log hoops time after infernal time. It was necessary, but Jane tired of it quickly, especially having to sweep up time and again after Will or Ab trailed in bark and dirt with the firewood. With so many children and so many rooms, it was a constant battle to keep the fires fed.

It was easier to get aggravated with her family in winter. Jane caught herself yelling like common riffraff at her children when she spied a bit of mud on the floor in the hallway and up the stairs. Seemed like the girls could never keep on top of Alice and Gilbert's propensity for bringing the outdoors in.

With Joseph, she'd emerged from a winter that had lasted for years. The sourness of winter gave way to the hope of renewal. And what greater sign than his suggestion that they have this picnic by the river? Here they were, just the two of them, and on a Wednesday afternoon, for goodness sake. Jane looked at Joseph beside her, intent on pacing the horse. He was handsome, she thought, imagining the strong, muscular arms under the heavy cloth jacket he wore. Jane looked at him with new eyes, as though he were a different person than the father of that brood at home.

"Such a fine day," Jane said to Joseph, stretching her arms out in front of her. "I really needed to get out of the house. This rain has been driving me to distraction."

Joseph looked at her with a smile. "Well, Brown's store and the mill are closed for the afternoon. Figured I could, too."

"Well, Mr. Morgan, they close every Wednesday—yet you usually work all day in that hot old shop. Are you sure you're not trying to woo me to get some favor?" she said with a wink.

"But this isn't anything unusual," Joseph protested with mock grievance. "I take you places!"

"Yes, to the Dalton market on Saturday—"

"Don't forget that it was a market where I fell in love with you," he said, squeezing her waist. Jane remembered the day and her pink dress.

"Well, we could accept one of Gideon's invitations to a ball and kick up our heels once and a while." Jane saw Joseph suddenly frown. "What is it, Joseph?"

"Nothing." The frown went away, but he remained serious. "I just was thinking how much I enjoy our time in the evenings. I'm feeling satisfied as I haven't been for many, many—well, for a long time."

It was a relief for both of them to be on better terms. Joseph had been relentless in his desire for her. One night he cried, telling her he'd felt he'd just been through a terrible drought, holding an empty dipper in a hot Georgia field with no water in sight. He compared himself to one of the useless old crocks they'd put on the shelf because it needed mending.

"It's good to feel whole again," he'd said, pulling her close to him once more.

Jane felt a bit tired, but also whole. Today she was so excited she could hardly breathe, especially with her corset pulled tight across her rib cage. However, it gave an attractive shape to the waist of her dark blue and green plaid cotton walking dress. There was a tingling in her spine as she sat next to Joseph. To find herself wooed by her husband so, and she already thirty-three years old and the mother of six! Lots of women didn't live that long; others became disabled from childbirth or mentally deranged from all the responsibility. Many women had back problems or were deeply crippled from arthritis after years of working over hot fires with heavy iron cooking pots, stirring lye for soap and emptying huge pots of simmering lye water for making hominy. Some broke limbs holding house beams and otherwise being the helper their poor farmer husbands couldn't afford to employ. Having a wife to help was the only way to construct an addition to a cabin or home if neighbors or relatives weren't available. Jane had been spared that hard labor.

She knew a woman who died from a kitchen fire when her skirts became a torch, but the gossip—always whispered over a pie crust being rolled out or a child's dress being rubbed clean—was that the woman's death actually was caused by a cruel husband who beat her.

Josephine was mistreated, Jane felt sure. Gideon's wife was so visited by bouts of melancholy that Jane wondered if she were looking after her sons. Gideon's house servant told Miriam that Josephine barely stirred before noon each day. Gideon was so mean when he addressed his wife in the presence of others that Jane didn't blame Josephine for staying in bed. Jane had spoken to Joseph about it several times.

Many was the time Jane wanted to stay in bed herself, but not because Joseph dishonored her—far from it. Especially lately, with Joseph's attentions draining her more, she'd wanted to stay abed long after cockcrow. Sometimes the only thing that propelled Jane Morgan from the warmth of her deep feather tick was the thought that such a scandal would set the tongues of her mother-in-law, her neighbors, and everyone for miles around wagging as fast as a quilts flapping in the breeze on a windy March day.

What a wonder, this newfound love and affection! Thank you, Lord, Jane said, for the man next to me. Her body warmed slightly as she thought about the tenderness of the night before. Was this a new man? Rebecca said William Morgan had been a new man after they were married twenty years.

"Maybe he felt surer that I was going to be around to help rear the passel of children we'd had," Rebecca had said. "Maybe he was taking a cure unbeknownst to me. But he was sure different," she'd said, a shy smile across her face.

Jane remembered thinking—but not running the chance of offending Rebecca with the thought at the time—maybe, just maybe, it had to do with the fact you'd gone through The Change, and he knew you could no longer birth babies.

Jane stroked her stomach as she rode beside Joseph.

"Something going on in there?" Joseph asked.

"You don't miss a thing," she said, tweaking his nose gently with the hand she lifted from her skirt. Joseph reacted a bit more somberly than she would have thought, not saying anything. Jane knew he had something on his mind. But he was a cake on the hearth in a spider pot. He wouldn't be ready till he was ready.

A solid bump stirred them. Jane was jostled forward as the wagon wheels trailed across deep ruts in the muddy road.

"Better keep your eyes on the road, Mr. Morgan," Jane advised, smiling.

When they arrived at the bridge, Joseph turned the wagon south along the riverbank and sought an area that was level. Across the river, they could see that the road they'd just left emerged on the other side of the deep stream, then climbed a steep hill. The adjacent wooded slopes anchored trees growing along and below the water's edge, some of them half-drowned in the rain-swollen river. The land on the side Joseph chose was sloped gently to the riverbank. They found a somewhat even spot, stopped the wagon, got down, and laid out the quilt. They dined well on ham, biscuits with butter and blackberry preserves, and a small crock of pickled green beans.

"Something's wrong in Gideon's house," Joseph began, as he set the crock back in the picnic basket. Jane was stretched out on the quilt, enjoying a feeling of fullness and relaxation from the meal and the spring air. "I need to talk to you about it."

Jane pulled herself to a sitting position. Now she knew why her husband had left the shops empty in the middle of the week. There was some bad news.

"Gideon's abusing his slaves, and it's reached a point where his corruption is affecting our household," Joseph said.

Jane looked at him, her brown boots stretched out in front of her, then at the deep, muddy waters swirling west between her two feet. "Wh-What do you mean?" she stammered.

Joseph then told her about the events of last Saturday. She put her hand to her mouth as if to scream when he told her about James' tempting Ab. Then he described his confrontation two days ago with Gideon. Something heavy pressed on Jane's breast as she heard of his break with his brother.

"He's your brother, Joseph," she said when he had finished. "But his boy's done such an awful thing—hurt my boy, tried to get him to sin so horribly. How can we stop them?"

Jane felt Joseph grab her face in his hands. He looked at her and said nothing for a moment. "We cannot help Gideon," Joseph said. "We can only let him know how depraved he is. I'm going to have to find a way." Joseph's slow, measured sentences fell on Jane's ears like someone else was speaking. She found his words unbelievable. He related what his mother had told him about the reason why William brought the family west from South Carolina.

Joseph now sat with his hands beside him.

"Your father must be spinning in his grave," Jane said, wanting to reach for his hand.

"Now I know," Joseph said as he looked out over the waters, "why he talked so negatively about planters. Mother told me she and father worried over Gideon's arrogance, but they didn't want to interfere with family harmony. That was my father, though, and I ain't him. I can't have Gideon flaunting his sins.

"We moved from South Carolina because of slavery. We moved from Atlanta because of the lawlessness. Here we put down our stakes on a way of life where we can own as much land as we need and pray the railroad brings us more prosperity. But the whole time, we've got this ugly specter lurking about in the barn, waiting to spring.

"The blacks could rise up and slit our throats some summer evening while Gideon's on Fort Mountain for the hot months. It came within a hair's breadth of happening in Charleston. It was the ones who didn't own slaves who were going to be murdered.

"You, me, our sons and daughters—all could be slaughtered. Failing that, those who want to secede from the Union could drown our hopes of prosperity like unwanted curs in the Conasauga. All for their precious slavery."

Joseph quieted for a moment. Jane smoothed his sleeve, then reached up to stroke his clean-shaven face.

"Such awful choices! Are we that near to giving up?"

Joseph looked intently at the river pushing orphaned tree branches or an occasional whole tree trunk west toward Rome. The tree trunk might follow the Conasauga as it became the Oostenaula and end up on a riverbank there in the center of Rome, where the Oostenaula joined the Etowah. Or it might speed along, caught up in the much larger Coosa, in a relentless fall towards the Gulf of Mexico.

"Our only hope is that our state, the only one that kept the South from seceding so recently, will continue to hold the ground," Joseph said. "You'd be surprised to know this, but the other day Will told me his teacher said that Georgia outlawed slaves when it was first formed. Said the colony was meant to be a place for yeoman farmers, not full of planters like South Carolina. Oglethorpe knew he needed strong defenders because the Spanish in Florida were ready to claim Georgia—he didn't want slavery because planters were lazy, unwilling to fight."

"Goodness, do we still have a teacher?" Jane asked, worried about the brazenness of the poor school instructor. He had to be very brave or very foolhardy. She knew talk about slaves was rare and frowned upon in the community—unless it was the menfolk talking among themselves. As Joseph talked, her sympathy gradually turned to fear. Joseph was a slaveholder, too, so what would happen if he went by his convictions, which seemed to be for abolition? What would happen to Miriam? What would the neighbors' reaction be? She knew her family could as soon become the town pariahs as the local heroes for a stand like Joseph's. "I sympathize, Joseph, but I wonder what would happen to our family if the word got around that you were shunning your brother because of slavery—"

"Not merely because of slavery, but because of his abuse of Matilda, and who knows who else—"

"But what I mean is, your children would be objects of ridicule. We could become socially undesirable. What about church—? "

Joseph looked hard at his wife. "Jane, we will one day have to make a choice, I feel sure of it. So you'd best get prepared to choose. It's thinking about the loss of social position that's allowed this unholy form of labor to grow. Every man with twenty slaves probably says that about his people—'they'd starve if I didn't feed 'em,' I've heard 'em say. It's become an excuse.

"If people want to exclude us because of my opinions, I'm afraid we'll have to bear up. We might miss an occasional ball at Gideon's—"

"Exactly, Joseph," Jane said. "Those are important for our daughters' and sons' social opportunities, and—" she let her voice drop. "I'd miss the chance to waltz with you, my husband. Remember, I fell in love with you back in old Marthasville, dancing at Mrs. Scogins'."

"Jane, Jane," Joseph grasped the back of her neck to keep her facing him. "Don't you see? We can't be concerned about dances. This is too important. Our survival is at stake here. This area could become dominated by planters' interests and their ways, just like Abbeville. I can't take that risk.

"You and I have just come through a peck of problems. We didn't love each other properly for some time because I wouldn't discuss important decisions with you. I'm changing my ways. I'm tryin' to tell you what's around the bend. And I'm askin' you to support me. I hadn't thought about the dances. But I have thought about what could happen as I sever my relationship with Gideon.

"There are so many forces working on us—it's hard to make the right choices. About anything. How to shield our sons and daughters from those who allow evil in the pursuit of wealth. How to provide for people brought here against their will, who have no resources to survive on their own. If you take a stand on your beliefs one day, you're likely to be knocked down the next by those who believe differently."

Joseph looked straight ahead, his voice sad.

"It's like drawing a line in the water out there in the river," he said, nodding toward the water. "Your position is certain about as long as the line lasts, but you have to take that position anyway, and figure out the rest as best you can," Joseph said.

"If I denounce Gideon, there will be bad feelings. But he and his kind will continue to grow in importance and ruin our chance for a permanent home, the one we've sacrificed and moved you from your family for—"

Tears came to Jane's eyes as she thought about her mother in Atlanta. She felt Joseph's thumbs, dry and cracked from work, wiping the wetness from the corners of her eyes.

"If you'll support me, Jane," he said, "I'll support you in your loss, and I'll try and make it good for you and for all of our young ones."

Jane felt squeezed in a vice between her love for Joseph and her anger about the world her menfolk were making. Tarnation on Gideon and his lustful ways! Why couldn't he make his wife happy and spare the rest of them this misery? Why did Joseph have to be the one to right the world's wrongs—he didn't start the problem, and he was just one man; how could he stop them? Would it be a better world if women had some say? What could she do to make things better? How could she separate herself from her husband after they'd just gotten back together?

"Oh, Joseph," she threw her arms around his neck. "You're right. How can I be concerned about dances when my sons were so near Satan's door? What if you hadn't overheard James and Ab?"

She thought about tall Ab and Brother Will. And the girls. What if James tried to molest one of their girls? It could be awful.

"You work so hard. I know you've carried most of this burden for us. Forget the dances. Forget Gideon and sad Josephine. Of course, I'll support you. I'll love you forever."

Jane felt his arms around her, holding her tight as they sat there on the riverbank. He kissed her deeply and lay back with her in his arms on the quilt. Jane sensed the heaviness lift from her body. What lay ahead might be difficult, but they were together in the struggle. Tears sprang to her eyes.

"I'm behind you, husband," Jane said after a long silence. "Do what you must." She felt his strong arms hugging her to him again.

"It won't be easy, but after you've lived a lifetime believing in doing the right and just thing, you can't turn away from it," Joseph said quietly.

The air was cool across their bodies, and the brilliant green buds on the trees overhead invited them to celebrate the newness of their love. Jane wanted more, but knew that this was not the time or place to indulge in scandalous behavior. She enjoyed more kisses, then snuggled close to Joseph, and placed her head on his shoulder. The afternoon sun cast shadows of trees across their resting bodies.

Chapter 12

A DESCENDING CURTAIN

A dark shadow swept over the ground in front of Joseph as he rode toward Gideon's big house. Joseph looked up to see the source, but saw nothing. Again, the shadow fell across his path. Again, he saw nothing. Joseph felt he was being guarded on his way to his brother's. It was as though he were being protected by a spiritual covering—something that was there, but not clearly seen. Keeping his hand to his eyes to block out the sun, he looked up and far to the right. Joseph spied a hawk flying swiftly to a nearby oak tree. There the bird perched as though in wait.

"Lord, I need the covering," Joseph breathed to himself. He let the horse plod at a comfortable pace. He was in no hurry. He even hoped Gideon wasn't at home.

Joseph paused atop the ridge above the two ribbons of the river that formed a sharp bend around Gideon's land. Gideon had so much acreage on both sides of the river's tortuous switchbacks that anyone looking at a map of the state could pick out his brother's holdings. Did it bother Joseph? He knew Gideon worked hard, and he was smart, smarter than Joseph about making money from land. In the early mornings when Joseph woke and couldn't get back to sleep, he thought about Gideon and his land, and he tried not to be envious.

The rain had just left. It had hampered everyone's work and muddied the roads, and yet what a blessing it was for the new cotton crop and for his own food crops so recently put into the welcoming ground.

Everything looked perfect, like God intended it—clear skies, a warming sun, crops being planted in rich soil. Joseph saw Gideon's crew working over on his left. Most of Gideon's people were out, even the small children, each dragging a tow sack of seed for the others to plant. Two older women bent over the ground, letting the tiny pellets fall into the fresh-turned earth. Four men followed behind, turning the soil over the row. The younger women were probably in the house.

Joseph prayed for fortitude, wisdom—all the virtues in the Bible he could think of. Should he be more compassionate? Joseph remembered Ab's anger with him, and he thought of Will. Would James try to entice his younger son, too, trading on Will's famous trust? And Susan, now twelve. How would she react to news of her older cousin fathering a child? Would Alice Jane, Gilbert and Catherine grow up amid stories about their dusky relatives?

As Joseph moved down the road to Gideon's house, he thought about his father's unhappiness about Gideon. He tried to imagine the pain it caused him when he saw Gideon purchasing first one, then three, then seven slaves while he lived in Griffin. William must have wondered why he had worked so hard to make a life in Georgia when he saw his oldest son grow up to be so like the people he fled in Carolina. What could he, Joseph, do to make both his and his father's dreams come true?

"Keep the family together. Family's all you've got." Joseph heard the words from the raspy voice of his dying father. Family's all I've got, but what a family! Joseph thought.

Pa, you didn't leave easy directions, Joseph said to the air around him. How am I supposed to keep the family together when the family is spreading licentiousness? You wouldn't want that, I know.

Walking his horse down the road, he remembered a story that his grandmother had told his father about seeing the over-the-mountain men. Joseph recalled it clearly.

He pictured the long rows of men riding single file over horse paths beat out from Indian trails. They gathered more men in each backwoods settlement they came upon and from rendezvous points they'd arranged in cozy gaps lying between mountains whose blue heights were often hidden by opaque white scarves of clouds. Gradually, hundreds of gaunt, determined men, their long rifles strapped across their saddles, would stream in from mountains that rose a mile high and spread over what were now five states in the Blue Ridge. When his grandfather encountered them, it was fall, with a slight breeze stirring golden yellow hickory leaves as large as the biggest feathers a Cherokee chief might wear. Light brown beech trees perched near water, and loblolly pines reached for the sky; brilliant scarlet maples stood next to spreading dark green hemlocks and colorful oaks of every description—red oaks, white oaks, black oaks, Spanish oaks, and water oaks—the weak oaks with the shallow roots that were the first to fall in huge windstorms.

He could smell fire, as autumn wildfires seared the drought-filled land. If a rider got too close to another man, a man's breath would be smothered by the smell of the other man's body awash with sweat trapped under deerskin pants and shirts reeking from several days' ride with little rest. His own horse's feet would pick up smelly droppings hitting the trail in front of him, and sweat would run down his horse's graceful, bent neck.

Joseph heard the sound of hardwood leaves crunching under horses' feet. Riders talked to their mounts, urging them up difficult rises or down treacherous slopes. They talked to the horses in quiet voices, in keeping with the general silence along the trail. He heard their voices calling "Whoa," and "Hyanh," and "Easy, boy" to their horses. All along came the sounds of the rattle and crack of leather saddlery and the clink of tin cups for drinking deeply from mountain streams. The men wore slouch hats or raccoon skin caps over long, stringy, hair that ranged in color from blond to brown to black. Some caught their hair back Indian-style, using leather strips or brightly colored cloth. Some wore beads strung on deer sinew around their necks. The riders' eyes would be red from riding long hours with only brief rests under the night skies.

When they stopped for water and food for their horses, the sound of their voices drifted up with talk of taking care of the English finally and forever. All knew people who'd been killed earlier by Indians—whom the English inspired to wage war against the mountain settlers—or more recently by Tories. They'd already engaged the Loyalists in several battles in the Carolinas. All were alarmed at the cruelty of the British soldiers being headquartered in homes—how they turned households upside down, ate their food, and threatened the families. They knew about the quick and vicious hangings. The over-the-mountain men were determined to take care of the Loyalists. Tea and taxation were not the issues—domination through cruelty and violence was.

After years of British insults to the folks in upcountry and low country South Carolina, in Georgia, and in North Carolina, the mountain men banded together to protect their neighbors. What would happen today if there was a similar threat, Joseph wondered. Would it be wise to aggravate his brother and risk not having support? That's probably what Pa meant. Family is everything. It's family who help raise the barn or the house, who share food and buy services, and who are the first to give aid when famine or war take over.

Either he or Gideon would be cut off from aid and support, Joseph thought. Was it fair for him cut off his brother from the rest of the family? A man excluded from his family was disgraced. If he disowned Gideon, his brother would find it difficult to hold his head up in the neighborhood. If he took the matter to their church, Gideon could be barred from attending services in the only church around. Joseph thought back to the mountain men guiding their horses down steep slopes bordered with mountain laurel and rhododendron, on to the slaughter at King's Mountain, traveling hundreds of miles to take a stand for their homes. This was his home. Like them, he had to fight for it.

Joseph's body felt heavy. He shrugged his shoulders as if to shift the burden, then straightened again. He looked at his tanned, wrinkled hands and dirt-lined fingernails. He thought of Gideon's hands, perpetually soft and always clean, the nails trimmed evenly.

Joseph and his family had moved from Carolina to Georgia. Watched as Atlanta grew up around them, and left because of the wickedness there. Followed his brother here, bought the inn, built the shops, girdled trees, and hustled the farm into its splendid state. Gideon had built his home and planted his lands with slave labor, and committed the sin of infidelity with women he owned.

Joseph could pull up stakes and go elsewhere, or stay and fight. His body was tired, and he let his shoulders feel the relief of an imagined touch from Jane. He bathed in a memory from early this morning. He pictured a cool mountain stream running down a hill, skirting huge, moss-covered rocks in a forest so deep the sun scarcely warmed the rocks, a stream that drew the mountain men to water their horses and themselves. He couldn't flee. He was too old.

"Lord, I believe you love those who labor with their hands," he whispered, holding the reins high as if in prayer. "With my hands, I try to provide for my family, as you told us in Scripture you would help us do. I don't know if this is right. I can only go by your words of love for those who labor and your anger at those who violate your laws."

Joseph watched in awe as the red-tailed hawk flew past him at near shoulder height, pounced on the ground, and ascended with a small rabbit in his talons. The hawk rose to the top limb of another nearby oak and proceeded to hack at his prey with his sharp beak. A chill went down Joseph's back. May he be the hawk, not the rabbit, in his encounter with Gideon.

Gideon clearly did not expect him. He looked hurried as he came in response to Cicero's summons to the parlor. The brothers stood in the hallway where they danced at Christmas. Gideon pulled at his frock coat, tugged at his stiff collar.

"Well, brother, I thought you didn't want me and my family on your property," he said. "I guess we need to clarify the circumstances under which you are welcome here."

"I came because I had not finished with our discussion of Monday," Joseph said evenly. "I need to make it clear that you are not welcome in this neighborhood at all, not just in my home."

Gideon made a fake choking sound. "Wh—what did you say? 'Not welcome in this neighborhood at all?' You've got to be deluding yourself, brother." Joseph felt a chill run through his body at the word "brother." What a mockery of what was once a close bond!

"Who do you think is most respected in this neighborhood?" Gideon said. He thumped his chest with his fist. "You're looking at him!"

"I'm planning to expose your outrages against your blacks at the next church meeting," Joseph continued. "There are enough self-respecting folks in that group to vote to exclude you."

He was bluffing, of course. How did he know how people would vote? The Methodist and Baptist churches had split with their parent churches only two years before over slavery. In their own primitive Baptist church, most people were hot about Northerners telling Southerners what to do. But they were also against fornication. Was it fornication if a slave owner assaulted a slave? His church might vote to exclude Gideon, but it might not.

"Leave now in the midst of a cotton boom? You've got to be crazy!"

"You've had your land long enough now to make your next move. The boom in cotton will help you sell out at a terrific profit and move on. I won't have my family sinning like you and your son are."

"Now look here, Joseph—"

The younger brother eyed the older. Joseph did not blink. His gaze held steady.

"You're going off half-cocked, little brother," Gideon said. "I'll crush you if you try anything to blemish our family."

"A little late, isn't it Gideon? My son's been poisoned by your sins. He'll never regain his innocence. What about your sons?"

"I'll speak to James."

"You'd 've done better to have reined in your own desires, rather than acting on 'em. Your son learned from you to give in to his lusts, then he tried to get my son to do the same."

"Brothers can't go against brothers," Gideon said, desperation mixing with anger in his voice.

For a moment, Joseph felt sorry for Gideon. "We promised our father to grow up decent and God fearing, loving the Lord. You are filth, trash—and I don't want to be associated with you, in person or in the minds of any of my neighbors. I'll look for your 'for sale' sign soon. I don't care where you go. You can go west, you can go south, I'm sure you won't want to go north. You can't stay here. If you want to fight me in the meeting, go ahead. But if you look around, you'll find people who come to your fancy balls but who loathe for your whoring ways.

"There are a few who may not hate what you do," Joseph continued, "but they hate you for your wealth, and they'll join in the vote, too. I'll bring it up unless you start preparing to leave." Joseph couldn't believe his own ears. Who knew how they'd vote?

"You little nothing tradesman," Gideon sneered. "You and your so-holy family. You've always held yourselves above everyone else. So righteous and without blemish. You are nothing—a speck, compared to me. You've always been envious—wanted to have a big house and large acreage like me, but you always got there just a little behind me, always just a little late. If I *choose* to leave, I'll leave you in my dust. You can't wish us away, Joseph. We're here to stay. And you know what? The blacks are the only things that give you any class. If it weren't for the slaves, where would you be? On the absolute lowest rung of the ladder of society.

"We're the elite, and you are semi-elite, only because you're not black. Without slaves, we're reduced to the winners and the losers, the quality people and the inferiors. And you're the losers, Joseph, you and your fine family. You'd better hope a few blacks are around to elevate you."

Joseph could ignore Gideon's blustering ways most of the time, but his fingers itched for revenge. It was so tempting to let fly with his anger as he had in the smithy. Yet this was a moment when he must press on.

Joseph focused his eyes more strongly on Gideon. Gideon's light-skinned nose seemed even more sharp and patrician than Joseph remembered. He knew what a contrast he was, his own skin tanned from the forge fires, the wind, and the sun. Joseph kept a close eye on Gideon's slender hands.

"When did the curtain fall, Gideon?"

"What curtain? What are you talking about?"

"The curtain that hides the truth from you. You're an intelligent man, well read—you associate with the finest society in Dalton. How did you let that veil fall over your intellect where you can't tell the truth from a fairy tale? It's a storybook life you're leading. Those who want to continue this evil system have erected a heavy lace curtain and lowered it over the minds of men like you. You're intelligent, but fooled by the fancy arguments that obscure the truth.

"You want to drop that curtain over all of us, so we won't see either. The truth is, this system is corrupt, and it's corrupted you, and now it's spreading to the rest of the family. You've got to go."

"Look," Gideon steamed, his face red. "You keep your distance from me, and I'll keep mine from you."

"It's too late. Seeing you reminds us all of the disease you've brought." Joseph placed his hat firmly on his head. "I'll expect to hear soon of your imminent sale and departure."

Joseph nodded towards his brother and strode out the door. As he left, he heard the solid sound of hardwood slapping hardwood behind him.

The blacksmith's shop was full of visitors. Five men stood around swapping tobacco plugs for seeds or offering news of other farmers not present in the group. They watched Joseph carefully shoeing a mare still covered in red dust from the heavy clay fields, his tall frame cramped under the horse's belly where he could hold the mare's front leg bent back and drawn through his own legs while he faced away from her. Shoeing horses was the one time he wished he were shorter.

"Y'couldn't take a little more time with that, could yuh?" asked Reuben Daniel. He spat his wad close to where Joseph stood. Joseph awkwardly balanced the mare's hoof on his knee while striking with his hammer.

"Y'couldn't try to be a little more careful where you spit, could yuh?" Joseph retorted, not looking up. Why the man was trying to fool with him, he didn't know. Usually this was a friendly group, as companionship was rare in these parts. The only other place in the settlement people could gather with impunity for not working away at the everlasting farm chores was at a church meeting. But these were not churchgoers.

"Waal, it's just takin' you an awful long time," Daniel said. "I thought you'd be done before my horse died of old age." The man let out a laugh that went into a high wheeze, reminding Joseph of an ass' bray. Joseph, who judged the man to be around forty, looked sideways as the fellow pushed his black wool hat back off his face. The man's face, all pink with folded skin around his mouth when he laughed, reminded Joseph of a pig.

"Well, you could try attaching your own hoe head, or shoeing this mare by yourself, thankee kindly," Joseph said, barely hiding his irritation. What was wrong with Daniel? He wasn't a man with a lot of smarts, but he usually didn't act like a horse with burr under his blanket.

"Hey, what're yuh chargin' these days for a coupla wagon tires?" James Benson asked. "I got me a broken down old wreck I gotta get goin' 'fore harvest this summer."

"Ain't gonna set you back much," Joseph said. He grabbed the mare's hoof to still her while he bent the last nail. "Prob'ly a couple dollars for the iron, then a dollar each for sitting the iron. You gotta have 'em filled or are the old spokes all right?"

"Wha'd you say the arn cost?"

"Couple dollars."

"Land sakes!" Benson gasped. "You mighty proud of them arn prices." Joseph looked up just in time to see him winking at Daniel.

"What's your problem? You gonna go down to the Etowah mills and get your own iron? Bring it here when you do, and I'll work it for you!"

"Well, why's the cost gone up? Last year it woulda cost me a lot less."

"Costs more 'cause I get charged more. Railroad's raised the prices for deliverin' the stuff by a half cent a pound. There's seventy pounds of iron in each tire. The iron is two and a half cents a pound. That means the price for seventy pounds is two dollars and ten cents. I gotta pay that, and you get to pay it 'cause I pay it."

"Don't seem right to me," Benson grumbled.

"What's the problem?" Joseph asked.

"Waal, we sure wouldn't want to get overcharged at the only blacksmith in town," Daniel broke in. "We hear you been overchargin' us somethin' fierce lately.

"Cain't have that kinda thieven' goin' on in this neck of the woods," Daniel said. Joseph looked up. Now that his mare was shoed, Daniel was a lot freer with his tongue.

"Take my business over to that Irishman near Sugar Valley," Daniel continued.

Joseph had been pulling the mare forward to check her step now that the new shoes were on. He looked around at the group of men. Daniel was the stationmaster's brother-in-law, and Joseph had always considered him at least a neutral friend. Benson was sort of new in the area, but he had no cause to get on wrong side of the blacksmith. He looked at James Wilson, a close friend Joseph trusted to watch the shop when he had to go to Dalton.

Wilson was looking at his feet, shuffling them nervously. As he shuffled, his shoe brushed a metal oil can from a locomotive. It was the kind of can that was suspended on a rod in front of the headlight of the locomotive. Train crews carried this large can to fill the smaller, long-spouted cans that lubricated the train's moving parts. When an engineer was out of oil, he carried the empty ahead to headquarters and pulled a full one off a train headed north, away from Atlanta. Then he replenished the oil can back in Atlanta and hung it out for the next southbound engineer. The engineer merely grabbed it from the rod on the front of the engine, saving the time and avoiding keeping large supplies of oil in the engine cab. Joseph was reminded of his pressing work to make repairs for the W&A Railroad. Here was a bail he had to fix to go back on the early train tomorrow.

Joseph didn't have time to squander on neighborhood trouble. "I don't think I'm cheatin' you, if that's what you're implying," he said. A clammy heat stole over his chest. This arguing was disturbing him. Being called a cheat was serious. "I give you honest work and only charge what's fair."

"'At's not what I hear," Daniel said. "Ever since you went up two cents on the horseshoein', word's been gettin' round that you're takin' your customers for a ride."

"The railroad's increased its rates bringin' the iron here that I work and then put on your horse," Joseph repeated, trying to be matter of fact. Why was Daniel objecting now? He'd raised his rates two months ago. Joseph decided the best course was to remain calm. He thought he was hiding his irritation well, but he was on edge.

"Next you know," Daniel said, "folks are going to be trying to find someone who'll be fair with 'em." Joseph felt the hair on the back of his neck slowly rising. That was the second time Daniel said he was going to find someone else to do his work. O'Connor, that was the Irishman's name. Joseph felt a chill.

Gideon. He'd been spreading rumors, trying to ruin his business. If people believed he was cheating them, he'd lose work. He couldn't raise the prices of meals and rooms at the inn too much; folks'd find a way to pass his stop without eating or sleeping. Joseph, with a huge household, was very vulnerable.

Joseph shivered under his heavy shirt and leather apron. He was not about to let on how nervous he felt. Let them find other people to do their work.

"If you feel you're gettin' cheated," he said loudly, staring in turn at each man, "then maybe you ought to take your work to someone cheaper." His friend Wilson looked straight at him, solemn as a judge. Joseph knew it was important to call Daniel's bluff. He moved over to his father's desk to write down the charge for the horseshoes.

"For sure, you need to go ahead and settle up your bill so's I won't be carryin' you and never get paid." He heard guffaws as two men laughed at Daniel, who'd just lost his credit.

While he sat at sundown on the back porch replacing the clabber on the butter churn dasher, Joseph fretted over the morning's scene in the smithy, like a dog mauling a fresh bone.

As Joseph placed the newly sawed dasher head on the end of the long handle, he thought about his brother. What had happened to their camaraderie? How could Gideon turn on his family like this? If Pa were here, he would have lit into Gideon in a big way, Joseph was sure. He'd no longer be able to strap his son, but he could have shamed him good, made him straighten up, and forced him to do right by Josephine and leave the colored women alone.

Should he be the one to move instead of Gideon? There was land out in Texas just waiting for settling. Water was a problem there, though. He'd heard people could make a prosperous living in Ohio. Joseph couldn't imagine himself in such a place. Floods of immigrants from countries where English never dinned their ears. Fast-talking, scheming, business people. Public ridicule and contempt for Southerners throughout the Northern state. People not caring for each other. Like here, he thought wryly.

He looked out past the pigpen and the barn. The sun was setting, its warm glow falling on the farm. Here and there he caught a last look at dazzling redbuds with bright pink blossoms showing up like jewels next to the dark slender branches. What beauty, he thought, and what rancor, side by side.

He longed for a peaceful home where he could feel safe with his family. And who was family? If a brother turned against a brother, was he still family?

He felt the pain in his chest again, a pain that visited him intermittently. He'd never heard his father complain about such a pain, yet he knew his father tired easily during his last years of life. It was "new monya," as Doc Gilbert called it, that took William in the end.

Across the broom-swept yard, small Gilbert came running toward him from under the water oak, where the long hemp rope swing was hung and where the children played on a flying jenny Joseph had bolted to a stump.

"Papa," Gilbert called. He ran towards the house, climbed the stairs with an awkward five-year-old gait, then moved to Joseph's side. Joseph remembered Ab and Will at the same age. They were more coordinated at that age than his third son.

Joseph put the dasher in the churn and slid the round top over the handle. He grabbed the two handles, slid it aside, and reached down to pull Gilbert on his lap.

"What's a pair more?" Gilbert blurted.

Joseph sat confused by the words his son struggled to say. A pair more, he repeated to himself. He looked at his son and was about to ask him to say it again.

"Unc' Gideon says you need to get one, Papa," Gilbert announced. "Do you need to get one, Papa? What is it, Papa, a pair more?" Gilbert looked up at Joseph, with inquiring eyes. His blond curls fell around his face.

Joseph could not breathe from the pain. He held his breath. Gideon again!

He tried to draw air. The pain lessened, but still prickled him in his chest. He put his head down and stroked Gilbert's blond hair.

"Perhaps Uncle Gideon thinks I need a pair more of hands," he lied. He held up his two large hands so the youngster could see. "Maybe he thinks I need more of these to get my work done. Or he may think I need some help in the blacksmith's shop, meaning some workers," Joseph said, searching his head for explanations. "Workers are sometimes called 'hands'."

"Would you have slaves like Uncle Gideon?" Alice Jane ran to her father's side. She'd followed Gilbert from the play area and was breathless as she joined them.

"No, I wouldn't, honey," he said, stroking her long blond hair and pulling it behind her ears. He put his arms around her and around Gilbert and hugged both of them to him. Then he held both of them out to look at them. "Your papa doesn't have slaves do most of his work—"

"Joe Morgan!" A shout came up from outside.

"Joe Morgan, come quick! There's a fire at the wood station south of town!" James Wilson rounded the corner of the house, limping from the fast running he'd been doing. Wilson turned to go.

Joseph stood up. The pain from his chest was gone.

"I'll follow right behind!" he cried.

He pushed the two children toward the stairs that led off the porch. "Go find your brothers and tell 'em to saddle up and come with me. We've got to go put out a fire down at the woodshed! The whole neighborhood could burn!"

Ab and Will ran inside the barn, breathless.

"C'mon boys," Joseph yelled. "Get these sacks wet at the horse trough, grab all the buckets you can, and bring it all with ya!"

Dipping the sacks, Joseph felt his body shaking. The woodshed south of town was a half-mile long. Tilton was a wood and water stop for all the locomotives going up and down the W&A Railroad. Some trains made stops for wood only at the longest shed, at Green's Wood Station, about a mile and a half below town. Then they continued on to Tilton for water, where they also stopped for meals and beds at the inn. What good the wet sacks would do, only heaven could say. Burning unchecked, this fire could bring disaster.

Joseph led his sons out of the farmyard and spurred his horse to a gallop down Tilton Road. They whipped past the Methodist Church brush arbor on the left. If only the church were built, its bell could summon help from miles around. As it was, the Tilton area depended on people going door to door.

They turned the sharp curve toward the railroad crossing and broke free of the heavy cedar trees blocking their view to the south. Heavy gray smoke was rising in the distance. Darkness fell quickly and, by the time they reached the railroad crossing just south of town, almost everything was obscured. Joseph knew they had another mile to go. As he thought about the hopelessness of quenching a fire eating away at well-dried hardwood, he felt a heaviness in his shoulders, arms and legs. A lead weight bound him to the saddle.

The skies were red against the black night. The darkness gave way to intense, flickering light, as they arrived at the shed. The middle part of the north end was afire, burning with a fury like Joseph had never seen. Steady winds kept the fire going. It was like the yellow fire in the forge, only this was huge. Flames leapt skyward. Sparks sprayed around the area inside the shed.

The structure was at least twelve feet high; it was filled head-high all the way down its half-mile length with hardwood fuel split in three-foot lengths. Entire tree logs lay strewn about it in readiness for cutting and splitting, a testament to the fact that the job of filling the iron horse's gut was never-ending. The flames reached twenty feet high across the middle of the north end.

They dismounted, tied their horses well away from the flames, and held their heads together to talk above the roar of wind and flame.

"It looks like there's only one way to stop this," Joseph yelled over the sound. "We've gotta tear out the north wall to get some logs rolled off!"

"Pa," Ab said, "let me go rip the end out. I can do it!"

"We're gonna have to all three pull at it," Joseph shouted. "Got your gloves? Let's go!"

They pulled leather gloves off of their saddles, the gloves they used in the smithy for extended work at the forge. They ran for the north end wall and began pulling.

"We need a sledge hammer to take this thing down," Joseph cried. "Run back to the smithy and get a hammer and an axe!"

At that moment, James Wilson came riding up, followed by three other men on horses.

"I got all the help I could," he cried, "but nobody's home!"

"We're not goin' to be able to stop the fire," Joseph yelled. "Water's too far away, an' there's too little of it! I got my boys runnin' back for a hammer and axe. What say we try to offload some of the fuel in the middle so the fire won't spread there?"

Joseph and the others ran to the open side of the shed, and two smaller men climbed up to the top of the pile closest to the fire. They began throwing wood down to Joseph and the three others below, who then shoved the fuel away from the burning inferno. Flames shot up high above the roofline of the shed. Hot wind whooshed past Joseph's face; heat seared the backs of his hands as he shoved and kicked the wood. The cauldron of fire kept up a constant roar in his ears. Hundreds of trees had been felled to make this pyre. Joseph, pushing the logs with all his strength and stopping to catch his breath a few times, thought about the awful waste of timber the fire was.

"Hey, look what I found!" a man on the ground called. "A big oil can."

Joseph and Wilson ran over to him. Enoch Jones held up the three-gallon iron can with both hands. The bail hung awkwardly from its one hinge. The oil can from the smithy!

Jones looked up at Joseph suspiciously, the large can gleaming in the firelight. "This a home-cooked deal or what?"

Joseph froze, his heart, head and chest full of fear.

"That can was in my shop for repair," Joseph admitted. "Someone must have taken it. I got no cause to do in my livelihood!"

Jones's and Wilson's faces were lit by the fire behind them. Joseph could see them looking at him. They knew that there'd been rains recently, so drought hadn't caused the blaze. They could figure out that it was a manmade disaster. The evidence, all of it, Joseph knew, pointed to him.

Joseph held his breath. Neither of the two men spoke. They just looked at him with disgust, then returned to hoisting and shoving logs. Joseph finally regained his composure.

"Look for more evidence as you work, men," he called. "Then we can make guesses that are closer to the mark! At least now we know why the fire is raging with such a fury."

He shoved an oak log not nearly so heavy as his heart at that moment. He kicked it with a fury.

Who had taken the oil can?

The night was pitch black all around the shed. Flames, bright orange tinged with white and purple, shot up to the dark heavens and kept up their terrible roar.

Joseph walked off away from the heat. He felt like his mouth was full of dry brush. His lungs felt burned. He wandered over towards the creek. He looked along the ground for a pail, a pan, or some other discard he could use to carry drinking water back to the others. There wasn't a lot of hope of finding anything. He knew that people used their utensils till they gave out. If a vessel couldn't hold water, it might instead hold oats or meal for horses or dogs.

After a long walk, he reached the small branch and bent over the water, scooped it up, and threw it on his face and chest. How cool it was! His skin was burning. His lungs were dry. He bowed to the water again to drink all he could in cupped hands. As he drew in the wonderful coolness, he noticed something dark in the grass near the bank. He reached out and pulled up a man's wool felt hat! Joseph knew the wearer—Reuben Daniel. Joseph couldn't believe his fortune. Here was evidence. He had to find a way to have others discover it.

He heard a commotion up near the fire. Ab and Will had returned with the tools. He ran to meet them, leaving the hat behind. Joseph took charge as soon as he arrived at the shed.

"I'll get on top of the pile," he yelled to his sons, "and whack at the planks from behind, so you can wedge 'em out from below. You give me the hammer when I get up there."

"Be careful, old man," James Wilson called. "The fire'll be eatin' at your back!"

Joseph grasped ends of logs sticking out from the pile to rise up over the long line of stacked logs, ever watchful of the fire that burned there near the north end. He pulled atop the pile, which stood six feet from the ground, and then reached down for the sledgehammer.

Joseph let go with a powerful swing at the planks on the north wall. He stood atop a gap in the wood where the man had worked to throw down logs, so he could reach the backside of the shed's end wall and yet escape the brunt of the flames.

Wham! Wham! Sweat collected on his hands as he hit. Fire blazed at his back and his shirt soaked through with perspiration. Boards groaned and cracked. Ab and Will had toted long iron rods from the smithy, and they made quick work of inserting them behind the boards Joseph pushed out from the wall. Then they leveraged the boards off the posts and sent them clattering to the ground. One by one they fell, leaving only posts where there'd been a solid north wall.

"Now, get the axes!" Joseph called as he climbed down from his hot perch. "You boys sure did right to bring those rods and axes!"

Joseph and Ab began slicing at the twin posts that held up the roof. They chipped at angles first from above, then from below, and then across the middle of the cuts. Chips flew like rare January snow. No longer was Ab a worrisome sapling to Joseph; he slung the axe with a fury, raising Joseph's admiration.

Within a few minutes, they had the posts whittled to precarious hourglass shapes. Joseph knew one push would send the whole shed collapsing, hopefully smothering the whole blaze.

"Ready?" Joseph asked Ab. He looked at his son, full of the energy and purpose of battle. Ab, his face dripping with sweat and his eyes brighter than Joseph had ever seen, nodded with a grin. "Then get ready to run!" Joseph called.

Joseph and Ab moved in unison at the critical moment, hitting the concave posts simultaneously. They heard a huge double crack; both leapt away at the same moment, then turned and looked back. Joseph saw the huge roof quickly slump, crushing the firewood underneath, while the posts, knuckling like knees, fell underneath. The posts at the next juncture of the shed cover slumped forward under the weight and pushed against dozens of cords of wood. As the roof fell, firewood spit out in front of the roof, cascading like a mighty river, moving to overtake the men who stood in her way.

"Run!" Joseph's cry was so desperate it was almost inaudible.

Wood shot out from the shed like bullets from a gun. One piece caught a man in the face and knocked him down. Another slashed across his shin and caused him to tumble forward. Ab rushed to block his fall. He ducked and pushed the falling man out of the way.

Men ran gasping and wheezing, trying to escape the freefalling logs. Finally, they drew together at a safe distance. Some coughed. They breathed heavily and watched the roof collapse.

"Look!" Wilson called. The fire had subsided, smothered by the sloping roof. "We can put those logs out with no problem!"

"Couple of you go get the burlap bags soaked with water!" Joseph commanded. "We might be able to lick this thing yet."

Joseph, his sons, and another man sat on the ground, their legs spread out in front of them, still panting, still trying to draw even breaths. Hats lay strewn about them. They talked little and used their hands only to wipe dripping sweat from their faces, necks, and arms. Fighting the fire had been exhausting.

The scene around them, with the long-spined woodshed roof collapsed into the racks of firewood, surrounded by logs that had been awaiting splitting and stacking, resembled what Joseph thought an earthquake would look like. He could only speculate; he'd never seen a picture of that natural disaster.

Joseph saw the connection. It was backcountry revenge. In South Carolina, Tories and revolutionaries attempted to burn each other out. In Atlanta, the Moral Party convinced Joseph the only way to clean out Slabtown and Snake Nation was with fire. Back in Abbeville, when his pa spoke out against the reliance on cotton, the disagreement was settled with a torch and gossip. It was a never-ending circle, old as the settlers' fight with each other back in the 1770s—and still going on nearly a hundred years later.

Joseph saw James Wilson approach, clutching in his tanned fist the bags he'd taken to soak in Swamp Creek. He was agitated, gesturing towards a hat he held in his other hand. Joseph held his breath.

"Look 'ere what I found!" Wilson shouted.

"Whatcha got there?" one of the other yelled.

"It's Reuben Daniel's hat." Wilson looked at Joseph. Joseph wondered what was going through Wilson's mind. They looked at Joseph.

Joseph was reminded of how he'd heard the ancient Brits tried a suspect by binding his arms and throwing him in a swirling stream. If he extricated himself and lived, he was innocent. If he drowned, he did the crime. Similarly, Joseph knew it was important not to look nervous, or he would be judged guilty. He took a deep breath and looked squarely at Wilson. He knew these men had been swayed by Gideon's talk against him. He also knew they were honest. What would their verdict be?

Wilson leaned his head to one side and squinted at Joseph.

"Why'd Daniel want to lay this on you?" he asked.

Enoch Jones came up behind Wilson into the circle of firefighters.

"I seen this hat by the crick back there," he said, approaching Joseph. "I says to James, here, I didn't see how it could be you, Joe, when here's Daniel's hat pleadin' guilty to the crime."

"I told you I didn't have no cause to go settin' a fire," Joseph said quietly.

"Old Daniel's the culprit, not old man Morgan here," Wilson said, turning to the others and holding up the hat. "Here's proof."

Jones shuffled his feet, embarrassed. "I'm the one whut accused you. That warn't right and I'll be obliged if you forgit I said anythin'," Jones said. He held his head low and extended a hand.

Joseph got up, dusted himself off, and reached for the man's hand.

"You didn't know," he said. "I've a mind that Daniels was settin' me up because of some business between my brother and me. He figures to get me in trouble."

"Yeah, come to think of it, I have heard your brother talkin' kinda rough about you," said Jones.

"Well, you don't need to worry about it. This is just between me and Gideon," Joseph sighed. He turned around to the others. "Go ahead and put those flames out—I'm headin' home!"

Joseph moved toward his horse and called back to his sons. "Ab, Will, git on over there and help Jones and Wilson. I'm headin' back. I've got some figgerin' to do!"

Joseph felt his body float above the horse's canter. He prepared himself for each of the horse's leaps forward, leaning back and letting his body roll slightly to absorb the heavy thrusts. He felt lighter, like a man who'd just escaped a sentence in jail. The quick assessment of the neighbors that Daniels was the firesetter gave Joseph a welcome reprieve. It was a narrow escape. The whole incident showed how Gideon's perfidy was infecting the whole community.

He let the rhythm of the ride overtake him as he cantered north on Tilton Road. The moon had risen and was bright enough to light the road. He could see dark lines of trees on either side, see the railroad tracks he crossed, and hear whippoorwills, grasshoppers, frogs, and bugs singing in the trees along the way. As he passed the Methodist brush arbor again, he tried to think what to do.

If he went to Gideon's to confront him, it would take almost an hour to get there. By the time he arrived, Gideon and his family would be going to bed, not a good time to talk heatedly with anyone. Joseph decided to ride through town, past the inn, and down to the river. The river was always a place to go to get things straight.

As he gently tugged his horse to the right to head down to the river, the gray luminescence of moonlight showed him the train tracks, the depot, and the stores collected around the depot. There were no people about. Near the general store, a dog looked up from the side of the road, too sleepy to bark.

At the bridge over the Conasauga, Joseph got off of his horse and walked him to look over into the water. The moonlight lit the swift-moving water below. Joseph could see tree snags reaching up out of the swirls, but he knew they wouldn't be there for long. The river quickly claimed its prizes, taking them under or swiftly propelling them toward Rome.

Joseph's body ached from fighting the fire, and he felt fatigued. He slumped, wedging himself between the bridge rail and his horse, and stared at the water for a while.

He then pulled the horse behind him and crossed the breadth of the river, catching glimpses of the dark water flowing and glinting beneath the wide gaps in the planks. He smelled the night air, fragrant with the scent of wild honeysuckle and new grasses, wisteria, and tulip poplar blooms. The inky sky bloomed with distant constellations, their stars winking at him as though on familiar terms. Joseph was filled with wonder at nature's gifts.

He looked steadily at the stars and told himself that one was William, another was his grandfather Joseph, still another pretty blond and blue-eyed Nancy, the sister who died in Abbeville District before she could speak his name.

"Pa," he appealed out loud to the sky. "What am I to do?"

There was no answer. Joseph remembered a phrase from Scripture that had a way of stealing into his mind when he was trying to make an important decision.

"So great a cloud of witnesses." The phrase echoed in his mind. Joseph had to think a minute to recall whether it was New Testament or Old. And how did the passage go?

He recollected. It was St. Paul appealing to the newly Christianized Hebrews and naming all the old patriarchs: Abraham, Isaac, Jacob, Joseph, Moses. The letter exhorted the new Christians to be steadfast, like runners in a race. "Compassed about as we are by so great a cloud..."

We're surrounded by these folks, Joseph knew. They're watching from above, just as they did from the porches and verandas here on earth. He thought of his pa, his long-separated uncle Samuel Morgan, and his cousins back in Abbeville. He thought about the Thurman relatives and the Manns and the Terrys and all the people they'd known in west DeKalb County before it became a terminus and then Marthasville and then the town of Atlanta.

They were Joseph's witnesses, those who watched and prayed with him so that he would live a righteous life.

Joseph thought to Joseph of the Old Testament. He recalled the story of Joseph being set upon by his brothers and sold into slavery. The story from Genesis was raw, full of the deeds of jealous brothers. As a boy, he'd read and reread that dreadful tale of the brothers dipping Joseph's wonderful, colorful cloak in the blood of a lamb and taking it to a grieving Jacob to show proof of his beloved son's death.

But Joseph survived and ended up a favorite of Pharaoh's court because of his ability to interpret dreams and see visions. In the end, he was reunited with his brothers and forgave them, bringing peace and prosperity to his family.

"Lord," Joseph prayed out loud, "I am not a seer like Joseph. But I pray you will give me some sign that you are with me!"

"I need a sign!" he shouted at the skies. He lifted his hands in prayer, his palms clasped together, the horse's rein threaded through the fingers of his right hand. He looked at his hands illuminated by the moon and held them there for a moment. Then he quietly led his horse back to the entrance of the bridge, remounted, and began the short ride home.

He took out his handkerchief to wipe his forehead and hands. He felt exhausted, like the biblical Joseph at age one hundred-ten. Night frogs serenaded him, and he inhaled the strong scent of wisteria, wild honeysuckle, and oak flowers as he slow-walked his horse back to the inn. An open field lay exposed in the bright moonlight, reeking of moist clay. Glints of mussel shells from an Indian shell midden dispersed in the field caught the moon's rays and reflected back to him like so many earthbound stars.

"Joseph!" Jane called to him from a veranda lit with oil lamps from inside the house when he arrived back at the inn. "We've had news!" She beckoned him to an oak-splint bottomed chair on the porch.

Jane's eyes gleamed. She'd changed to a rust-colored dress with three-boned hoops that set off her slender waist. Joseph, tired from his long ordeal with the fire, wondered why she was dressing up.

"Cicero came by earlier," she said softly, stroking his hand as she sat beside him. "At first, I was aghast that he rode by himself. Gideon doesn't usually let his people go anywhere by themselves. Gideon has sold all his land and is moving to Dalton."

Joseph leaned over Jane, moving his arms around her. As he pulled her to him, he let his shoulders drop their weight. "I'm sorry for getting your nice dress dirty," he said heavily. "I need to hold you right now. I couldn't have asked for better news than if you told me I had just won sixty more acres of land."

Joseph collapsed his arms around Jane. Her fragrant hair lay under his chin. Neither talked as his heavy breaths gradually lengthened and grew shallower.

A high noon sun hung in the early June sky as Joseph leapt on the Tilton station platform. He lunged forward, then quickly pulled his long body up and over the edge just as he felt himself falling backwards.

"Used to be able to make that without a blink," he told himself. "Gettin' old." Recovering, he strode across the rough boarded walk, heading for the stationmaster's window. "Train on time?" he asked John Hogan. Hogan was in shirt sleeves and wore an open vest.

"Are there bears in the woods?" Hogan joked with him.

Joseph remembered his near escape from the she-bear and wondered if the word had gotten around. Of course it had, he told himself. It was a small settlement. He grinned at the stationmaster. "Hear tell there are," he said with a wink. "At least my boys tell me so."

The people waiting at the station were far better dressed than when he and his family had first come to Tilton. Women were not so numerous a few years ago, either. Now folks readying for trips to Dalton and Chattanooga were gathered on the platform, five of them women. Two wore dark traveling suits, while the others were dressed in becoming dark blue and brown skirts and waists with bolero tops, covered with fashionable capes. The women wearing the more tailored garments sported crisp-looking felt hats trimmed in feather and ribbon, while the women wearing capes wore bonnets with equal adornments. Their four male companions wore frock coats and dusters over black pants.

Joseph noticed the men's shoes. Well-made boots, probably purchased from Atlanta stores, imported from Boston. Generally a moneyed bunch, he concluded. They had the leisure time and the money to travel to other cities to visit relatives, transact business, or shop in the stores that now populated the nearby towns. Very soon, there'd be an onslaught of summertime visitors getting off the train at Tilton for the wagon ride east to Carter's, the crown of the Coosawattee River plantations. Carter had thousands of acres under cultivation, most in cotton, lots of it in oats. When there was discussion of anyone having a lot of money, folks would say he had more of it "than Carter has oats."

As Joseph heard the eerie whistle of the approaching train, a murmur of excitement passed through those gathered on the platform. As the noisy, sooty train pumped its way into the station, they moved inside the depot to avoid the cinder shower. Joseph stood where he was, as he was used to soot. He wanted to make sure he caught the eye of the man who'd lift off his iron bars so he could load them quickly in his wagon and return to his smithy.

Joseph never saw a train approach without catching his breath. It seemed miraculous to him that the big, dark giant could traverse land so easily while a road wagon was bedeviled by rain, washed-out roads, and wheels breaking down under pressure from rocks, mud, and general wear and tear. A train could carry fifty or more people, the day's news from Atlanta and beyond, foodstuffs from Florida, and steel from Allatoona, Georgia or Altoona, Pennsylvania—or even from London, England—all in the same load. What a wonder he'd lived to see!

Pa would have been astounded. He'd be right here, aching to load and unload the boxcars carrying their goods, admiring the iron makers' work on those long, huge rolling wagons. He'd wonder at the large wheels with their convoluted surfaces designed to mount and ride the long, narrow rails and at the massive iron undercarriages. They'd both wonder at the factories that turned them out.

The train pulled alongside the platform, its wheels squealing, its smokestack belching, and its engine shuddering under the reverse gear, rattling with its own power. Joseph heard loud voices. For a moment he forgot his bars as he saw men, all soldiers, jump off the first car before the train even stopped. The six men were clad in deep blue uniforms featuring high standing collars, and they wore snappy looking hats.

But most of all, Joseph noted their guns. Two men carried rifles and stationed themselves at one of the supply cars, casually, yet carefully, keeping guard. The long, polished barrels of the rifles gleamed in the spring sunshine, and Joseph guessed they were Harper's Ferry issue percussion, but with some changes.

Like those in the army wagon that struck Will in Atlanta, the rifle barrels were identical and the fittings uniform, made from precision dies. Tooling and dieing could make even bullets interchangeable from one gun to the other, eliminating the tedious job of making bullet molds for each rifle, something Joseph still did. How quickly the government could turn out arms! It was amazing.

He figured the guards were there for the gold pieces transported from the mint in Dahlonega. Four other soldiers lunged toward the stationmaster's window, laughing and guffawing. Joseph saw their pistols hanging from their right sides, and he followed them at a discreet distance to catch a better look. The pistols were encased in hard, new leather holsters, and it was difficult to see the make.

"Yeah, this is Georgia, boys," one of the soldiers was telling the others. "Why, I knew a first lieutenant one time who spent a bit of time here once, and he talked and talked about its rolling hills. So you see, I've already been here, he told me so much about the area. That guy bent my ear jawin' about riding from Marietta—that's where we stopped earlier— then taking his horse and going up as far as Allatoona, and then going over to the old Indian mounds on a Colonel Tumlin's plantation.

"Man would drive you crazy," the soldier continued, "talking about his riding 'round looking at mountains and valleys in this area. Atlanta was called Marthasville then, so it must have been a long time ago. You've never seen a man who loved to look at mountains and valleys so much."

"Hell, you'll say anything to pass the time, you spend much time around a campfire," his companion said.

"Campfire, nothin'," the private responded. "Damn West Pointer—Sherman was 'is name. He was all the time goin' to balls and socials with them folks in Charleston where we was."

"Shudda gone to some balls yerself, maybe you wouldn't be no private no more, Schultz," hooted a third man. Boisterous laughter greeted the comment.

"Hey, Mr. Stationmaster—where c'n we get some grub around here?" asked the fourth man in the group, a medium-sized stocky private with greasy black hair. He leaned his arm on the office window and placed his nose within inches of Hogan's. There was an unintelligible answer. "I said, old man, where's some grub in this godforsaken little filthy village!" He turned to the other three. "Dirty, foot-draggin' Southerners," he said in disgust.

"Hey, mister, can't you understand plain English?" he yelled at the man in the window. The private was enraged.

Joseph stepped up to the window to aid Hogan, forsaking his delivery of iron bars for the moment. The other three men fell back.

"Here, here, what's yer problem?" Joseph asked. "Why're you being so rude to this gentleman?"

"Hey, pop, what's your problem?" The soldier turned his head, still leaning on the window, then slowly straightened as he saw Joseph's long, tall form next to him. He ever so slightly brushed his pistol cover with his hand then let it fall beside him. "Remember, we've got the authority of the U.S. government here."

"I don't care whose authority you've got," Joseph said brusquely. "You'll do well to mind your manners wherever you are. If it's food you're hunting, my inn offers a bountiful lunch. However," he said, motioning to the passengers moving off the train and on down the platform in the directions of the Morgan home, "it looks like the ladies and gentlemen in the coaches behind you have already started for the house, so the table's already full."

"Well, by God, we're protecting this load of U.S. gold coins, so we'd better be first at the feeding trough," the man said.

"I understand you have duties as sentinels," Joseph said, barely disguising his disapproval. "If you go to the kitchen of the inn I give you directions to, I'll be glad to see that you get a basket of dinner, but there'll be no room at the table."

"No room at the table, my eye," the soldier grumbled half to himself. "All right, old man," he said, quickly recovering. "Since you're the only host in town, we'll have to take what we can get, hard biscuits and all."

Joseph, seething with anger at the soldiers' insults, quickly gave directions. He realized he'd made enemies of the private, but he didn't care. Rudeness deserved rudeness. He was surprised at how little respect he had for the soldiers. Only a few years ago, he had been impressed with the regular army, but these men were despicable in their behavior and as arrogant and boisterous as the bear wrestlers. Such language and demeanor befitted a mountain man or a rowdy, but these were our nation's defenders. Or were they? Joseph wondered if they would defend areas they spoke of so disparagingly.

He was also bothered by the way the man broke military security by announcing the load of Dahlonega gold coins. They weren't much better than the riff-raff Joseph had thankfully left behind in Atlanta.

Joseph wondered why the blue-clad men rankled him so. Then he knew. He could tell from their voices that they were all from outside the South, probably New York or Ohio. Fast-talking, rude sons of guns, Joseph thought.

Joseph's own bias was showing, he decided, but to him they were despicable.

Joseph crossed the railroad tracks in front of the locomotive and went towards the freight car where he'd parked his open wagon. As he walked beside the train, he stepped aside, allowing a double team wagon to pass on his right. He saw it was Gideon driving with Cicero by his side. The bed of the wagon was stacked high, with trunks and crates piled above the wagon's sides.

"Whoa," his brother called to the horses. "Cicero, get down and see if my brother will give us a hand. I know he'll be so glad to see us go he'll do anything to help!"

Cicero's eyes showed his great discomfort in having to address Joseph.

"Of course, I'll help," Joseph said. "Where're you going?"

"To Dalton, my lad," laughed Gideon. "You were right. I got a good price for my land. I'm ridding myself of these slaves, and I'm going to deal in cotton in the fair city of Dalton. Of course, I'm selling Cicero here and all the rest. Need some good bucks, Joseph?" His brother laughed at his joke.

Joseph helped Cicero lift trunks into the freight car. He said nothing as Gideon stood puffing on a cigar.

Joseph felt a cramping in his stomach and then realized he hadn't eaten dinner, but he gradually found the strength to continue helping load the goods. He hoped Cicero and Gideon's other slaves didn't end up at Carter's Quarters. Joseph didn't know much about the Quarters, except that the old Indian judge John Martin had sold eighty slaves and all his land to Carter when he'd gone to Arkansas. Carter had brought two hundred more slaves from his plantation in Milledgeville. Cicero and the others would get lost in that town-sized population. Joseph tried to imagine what such a place looked like, then put it out of his mind.

Finally, Joseph was able to claim his own iron bars and carry them to his wagon.

After the train bearing Gideon's shipment had gone, Joseph grasped Gideon's hand and wished him well.

"I hope you'll come to see us before you leave," Joseph said, knowing he didn't want and Gideon wouldn't attempt a visit. He left Gideon leaning against his empty wagon.

There was a sudden lightness in Joseph's stomach and in his shoulders as he drove to the house to join his family for dinner leftovers.

"So Gideon is really leaving?" Jane asked. She placed warm cornbread, ham in field peas, butter, and preserves in front of Joseph at the eating table.

"Yes, he says he's going to deal in cotton in Dalton," Joseph said.

"Well, that's a big change from planting," Jane said. "At least the boys will have a chance for a better education. I hope Josephine will fare better."

"I'm sure Gideon has thought it all out," Joseph said.

She placed her hand on his shoulder, watching him as he ate.

"Well, I'm satisfied he's leaving. I see the advantages of Gideon's family being out of our lives. I think Ab needs more mature companions, definitely ones who'll have to work for a living. He and Will can expect to do hard work all their lives."

Joseph reached up, took her hand, and sat her down next to him at the table.

"Yes, they'll have to work hard, just as I do," Joseph said. "That appears to be a consequence of having a large family."

Jane looked at him with dark, dancing eyes. She smiled at him and squeezed his hand. "Well, I hope you're prepared to keep working hard because I think there's going to be a new baby in the family in a few months," she said.

"Really?" Joseph said with a broad grin. "That's real good news. We're really blessed with so many healthy children. May we continue to be so graced.

"Since you've shared your good news with me, and since I said I'd try to do better and tell you about major decisions in my life, I'm going to let you in on a secret."

"A secret? Oh, good. What is it, dear?"

"Gideon's decision wasn't his own. I had to help him with that one."

"Well, aren't you smart? I always knew your brother needed to rely more on your good sense. What advice did you give him?"

"It's a long story, one I'll have to tell you when we're in bed."

"I can't wait," she said, tweaking his nose.